D0406091

# THE FIRST MAN

Also by Xavier-Marie Bonnot in English translation

*The First Fingerprint* (2008)
*The Beast of the Camargue* (2009)
*The Voice of the Spirits* (2013)

*Xavier-Marie Bonnot*

# THE FIRST MAN

A COMMANDANT DE PALMA INVESTIGATION

*Translated from the French by*
*Justin Phipps*

MACLEHOSE PRESS
QUERCUS · LONDON

First published in the French language as *Premier homme by*
Actes Sud, Arles, in 2013

First published in Great Britain in 2015 by
This paperback edition published in 2016 by

MacLehose Press
an imprint of Quercus
Carmelite House
Victoria Embankment
London EC4Y 0DZ

An Hachette UK Company

Copyright © Xavier-Marie Bonnot, 2010
English translation copyright © 2015 by Justin Phipps

Published by arrangement with
L'Agence littéraire Pierre Astier & Associés

All rights reserved

The moral right of Xavier-Marie Bonnot to be identified as
the author of this work has been asserted in accordance
with the Copyright, Designs and Patents Act, 1988.

Justin Phipps asserts his moral right to be
identified as the translator of the work.

All rights reserved. No part of this publication may be
reproduced or transmitted in any form or by any means, electronic
or mechanical, including photocopy, recording, or any information
storage and retrieval system, without permission in writing
from the publisher.

A CIP catalogue record for this book is available
from the British Library

ISBN (MMP) 978 0 85705 393 0
ISBN (Ebook) 978 0 85705 391 6

This book is a work of fiction. Names, characters,
businesses, organizations, places and events are either the
product of the author's imagination or used fictitiously.
Any resemblance to actual persons, living or dead, events
or locales is entirely coincidental.

2 4 6 8 10 9 7 5 3 1

Designed and typeset in Minion by Patty Rennie
Printed and bound in Great Britain by Clays Ltd, St Ives plc

*For Frédéric, who uncovered some of
the secrets of our ancient earth.*

*For Michel, so erudite . . .*

"But by what myth does man live nowadays?

"The Christian myth, possibly."

"Do you live it?" I asked myself.

"If I am truthful the answer is no. It is not what I live by."

"So we no longer live by myth?"

"Apparently not."

"What is your myth then – the myth by which you live?"

C. G. Jung – *Memories, Dreams, Reflections*

# PROLOGUE

The first print appeared on some folds in the rock. A child's hand, a few metres from the large slab that sloped into the dark water. The sign of First Man.

The diver shivered. He had a lump in his throat. A fresh hand rose before him and then another: both negative impressions. Some were amputated, others with a red line through them.

Further on there were scrapings on the rock. Lines forming curves and tracery. Petroglyphs, then fantastic figures. A carved being: half-man, half-beast. Deep scratches along the long, chiselled body, though not on the birdlike skull or stag's feet.

The diver was entranced. He had been searching so long for this. It made him reel in the depths of time, the source of all myths, where man first set out on his journey of discovery, never to stop again. He loaded his camera and pressed the shutter. Once, twice . . . He moved forward again until compelled to bend double by the ceiling. An object lay on the glistening ground. He went closer and using his flash, took a succession of photos.

It was then he heard the lament. Barely audible words, like a prayer muttered in hoarse tones. Faster and faster. From one great rock face to another. Then silence. Heavy drops falling again onto the rusty ground. Drip. Drip.

The diver held his breath. A shudder of anxiety ran through him. He undid his wetsuit, as if to free his pounding heart.

To his left the rocks formed a damp labyrinth receding deep into the darkness. The air, saturated with humidity, had a sour taste of camomile.

The diver turned off his torch and crouched down.

The singing returned, closer now. More terrifying still.

He tried to think rationally. His hands were trembling. It was not his first visit to an underwater cave. Perhaps the wind was coming in through some great stone columns, pushing tremolos deep into the bowels of the earth.

But there was no breeze that day.

He switched on his torch again. The chanting ceased. There was nothing but the cold, unchanging rhythm of drops falling from the roof. Drip. Drip. Like the endless ticking of a clock.

The diver shrank from the danger. His equipment was by the shaft. He loaded the cylinders as fast as he could, clumsily putting on his mask and flippers as his panic grew.

He didn't notice the soft padding of feet just behind him, or the monstrous shadow.

# PART ONE

# The Mad House

Prehistoric man has only left us truncated messages. He may have placed a pebble on the ground at the end of a lengthy ritual where he offered up a roasted bison's liver on a bark platter painted with ochre. The words, the gestures, the liver and platter are all gone; as for the pebble, barring a miracle we cannot distinguish it from the surrounding pebbles.

André Leroi-Gourhan – *Les Religions de la préhistoire*

# 1

23 July, 1970, was a blazing hot day. Fires had ravaged a huge expanse of forest across most of Haute-Provence. The rains were late in coming and day after day nature was dying, consumed by thirst and fire.

Light wavered over the trenches at the prehistoric dig at Quinson. As the late afternoon sun set towards the dark mountains enclosing the Durance valley, a mild, fresh wind came down from the Verdon hills.

It was then that death passed by.

Death in a green four-door saloon, that raised the ochre dust as it rounded the bend in the road leading to the cool gorges of the river Verdon. Pierre Autran did not know, he didn't notice anything. He glanced at his watch and called out to Professor Palestro.

"Shall we call it a day then?"

He carefully lined up his trowel, scraper and brush on the edge of a large sieve. Pierre Autran was a man of order, precise in everything he did. Sunset was time for a beer. Chilled cans awaited in the fridge in the hut at the other end of the site. Autran needed little persuading.

The dig was on a plateau of harsh scrubland strewn with rock-roses. Further away the slope rose towards grey cliffs. A path ran through some green combes and smudges of red earth, then disappeared among shrub oaks scarcely bigger than a man towards the coastal roads leading to the Baume Bonne cave.

Pierre Autran leaned against the side of a barrow full of rubble. He handed Palestro a Kronenbourg.

"Cheers!"

Palestro was about thirty years old. A tall, gangling figure with drooping shoulders, he always wore military surplus trousers. He had an ageless hat on his head. He was attached to the department of prehistory at the University of Aix-en-Provence. Autran was roughly the same age, but more sturdily built. He was one of those volunteers in canvas hiking boots who toil away at the rubble for the joy of taking part in the great pursuit that is research. The team had done quite a job. The excavation went down like a giant staircase into the belly of the earth as far as the Gravettian layer.*

The site had grown considerably during the course of a month. Palestro had asked them to dig in the direction of the hills, towards a partly filled gap at the foot of a cliff that looked like a Palaeolithic hunters' hut. The assistants had put down rulers and stretched lines to indicate the levels; and a surveyor checked everything regularly. Layer upon layer, the harsh soil reluctantly revealed snatches of history. Man had been living here for four hundred thousand years.

Jérémie Payet, a doctoral student, lingered in the lower layers. Kneeling by an embankment he worked his brush over a darker line at ground level. He was probably the most tenacious of them all. A real explorer! He had already found quite a few objects.

Autran took a swig of beer and ran his tongue over his cracked, dusty lips.

"So tomorrow's the great departure then," Palestro said.

"Yes, I'm a bit sad about that."

"Oh well, you'll be back next year. We always need volunteers with your experience. And you can always visit as a friend. An enthusiast."

---

* From La Gravette archaeological site in the Dordogne. It designates the cultural and artistic traits specific to the upper Palaeolithic period (28,000–22,000 BC). The Gravettian is noted for the production of ivory female figurines.

"Who knows where I'll be in a year's time?"

The pre-historian chucked his can into a metal drum used as a rubbish bin.

"Thinking about your children?"

"Yes," Autran said. "I miss them."

"You'll have to introduce me one of these days!"

Autran opened his wallet. Inside there was a slightly faded photo of his twins, Thomas and Christine, in the plastic sleeve over his driving licence.

"That's Christine," he said, showing Palestro the photo.

"A beautiful young lady!"

"She's brilliant, interested in everything."

"Is that Thomas next to her?"

"Yes, he was born just eight minutes after his sister."

Thomas had a miserable, dark, troubled expression. A teenager's face with some childish features. His eyes carried the terrible glint of an illness his father never spoke about. Thomas was still afraid of the dark. Sometimes he would cry out and struggle until he was restrained by his relatives, tied up and sedated. He was passionate about prehistory, devouring texts by great authors such as Leroi-Gourhan, Abbé Breuil and Lumley.

"Why don't you bring your kids with you on digs?" Palestro asked.

Autran's expression hardened. He rarely talked about his family. Probably through natural reserve, but also because of the cruel secrets that weighed upon him and left him tongue-tied about himself and those close to him.

The church bells in Quinson rang the Angelus. The hollow notes bounced off the limestone cliffs and dispersed across the clear waters of the Verdon. Jérémie Payet stood up.

"Hey, come and look!" he exclaimed.

Palestro and Autran strode across the site. Payet pointed to a brown line two metres below the ground.

"There, in the Gravettian!"

A long, dark object, still covered in a coating of clay. Jérémie Payet crouched down and ran his brush over it.

"It's a statuette, that's for sure."

"Great find," Autran said. "Well done, Jérémie!"

"It's extraordinary!" Palestro added, without taking his eyes off the figurine.

The pre-historian pushed the student aside roughly. He worked away painstakingly for about ten minutes. From time to time he stopped to take a photo, having placed a yellow and black ruler beside the figurine. It was about twenty centimetres long. The feet were crudely carved; the body perfectly proportioned. A hole at chest level meant it was possible to see inside.

"Looks like a mammoth's tusk," Payet suggested.

"I think you're right," Palestro replied. "You can see the ivory clearly here."

The head was intriguing. The chin was shaped like a cervid's muzzle. And the brow was topped with hair that stood on end and deep notches like antlers.

"I think it's a man with an antler head," Palestro said. "A horned sorcerer. Half-man, half-beast . . ."

Jérémie Payet went over to the hut and came back with a rectangular box. Palestro laid the figurine inside on a wad of cotton and replaced the lid.

A car horn sounded. The three archaeologists looked up.

"It's for me," Pierre Autran said, shading his eyes with his right hand.

Death stopped by the fence enclosing the site. A metallic green Mercedes 300 that Autran had bought six months earlier. His wife was behind the wheel.

Autran brushed the clay off his trousers, put on his sunglasses and went down to see her. Neither his wife nor the car should have been there.

# 2

*Marseille – forty years later*

For three days the Mistral had been tearing through the streets of the city. Above the cliff tops that bowed down to the sea, the brittle blue sky had a cold purity about it. If the wind dropped, the forecast was predicting unprecedented snow. December promised to be freezing, but in Marseille they had long since stopped taking any notice of prophecies of this kind.

On the second floor of the Évêché police station, the telephone had been ringing for a while.

"I'll get it," Commandant Michel de Palma shouted, blowing on the coffee cup that had just been dispensed by the machine.

He raced down the corridor and picked up the receiver.

"I'd like to speak to Inspector de Palma."

"It's Commandant, and has been for God knows how long . . . De Palma speaking."

"Oh, I'm so glad I've caught you. I was about to give up."

A quavering female voice. De Palma settled himself in his armchair and stretched out his long legs. He was tired and alone. He didn't want to speak to a neurotic, emotional woman.

"What do you want?"

"Have you seen this morning's paper?" the voice replied.

"I don't read the papers."

The voice paused. Down the receiver de Palma could hear the purring of an engine. A diesel engine from a boat, he assumed.

"I'm in charge of the dig at Le Guen's cave and, you see, two days ago one of my colleagues, Rémy Fortin, had an accident. A serious one."

De Palma tensed.

"In Le Guen's cave?"

"Yes. Well, not exactly. More like just inside the entrance."

"How deep?"

"Thirty-eight metres."

"Decompression sickness?"

"That's what the experts say."

"Diving in Le Guen's cave is dangerous. You know that. What's your name?"

"Pauline Barton."

De Palma scrawled the name on the back of his cigarette packet.

"So you think it wasn't just an accident?"

"That's right," Pauline Barton replied. "I don't know how to put this, but since it happened I've been reading everything I can find. You know that terrible business at the cave all those years ago? I keep thinking it didn't just happen by chance. Do you remember?"

"The Autran case, ten years ago. How could I forget?"

The team led by de Palma had arrested Pierre Autran's son, Thomas, who had killed three women. More perhaps. The police had never managed to establish the true picture. He had left a negative impression of his hand beside each of the victims. A signature, just like the Magdalenian cave paintings.

Autran had never confessed to a judge or to the police. The criminal court in Aix-en-Provence had handed him a life sentence, with a minimum term of twenty-three years. At the time, his twin sister, Christine, was professor in Prehistory at the University of Provence. She had been given twelve years for aiding and abetting. The court knew how to be lenient.

De Palma scanned the news from the world of predators. There were no reports of any escapes. No wanted notices. Nothing on the Autran twins. It was a long time since anyone had mentioned them or talked to him about Le Guen's cave. It was not a good sign. He assumed a more commanding tone:

"We need to meet right away. Five o'clock?"

"Er, yes . . . I'm at Sugiton. I'll be above ground by then."

"O.K. I'll come over and see you. The two of us can get the boat back."

De Palma hung up without saying goodbye. He threw his coffee cup in the bin. It had been a terrible start to the day. The tenor bell from La Major cathedral tolled three times. In rue de l'Évêché the Mistral started to howl, scooping up bits of paper and plastic bags and lifting them as high as the upstairs windows.

Faced with all this, there was good reason to ponder twists of fate. Why Le Guen's cave? Why a suspicious accident?

De Palma spent an hour on the phone. The Directorate of Cultural Affairs confirmed a dig was underway at the cave. The *Gendarmerie Maritime* and the Sea Rescue Service both verified that a diving accident had taken place at the entrance. Rémy Fortin had been recovered in a bad way. The Rescue Service put him straight in a decompression chamber and then took him to Timone hospital in Marseille.

From nearly forty metres below sea level Fortin had risen to the surface in just a few seconds. The nitrogen, which expands under pressure, hadn't had time to revert to its normal state and had formed bubbles in his blood and muscle tissue.

"It's a miracle!" the doctor said.

De Palma was sceptical about everything, miracles included. Divers of Rémy Fortin's calibre didn't just lose their cool. But anything could happen at the bottom of the sea: strange encounters with killer sharks that had lost their bearings, dolphins in need of affection, or even nutters like Thomas Autran. The thought triggered an intense desire to have a cigarette. But de Palma hated going down to the yard in the middle of a blizzard – for a Gitane, in the company of the police force's latest nicotine addicts.

He walked round and round his office. A memo from the new head of the C.I.D. lay by the computer. His boss was giving priority to the struggle against organised crime and restoration of the rule of law in the northern districts of the city. A real crusade. In the space of twelve months four petty crooks had gone to join their mates at the great gig in the sky. More serious still was the war raging on the estates between la Rose and Castellane. Six kids wasted. Vicious stuff, with Kalashnikovs. De Palma tore up the memo and chucked it in the basket.

The door opened. Karim Bessour put his head into the office. De Palma was taken aback.

"Oh, you're here, Baron," said Bessour in surprise.

"Where else do you expect me to be?"

Bessour frowned. With his emaciated face and tall, slim body, he always gave the impression he was a soldier marching off to war.

"Have you forgotten about my promotion do?"

Bessour had put on a white shirt for the occasion, with a wonky blue tie. His long arms stuck out of the sleeves.

"You're going to be a Captain," de Palma said. "At your age you could end up as Commissioner."

"Don't take the piss!"

"You could, son. We haven't got ten like you in this dump."

"You've taught me everything I know, Baron."

"'Fraid so."

De Palma frowned.

"In three weeks, I'm out of here. There'll be no more Barons."

Bessour felt somewhat superfluous in the midst of all this nostalgia. He glanced at his watch to create a diversion.

"It's a bit like a confessional in this office," de Palma went on. "With no priest. I get to see some sad characters sitting here. Their wrists – it's always the left one – attached to this ring. Blokes pro-

12

testing their innocence. A few women. A handful facing the death penalty. One of them about to be sent to the guillotine. I can't forget the face. Those bulging eyes behind the square glasses. I still struggle with all the crying, the shouting, the pleading . . ."

"We've had some big cases all the same. They don't call you the Baron for nothing."

The conversation was starting to get on de Palma's nerves, so he grabbed hold of a cardboard box he had salvaged from the fruit and veg shop on rue de l'Évêché.

"I'm going to pack my things."

He unlocked the drawers and emptied them into the box. Odds and ends rained down: business cards, old rubbers, spent cartridges, chewed pencils and scraps of paper with trivial notes scrawled on them. When all was said and done thirty years in the squad didn't really amount to much.

"Don't forget, you've still got three weeks to go," Bessour teased.

De Palma put on his jacket and stuffed his weapon into its holster.

"Got to go. I've a meeting with some pre-historian woman and it's not exactly nearby."

"Oh yes?"

"A diver nearly drowned at Sugiton. That's where I'm going."

"Do you want me to come along?"

"No way, you need to go and pop some corks!"

De Palma placed three fingers on his shoulder to indicate the stripes Bessour would get when he was promoted to the rank of Captain.

Bessour never reacted to jibes from his boss, who, as it happened, had little time for hierarchy, authority or stripes on uniforms. He looked serious.

"An accident at Sugiton? I think I read about that in the paper. Was it at Le Guen's cave?"

"Just by the entrance. Thirty-eight metres down."

"It wasn't an accident then?"

"No idea, son. But when it comes to Le Guen's cave I always expect the worst. If you know what I mean."

"Yes."

"Did you say it was in the paper?"

"Er, yes."

"That's all we need."

Bessour turned and went out. De Palma had a horror of any kind of do: promotion dos, leaving dos – he could do without them.

# 3

On the 1959 model of the Alfa Romeo Giulietta, the radio was to the right of three large chrome dials, just below the rear-view mirror attached to the dashboard. Finding the stations required a certain dexterity: you had to turn the right-hand button slowly, otherwise the tuner went haywire. The Baron had long since given up adjusting the thing and forbade anyone else to touch it. For decades the radio needle of the legendary coupé had been stuck on *France Musique*, and hadn't shifted.

As he came out of the Évêché underground car park, the radio crackled for a few seconds. Then he heard the final bars of Radames' great aria from the first act of "Aïda":

*Egerti un trono*
*Vicino al sol . . .*

De Palma recognised Placido Domingo's voice. The year of the recording was 1974. After the heroic long B flat he was expecting the entrance of Amneris and Fiorenza Cossotto's stunning voice. The presenter came on air instead. It was a programme about the great classical heroes. De Palma listened absent mindedly. In any event, the tunnel through the city (from the old deep water harbour to the Timone district) would soon silence the presenter for quite some time.

The journey took another half hour, crossing through the districts backing on to the steep slopes of Mont Saint-Cyr and the Col de la Gineste, as far as the outlying houses.

Marseille stopped at the entrance to the Massif des Calanques. Beyond a rusty barrier a line of fire rose towards the Col de Sugiton.

The path climbed first to the pass between wind-lashed white oaks and pines replanted after the great fires that had ravaged the valleys. Beyond a gorge, a combe ran over towards a creek. Posidonia formed dark patches on the clear seabed. Thirty-eight metres below sea level, a tunnel led into the belly of the mountain and to Le Guen's cave, a hollow space where one could breathe, adorned with prehistoric paintings and drawings.

A sharp cry broke the silence. A Bonelli's eagle took flight over Sugiton, seeking out the rising currents along the cliffs.

De Palma raced down the path and found himself on a rocky ledge that served as a land base for the divers. Pauline Barton surfaced a few minutes later and waved to the detective.

Technicians from the Department of Maritime Archaeology were bustling round a waterproof container tied to the end of a rope. Pauline hoisted herself aboard the *Archéonaute* and disappeared for a few minutes – time enough to knot a towel round her hair and put on an orange fleece and some faded jeans.

"Good morning, Monsieur de Palma. Thanks for coming over."

The handshake was firm. She wasn't wearing make-up or a wedding ring. Diving and sunburn had furrowed her long face with its alert, grey eyes.

"Any news on Rémy Fortin?" de Palma asked.

"The doctors aren't very hopeful. Come on board. It'll be easier for us to talk. You don't mind the rolling?"

He smiled.

"I come from a family of sailors."

The *Archéonaute* was about thirty metres long. Its pointed stem sliced through the water like a blade. The white hull with its three lines, red, white and blue, was spotted with rust below the portholes.

Pauline Barton led the way into the wheelhouse, which was furnished with an imitation wood table and two leatherette bench seats.

"What happened exactly?" the Baron asked, coming straight to the point.

"It was a decompression accident. A bubble of nitrogen went straight to his brain. He's still in a coma. His condition is life-threatening, as the doctors say."

"What makes you think it wasn't an accident?"

Pauline glanced towards the gangway, to make sure no-one was listening.

"Rémy was easily our best diver. Not the sort to panic for no reason. When I visited the place where he inflated his B.C.D.* there were some clay particles still floating in the water."

The slightest false movement could cause the clay carpet on the bottom of the underwater passages to rise, turning the water completely opaque. This was one of the hazards divers most feared.

"Rémy lost a fin," added Pauline in a low voice. "His guideline was cut."

De Palma took a notebook from his jacket pocket.

"Do you know the history of Le Guen's cave?"

The scientist looked surprised.

"I should think I do! I've been working on it for years . . ."

"I'm sorry, I meant its recent history."

"What about it?"

De Palma turned to the gangway. The chief engineer had just left. They were alone in that part of the boat.

"Christine Autran and her brother Thomas – do the names mean anything to you?"

"Everyone in the prehistory world knows Christine Autran. Palestro's favourite, not to mention his mistress! She was my teacher . . . I've read her work. It's brilliant, I have to say. And of course I've heard all about that terrible business in the cave. I was working on

---

*   Buoyancy control device – allows divers to remain effortlessly on the surface or come back up in case of a problem.

the Ariège site at the time. I don't know anything about the brother though."

De Palma hesitated before continuing. Pauline Barton had notified the *Gendarmerie Maritime* about the accident. The officer on duty, a laid-back old cop, hadn't taken her seriously when she spoke of an ambush. He had written his report in a kind of shorthand, sprinkled with legal jargon from a bygone era, but Pauline hadn't given up. Once she got home she had surfed the net. De Palma's name had appeared in several articles on the Autran twins. Despite her dislike of the police, Pauline had contacted the murder squad.

"Do you think Rémy Fortin was afraid before his accident?" the Baron asked.

"Yes."

"What makes you say that?"

"He was found with a fin missing. He'd lost his knife."

"Knife?"

"He always had a diver's knife, attached to his calf. Why would he take it out?"

"To cut the line."

"In that case why did he lose it?'

She always had the last word. But de Palma persisted.

"So you think he used this knife before his accident, probably to defend himself. But surely it's also possible one of Fortin's feet got caught in the line and he was trying to disentangle it. First he lost his flipper and then he cut the line. It's also possible there was a problem with the regulator. A malfunctioning valve. In those situations an intermittent breakdown can be pretty scary."

"You don't believe what you're saying! There's a curse on that cave."

"I can believe it."

A young man came in and put some white boxes down on the table. A student no doubt, or one of the many volunteers that help out on digs. De Palma took a mental snapshot. As a policeman he had learned to mistrust everyone.

"These are precious finds," Pauline said. "New carbon samples that are definitely over thirty thousand years old. We're going to do some tests. That's the second set . . . they're more interesting than the first ones."

Her eyes melted as they settled on the black pieces, which meant nothing to the layperson. The specialist press would devote long articles to the dating and the pre-historians' topographic data. Pauline was a star in *L'Histoire* magazine, which suited her just fine.

"In three weeks time I'll be gone," de Palma said. "To be honest I don't know if I can really help. I'm just a Commandant who's about to retire and lay down his weapons. That's all."

"There's a lot you can do," Pauline retorted. "You know Rémy wasn't the victim of an accident. I haven't told you the full story."

There was a dull throbbing from the engine, then a clattering of metal. The boat shuddered. The chief engineer began manoeuvring his way out of the Sugiton bay. The propeller traced a semi-circle of foam in the still water.

"There are some photos," Pauline went on. "Shots that Rémy took before the accident, without telling me. We got the camera back intact. He'd put it in its waterproof case."

"Can I see them?'

"You'll have to come to the lab."

They had just passed Cap Morgiou. Its ridges were still bathed in the last rays of sunlight. Darker and a little further off, the Pointe des Merveilles took shape. The student came to sit in the wheelhouse.

"It's cold outside," he said.

"You'd expect that in mid December, wouldn't you?" Pauline said.

Even with some chapping caused by her daily dives, de Palma was moved by her beautiful, pure face. He liked women who did crazy things, such as diving in the Calanques in winter to save bits of charcoal that Cro-Magnon had left behind.

Past Cap Croisette, the huge bay of Marseille was churned up by the Mistral. The *Archéonaute* mounted the waves that crashed against the port side. The sea seemed to be filled with unexpected shadows. They rose from white crests only to disappear again in dark troughs. Towards Château d'If island, an enormous mass of metal and light appeared: the *Ibn Zayyed* ferry was heading for La Goulette port in Tunis.

The *Archéonaute* landed at the customs post, right by the square tower of Fort Saint-Jean. De Palma stepped ashore and then waited for Pauline Barton to disembark. The swell came in through the Passe Sainte-Marie, beating against the rocks at the foot of the ramparts, which were covered in red seaweed. On the quay an elderly North African, wrapped up in his sailor's jacket, had cast out two lines.

"Anything taking?" de Palma asked him.

"Shoya, shoya," the old man replied, wiping a drop from the tip of his hairy nose. "It's too cold."

"You sometimes get bass here . . ."

"Insh'Allah!"

The prehistory lab was housed in the old greyish naval buildings, right above the fortress. It was surrounded by beams and building materials. The renovation works were taking forever.

Pauline Barton and de Palma went to the room where they kept the finds from Le Guen's cave. A skull with a missing jaw lay on a grey metal cabinet.

"Take a seat and move anything that's in your way," Pauline said.

Files and scientific publications were piled up to the ceiling. A photo of a stencilled hand was pinned to a cork board. The thumb had been amputated.

"That handprint intrigues me," the Baron said. "You'll see why in a minute. To really understand things we need to recap a bit and talk about the Autran case."

He showed Pauline a photo from the Criminal Records Office. It was the most presentable one he could find on file. She reeled when she saw the strange signature the police had found by the women's bodies: on a sheet of paper was a print, identical to the one on the wall.

"I've never known why a man like Thomas Autran would attach such importance to these stencils!"

"I don't know if there is a meaning," Pauline replied. "I suppose that for him there is one. His sister wrote some remarkable articles on the symbolism of hands, even if they were just theories that still needed to be verified. She used to talk of medicine men coming to collect substances in these caves."

"Such as?"

"There was something called moon milk. In fact it's calcium carbonate. A substance found on the walls of caves and stalactites. When you reduce it to powder, it's very effective against certain illnesses, particularly bone diseases. It's also said to help increase the flow of milk in pregnant women. Nowadays calcium is very well known, but at the time . . ."

Christine Autran had suggested that magical rites had taken place in Le Guen's cave. She went so far as to suggest that Magdalenian shamans dosed their patients with moon milk and other substances. From there it was just a small step to thinking that the powder possessed magical powers. And Christine would probably have done so, had she not retained a little academic restraint.

Pauline Barton crossed the office and opened a steel cabinet.

"There's something I must show you."

She came back with a tablet and put it down on her desk.

"There," she said, switching on the touch screen.

With her fingertips she brought up some icons and opened the photo library. The first two images were general shots of a huge cave with a rather low ceiling. The third was of some enormous stalagmites. There were drawings of two stencilled hands on the rock, in a corner.

"This is what interests me," said Pauline. "Do you see that shadow?"

At the bottom of the sinkhole a huge shape was clearly visible. Two arms and legs, and an excessively large body, completely out of proportion with its limbs.

"Careful," de Palma warned. "It could just be a silhouette caused by the flash. There are so many stalactites and strange shapes in that cave. Depending on the lighting it can turn into a shadow puppet show. They start to look like monsters."

"Of course," Pauline replied. "But it was the last shot he took. He'd taken other photos before that."

She brought up another image. An object shaped like a branch, resting on a shiny stalagmite, some twenty centimetres long.

"What's that?"

"That's what I'd like to know."

She selected another photo and enlarged it. The shape of a statuette stood out clearly against the ground.

"Do you have any other photos?"

"There were six in all. Here."

She displayed the pictures on the screen. All of them close-ups.

"You know, Monsieur de Palma, I think what we have in front of us is one of the oldest depictions of humankind. A sort of man-beast probably sculpted in a mammoth tusk or cervid's antler. This type of object is often found in the upper Palaeolithic, or Gravettian, period.

She chose a shot in profile and enlarged it. The figurine's neck and chest were perfectly worked. The lower part of the face was like a muzzle, with barely a hint of any eyes. Numerous horns perched on the forehead.

"It's definitely a man with an antler head. A magic creature. People don't always appreciate the Gravettians were capable of such delicate work."

"Is it a significant sculpture?" the Baron asked. "I mean important at a symbolic level?"

"Of course. There's an obvious magical dimension, and a mythical one too. In ancient Greece you had Actaeon, the god who was turned into a stag by Artemis. The Celts had Cernunnos, the horned God with antlers. It's a figure that recurs in different civilisations, until Judeo-Christian mythology gets the upper hand. In the past researchers likened it to the Devil. It seems cervids were considered the king of animals. Think of those trophies displayed in hunters' dining rooms. You're never far from the magic of the hunt . . . Christine Autran used to say that shamans invoked stags or reindeer in order to appropriate their strength."

"Why did she say that?"

"Because you find them in all the painted caves . . . but it's only a theory."

"And this statuette?"

Pauline held her breath for a few seconds.

"I've never seen or heard of one," she said.

"So it must be important."

"Yes, definitely. I would say extremely important. Otherwise why would Rémy have taken the photo?"

"Can you be sure it's authentic?"

"As a scientist, I'd say no, because I haven't examined it myself. But I trust Rémy, so I'd say yes, definitely."

She switched off her tablet and put it away in the desk drawer.

"These objects are the oldest human representations. In cave painting animals are by far the most common motif."

"Do you think that man with the antler head comes from Le Guen's cave?"

"Good question. No, I don't think so."

"Why's that?"

"It's clearly been restored. You don't find them in that condition. Most of the time they're under several metres of earth or concretions."

She took a tome from a shelf, an enormous study devoted to statuettes found at Brassempouy, a tiny village in Les Landes. The illustrations were old. Two moustachioed men in round glasses stood above some workers leaning on shovels. They were working on two Palaeolithic deposits: the Gallery of the Hyenas and the Pope's Cave, veins that lay about a hundred metres apart.

"The Pope's Cave was studied in the 1880s by a local scholar, Pierre-Eudoxe Dubalen, and then by Edouard Piette. Those old scholars didn't excavate the way we do nowadays. There was nothing very subtle about their digging. Piette didn't do too much damage to the strata. He discovered several fragments of female statuettes, one of which was the 'Lady with the Hood', the oldest human representation. It's five centimetres tall and about three centimetres wide . . . there's nothing human about the proportions of the head. No-one has a skull like that. You have to allow for artistic licence. The forehead, the nose and eyebrows all stick out, but there's no mouth. When you look at her you get the impression the lips really exist. No eyes, just eyebrows. But there's a smile on the face. Today the Lady with the Hood is in the Museum of National Antiquities at Saint-Germain-en-Laye."

"Is there any theory about the significance of these sculptures?" de Palma asked.

"That's a question many researchers have asked. Particularly about the female figurines. Some say they're virgins, in the image of Christ's mother. Others claim they're priestesses. Nobody really knows. At best we assume ethnographic comparisons can help explain these things. Not so long ago among the Tungus in Siberia, shamans used to disguise themselves as stags for clairvoyance or healing ceremonies. So some researchers suggest, by analogy with the present, that these figurines might be shamanic objects. Not everyone agrees, as is usually the case in this field."

De Palma remained silent for a while as he tried to recall something. Christine Autran had published an article on the mysterious symbols of the Gravettian and Magdalenian periods.

A long study entitled: *The Time of the Magicians.*

"Papa, do you think I'll get better?"

"Yes, son. With willpower you can overcome anything."

"Willpower? What good is that against madness?"

At the beginning of the autumn Thomas had a fit. They took him to hospital and locked him up in a secure cell, to calm him down. He didn't really understand why.

Why a cell? And why on his own?

A blue-and-red checked blanket, thrown over a mattress on the ground. A stupid teddy, like the one on T.V., that cuddly toy which flew away on a cloud with Pimpernel, the programme with the music he hated, because it scared him.

The yellow walls shone faintly in the harsh light. There was just one opening, a half-moon covered in vermilion paper. The whitish neon strip was reflected in the centre. Seen from below the window looked like a no entry sign.

Thomas tried to sleep, but he couldn't take his eyes off the no entry sign. The sign that no-one was allowed to cross. That forbidden life.

He couldn't get out. He cried.

His father had taught him the meaning of the road signs. When they went up Avenue du Prado they played a game to see who could say the names of the signs first. Thomas was most afraid of the no entry sign. He had told the doctor about it, but the doctor didn't give a damn.

A few days after his fit, Thomas left the ward for disturbed patients. He had a face like a church candle, no eyes, no mouth, arms like marble and grey veins under his pale, delicate skin.

His mother didn't dare come and visit him. She didn't love him any more.

"Papa, do you think I'll get better?"

"Yes, son. With willpower you can overcome anything."

Papa was sitting on the edge of the bed, stroking his hair with his powerful fingers.

"I had a funny dream last night," Thomas said.

"Do you want to tell me about it?" his father asked.

Thomas sat on the bed, his back propped against a large pillow. Outside the wind whistled through the oak trees in the grounds.

"I dreamed I was by an endless sea. There were these thin trees on the beach. Fine, golden grass. It was cold. The cliffs seemed smooth. In the middle of the beach a naked man was fanning a huge fire. I went over to him. First he smiled at me, then he hit me very hard. I collapsed and my soul left my body."

Thomas bowed his head. A huge hideous crease ran across his forehead. His father took his hand and held it tight to reassure him.

"Then the naked man cut up my body and threw the pieces on the flames. Everything burned, the body sizzled. A large black cloud of smoke rose into the sky. And then the naked man said: 'Now you're dust. Can you count the dust? Can you count your limbs and feel your flesh?'

"Then the wind began to blow and all the dust was scattered in the long grass."

"Your body went up in smoke!" his father said in surprise.

"Yes, and then the naked man started to sing and dance in the ashes. It caused a whirlwind. And the ashes came together again and my body reformed. Only the head was missing. It looked like a dry skull. The naked man held it in his hands. He gave it back the flesh. Then he tore out the eyes and replaced them with the eyes of the bird from the cliffs."

"The bird from the cliffs?" Pierre Autran exclaimed.

"That's what the naked man told me. He said: 'Now you will see the truth of everything.'"

"And then?"

"He burst the eardrums in my head and said: 'Now you will

understand the language of everything. Of all the animals and plants.'"

# 4

The workshop bell reverberated round the walls of the prison. Cold and dismal, the day was coming to an end.

Thomas Autran put both hands through the steel bars and checked his biceps under the fine, clean-shaven skin. He clenched his fists a few times and flexed the powerful tendons in his fingers. For some time he had increased his daily quota of exercise: three hours of pull-ups and press-ups in his cell, and two hours in the gym.

Beyond the huge prison ramparts the countryside was gripped by frost. Autran stared out at the fields overlooking the byroad. Nine years in gaol. Icy mornings, workshops, time wasted making espadrilles or dismantling electrical systems. The confined yard and the watchtowers that looked like the gangways on a warship. The harsh silhouettes of the screws armed with their sniper rifles.

The yard was deserted. In the middle of the main path was a small monument to the Clairvaux martyrs: engraved in gold letters two granite plaques in memory of the prison officer Guy Girardot and nurse Nicole Comte, murdered by Claude Buffet and Roger Bontems during a bloody hostage siege in May, 1972.

No-one ever escaped from Clairvaux. It was a maximum-security prison.

He had been locked up there forever.

The door flap opened.

"Thomas Autran, reading room?"

28

"Yes, boss."

In that type of prison the cell doors were left unlocked. The prisoners – lifers for the most part – could move around as they pleased. Autran was a 'Prisoner under Surveillance'. He was therefore someone feared by the screws. He had asked to be kept apart and placed in solitary confinement. He had been going to the reading room at the same time each day for the nine years he had spent in gaol. It was his sole form of escape. The great world of words, bigger than a hundred continents. No-one had ever escaped from Clairvaux.

The bolts slid back. The prison officer's silhouette appeared in the white doorway. A fair-haired lad, whose uniform didn't fit.

"Shall we go then, Autran?"

"Yes, boss."

The B block reading room had several Formica tables separated by low shelves lined with books. That week the prison infirmary had organised a little exhibition on A.I.D.S., with posters on prevention and one or two educational magazines. Some baskets filled with condoms had been placed around the room. Martini, a prisoner from cell 18, stuffed a handful into his trouser pockets.

"What are you gonna do with them?" yelled Gilles, a lifer, doped up on tranquillisers prescribed by the doctor in charge.

"They're for when I bugger you! You nonce!"

Gilles raised his fist like a sledgehammer.

"Keep your cool, Gilles!" the officer said. He had held up his hands in a conciliatory gesture. "And Martini, you leave off. Get back to your cell."

"Alright, boss!"

Autran was engrossed in his reading. He tried to ignore the scene.

"Back to your cell, Martini."

Gilles leapt up, threw back the chair and hurled his books across the room. Autran gritted his teeth. Short-circuits flashed in his brain. He went over to the magazine-and-newspaper rack to find something to read, as he did every day. *Le Monde* led on victims of the cold spell and the next G20 summit. *Paris Match* had a photo of Alain Delon with a young woman draped round his neck; inset, a picture of a homeless person in Paris who had died in the snow on place de la Concorde.

Autran glanced through the different titles until he came across *l'Histoire*.

In the centre spread there was a photo of the entrance to the cave.

*Will we ever know what caused the terrible tragedy that claimed Rémy Fortin as a victim? Decompression sickness? Panic? Thirty-eight metres below sea level the slightest problem can turn to disaster . . .*

Thomas didn't read on. His mind was getting all muddled. It was as if he'd been kicked in the guts. He couldn't stop his hands from shaking. Everything around him started to wobble. He muttered:

"This is the sign!"

"What sign?"

Thomas stared. He recognised the officer with the chicken face standing there in front of him.

"Something wrong, Autran?"

"No, boss. Everything's O.K."

His voice was plaintive, barely audible. It was the voice of a sick child. He waited for the screw to return to his magazine. The C.C.T.V. was behind him. His hands couldn't be seen. Slowly he tore the pages one by one from the centre spread and stuffed them inside his shirt.

"This is the sign . . ."

# 5

Rémy Fortin had been transferred to the recovery room on the top floor at Timone hospital. He was in a stable condition. The nitrogen bubbles exerting pressure on his brain had resolved, but at a price: he was left almost totally paralysed. He could understand but was unable to respond. He was incapable of uttering a single word, let alone make gestures.

In the evening, visiting hours ended at eight o'clock sharp. De Palma had to use all his powers of persuasion to gain entry to the intensive care unit.

"Can we have a word?"

"Any stimulation is good," the doctor replied. "He can only move his eyes."

They went down a long corridor. Patients were waiting for their evening meal. The smell of bad soup and overcooked meat was all-pervading. The doctor stopped outside room number eighty-seven.

The door was open. Pauline entered first and slowly walked towards the bed. She tried to hide her feelings and adopt a reassuring expression. Fortin followed her with his restless eyes, shining bright in a face like marble. He was tall and broad-shouldered, with a determined chin and powerful arms. Not the sort to let himself be pushed around.

Pauline planted a kiss on his forehead and adjusted the sheet where it had slipped.

"I'm so glad the worst is over. The doctor told me you can understand what people say."

He closed his eyes and opened them again.

"How do you feel?"

He blinked twice, then his eyes settled on de Palma.

"I've brought a detective with me."

Fortin's expression clouded over. He blinked several times.

"Do you think you could answer some questions, Rémy? We'd like to understand what happened. Blink twice if you agree. Three times if you disagree."

His eyelids closed twice. Pauline turned to de Palma.

"Hello, Rémy. Michel de Palma, Commandant at the serious crime squad. I'm here in a personal capacity. Pauline thinks, and I agree, that it wasn't just a diving accident. Is that right?"

Fortin blinked twice.

"Did the accident happen after you returned to the entrance?"

He agreed once again.

"Was it you who cut the line?"

Fortin took his time. His face betrayed the memories that must be going through his mind. Eventually he closed his eyelids twice.

"Why was that? Was something pulling you back?"

He agreed.

"Did you see something?"

The answer was negative.

"You don't think the line might have got caught in the rock and held you back?"

No hesitation. No, once again.

"Was there a struggle?"

His eyes moistened. He stared intently at the ceiling.

"Did you have a fight with someone or something?"

He blinked twice then his face tensed and started to tremble. His heartbeat accelerated. The doctor intervened.

"We have to stop now," he said. "He's too weak to continue."

"When can we come back?" Pauline asked. "We've got some extremely important questions to put to him and some photos we need to show him."

The doctor assumed a stern expression.

"Not for at least a week for that type of question. Stress can be very dangerous for someone in his condition."

"Alright, understood."

Once they were out in the corridor the Baron took the doctor aside.

"Any sign of blows or haematomas?"

"No," the doctor replied, "Nothing at all. But he was wearing a diving suit. A dry suit. They're very thick; they cushion any blows."

A nurse crossed the corridor and entered Fortin's room. The light went out, and then she came back.

"I can't tell you anything more," the doctor added.

As they came out of the hospital, Pauline stopped for a few moments to take a deep breath of the cold air.

"He confirmed just what I feared," she said.

"I'm puzzled," de Palma replied. "He lost his knife. That seems to support the idea of a fight, but who with? Was someone waiting for him down below, near the entrance to the cave?"

"It's possible."

One of your team, perhaps, de Palma thought.

"Does anyone keep an eye on the cave at night?" he asked.

"In theory, yes."

"In theory?"

"There isn't always someone there. We don't have enough people to keep watch ourselves and we can't afford to pay for a guard."

"Is there anyone there tonight, for example?"

"No, not tonight. This accident has thrown us a bit. But there'll be someone there tomorrow."

"Who normally does it?"

"Rémy."

Pauline looked up at the illuminated upstairs windows and added, "It was his passion. He used to sleep at our headquarters – and sometimes in the cave itself."

# 6

De Palma lived just round the corner from Timone hospital. He left Pauline, retrieved his Giulietta and drove back up the long dark boulevard bordering the Saint-Pierre cemetery – the largest in Marseille. His flat was in the Résidence Paul Verlaine in La Capelette district: three concrete blocks, a car park, and some maritime pines and Judas trees, set in the gardens of the old Sisters of the Apparition convent, between the motorway bridge and the Italian quarter.

The roads in La Capelette bore the names of members of the resistance movement who had been deported, or killed by the Nazis. In this low-income district the communist party had once been all-powerful. But since the closure of the steel works, and the factories producing playing cards and colonial hats, there were hardly any commies left. Those workers that remained were more likely to wear brown shirts than red.

De Palma had been born in La Capelette and would never leave. Not out of love or loyalty, but through sheer nostalgia.

As was his wont, he opened the door of his flat, put the revolver on the table beside the phone and in-tray, and went through to the living room. The little ritual ended with some music. He put a Georges Thill compilation in the C.D. player and turned up the volume. The smooth tenor voice sounded dated and scratched by the passage of time.

"Haven't you got anything new?" Eva shouted from the kitchen.

De Palma raised his eyes to the heavens in despair. Moments of nostalgia were strictly rationed since he'd been living with her.

"He was the greatest French singer ever! No-one has ever sung Werther like that. Just listen to the phrasing."

Eva appeared in the doorway. She wasn't wearing any make-up, which was unusual.

"I think my great-grandfather liked him a lot. Shame you do too."

De Palma disarmed her with a smile. Then he hummed along to the music.

*Why do you wake me, oh breath of spring?*
*Tomorrow the traveller will come into the valley*
*Remembering my early glory.*

Eva retreated to the kitchen, de Palma followed.

"One of these days we'll go and see 'Werther'. It's very romantic. You'll like it."

"A bit dated for me," Eva replied.

He whispered in her ear:

*On my forehead I feel your caress,*
*And yet comes the time*
*Of storms and sadness!*

"I have to admit it's lovely. Not very cheerful, but that'd be asking too much."

Eva was still a beautiful woman, a brunette with enchanting eyes. Sometimes they were full of laughter, sometimes mischievous or piercing, depending on her mood. The first time de Palma had kissed her was at Le Royal cinema, as they watched an epic Italian film whose title he couldn't remember. The cinema had become a multi-storey car park at the end of Avenue de la Capelette. No more gladiators' oiled bodies or cowboys in their hats. Instead a quick oil change and new brake pads! Just opposite Le Royal, on the site of the old steelworks, the council had built a huge skating rink.

Whenever Michel met Eva after school, he used to carry her satchel and thump anyone who laughed at this. The path followed the struggling factories that had now almost all disappeared and ended up in the streets with single-storey houses. Always there would be two or three old women chattering away in a mixture of French and Neapolitan. Always a smell of cooking – garlic and tomato – and husky tunes.

Once Michel and Eva grew up they had gone their separate ways. She hadn't forgiven him for his departure to 36 quai des Orfèvres in Paris, or his marriage to Marie.

For de Palma everything wobbled until Eva appeared again at the other end of his life. He began to hum:

*In vain his eyes will seek my splendour:*
*Finding only mourning and misery. Alas!*

Eva was still not ready to let herself be swayed. She turned away and threw two thinly sliced onions into the casserole with some pieces of lamb shoulder. She browned them for a few minutes and then sprinkled in some cinnamon, saffron and ginger.

"What are you making?"

"A tagine."

"Fantastic!"

She plunged a wooden spoon into the casserole and gave it a good stir. De Palma found it amusing when she wore her grandmother's flowery apron. Her new haircut showed off her slender neck. There were two dark kiss-curls on her cheeks.

"Where were you?" she asked.

"At work. How about you?"

"Down the job centre . . . I don't want to talk about it."

She tasted the sauce.

"I'm going to cover it and leave it to simmer for a bit."

He stared at her. Her expression changed. She sensed his anxiety.

"Tell me what's going on."

"It feels like something disturbing is about to happen."

"Well, that's not surprising in your line of work."

She had always been able to read the Baron's eyes. That evening she could sense he was teetering on the edge.

"How do you mean, disturbing?"

"It's just a feeling. It's like you've lost your sense of balance all of a sudden. You tell yourself life is sending you confusing messages. But they're like hieroglyphs; unless you're Champollion you don't know how to interpret them. The worst thing is if you do ever manage to work them out, it's always too late."

"You've spent too long mixing with the dark side. You need to lighten up a bit."

Georges Thill was starting Faust's serenade:

*Hail! Chaste and pure dwelling,*
*Where one can feel the presence of an innocent soul . . .*

Eva focused on the old tenor crooning. The melody touched her, but she was even more affected by the sentimental words that told of the things a man can do when he seduces a woman. Sometimes she thought opera was a bit like those old hits by singers with their permed hair that had been the soundtrack to her early years. De Palma removed the C.D. before the Devil arrives on stage and shatters Marguerite's life.

"Anita rang this afternoon."

Relations between Eva and her only daughter were as ferocious and raucous as the Mistral. The slightest word out of place caused a storm. Anita had phoned to say she was two months pregnant. In theory this should have been great news, but the father-to-be wasn't exactly ideal. He supported *Olympique Marseille* more than was perhaps sensible, drove a black B.M.W. and found his own ways of making ends meet. He was common and proud of it. Five fingers, six rings! Eva erupted, using harsh words she later regretted.

De Palma decided he belonged to a generation that didn't get involved in all that. And he had better things to do, so he tiptoed out. An idea was forming at the back of his mind. There was a large cupboard on one side of the hallway. He opened it and searched among the thousand and one objects stuffed at the back. He found a pair of hiking shoes that he hadn't worn in donkey's years. It was reassuring that they still fitted.

"Where are you off to?" Eva asked.

"I have to go out this evening."

"You mean right now?"

"Yes."

"Where are you going?"

"To the Calanques, to Le Guen's cave. I won't be long."

Eva took off her apron and flung it on the table.

"People say that cave is unlucky," she said.

"Well, maybe they've got a point."

"And what am I supposed to do with my meal?"

"We won't be late.

"Who's we?"

"Maistre and me."

He shot her a sheepish smile. For a second time Eva relented. De Palma and Jean-Louis Maistre were like brothers. They had got to know each other at crime school, on the quai des Orfèvres in Paris. Maistre had retired three months earlier. The Baron dialled his number.

"Hi, Jean-Louis. What about a little stroll down the Calanques?"

"Sugiton?"

"Yes."

"When?"

"How about right now?"

He hung up. Maistre rarely asked any questions. He agreed or he didn't, but he never wavered.

"Can you at least tell me what this Sugiton business is all about?" Eva asked.

"There's something I want to check. Do you want to come too?"

She sat down, at a loss.

"It seems to me you've totally lost it with this case."

He sat beside her and gave her a hug.

"I think you're right, but I have to see things through."

"See what through? Men always want to see things through. It's like you're on a divine mission or something."

"It's an old story and I've had enough. That's all."

"The Autran case."

"Yes. One of these days I'll tell you about it."

"Save your breath. I know enough."

She lifted the lock of hair that fell across the Baron's forehead. A livid scar formed a star near the hairline.

"Was it him who did that?"

"Yes."

"I hope you're not thinking of getting revenge?"

He struggled for words.

"You know very well I'm not."

"I'm not so sure."

"That's ridiculous. Autran's in gaol."

"So? He's obviously not the only one involved in this."

# 7

The moon cast long shadows over the milky-white cliff faces that jutted into the sea. Here and there pine trunks rose like deformed bodies from between the rocks.

"Are you sure something's going to happen tonight?" Maistre asked.

"You can never be sure about anything!" the Baron replied, doing up the straps on his rucksack. "But it's possible he's found out we've just been at the hospital. He knows there's no-one keeping watch on the cave tonight. And that won't be the case tomorrow."

"Who's this 'he' then?"

"Our enemy, you eejit. A bit of a virtual character, but we have to call him something."

"I see."

Maistre stood tall in the breeze, his massive form silhouetted against the pewter sea. The rocky inlets held no secrets for him. He had walked here hundreds of times with his children.

The only access to the inlet was by footpath, sea or the pass at Col de l'Ange. For the latter a rope was needed, and you then had to abseil for twenty metres – something you would only attempt if you'd done that kind of thing before.

Despite his paunch, Maistre was completely at home in the maze of winding paths, sheer drops and plunging valleys. He had brought a rope with him, sixty metres long.

"Just think what the world was like thirty thousand years ago," de Palma said. "The sea used to cover everything well beyond the islands. Can you imagine? There was snow where we are now. Bison, mammoths and bears."

"And now there are nudists reeking of sun cream, and then only in the summer."

"You're a born poet!"

They walked for a long while along the ridge as far as the Pointe des Pierres Tombées.

To the left was a cliff overhanging a deserted combe. A breath of air rose from the rocky ridges. Down below the sea beat against the boulders. There was a small building fitted out for abseiling, with two pitons and a chain placed to secure the rope.

De Palma went closer to the cliff face. His legs felt unsteady. The sea was black and barely visible through the rock arches. He sat on a ledge and put down his rucksack, suddenly cursing himself for being so old and incapable of mastering his fear. Maistre stood just a few centimetres from the abyss.

"Come back," de Palma said, "You're scaring me shitless. We're too old for this sort of crap."

"Well, there's a first!"

Maistre took a few steps towards the gap and jumped on to a rock jutting out from the cliff. From there he could see all of La Merveille cove.

"Come and look," he said, suddenly lowering his voice.

De Palma went as close to the promontory as possible. He had butterflies in his stomach. Maistre pointed to a small pebbly beach directly below.

"There," he said.

A beam of light, barely visible in the water.

"There's someone down there. A diver."

In a few minutes the light focused to form a yellow circle with a sharp outline. The diver was coming to the surface. Maistre stepped back from his vantage point and glanced towards the two pitons.

"Feel like going down?"

"Abseiling?"

"Unless you're planning to fly, I think that's the only way."

"We could always go round."

"Can I remind you the reason we're here is because we need to keep a low profile. If we go round, the frogman will see us coming and push off."

"O.K., point taken," de Palma grumbled.

Maistre opened his rucksack. He took out the rope and slipped it through the chain. Then he bent forward and flung it with a sweeping gesture. The nylon whistled.

"Put on your harness," he ordered.

"I'm scared."

"No time for that. You've done it before. You want to see what's going on. So either you go down, or else we go home and have a nice whisky."

Maistre had never seemed so commanding. He fixed the rope to the harness in a figure of eight and checked that the straps went between his legs. The Baron tried to clear his head. He caught the rope in front of him in his right hand and the rest in his left.

"Come on big boy, let's go," Maistre said. "Feet flat, body at a right angle, like in training."

"I did that that in the army."

"Great. Don't look down; look straight in front. Let your feet guide you. Breathe the fresh air. Breathing is important."

"You're just like my old staff sergeant. We used to call him Plonker."

"Down you go!"

De Palma positioned himself above the drop and clumsily took a first step backwards. He nearly slipped and found himself hanging over the edge.

"Keep your legs wide apart, so the rope doesn't keep spinning round."

"I'd like to see you do it."

He took another step then a third, without too much difficulty. The rock went down about ten metres to a broad ledge, where a pine tree had grown. Maistre put on his equipment without taking his eyes off the seabed. The circle of light hadn't moved. There must be a few minutes left to go for the decompression stage.

"Where have you got to, Michel?"

"I'm on the ledge."

"O.K., sort yourself out and wait for me there."

In two bounds Maistre joined him.

"Alright?"

"Just about," the Baron replied. "My legs feel all wobbly."

"Don't think about it. You've done the hardest part."

"I hope so."

"It's twenty years since I did any climbing," Maistre shouted, puffing out his chest. "Makes you feel good."

De Palma felt some drops of icy sweat trickle down his spine. He raised his head and glimpsed the moon between two jagged rocks. Maistre pulled in the rope and fixed it round the trunk of the pine tree. The light in the water had just moved. De Palma wasted no time. His movements were more assured now, but his limbs ached. His muscles contracted painfully. In a few minutes he covered the final stretch down to the ground. As Maistre left the ledge, the diver came to the surface. A jet of oxygen whistled through the rocky inlet. De Palma removed his harness and hurried on.

"Careful, Michel!"

He clambered from one rock to another. Maistre followed two metres behind. Their cold shadows lengthened each time they rose to take another jump. The diver sat on the pebbly beach and swept the bay with his torch. De Palma and Maistre hid behind an enormous boulder.

"Let's jump him," de Palma said. "He can't be armed."

"Careful, he might have a blade."

De Palma emerged slowly from his hiding place. The diver had put down his torch and was picking up his mask.

"Don't move!" the Baron shouted.

A piercing cry rang round the cove. The diver grabbed his torch and plunged into the water.

"Shine your light on him!"

Maistre pointed his torch towards the stranger.

"Oh shit! He's out of reach already!"

The diver had disappeared, swimming just below the surface, so he could paddle fast without being seen. Maistre sat on the beach and put his torch down by his feet. De Palma stood for a long while facing the dark expanse of sea. After about ten minutes, a powerful engine roared off into the night.

"We'd thought of everything except that. He came from the sea."

Maistre stared at the silvery horizon. In the distance the Riou cliffs looked like black lace.

"We'll have to come back tomorrow," the Baron shouted.

"Calm down, Michel."

"I want to know what happened tonight."

"A bloke's just given us the slip. That sort of thing's happened to us hundreds of times. I hope tonight's going to be the last. I'm not in the police any more and in three weeks you won't be either."

"The bloke who's just escaped knows it's a Friday and there's no-one here to keep watch. And he's a killer."

"Who told you he's a killer?"

De Palma snorted.

"Alright, no-one."

Maistre couldn't see his friend's eyes, but he sensed he was very upset. He tried to cheer him up.

"Would you like to go out in the *Juliette* tomorrow? We could do a little outing just for you."

"Where to?"

"Here, you wally. Just to check a few things. You always told me you were ace at diving."

"You should see me . . . I make a grouper look like a toad!"

# 8

The Mistral had dropped during the night. Towards Pointe de la Merveille, Maistre's boat hit a big wave. Eva stared at the coast and the sea-splattered reefs. She was wearing a yellow oilskin and she let her hand trail along in the cold water. Every now and then de Palma shouted out some remark about the passing capes and seamarks. Family memories.

He was nearly fifteen. His grandfather took him fishing near Riou and Plane islands when the east wind wasn't too strong. Michel was at the wheel. He had to put the Baudoin engine in neutral when instructed to do so. The older de Palma stood in the centre of the craft, his neck rigid, arms at a right angle, his eyes half closed.

"Keep rowing, Michel!"

As reliable as radar, he pointed at Cap Morgiou with his right arm.

"Just a jot more."

This meant a single stroke, not more. His left arm was aligned with Les Impériaux.

"Right, stop now. Time to cast."

The lines, each bearing several hooks, went straight down. The fishing was always miraculous. After fifty years on the world's seas, visiting each and every gulf and harbour, grandfather de Palma still spent most of his time on the water. His grandson worshipped him, because, like everyone who's spent too much time staring at the ocean, he had narrow eyes and his face surpassed any book with its tales of the southern seas.

Eva guessed that de Palma was deep in the past.

"You're daydreaming, Michel."

"Yes."

There were only five minutes to go. Le Guen's cave could be seen in the distance: a long limestone overhang silhouetted against the dark blue sea. Some solitary pine trees had grown between the natural stone pillars.

After the forbidding faces of the Trigane, a long rocky inlet appeared in the shadow of the cliffs. Some huts nestled around the port of Sormiou, barely concealed by the few pines that had survived the fires. Further to the east the long ridge of Morgiou became a chiselled headland. The water was darker there, especially at the bottom of the cliffs above Voile and in the Calanque de la Triperie: a huge mouth, framed with black-and-white stone, where the sea danced.

"He must know we're around," Maistre said.

"Of course he does, but it doesn't matter. If he opened the gate to the cave without forcing it, that means he's managed to get hold of a duplicate set of keys. He'll be easier to find."

Squeezed between the giddy cliffs and Crêt de Saint Michel, the hamlet of Morgiou shone in the sun. Maistre left the headland behind, the movement of the waves carrying the *Juliette* along.

An expanse of flat rocks sloped into the sea. To the left were the little pebbly beach and the ledge that served as a resting place for divers before they descended to the narrow entrance of the cave. It was underwater because of changes in sea level since the time it was inhabited.

De Palma took a wetsuit from his worn sports bag. He spat into his mask and carefully spread the saliva over the glass to stop it misting up once he was in the cold water. Eva watched him anxiously.

48

"I don't mean to be unkind, but you're not twenty any more, you know. And I haven't seen you dive in a long time."

"Thirty-eight metres isn't much. If there's a problem, I'll come straight back up."

Eva glanced overboard. The sea was suddenly dark and hostile.

"If I'm not back in an hour, you can call the *Bonne Mère!*"*

"Oh, very funny," Eva said. She wasn't really in the mood for joking.

De Palma squirted some air from the cylinders, put on his weight belt and sat on the edge of the boat.

"Got any Pastis, Jean-Louis?"

"What for?"

"Pour a few drops in the water; it'll taste better."

He loaded the cylinders onto his back, adjusted his mask and toppled over into the water.

The cliff receded into the dark. Sea bream were searching for small shellfish around a cluster of coral. Some gorgonians swam past in the poor light. The Baron glanced at his depth gauge and paddled closer to the reef drop-off.

Twenty-eight metres down, thirty ... the concrete blocks dropped by the Department of Marine Archaeology appeared. The entrance to the cave gaped like a sleepy mouth.

The sea pressed on his eardrums. Fear entered him like cold venom. Losing no time de Palma pointed his torch at the gate and carefully examined it. There were fine traces of scraping on the ties on the rocks. Some seaweed had been torn away. No saw marks were visible on the bars.

Between two concrete blocks a piece of metal glinted in the beam: a small diver's torch, about ten centimetres in length. The surface was clean, a sure sign it had not been there for very long. De Palma struggled for a while to reach it. Only by using the tip of his knife could he manage to slide it towards him.

* Name given to one of the sea rescue craft in Marseille.

"Hired equipment," Maistre thought, inspecting the base of the torch. "There's a number engraved and the name of the hire company."

*

Scubapro was a newcomer to the exclusive world of scuba diving. The man in charge confirmed that he had indeed rented out a pair of cylinders together with all the diving gear. The equipment had been returned in the morning, except for one torch.

By sea it took an hour to reach Montedron district, where Scubapro was based. Maistre started up the *Juliette*. The waves and currents forced him to keep a fair distance from the coast.

Once they had passed Cap Croisette, the sea became calmer again. They pulled into a creek beneath some old fishermen's huts. The Scubapro shop was in the middle of a cul-de-sac; at the end was a low stone wall overlooking the sea.

Inside the shop dozens of yellow-and-white cylinders, mostly new, were stored either side of a compressor. The equipment smelled of rubber, salt and dried seaweed.

"The bloke who hired the gear told me he'd lost it," the owner said. "Often happens. Especially if you forget to put on the wrist-strap. Nothing serious, I hope?"

"No, no, don't worry", de Palma assured him. "What was he like, this man?"

The owner hesitated for a few seconds.

"Small, he was. A bit of a belly on him, balding and fifty. Given the size of him I asked if he could dive. He showed me his certificates. I couldn't see a problem. "

"Do you have his name?"

"Couldn't tell you. He paid cash. You know how it is."

"Can you show me the rest of the equipment he hired?"

The Scubapro boss disappeared behind a wooden panel and rummaged around in some equipment. He returned after a few minutes with two ten-litre 230 bar Scubalung cylinders.

"Did he rent any other torches from you?" de Palma asked.

"Yes, two. That's normal."

"Have you recharged them since?"

"No, it's a bit of a shambles here at the moment."

"Could you check the batteries, please?"

The owner disappeared once more behind the wooden partition.

"So there was a 50-watt light and a 100-watt Vario. The 50-watt one is 70% charged and the Vario is almost fully charged. He didn't use them much."

"How long?"

"Half an hour at most. Bearing in mind batteries lose a bit of power when you don't use them . . . Yes, I'd say half an hour."

The diver hadn't ventured down the long tunnel at Le Guen's cave. He hadn't crossed the threshold of the sanctuary Otherwise at least one of the torches would have run out of battery.

On leaving Montredon, the *Juliette* passed Pointe-Rouge and the Prado beaches. The sounds of the city were barely audible, as if kept away by the sea breeze from the blaze of the setting sun. De Palma sat by Eva and held her tight. They remained silent till they reached the entrance to the Old Port. Maistre moored his boat at a landing stage by the city hall. He waited for the last launch from Frioul, and then changed direction.

A piercing beep signalled the arrival of a text. It was a message from Pauline Barton: "Rémy Fortin has passed away."

*

"Look, son. Look!"

Pierre Autran had a small box under his arm. He helped Thomas to sit up on his bed. The sedatives he had been given the day before had weakened his muscles.

"What is it?"

"Close your eyes."

Thomas heard the cardboard lid slide against the box. Then a rather sharp sound of rustling paper, reminding him of Christmas presents.

"Make sure you don't open your eyes."

Pierre Autran put a strange object in his son's hands.

"Tell me what you feel, but make sure you don't look."

"Yes, Papa . . ."

Feverishly Thomas explored the object with his fingers.

"It feels like a piece of wood, but it's cold. What is it?"

"Shh! Try to guess."

Thomas's eyelids trembled. He tried very hard not to open them. His fingers reached the end of the object.

"It's a statue! I can feel the shape of the face and here are the legs."

He kept fingering the object.

"It's the man with an antler head," Pierre Autran whispered. "There's a spirit that lives inside him. He will cure you. You can open your eyes."

Thomas raised the statuette to eye level and slowly turned it round.

"Was it First Man who made it?"

"Yes, son."

An anguished expression appeared on Thomas' face.

"It's funny. It's all cold."

# 9

*Clairvaux Prison, 7 December*

Thomas Autran put down *L'Histoire* on the table. He had been reading the same article for three days now, obstinately dissecting every passage, every word. Half a page described the curse on Le Guen's cave. Inset there was a photo of his twin sister. He hadn't seen that face for nine years. She was beautiful and still a little severe, with that smile which didn't really make her seem happy. He tried to imagine her how she was today after all the time in prison; the loneliness. He felt torn apart. There was a schism in his life, as if a scalpel had dissected every part of his body. The other bits were elsewhere, in another prison. Without Christine he felt incomplete.

He closed the magazine.

The library was quiet, the prison officer down at the other end. He was idly flicking through a comic book. Two prisoners were sitting at a table, talking in low voices. They were there to make a good impression on the probation service, but they never read a thing.

Autran stood up slowly and pushed his chair under the table. He looked straight ahead, as though he was about to pass through the prison walls. He struck the table. The screw looked up.

"Anything wrong, Autran?"

"It has come to pass!" Thomas shouted, ignoring the looks in his direction.

The officer put down his magazine.

"Keep your cool, Autran! Now!" he ordered, raising his voice.

"It has come to pass!"

"Alright, sit down or it's back to your cell."

Thomas looked at him with dead eyes, then turned and headed for the double doors at the end of the corridor.

"Hey! You nonce!" shouted a prisoner from another table. "What's your fucking game?"

Autran stopped. Morales 'the gypsy', an armed robber from an East Paris estate, pointed a finger at him.

"You nonce! We're gonna screw you. I swear we're gonna fuck you over."

"Shut it, Morales!" the officer barked. "Otherwise it's the block."

The screw positioned himself beside a shelf and glanced around the room. He was on his own. Discreetly, he took his whistle from his shirt pocket.

"Want to suck on it or what? You poof!" Morales whispered, moving closer to Autran. "See my hard-on? Take a look. C'mon!"

Autran rolled his head round on his shoulders to loosen up his vertebrae.

"C'mon, you gonna suck on it?"

Autran raised his right hand up to his eyes and slowly closed his thumb. The four remaining fingers stood straight as arrows.

"This is the sign."

He bent down his middle finger and moved towards him. Morales squared up for a fight.

"What sign? Poof!"

He took a step forward.

"O.K. then, I'll give you one. Come on!"

The blow came like lightning, delivered with incredible strength. Striking the carotids with both hands. Morales had no time to react. He collapsed, his mouth full of blood. Autran seized him by the hair and smashed his face on the corner of the table.

"I'm First Man. Your life is mine . . ."

54

His voice quavered. He picked up the bloody head and banged it once more with all his strength. The frontal bone split, snapping like dry wood. Terrified, the other prisoners retreated to the back of the reading room.

Then Autran dipped his hands in the blood as it spread across the shiny tiled floor. He smeared his face.

Bird cries rose from his chest. Like the screeching of an eagle.

# 10

Professor Palestro was not a happy man. And not in good health either, but that wasn't something to which he paid much attention. He seemed to be waiting for death, having withdrawn to the low-lying Verdon valley, not far from the Baume Bonne cave above Quinson. He had done his first dig there in the summer of 1970. His research had then taken him to the Dordogne, that great sanctuary of Franco-Cantabrian art, to Paris, and finally, back to his native Provence. His last excavation had been at Le Guen's cave. It was the most important and also the most dramatic.

Coming off the side road Pauline Barton turned right and drove up to the village. Amidst the red-tiled roofs, Quinson church tower glinted in the sun. Beyond this crib-like scene a huge rift, cold and dark, cut through two limestone faces.

Pauline hadn't been here for a couple of years. She was Professor Palestro's last doctoral student and his favourite. One of the rare few permitted to visit his home without an appointment.

The old scientist rose early. He hardly ever went out except to buy essentials in the village or to wander along the banks of the Verdon. People said he was unhinged and prone to hallucinations. Pauline had never managed to work out which of the rumours were true. She knew he was eccentric, but that didn't bother her. Quite the contrary.

The pre-historian's home was an old farmhouse built of large blocks of grey and white stone, backing on to sloping scrubland.

Some drystone walls that belonged to him ran over to a grey cliff, enclosing a vine and some fruit trees that were slowly growing old.

"Hello Pierre," Pauline exclaimed, slamming the door of her old Peugeot 205.

"Pauline! How are you?"

Palestro must have been wearing the same trousers for a month or two, longer perhaps. The fabric was shiny at the knees. As usual he was wearing his walking boots with the leather laces. The wind had raised a tuft of hair on his head. His stoop had got worse since they last met. But he still had the same eagle eye, and sharp, troubled face. Pauline kissed him on both cheeks. She noticed he stank more than ever.

"I've got some bad news," she said. "I wanted to tell you before you read about it in the press."

"Oh," he said, looking towards the village. "I haven't looked at the papers for a long time. So what is it, then?"

"Rémy Fortin is dead. Decompression sickness."

Palestro scratched his head. He couldn't seem to take it in. He hadn't known Fortin very well.

"Poor boy. Diving in those caves is always dangerous. You should be careful yourself. The place is unhealthy, whatever they say."

Pauline didn't know how to express her feelings about the accident. She knew Palestro was volatile and capable of suddenly shutting down without warning. Or perhaps even throwing an epic temper tantrum. If that happened she would have to leave. But she had come to talk to him about the man with the antler head.

"So, do you still hear from your colleagues?" she asked in an attempt to change the conversation.

Palestro raised his arms in the air to indicate he no longer really cared either way.

"In our field they don't find much any more. These days all they do is speculate, and I distrust that. The only thing that counts is D.N.A. Those chemists are going to end up replacing us!"

He gave her a fond look. His lower lip trembled, as it does with old people when they want to hide their feelings.

"You were my best student."

He took a few steps towards the house, and then stopped.

"In my entire career, I only had two brilliant students: you and Christine Autran. The others just repeated what they'd read. Like parrots."

Inside, the house was plunged in darkness. Pauline was fond of it. While she was working on her thesis, Palestro used to invite his favourite doctoral students to his hideaway for weekends. That was before he went to seed and became a recluse with an unpredictable temper.

Saturday afternoons were invariably spent walking by the Verdon. Sometimes they went as far as the Baume Bonne cave. The evenings ended up in front of the fire, chatting about prehistory and eating roasts – Palestro's speciality. Meals fit for Solutreans, he called them, except that he washed them down with copious amounts of Haut-Var wine.

"Sit down," Palestro ordered in a baritone voice more attuned to lecture theatres. "Let's have a drink and then we'll go out. This evening I've got some charcuterie someone brought me back from Corsica. An old friend, I'll introduce you one day."

He put his hand on Pauline's forearm and whispered, "Tell me about the accident."

"We went further in. Beyond coordinates 306 and 307, where you'd stopped."

He remained silent and closed his eyes. His mind was in the cave beneath the sea.

"We found a fireplace. The charcoal pieces match the outline of the small horses and the large bison. The lab is quite certain."

"Oh good, that's very good," Palestro muttered. "You're starting to re-create the workshop. That's excellent."

He opened his eyes and stared at her.

"I looked for that fireplace, but with everything that happened I didn't have time to find it. I look forward to reading you on the subject. What about the accident?"

"Fortin must have used his emergency buoy while he was bringing a box to the surface. That was fatal."

"Why would he do that?"

"It's a mystery."

A long silence ensued. Palestro seemed distant, his face blank as though nothing around him existed. She would have liked to continue, but decided to wait.

"Tell me what you found," he said, seeming to have forgotten about Fortin's death.

She showed him the photos she had taken of the different stages of the dig. Palestro nodded, occasionally pursing his lips, whenever a detail reminded him of something. As he came to the last shot of the large cave he stopped, his expression strangely fixed.

"That's the riddle," Palestro said. "Your last hurdle. The big cave."

"What's your theory then?" Pauline asked.

A ray of sunlight crossed the room and traced a golden circle on the Persian carpet in front of the fireplace. Palestro threw an oak log on to the dying fire.

"You need to look at the topography of the cave," he said, raising his arm in front of her eyes. "The floor goes up. Rising from a depth of thirty-eight metres, very soon you're a good few metres above sea level."

The log caught fire, throwing yellow smoke rings over the dark walls of the fireplace.

"There's no reason why there shouldn't be a second chamber or even a third. There's more than we found the first time, that's clear."

His eyes rested on Pauline and he watched her for a few seconds.

"Don't you agree?"

"Yes, Professor."

"But be careful, it's an evil place."

"Why?"

"You know Christine did a lot of research on those tales of magic in the Solutrean and Magdalenian periods. I never really found out what she discovered – she kept that part of her work to herself."

He checked to see Pauline's reaction before continuing.

"Did you know she tried out some magical rites herself?"

"No, I didn't."

"She followed Carl Jung's example. Jung was one of the founding fathers of psychoanalysis. He spent a long time with the Pueblo Indians, as well as in African societies. He never really talked about it. It was like his scholar's private domain. He didn't want people to laugh at him. But most people who knew Jung at the time say he was profoundly affected. Afterwards he began producing some impressive work that would transform our understanding of psychology."

He caught his breath, moved by some unexpected memory.

"I knew Christine very well at that stage of her life and I can tell you these experiences really changed her. She had connected with the magic of man's origins. She had crossed a boundary we see as taboo, because we're worried about disapproval from our colleagues. Believe me, Christine doesn't know the meaning of the word fear!"

He sank further into his armchair. His tweed jacket collar had slid up the back of his neck.

"Whether we like it or not, we live by Judaeo-Christian mythology and our whole culture can be explained by it. Palaeolithic man, like other early peoples, didn't know about that. That's the secret Christine wanted to discover in order to explain cave painting and early man's thinking. Nobody has ever managed to do that. It would represent a real leap in our knowledge of humanity."

"But that's just hubris!"

Palestro stared at Pauline.

"You don't achieve anything without it!" Then he whispered: "The well at the bottom of Le Guen's cave is about twenty metres deep. Beyond that nobody knows. It could be there's nothing, but equally there might well be galleries. Be careful."

"How do you mean?"

"You don't go into the sanctuary of First Man without taking risks."

# 11

With its sharp lines and angles, the Centre Bourse resembled the set from a bad science fiction film. It overlooked the ruins of Lacydon, port of the Ancient Greeks. Marseille had chosen to dump a hideous shopping centre on top of it, burying the past. During the holiday period, half the population tramped mindlessly through. That morning the Baron was following the herd, in search of a Christmas present for Eva. He wanted something different – not perfume or jewellery – something with a bit of class. But what could he get her? His brain kept coming up against what seemed like an insurmountable obstacle: the gulf that separates male and female tastes. He himself would have been happy with a box set of opera C.D.s, as long as it was something he didn't already have, which made it virtually impossible. But for her?

De Palma passed swiftly through the lingerie department. He couldn't see himself buying that kind of nonsense, especially since he knew nothing about sizes. The sales assistant, a sassy platinum blonde, gave him a ferocious glare, as if he was trespassing on forbidden territory. He stopped by the handbags. Eva's bag was too flashy for his liking. He wanted something that would come as more of a surprise. He thought of Pauline Barton's touch-screen tablet. He had been blown away by its double dose of technology. Bessour had assured him you could put an entire music library on the one small machine. Eva would like that. He headed for the computer shop. But just as he came off the escalator Maistre called.

"I've got something on Fortin. A witness. I think we need to see him right away."

"Where?"

"Porquerolles."

"Nice spot. You going to come?"

"No."

"Why?"

"I'm going to the Centre Bourse to do some Christmas shopping."

"O.K., I give in."

"The bloke you need to see is called Manfredi. He's the Captain down at the port. Knew Fortin well."

*

The east wind wound between the Levant islands and Port-Cros, carrying the scent of pine and eucalyptus. Porquerolles jetty was wet with spray. The port authority was housed in a white prefab building at the end of the quay.

"Pleased to meet you," Manfredi said, his cap stuck firmly on his head. "I've been waiting days for this moment."

"How come?" de Palma said, throwing away his cigarette.

"Well, I don't believe Fortin's death was just an accident. He was an exceptional diver. Swam like a fish. The sea held no secrets for him."

The captain was a skinny man. He wore deck shoes and a rather worn oilskin. He invited the Baron inside. Several nautical charts lay on a blue Formica desk. A dazzling sun beat against the windowpanes. Manfredi pulled down the blinds. De Palma removed his jacket and took a notebook from his inside pocket.

"Did Fortin live here?" he asked.

"Not all the time. He lived on a boat called the *Aranui*."

Manfredi kept passing his hand across his mouth, as alcoholics do when they're suffering from withdrawal symptoms.

"The day after Rémy died there was a bloke came here. A Parisian. Yeah, very smart he was. He says to me: 'Can you show me Monsieur Fortin's boat?' So I tell him the *Aranui* is in Toulon because the *Gendarmerie Maritime* took it . . ."

"You mean Fortin's boat has been impounded?"

"That's right."

"Do you know why?"

"Debts, I should imagine."

"When did that happen?"

"Six months ago."

"Tell me about this man who came to see you. What was he like?"

"The guy was loaded. You could tell from the way he was dressed. He was getting on, sixtyish . . . Receding hair, small glasses, average height."

Manfredi stood up and grabbed a packet of Marlboro lying on the computer.

"So this bloke, he was like this: 'Could you be sure to contact me in person as soon as Fortin's boat is returned?' And he gave me a card with a number on it."

"Have you still got the card?"

Manfredi blew some cigarette smoke out through his nostrils.

"There it is. Just a phone number. That's all."

"Why didn't you mention this before?"

"I did, but the police and the *Gendarmerie* didn't want to know."

"Do you know where the boat is?"

"It's right here. The Gendarmes brought it back two days after he died."

"Did you tell that visitor of yours?"

"No," Manfredi said.

The *Aranui*, a fine tuna boat, was moored at the end of a pier, beside some slowly rotting old tubs. The straight stem on the prow was painted bright red, with the registration number in bold white letters. Two windows on the bridge were cracked in a star pattern.

De Palma jumped on to the deck. The wheelhouse door creaked. There was a diver's mask beside the mahogany helm. Fortin couldn't have been very careful; a jumble of objects lay beside the navigation instruments.

The drawer contained some large 1/50,000 scale maps, showing sections of the coastline between Marseille and Nice. Off the Calanque d'en Vau, Fortin had drawn two semi-circles with a compass and marked in red a route leading to Le Guen's cave.

A ladder led down to the former fish hold. Fortin had converted it into a sizable rectangular room, with a kitchen area on the left and a large table covered in a red checked oilcloth. A fan was attached to a shelf lined with books that had been warped by the sea air.

A second, much larger cabin was used as a bedroom-cum-storage space. A mattress had been turned over in a bunk. A yellow kerosene lamp hung from the ceiling. At the far end of the room, in the triangle at the stern, Fortin had created a cupboard for his diving gear: two old wetsuits, a collection of masks and some boots . . .

De Palma turned everything upside down, but found nothing. He retraced his steps.

Beside some dividers, a pile of maps was stored in a large drawer under the table. Most were of the coastline. Several journeys were marked out between Cap Morgiou and Pointe de la Merveille. A mass of crosses indicated rocks or small islands. One route led to Le Guen's cave.

De Palma put the map on the table and took out another. A set of coordinates was marked in red.

2° 43' 57" E

42° 37' 3" N

It was somewhere on a hill near Marseille. Between nothing and more nothing. He rolled up the two maps and tied them with a piece of string lying on the floor. Up on deck and away from the wind and spray, he dialled the number the captain had given him. A rather worn female voice answered.

"Dr Caillol's secretary. How can I help you?"

"Er, sorry," de Palma apologised. "I must have got the wrong number."

He hung up. Dr Caillol was an old acquaintance. A psychiatrist who had treated Thomas Autran for many years.

## 12

Pauline Barton never dived alone. That morning she was accompanied by Thierry Garcia, a young man with a doctorate in Magdalenian studies, who had replaced Fortin.

The descent below the surface of the sea to the entrance of the cave went off without a hitch. For the first ten metres the rocks retained their emerald reflections, scattered here and there with dark patches of sea urchins. Rainbow wrasses nudged against coral reefs. Garcia pointed out a spiny lobster as it retreated into its lair, its antennae at half mast.

The two archaeologists descended slowly towards the pale drop-off. A little lower down, a pile of rocks balanced on top of each other. At eighteen metres the light began to dim. The colours slowly disappeared into the darkness of the depths still steeped in blue.

Pauline released long streams of oxygen bubbles at regular intervals. Above lay the silvery surface of the sea and the long guide line that disappeared in the bright light.

At about thirty metres down, Pauline carefully shone her torch along the rock face that jutted out over the barely visible ocean bed. She never failed to notice things. Some seaweed had been torn away and the tube of a bristle worm was partially uprooted. She made a mental note and moved away.

Thirty-eight metres down. She peered through the water towards the cave where Garcia was waiting at the gate. Two technicians and an engineer had gone ahead of him. A stainless steel sign bolted to the rock over the entrance read:

MINISTRY OF CULTURE — NO ENTRY

Thierry went first, with Pauline following two metres behind. Twice the cylinders scraped against the rock and the sound of steel against the limestone grated on her eardrums. With each slow breath the hissing of the regulator was sharper, more obvious.

Pauline tried not to think until she had reached the end of the long, narrow tunnel. She felt as though the cold water was closing in around her like a vice. As she came into the first submerged chamber she thought she saw the flash of a diving lamp down one of the countless passages that disappeared into the bowels of the mountain.

She came out on to the rock with some ropes and an aluminium tray for the diving equipment. She stood up straight, her legs still painful from the cold and from crawling along the tunnel. This world of bumps and streaks had become like a second home. Removing her flippers and pulling back her hood, she walked towards the long yellow and black rulers that served as landmarks for topographical data.

"We need some more light over there," she said to one of the technicians, pointing to a patch of darkness. "We're going to be working here today and in the coming days."

Pauline's words resounded strangely under the roof of the chamber at the back of Le Guen's cave. Richard erected a projector on a retractable tripod and flooded the cave with a powerful light. It was like a giant wet mouth, spotted with rust. Above her three hands were clearly visible, each with missing fingers.

There were some diagonal scratches on the rock face. During the first stage of the dig, Palestro and Christine Autran's team had only cursorily explored this part of the cave. They had simply noted the fingerprints. Nearly all the work remained to be done. Pauline took a few photos, focusing carefully on each section of the walls and ground. Then she put down her camera.

"Let's light the torch," she said, opening her laptop.

From the beginning she had adopted a simple procedure at the cave: she tried to recreate the original lighting used by prehistoric men themselves. This allowed a better understanding of their intentions. Each session was shot in high definition and immediately transferred on to image-processing software. The camera could pick up on things that escaped the human eye. She took a resin-covered stick and lit it.

"Can you turn off the spotlight, Richard?"

A yellow flame danced in the darkness. Shapes started to move. Under the low light the scratches in the eroded rock were transformed into deep, dark wounds. As the flame moved a second drawing appeared: it had the body of an ibex, and what seemed like a bird's head.

"A bird of prey," whispered Thierry, who was now holding the camera.

"Could be, unless it's a second slain man."

She went up to the drawing, which seemed to come to life in the flickering flame.

"Look," Richard said. "It's like a body with limbs. The curved beak, here, is like an eagle's."

The drawing started on a wall and finished on the curved ceiling. Pauline pointed at the detail and ran her finger over it.

"These two large lines could be spears or something of the sort. What do you think?"

"It's just like the other slain man," Richard replied. "The one we found in the first chamber."

Pauline waved the flame to her left. The drawing disappeared and only the scratched lines across it remained visible.

"I'd give a lot to be able to date them," Richard said.

"It's possible thousands of years separate these two drawings.

We'll take some samples inside the scratched lines and see what the lab has to say."

"Are we going to send them to Gif-sur-Yvette?"

"Yes. You can put on the light now."

She dipped her torch in a bucket of water. "One thing seems certain," she said. "Those diagonal lines appear to contradict what's drawn below. It's a bit like a magical code. People come back, see the ibex and the slain man, and decide to deny it."

"But why?"

"That's the only real question," Pauline said sarcastically, "But we're no closer to answering it."

"Christine Autran did some work on that, didn't she?" Thierry said.

"Some of Autran's theories were pretty far-fetched," Pauline replied, "but by then she was mad. You can't explain everything by magic. She used to say calcium had been collected from these drawings because of its magical qualities."

Thierry bowed his head. From the outset Christine Autran's name had never been mentioned on the dig, as if it was taboo. No-one spoke of what had happened in the cave.

"Hey, look!" Pauline said suddenly. "There's a new print. A right hand."

She froze. The handprint was missing a thumb and part of the middle finger. It was just like in the photo from the criminal records office that de Palma had shown her. The outline was very clear, with ochre and red pigments around the palm and splayed fingers.

"Is something wrong?" Thierry asked.

"No, nothing. I just had a mad idea."

Pauline couldn't help shivering. She scribbled something in her notebook and made a sketch of the drawings.

Suddenly there was a growling sound. Thierry Garcia tensed and looked enquiringly at Pauline. She replied with a nod towards the back of the cave.

"I think it's a draught passing through the sump at the back. There used to be another entrance just above the shaft. It was blocked by a landslide six years ago."

"It's strange though, it sounded like a man's voice."

"I hope it's not some prehistoric shaman waking up," Garcia sniggered.

"It's not funny. You never know."

Two hours passed as they recorded the coordinates needed for a precise inventory. At around noon, Pauline turned her attention to the large charcoal spots that surrounded the handprints.

"We're going to take some pigment samples and get them dated." She paused to think. "We'll send them off to the lab today."

"I'll take care of it," Thierry said. His diving cylinders were still wet as he loaded them on to his shoulders. Julien Marceau, the engineer from the Department of Marine Archaeology, was in the process of setting up a video link with the surface. He watched sceptically.

"You going back up already?"

"I need to get this stuff off to the lab by tonight."

Marceau stared at the box Garcia was holding. "What is it?"

"Some pigments we found by the shaft. Pauline wants them analysed as soon as possible, and it's Friday so they need to go off today."

Marceau looked at his large diving watch. "You've just time to get to Marseille before the post office closes."

\*

Garcia released a little oxygen from his regulator. He did up his harness and lowered himself into the water. If he swam fast he wouldn't need a decompression stop. He decided to press on. In less than fifteen minutes he was thirty-five metres below sea level. It was only about ten strokes to the end of the tunnel. Beyond there was nothing but the open sea.

As he came round the final bend everything turned white. The clay carpeting the funnel had been stirred up, reducing visibility to almost nil. Garcia swore. He was dazzled by the torch on his forehead. The light reflected back in the water. It had turned murky as a result of the suspended particles. He caught sight of a darkish shape in front of him. A rock perhaps, or another diver? He couldn't make anything out. His depth gauge read thirty-eight metres.

The guide line suddenly rose: a sign he must be right by the entrance. He had to keep swimming through the pea soup. In his hurry to escape he followed the line.

As he kicked with his flipper, he felt something pulling him backwards. His right foot had caught in the line. He tugged nervously, but to no avail. In the dense fog he undid the strap on his flipper and released his foot. He tried to kick, but noticed his other leg was also caught. He took out his knife and cut the line.

Then all was confusion.

A strange dark form leapt out and struck him. His head banged against the rocks. He let go of the box of pigments and lashed out randomly with his knife. The shape was elusive and intangible, disappearing into the milky cloud each time he thought he could touch it, only to rise up again from nowhere and attack him anew.

Using all his strength he thrashed through the water to escape the trap closing around him, not knowing if he was heading to the surface or the bottom.

The shape didn't want to let go. It was moving faster than him. He couldn't make out what it was.

At the end of his tether, he pulled the cord on his safety jacket. The red air pocket inflated at once and propelled him out of the danger zone, up towards the mirror of the surface.

# 13

The police launch suddenly turned in the middle of the bay. Over Sugiton a bird of prey rose and then dived down towards the sea, letting out a piercing cry.

"That's a Bonelli's eagle!" de Palma said, pointing at the large bird as it glided along the rising air currents. "They're incredibly rare!"

"You seem to know your birds, Commandant," the brigadier said as he steered the launch.

"Not really. But it seems like every time I come across that bird something bad happens."

The brigadier cut the engine. Near the small pebbly beach, a group of first-aiders were bustling about on the deck of the *Bonne Mère*. They stood round a decompression chamber. Thierry Garcia had just been placed inside. De Palma jumped up on a rock, a few metres away from the rescue workers.

"We're lucky," the doctor shouted. "There shouldn't be any adverse effects from the return to the surface."

"How come?"

"He wasn't down there long enough. It was only a few minutes. There wasn't time for his body to be affected by the difference in pressure."

Pauline Barton came out of the tent that served as their head-quarters. She was still wearing her blue and black diving suit and her hair was tied up in a bandana.

"I don't understand," she said, looking strained.

"Thierry's alright," de Palma reassured her. "He'll be back on his feet tomorrow."

Pauline threw her mask into a holdall. De Palma beckoned her away from the first aid workers.

"Did you notice anything out of place?" he asked. "The smallest clue can be important."

Without thinking she replied, "This morning on my way down I saw a place where some seaweed had been torn away."

"Did that seem odd to you?"

"Well, let's just say I'm very observant and none of our divers removed any weed yesterday. I'm sure about that, but . . ."

"How can you be sure?"

"I don't know. I've been checking everything for some time now."

Pauline picked up some small pebbles and played with them in her hands.

"It could be nothing, but I prefer to make a note of it. You don't dive alone?"

"No, never. Thierry Garcia was with me. Sometimes there are two or three of us. We can all look after ourselves."

"Thierry's going to be O.K."

"Well, we're not giving up."

"I've arranged for two men to be seconded to keep an eye on the site. I think the powers that be are starting to believe us."

"About time."

He liked this strong, open woman. She had boyish manners, her gestures were assured, and she took risks with every dive. Nothing seemed to get to her.

"There's something that might be important," she said.

"Go on."

"You remember the print you showed me, the one Autran drew, with the thumb and part of the middle finger missing?"

"Yes, of course."

"I only know one other like it and it's right here beneath your feet."

"That's not nothing, Pauline. It's probably very important."

"You think so?"

"I'm sure it is."

She looked up at de Palma. "Besides, now I think about it, there's a problem."

"What's that?"

"Those prints weren't listed during the first stage of the dig. I think they hadn't been discovered."

"Do you just think that or are you sure?"

"No, I'm sure. Because the negative prints are in a quite inaccessible part, on the ceiling just above the pieces of charcoal I discovered. I know Palestro – he wouldn't miss a fireplace, let alone those hands. So they can't have been discovered."

The first-aiders had just started up the rescue vessel. Two technicians from the Department of Marine Archaeology were rinsing the diving equipment in fresh water. Out on the open sea a passing sailing boat caught his attention. The rainbow spinnaker bulged like a giant's belly.

"What else did you find," de Palma went on, "apart from these prints?"

"As I mentioned, the hands are in quite an inaccessible part. You have to go down a sort of narrow passage not far from the shaft. There's a load of drawings and handprints, which haven't yet been examined. I'm going to get down to it next week. It's a place where there are lots of scratches on the walls. There's a slain man too," she added in a whisper.

"A slain man? They discovered one of those during the first dig."

"Yes, but they've just found another one. He's in an area where the rock face has flaked away. I haven't yet analysed it all. This one is clearly a bird man," Pauline added, "Must be between eighteen and nineteen thousand years old."

Julien Marceau, the last person to have seen Garcia before the attack, came out of the dig headquarters. He was wearing a yellow shirt that glowed in the sun. De Palma shook his hand.

"Have you told him about the strange voice?" Marceau asked, looking at Pauline.

"No."

She turned to the Baron.

"I think it's something to do with the acoustics. It must be the wind coming in through a cleft and that makes a strange sound, like a man's voice."

De Palma looked up at the cliff faces.

"There used to be another entrance. A shaft that led directly into the big chamber. We went that way when we arrested the Autran twins. But that opening is completely blocked now. There was a landslide. The wind might get in between the rocks and it would sound like a whistle."

"But there's one big snag," Marceau objected.

"What's that?"

"There's isn't a breath of wind today."

For once the press hadn't found out. Beyond the small worlds of pre-historians and first aid workers no-one knew about the second diving accident in Sugiton bay. Pauline reported the attempted murder to the police. De Palma took a statement from her, in spite of Commissaire Legendre's reluctance to get involved. The commissaire didn't see the case as any of the squad's business.

Bessour spent hours trawling through Thierry Garcia's past, as well as those of his acquaintances. But there was nothing to establish a link with the Autran case. His connection with Rémy Fortin amounted to just a few work meetings, nothing more.

Two days later Garcia recounted what had happened to him by the entrance to Le Guen's cave. De Palma drew up a statement and pressed him to go into great detail.

"He was so at ease in the water it felt like he was a fish," Garcia said. "Only a top diver could do that."

He was unable to give the height of his assailant. He also couldn't say what the person looked like, or even whether it was a man or a woman.

"Do you think the same thing happened to Fortin?"

"Yes, I think so," Garcia replied. "But in his case it was fatal."

De Palma did some quick calculations about pressure under water. He recalled that the main factors to be taken into account were the depth and the length of time spent there.

"How long were you underwater for?"

"Very little time at all," Garcia replied. "That's what saved me. When you're not under for long, the nitrogen doesn't have time to expand and no bubbles form."

So, de Palma thought, Fortin had stayed for much longer than planned. He needed to revise his initial calculations. But there was only one route from the cave to the surface. Fortin had no reason to stay longer at thirty-eight metres below.

"What was the colour of your diving suit?" de Palma asked suddenly.

"It's blue and black. We all wear the same ones, ever since Pauline managed to find a sponsor for our equipment."

"The same ones," de Palma repeated.

It had just dawned on him. The man in front of him was not the person they meant to kill.

*

"Do you think they can cure you?" Thomas asked.

"Of course. But what's the point? Psychiatry shouldn't exist."

Bernard listened when he said the word "psychiatrist". Thomas thought he was doing it to poke fun, but he couldn't be sure.

"Why do you say that?"

"Because psychiatrists can't understand I'm happy with my visions. I don't see this hospital. It's like I'm somewhere else."

"Where?"

"I'm not telling you. That's my secret. You don't tell me every-thing either, but there's stuff I know."

"Such as?"

"Sometimes you talk in your sleep. When they haven't doped you up."

"What do I say?"

When someone asked him a question that disturbed him, Bernard wriggled his bum around on the hard hospital chair. He was scared of questions when he knew the answers might result in conflict. Harmony was important.

"What do I say in my sleep?" Thomas insisted.

Bernard scratched his head so hard he nearly ripped his scalp.

"Don't worry," Thomas reassured him, "I won't get annoyed. But dreams are so mysterious sometimes I'd like to know a bit more."

Bernard shook like a character from the Muppet Show. He wanted to say something, but he stammered instead. Nothing came out of that mouth of his.

So Thomas took him in his arms and rocked him. It must have reminded him of his father, or his mother perhaps. Thomas was strong. Bernard felt safe in his arms.

When he returned from his land of pain, Bernard wrote poetry. Beautiful verse that a publisher wanted to publish, though he did not offer an advance for it. Bernard didn't care. It wasn't his family. He self-medicated with large doses of poetry. That was the best anti-psychotic. The men in white coats couldn't get over it. No more Nozinan or Largactil.

Thomas couldn't self-medicate with poetry. The voices that spoke to him came from a world where nothing was written down. Sometimes he did some sculpture. He had been told he was very gifted. He made shamanic objects: the lion man and the virgin goddess, whose eyes and mouth you never saw. Objects that helped him to sing and call on the spirits of the elders.

Only Bernard knew his friend's secret. He had even written a poem about it called "The Man Who Wanted to be Sacred". It was about a young man who travelled the worlds and set foot in the paradise in the stars. Thomas swore never to tell anyone about the poem. Sometimes he whispered it to himself in a corner of the grounds. Even if he shook like a leaf because of the Nozinan, he would never tell anyone.

Madmen have secrets that no-one must know.

# 14

The prison infirmary lay at the end of a long white corridor. It had a shiny floor with metal gates at several points. The cells faced one another. Glass block walls let in the daylight.

The door to cell number thirty-seven was open and the inner bars were locked. A prison officer kept watch 24–7. Thomas Autran slept without a pillow or blanket, huddled up on the floor. From time to time his body twitched. He kept turning over and grunted without opening his eyes.

Since he had been under sedation no-one wanted to wake him, except at meal times when hunger overcame his lethargy. Autran devoured everything they gave him, using his fingers, and then relapsed into semi-consciousness, his pyjamas soiled. Several times the screws on duty caught his eyes with their steely expression. They talked about it amongst themselves, with some trepidation. The chemical cocktail hadn't succeeded in completely subduing him. The entire staff was waiting impatiently for the transfer of prisoner number 167485.

A few hours after Morales' death, there was a riot in the prison yard. They had to bring in the Special Forces to get the prisoners back to their cells. The Governor hadn't given in to the clamour for punishment. The matter was closed.

The nearest unit for problem patients, at Sarreguemines, had no spare capacity. Officially Villejuif was also full, but they agreed to a swap. Before Thomas Autran could be transferred, Clairvaux had to accept another patient. That was the rule in those types of establishment, buckling under the demand for people to be locked up. The least mad were allowed to leave, so the real hard cases could be admitted. Autran belonged to the second category. For more than a week he had been given massive doses of tranquillisers.

On Tuesday evening authorisation for the transfer came through. This triggered a wave of relief.

"We're on for tomorrow," the Governor told the small delegation of officers gathered in his office. "He's leaving at three o'clock."

"Three?"

"Yes, two reasons for that. The first is I don't want to have the whole prison howling death threats from their cell windows. And secondly the Gendarmes don't want to arrive in Paris in the middle of the rush hour. With a patient like Autran, that could be risky. So we need to prepare things this evening."

"I'm not sure he'll understand anything, with all that stuff the shrink has stuck in his veins," the supervising officer said. "His brain is like porridge."

"When I say prepare," the Governor continued, "I mean everything needs to be done before the Gendarmes arrive."

"He was singing just now."

"Singing?"

"Yes, stuff you couldn't understand. A bit like Indians in the Westerns!"

The Governor looked irritated and shook his head.

"That's what we have to put up with. Raving lunatics who shouldn't be here in the first place."

He glanced sadly round at the officers.

"Thank you, gentlemen. Nice work. I know it's not easy."

At two-thirty in the morning the van arrived at the prison lock-up. At that same moment two officers opened the door to cell number thirty-seven. Autran was fast asleep. Seemingly lifeless. Six other officers waited outside in the corridor. Two psychiatric nurses had made the journey from the southern suburbs of Paris to fetch their new charge. They surrounded Autran and tried in vain to wake him. His body wouldn't respond. It took them several minutes to haul him back from the dark night where he had sought refuge.

"We're going to transfer you," the older nurse said. "To somewhere you'll be better off. This isn't the right place for you any more."

Autran's eyes were dead. He stared at them.

"Nowhere's ever been my place," he said with difficulty, struggling to open his lips.

"How do you feel?" the younger nurse asked.

"Like a psycho who's been drugged up."

The nurses and prison officers exchanged glances.

"Let's sit you down. Can you manage on your own?"

Autran stood up with difficulty, his legs unsteady. He reached the stool offered by one of the prison officers.

"That's good, Thomas. We need to secure you. You know what that means?"

He nodded.

The nurses, assisted by two officers, put his arms in the sleeves of a straitjacket and fastened the Velcro pads at the back.

"You'll be safer this way," the nurse said in a calm voice. "Don't be afraid."

His colleague put some stainless steel shackles round his ankles. Autran was just a human package, barely able to put one foot in front of the other.

"I want to see the sky," he said abruptly. "The sky."

"We'll get you sorted in the van. Then you'll be able to see the road. No problem."

They went down to the office in silence. The nurses dragged Autran, his feet trailing behind him. The formalities of the transfer went on forever. He waited in a corner surrounded by the screws. His hair was tousled and his eyes missed nothing. He watched the scene being played out in front of him, catching every facial movement or clumsy early morning gesture.

"Right, let's go then," the head nurse said, stuffing the paperwork into his black leather briefcase.

Outside it was snowing. The flakes fell in long, shiny streaks against the reddish searchlight beams and the green rectangles of the watchtowers. A fine dusting already covered the cobbles in the small yard separating the prison from the administrative buildings. Autran shuffled along, his shackles clinking as he went. A Gendarme held him on a lead tied to a snap hook on his straitjacket.

"Put him in the first cell in the van. You get the best view from there."

"Why's that?" the Gendarme asked.

"He wants to look at the landscape on the way," the nurse grumbled. "Hope that doesn't bother you."

"How do you mean?"

"Him looking at the view."

The Gendarme didn't reply. He opened the side door and roughly forced Autran inside, the driver pulling him under his arms, the other man shoving his behind. Once inside the tiny compartment, Autran pressed his nose against the wire mesh and gazed out beyond the stone walls and the shiny slate roofs. The curtain of snow spread a vast silence.

The van set off. A car belonging to the *Gendarmerie* followed behind, together with another unmarked vehicle that had been used to transport the people from Villejuif. It was still dark as the cortège left Clairvaux. The deserted road ran alongside fields interspersed with bare trees. A stream of cold air passed between the reinforced windows and the body of the van. Thomas drank it all in and forgot about Clairvaux. He stared at the frozen mud and looked for the large animals that might inhabit those empty spaces. In the distance he caught sight of a stag.

# 15

The conductor raised his baton. The lights from the music stands traced golden butterflies on his half-moon glasses. There was a silence, and then he swung into action. Two short notes, followed by a long one. Agamemnon's motif. The first maidservant crossed the stage.

*Where is Electra?*

The second servant shrugged.

*Is it not the time*
*When for her father she cries*
*So loud is her wailing*
*From every wall it echoes.*

The five servant girls wore white tunics. Their long hair fell down over their shoulders. In the background, there was a dark wall and a large figure.

Each day at the same hour Electra wept for her dead father. None of her servants went near her. None of them dared face the hatred of her hellcat eyes.

*The other day she lay there*
*groaning . . .*

Electra was fed with the dogs. She received her meagre fare in a bowl. Aegisthus, the lover who had replaced her father in her mother's bed, treated her thus. Yet Electra was the daughter of a king. Vengeance would be hers.

De Palma had come to the opera alone. He was tired. He had never been so tired. Ever since he learned that Dr Caillol had tried to visit Fortin's boat, he felt plagued by ghosts everywhere. The psychiatrist couldn't be brought in just like any other witness. There had to be serious grounds and for the time being there was nothing to justify putting him on the list of suspects.

De Palma didn't know if he was going down the wrong track, pursuing every lead that came up. He felt the need to get away, find somewhere remote. Strauss's music was his private domain, a refuge he didn't share with anyone. Not even Eva. He knew each violin note, each rumble of the brass and kettledrum, each dramatic emphasis. How many times had he heard them? He had no idea.

The previous night he had seen his brother. It was a long time since Pierre had appeared to him in that way. His face was serene; he had a gentle expression and a playful smile. Pierre's lips had moved, he said something, but Michel hadn't understood and the dream came to an end at daybreak. He got up, his limbs stiff, feeling as exhausted as the day before. He made Eva some coffee and then went back over the strange dream. Before it all became incomprehensible his brother had mentioned a name: Electra! An opera by Richard Strauss. A masterpiece of dark intensity, which made the authors of tales of blood and gore seem mere amateurs.

When he checked to see what was on at the Grand Théâtre Municipal, de Palma found there was a performance of "Electra" the very same night. It would be difficult to get a good seat. His annual subscription had expired after the last production of "The Marriage of Figaro". He hesitated and then rang an old acquaintance who worked for a ticket agency.

Eva encouraged him to go. She sensed he was too tense for her to raise an objection. In any case, she had to go and see her daughter, Anita.

Electra's song was one of dread. It told of Agamemnon's murder in his bath. At the first dazzling bowing of the cellos and double bass, the hysterical servants became silent and fearful. Deep notes from the brass and then the lament:

> *Agamemnon! Agamemnon!*
> *Where are you, father? Do you not have the strength*
> *To bring your face to me?*

De Palma closed his eyes.
Electra spoke in a low voice. She was anger personified.

> *Now comes the hour,*
> *The hour when they cut your throat,*
> *Your wife and the man who shares*
> *Your royal bed with her.*
> *They murdered you in your bath,*
> *The blood ran over your eyes,*
> *And the bath steamed with your blood.*

De Palma pictured once more his first night alone.

He was twelve years old. His twin brother had just died. In the dark he listened for the sound of shallow breathing. Often Pierre would talk in his sleep, then gasp and nod off again. Michel strained to listen, but there was nothing, only the strange creaking of the shutter. It sounded like Pierre's voice calling for their mother. Michel cried. He had lost his other half. No-one could understand that. Only twins understood. The one thing he had left was memories. He must never lose those. The flame must never go out. Otherwise half of him would cease to exist. When he was alone Michel spoke to his brother so the flames would never die.

Tonight Pierre asked him to listen to Electra's terrible lament:

*Father! Agamemnon! Your day will come!*
*Just as time always flows from the stars*
*So will the blood of a hundred throats pour on to your grave.*
*Spilling as from overturned amphoras,*
*The blood of killers in their chains,*
*Like a torrent in spate, wave upon wave,*
*Carrying away their life blood . . .*

The end of the long monologue had a bacchanalian feel. The rhythm was heavy, in three-four time. Each beat accentuated the desire for vengeance. A waltz of hatred.

At the end of the opera de Palma didn't hang around in the crush room to rail against the singers. The performance had been pretty mediocre, he felt. Instead he went home, his mind still caught in the shapeless mass of his deductions. Nothing made any sense.

Eva greeted him with a smile and some news: "We didn't scream at each other for once."

"Has Anita started to mellow then?"

"Yes, I think so."

Eva had put on some intoxicating perfume. She wore make-up, with a pencil skirt and stockings. De Palma felt cornered, but put up no resistance. He delighted in undressing her and they quietly made love, shielded from dark thoughts, while outside a sea breeze tore at the pine trees in the garden. Their desire sated, they took refuge under the duvet in the peaceful warmth of their double bed. She snuggled up close to him. He looked at her and told himself he had never seen eyes with so much light. No-one could ever paint them.

Later that night as the Baron went off to sleep he recited aloud:

*Now comes the hour,*
*The hour when they cut your throat*

"What are you on about?" Eva asked, frowning.

"It's from 'Electra' . . . Richard Strauss."

"Did you enjoy the show?"

He nodded, then was silent. His eyes remained fixed on the ceiling. His lips quivered, the words seemed to die there.

*The blood ran over your eyes,*
*And the bath steamed with your blood.*

Eva didn't dare look at him. She moved her leg over his.

"The Leonie Rysanek production will always be my favourite," the Baron went on.

"Oh right," said Eva, "That's reassuring to know."

"Do you know why I'm thinking about it?"

No answer was necessary.

"When we were searching for the Autran twins," de Palma continued, "I had a recording of that opera in my car, with Rysanek in the lead role. It was wonderful. I used to listen to it on a loop."

"A bit like those Bach suites, when you're in the mood."

"Yeah, that's right."

"Just one small question," Eva said. "Why 'Electra'?"

"Thomas and Christine: it's a bit like the story of Electra and her brother Orestes."

De Palma pointed his finger in the air like a teacher and drew some lines between imaginary dots.

"Agamemnon, King of Mycenae, was killed. His wife, Clytemnestra, colluded in the murder. Seven years after the king's death, his son Orestes took revenge, with the help of his sister Electra."

*The dead are jealous: and for a fiancé*
*He sent me hate with hollow eyes.*

"You know it off by heart!" Eva exclaimed.

"That story's haunted me for some time. It's a bit of a mystery. I've a feeling it's going to keep cropping up and we'll have to find an answer."

Eva turned off the bedside light. Long blue shadows rose from the surrounding furniture.

# 16

The next day Pauline went back to Quinson. The sky was leaden. Snow had fallen over the Manosque hills and Verdon ridges. Down below patches of fog hung in the scrawny orchards and prostrate villages.

Palestro was standing on his doorstep with a gnarled stick in his hand, ready for a stroll. Winter was his favourite time of year. He often used to say that in cold weather he felt more in touch with prehistoric times.

"Only you can help us," Pauline said, shaking Palestro's hand. "I didn't tell you everything the last time we met. And there's been a second incident since then."

Palestro remained impassive as though he'd half expected another meeting.

"We're going for a walk," he announced. "Pre-historians gets their best ideas walking in the countryside. Never forget that man is a walker. Afterwards we'll have some supper."

They took a little shortcut leading down to the banks of the Verdon. The cliffs were creased like old fabric, dotted with black dwarf oaks and age-old rust stains. Emerald waters ran slowly between the rock faces and the sparse woods.

Palestro pointed to some tracks in the mud. "Wild boar," he said. "Definitely a large male. He was running."

"Do you still hunt then?"

"No, that's over now, I'm too old for all that. No more hunting, I'm just a gatherer. With a bit of luck we might find some black trumpets. There isn't much else at this time of year."

"You wonder what people found to eat in the Palaeolithic period."

Palestro stopped and sniffed at the cold air. "A whole load of things you'd never suspect. Roots, for example, and game. Today you don't see anything, but if you think about it, twenty thousand years ago you'd have come across some big birds, hairy beasts and I don't know what. Times have changed, sadly."

Palestro had published a study on the dietary behaviour of men in the upper Palaeolithic era. The tome had helped researchers in nutrition to develop new slimming diets. He stopped a little way from the Verdon. The waters were calmer and darker there.

"The same thing happened to Thierry Garcia that happened to Fortin," Pauline said.

"Garcia? I don't know him."

"A young guy from Bordeaux University. He survived."

Palestro grunted. He was becoming less and less concerned with anything that happened outside his own world. Pauline understood he was waiting for other news. She took the plunge:

"Shortly before he died, Fortin took some photos of a man with an antler head."

Palestro didn't seem surprised. His wrinkled face showed no emotion.

"You'll have to tell me more," he replied in a neutral tone.

"Apparently he found a statuette twenty centimetres high. The head's barely hinted at. Above the eyes, carved in the wood, you can make out some antlers like a cervid's. It's quite clumsy, but clearly visible."

"Have you got the photos?"

"Of course."

Palestro stared sternly at each photo.

"You haven't found the object Fortin took a photo of?"

"No," she said.

"Doesn't that seem inconceivable? Fortin takes photos of a statuette, which then disappears. It doesn't make sense."

She nodded. De Palma had asked the same question. But there was no answer.

Palestro picked up a pebble and chucked it into the clear water. The stone slowly sank before coming to rest on the bottom.

"It's like that stone. The sudden appearance of the irrational, in a theoretically coherent world. No stone ever falls in the water here. But it can happen, if a child decides to throw one, or an old professor like me."

He threw a second stone as if trying to convince himself of the soundness of his theory.

"Strange things have always happened at Le Guen's cave. At the moment it seems completely irrational for that statue to be there. It's inexplicable. That stone on the bottom only makes sense to someone who lives by the Verdon."

Pauline had stuffed her hands in her pockets, her eyes remaining fixed on the pebble.

"Stones don't just fall from the sky, Pauline. Do you see what I mean?"

"Yes, Professor."

"Someone put that figurine there."

"But that seems impossible."

He turned towards the lake.

"Someone or something," he muttered under his breath.

She shuddered at the idea that the scholar might be trying to alert her to a danger she refused to confront. Palestro continued to walk. The sun had passed between some rocky outcrops. The russet oak leaves fluttered in the warm breeze.

"Have you thought about the spirits?" Palestro exclaimed. He was just a few metres from Pauline.

"The spirits?"

"If men have come to this cave for thousands of years, there's a reason."

He pointed at the surrounding rocks and bushes.

"There are hundreds of caves in this region. From here to the Calanques and I don't know where else. So why Le Guen's cave?"

"Because it's the only one we've discovered!"

He gave a wan smile.

"Good point. All our digging and research only give us a very vague picture. The prehistoric world is how we see it. But I was talking about the exceptionally long history of this sanctuary."

"I understand," Pauline said.

"A period of time that is quite extraordinary."

His eyes blazed.

"It's up to you to explain that. You've already found the workshop of some of the artists who drew in this cave. We still have to find out the reason. That's the great mystery of cave painting."

She was disturbed to hear him talk of mysteries. Unlike Christine Autran, Palestro had never had fanciful ideas about prehistoric religions. Just brilliant deductions, drawn from impressive amounts of reading and research. He asked whether she believed in spirits. She replied that she didn't. Believing in spirits could well drive her mad, or perhaps even destroy her.

They walked to the Baume Bonne cave. The path climbed towards a plateau. Palestro stopped, out of breath.

"This was where I started out," he said.

Bushes now covered the excavations carried out by Palestro's team back in the early seventies. The roof on the site hut had collapsed.

Pauline went up to a trench. The archaeological layers could be seen perfectly.

"Do you know who was working on the 1970 dig?" Palestro asked.

"No."

"Pierre Autran. Thomas and Christine's father. We got to know each other a few years before that. He used to come to my lectures in Aix."

"I didn't know he'd been a pre-historian in his day."

"He was better than any professional."

Palestro walked alongside the rectangular dig towards his house. From time to time he glanced down at the deep holes in the barren earth. He stopped at the place where, in July 1970, Jérémie Payet had discovered the man with the antler head.

At the time Payet was finishing his doctorate. He had offered supervision to some students struggling with their M.A. dissertations. Finding the statuette was the result of his work and his intuition. It would have had an enormous impact on his career. But Palestro was in charge. He had identified the find and become its author. The world of eggheads is a cruel one. Payet had threatened to sue; he fired off some angry letters. But it was a waste of time. The man with the antler head disappeared just a few days after it was discovered. The police investigated Payet for a while, then Autran and Palestro himself. But it was all in vain, and the case went no further.

"This is it," said Palestro sadly, pointing to the slightly darker Gravettian layer, two metres down.

"What happened?" Pauline asked.

Palestro stared at her for a few seconds. "The man with the antler head in your photos . . . he was found here."

*

"Tell me about the history of the sacred cave."

Papa closed his eyes to concentrate, as he always did.

"For thousands of years, people didn't live in solid houses like we do. They built huts at nightfall when they had to stop hunting. Sometimes they found shelter by the cliffs. It depended. In those days men were free.

94

"One day a child about your age saw a great hole at the foot of a high peak. He went up and saw that it went deep into the bowels of the mountain. There was a long passage and at the end a faint light danced in the dark.

"Intrigued he walked inside, holding his breath. The caves were the sacred territory of the spirits. No-one could go inside except those who understood magic.

"As the young man walked towards the light, a strange voice starting to sing a song he had never heard before. He had to be really brave to carry on. The cave was cold and damp. Water ran down from a roof he couldn't see. It was freezing. He walked until he saw the silhouette of an old man sitting on an enormous stone.

"The old man's voice was frail, but as he sang every word bounced off the walls of the cave. It sounded like women wailing at a vigil. Suddenly everything went quiet.

"The old man went over to the wall of the cave. In the torchlight the young boy noticed some painted signs on the walls. The hands of sacred men. No child was allowed to see these magic symbols. When the man waved his torch above his head the boy thought he saw a large stag run across the ceiling. He crouched down and closed his eyes, afraid the spirit might come and carry him off.

"It was then he saw the old man put his hand on the rock and blow earth over it. A thumb and two fingers were missing."

# 17

Bang! A sharp noise resounded round the common room, then another. Thomas lifted his heavy eyelids.

Big Lulu was laying into the table football. He had boxer's hands. Savage grunts came from his stomach and filled the room. Opposite, Pierrot, his brain like porridge, watched the cork ball zigzag back and forth. His eyes were glazed from the tranquillisers. From the moment he'd arrived the nurses had given Pierrot the full treatment: restraint, the straitjacket and heavy medication – the kind that plays havoc with the nervous system and turns wolves into lambs.

More than three weeks had elapsed since Autran's transfer to the unit. For some time he had been allowed to use the common room. It was air conditioned and, unlike the other communal areas, it didn't smell of detergent, piss, and life gone bad.

Lulu was wearing his blue tracksuit, its trouser legs worn and shiny. The medication had turned his hair greasy and his pock-marked skin had an odd sheen. He had the face of a fallen angel: empty eyes, a fine nose and cheeks ravaged by anxiety. Lulu was a killer and Pierrot not much better.

The head nurse strode across the room. With each step his spotless white coat flapped like a cape. A murky light came through the large windows, the bleak day never ending. In the yard the chestnut trees stood like sentries, their scrawny branches sticking out from lumps in the trunks. Autran sat down on a bench. Its feet were fixed into the yellow, red and grey tiled floor. The head nurse crossed the room in the other direction and stopped by him.

"Feeling any better, Thomas?"

Autran didn't reply immediately.

"Are you alright?"

Autran nodded and gestured with his hand.

"Everything's good."

On the seat beside him, François, a lunatic with an ashen expression caused by years on medication, had pulled his T-shirt over his face, exposing the dark belly button on his smooth stomach. It was a habit he had adopted some time ago. When he wanted to shut out the faces of people in the mad house, he hid behind those few centimetres of cloth. To him the piece of fabric was the whole world and its delights; his visions of the hereafter with the colours of paradise.

Thomas closed his eyes and inhaled. He was no longer bothered by the clammy air. For some time Papa had advised him to keep calm and not attract the nurses' attention. Act the model nutter, the curable crazy one. The patient who could be tamed by medication, or moronic activities such as pottery or sculpture.

His time was coming. Papa had predicted it.

During exercise time he always sat in the yard in the same place: on the ground, beneath the chestnut tree, a few steps from the perimeter wall. Discreetly he put his hand to the ground and listened to the spirits, as Papa had taught him. From the bowels of the earth came the first incomprehensible murmuring: the wailing of souls. A distorted rumbling, followed by phrases that slowly came together, word by word. One uttered his name, then another, and another. A long string of voices, taking hold of him.

The singing from the world below ran through his fingers and entered him in thousands of dazzling pieces. He was the earth, the breath of animals, the strength of the trees and the vigour of the spring flowers. All at once.

The three nurses accompanying him had never questioned him about his attitude or that strange habit he had of listening at the gates of the hereafter. They wouldn't have understood anyway.

The biggest one often used to ask, "Want a game of footie, Thomas?"

"No," he would reply. "I'd rather read."

"Prehistory, eh? That's all you're interested in!"

"Yes. It was a time of infinite purity."

The nurses gave off a bitter smell. Fear gnawed away at them. They were afraid of First Man because he was the wonder of their conscience, their most noble instinct. The most repressed part of themselves. The primitive person; unsullied, intact. He had nourished himself with the strength of beings; he had absorbed the soul of the vanquished. The nurses didn't really know his power, but instinctively they feared it.

Once Thomas had overheard a conversation with a newcomer called Jacques. He was clean-shaven and built like a tank.

"Watch out for Autran. Number 17, ward 36. Don't let him out of your sight. He's been creeping me out ever since he got here."

"But you could say he's a model patient . . ."

"Yes, but he's the hardest nut of all."

Jacques had glanced discreetly in his direction. Thomas smiled back, without staring. Not that.

The next day at the same time three nurses left the common room; there was an incident in ward 38, the intensive care unit. The nutter with arms like hams was still having fits. The first day he'd been to the sculpture studio he had bitten Gilbert, the simpleton who didn't know why he was there.

Thomas Autran hid in the blind spot. Through the peephole he saw the doctor go past, with a straitjacket in his right hand. Ham Hands was due for some restraint. Which only made the disturbed even more disturbed.

He glanced rapidly towards the kitchen. The nurse couldn't see him. Thomas worked out how long it would take him to open the common room door and run to the tree. After climbing the tree he had to jump across the ditch and sprint to the perimeter fence. At the time of his transfer, when the police van had stopped in the general area of the hospital, he had time to look out through the slit and see the place where the wall was only one metre fifty high. At the speed of a great hunter, he was just four minutes away.

The hardest thing was to leave the cage for nutters. He had been preparing for this moment for nine years. With all the determination of someone who knows he will never obtain leave or remission. No indulgence. Nothing. He was considered too dangerous.

A glazed opening separated the kitchen from the room he was in. When the nurse looked over to the common room, he couldn't see Thomas in the dark corner.

Lulu was hunched over his table football. Pierrot's eyes were glued on the ball which went back and forth between the upright players, stiff as lead soldiers. François was still tucked away in his world of stars, motionless beneath his piece of cloth.

Thomas carefully opened the door and went out, remembering to close it behind him. He ran beneath the windows, bent double but nimble as a young athlete. The tree with the voices was outside everyone's line of sight. He scaled it, scrabbling at the trunk with his powerful hands. Once he reached the main branch he could see the people working in the hospital kitchens. Straddling the branch he hoisted himself up to the end, got to his feet and crouched low to obtain the maximum spring. Then he leapt. Three metres. Another person would have broken their bones.

The ditch was behind him now. He was by the outer wall of the hospital. A section of tarred road ran alongside a three-storey rough stone building. The perimeter wall was much too high on this side. He needed to reach the administrative buildings. More than two hundred metres across open ground.

A car appeared at the end of the main path. He hid behind an enormous dustbin. His muscles ached. His thighs twitched. In a few hours he would start to miss all that rubbish they had pumped into him. His whole body would cry out for it, but he would stay strong. He massaged his legs.

The day was receding. A blue light spread over the tarmac. Soon they would turn on the yellow searchlights on top of the walls. Thomas emerged from his hiding place and sniffed the air. No enemy around. He walked quickly, lengthening his stride. He was only a hundred metres from the place where the perimeter wall was lower.

A doctor emerged from C Block, with his nose in a file. Another joined him and lit a cigarette. Autran increased his speed. He passed some visitors, but they seemed indifferent.

Just sixty metres to go.

He tensed. The nursing auxiliary and junior doctor had their backs to him. Another car appeared at the end of the car park. The headlights swept the semi-darkness.

Forty metres. He hid behind a tree, then a delivery van. It was five minutes since he had left the unit. At any moment they would sound the alarm. He caught his breath. His muscles were hard as steel and racked with thousands of small contractions. His body seized up as though grains of sand were spreading through his joints. He had experienced the same feeling the first time he escaped, but not so soon. Every neuron in his body was saturated with medication. For years they had been stuffing him full of anti-psychotics and hypnotics. Injections and little pills of every conceivable colour. Depending on how restless he was, how dangerous he was to himself and to others, to use the fine words of the Public Health Code.

Thomas focused. One by one he unlocked the parts of his body. The sand retreated from his joints. He started to run. With every stride he was carried along by a sublime strength. With each thrust of his hips, his long legs lifted him as he tore away from the cage for nutters. He put both hands on the edge of the low wall and toppled over – into the other world.

# PART TWO

# The Wounded Man

The magic of the hunt sought to ensure a favourable outcome, taking possession of the animal to be killed and thus of the beast itself.

Jean Clottes and David Lewis-Williams
– *The Shamans of Prehistory*

# 18

"Weapons in your belts! Three steps: freeze, draw, fire!"

Robert, the shooting instructor, stood just behind the two policemen, with his ear protectors clamped down over his small, birdlike head. De Palma looked in Bessour's direction and stroked the grip of his S&W Bodyguard 38. He had never liked training sessions, but he didn't want to miss this one as it would be his last.

"I want every shot on target. Understood? Ready for my signal."

Robert whistled. De Palma took two big strides and adopted the firing position, chest straight, long legs bent. For a fraction of a second he stared blankly at the cardboard silhouette in front of him, then fired. Bessour was more relaxed, his arms loose. He was still young enough to like weapons and the sound of bullets.

"Weapons in your belts!"

De Palma removed his protectors as though being released from a straitjacket. His hair was plastered to his skull with sweat. An acid smell of cordite had spread through the firing range.

"Good!" Robert said. "Very good. Nice to see the Squad on target for once."

"Yeah, but at least we can read," de Palma said sourly.

"Well, I hope you can count too. Let's see how you've both done." The two policemen followed the instructor.

"Perfect, Karim. All six on target. Nice spread too. Well done. Immaculate. You can tell you've got your diploma."

"A lot of good it does me!" Bessour said, taking a second magazine from his jeans' back pocket.

De Palma looked for a few seconds at the holes produced by the three bullets lodged in the dummy's heart. They were all fatal. Two others had gone wide of the mark, and the last one was lost, somewhere.

"Michel, that's good, but you can do better. The two first shots are off target, so if the bloke returns fire you're dead!"

"I'm retired, not dead. This is my last session. Finito!"

Robert was probably about to have the last word when Commissaire Legendre appeared at the entrance to the range and waved to de Palma.

"Hello, boss," de Palma said. "Come to see if your men can shoot?"

"Oh, I don't have to worry about you now. Unfortunately."

De Palma stared at the Commissioner.

"You've got a face as long as a wet weekend!" he said with a smile. "Doesn't look good. Have you seen the Governor?"

"No. Autran's done a runner. He's vanished."

De Palma was shaken, but tried not to show it. He ejected the cartridges and reloaded with six .38 specials.

"Autran, that's all ancient history," he said in a cold voice.

"The judge has referred it to us."

"Why us? This sort of thing is head office's responsibility."

The Baron lowered the cylinder on his weapon and stuffed it back in its leather holster. Then he added, "Why have you come to see me? You've got other lads in your squad."

"Let's just say you're the best qualified."

The Baron gave his boss a hard look.

"In three weeks I'm going to hang up my boots. You won't have found him by then. Why don't you choose someone else who'll still be around?"

Legendre hissed through his teeth, "I know your file, Michel.

You don't have to leave in three weeks' time. I can put in for an extension."

"So?"

"I want you and Bessour to take on the case."

"So I don't have a choice?"

"That's not what I mean. We need you. Finish your session then meet me down the nick. We can take a look at things."

De Palma and Bessour went back to their instructor. He beckoned them towards the middle of the range.

"Right, last round. Don't freeze. Two steps, draw and fire twice. Another two steps, and fire. Got it?"

Bessour concentrated and reached for his Beretta. "No, Karim, arm by your side. Ready?"

A piercing whistle. Another round of dull salvos. De Palma emptied his cylinder into a circle about thirty centimetres in diameter, right in the bull's eye.

"Congratulations, Michel!"

"Anger is a great motivator," the Baron muttered.

*The dead are jealous: and for a fiancé,*
*He sent me hate with hollow eyes.*

The meeting room at the serious crime squad was a soulless place, with new, supposedly functional, furniture. Several imitation wood tables fitted together to form an oval shape. Legendre sat at the head and placed a file in front of him.

"Thomas Autran, a patient from the secure unit at Villejuif, escaped late yesterday afternoon," he said. "When I say patient, you need to understand he's a very dangerous individual. Capable of anything. Michel's team arrested this man ten years ago. I'll leave it at that. De Palma."

The Baron impatiently removed the ribbon from the old file and opened it, "Thomas Autran. Born 27 February, 1958, in Marseille.

Height: 1 metre 85 cms. Brown hair. Here's what he looks like."

The Baron turned over a photo from the criminal records office and passed it to Bessour who was sitting immediately to his left.

"He's the son of Pierre Autran, who studied civil engineering at the École des Ponts et Chaussées and died in September 1970; and Martine Autran, née Combes, who died in a car accident in March 1982. Last known address: 36 rue des Bruyères, Marseille.

The picture of Thomas Autran looked like a glossy school photo. With his strange, faint smile, he looked angelic. Two almond-shaped eyes stared nonchalantly at the camera, miles away from the moment. The photograph bore a prisoner number and the name: Marseille Regional Criminal Investigation Branch.

"He was arrested in Le Guen's cave," de Palma said.

"Le Guen's cave!" exclaimed Bessour, who was taking careful notes.

"Yes, in one of the Calanques near Marseille. Prehistory is his obsession: a return to the earliest stages of humanity. In fact he was about to sacrifice a woman called Sylvie Maurel, performing a primitive ritual."

"We need to get in touch with her right away," Legendre mumbled, as he made a note of the name. "In case he wants to finish off the job."

"Already done," de Palma said. "Sylvie Maurel is now living in South Africa where she works on archaeological digs. I rang her to give her the good news."

Legendre handed back the photo.

"Michel hasn't told you he was nearly killed by Autran when he arrested him. An axe blow to the forehead. And he wasn't wearing a helmet or torch either . . . isn't that right, Michel?"

"No comment, boss," de Palma said, opening a purple folder.

The first photo was unbearable, even for detectives hardened by years in the serious crime squad. Blood spread thickly over dead leaves, a woman's body, legs apart, stockings torn.

"Hélène Weill," the Baron explained in a flat voice. "Forty-five years old. Divorced. Found in a forest near Cadenet, about sixty kilometres from Marseille. The *Gendarmerie* did the report. It was the first time the pathologist had come across an act of cannibalism. Me too, I have to say."

Bessour tried to detach himself from the images that bombarded him. He passed the photo to the colleague on his right and took a second one that de Palma handed him.

"Autran ate the upper thigh and cut off her leg with a stone axe or rudimentary knife. We never could find out which. Her skull was crushed with a similar weapon."

The third shot was a close-up. Beside the body Autran had left a drawing of a hand on a plain sheet of A4 paper, using the stencil technique. His signature.

Hélène Weill had been abducted while attending a session with her psychoanalyst. Autran pretended to be a patient to seduce her. From the outset, his M.O. had been very sophisticated. He knew instinctively how to approach his victims and conceal his identity. He left nothing behind – no marks that could be used. Nothing except the painted hands.

De Palma moved on to a second set of photos. "Julia Chevallier. Found at her home. I'll skip the details. Let's just say it raised the bar of horror a notch or two. Same handprint. In this case it seems he pretended to be a priest. Julia suffered from anxiety and she'd asked for help from a man of God . . ."

The photos were passed from hand to hand. Bessour watched de Palma out of the corner of his eye. The wound on his forehead was covered by a curly lock of hair. His face clouded over at the mention of certain points in the investigation.

Autran's twin sister, Christine, had been complicit in the crimes. At the time she was teaching prehistory at the University of Provence. She was brilliant. At the trial the court accepted she was unbalanced, but took the view she still had legal capacity. The experts believed the twins' relationship was a fused one and most certainly incestuous. She was sentenced to twelve years' imprisonment for aiding and abetting.

"With remission she could be out in a year, or sooner," de Palma explained. "Maybe even tomorrow."

Legendre drained his coffee and pulled a face, "Shit. It's cold." Expertly he tossed the plastic cup into the wire basket. "Any questions?"

"What about the escape?" Bessour asked, fiddling with his pen.

"I was coming to that," Legendre went on. "From the prison authorities' point of view Autran is a D 339 . . . that's a prisoner who's been moved from prison to an acute unit for security reasons. And with good reason."

He took a large-framed photograph from a folder and briskly turned it over. A man lay on a white tiled floor, his skull shattered.

"Gregory Morales. Twenty-eight. Clairvaux prison. A gypsy, doing life. Armed robberies, homicides, the whole shebang. He was in the library trying to get himself a bit of education. Autran likewise. The screws were standing some way away. No-one knows exactly what happened or why. Autran smashed in his skull."

Legendre put back the photo and rubbed his forehead. "They think he ate part of the brain and . . . Let's leave it at that, shall we?"

Bessour couldn't take his eyes off the photos.

"Just to be clear," Legendre went on, "we're being asked to coordinate all investigations for the Marseille region. As things stand we've got nothing to go on. I'm waiting for the complete file to arrive any minute."

The Commissaire turned solemnly towards the Baron. "Thanks for staying on, Michel."

By way of response de Palma recited:

*Father! Agamemnon! Your day will come!*
*Just as time always flows from the stars*
*So will the blood of a hundred throats pour on your grave.*
*Spilling us from overturned amphoras,*
*The blood of killers in their chains,*
*Like a torrent in spate, wave upon wave,*
*Carrying away their life blood . . .*

# 19

Dawn. Thomas Autran felt tired. The back alley opened on to a bare courtyard with peeling walls. Window boxes filled with evergreens brightened up the top floors of the blocks of flats, the only ones to share the meagre Parisian sunshine. The ground floor flats belonged to the shops on rue de la Folie-Méricourt, or to craftsmen who had set up small businesses there. The patio was cluttered with polystyrene packaging and empty cardboard boxes.

He sat down on a step between two dustbins and closed his eyes. The shaking started in the arch of his foot, spreading in uncontrollable waves, first to his right leg, then his left. Then the muscles started to contract. He felt as if he was made of wood, full of knots and ties.

He needed to sleep, change his clothes and disappear. The night in Paris had worn him out. There were too many police: dozens of patrols, particularly near the bright lights and in the affluent parts of town.

A fresh wave of pain drilled into his guts. His heartbeat quickened. Like a faltering engine it slowed, then raced again. These were the side effects of the last medication they'd given him at the mad house. Escaping that mysterious security guard was perhaps more of a risk than meeting any police patrol. You didn't get much lower than the unit.

Scrawny tufts of grass had managed to grow between the cracks in the glistening cobbles. Thomas needed to be like those wisps of life, trapped in a hostile universe. To resist and find in tiny things the strength to live.

He stood up and went back to rue de la Folie-Méricourt. A man of a similar build to him turned into rue Oberkampf: a middle-aged guy wearing jeans and trainers like someone in his twenties. Fashion had hardly changed in the past nine years. He let the man hurry on for about fifty metres then started to follow him. The man stopped by a cash machine.

At that time of morning the streets were still deserted. Paris was overcast and at a standstill. The calm before the storm. Some delivery drivers dawdled in front of metal shop shutters; waiters with grey faces relished their cigarettes as they thought of that first coffee with bread and butter, a first small glass of white wine . . . In less than an hour the crowds would be bustling, yelling and pawing their way through the hubbub and the circumvolutions of the great sick brain that was the city.

The middle-aged man put a nice wad of notes in his wallet. The waiter from the Brasserie on the corner went back to his bar. The road emptied in the blink of an eye. The hunter's moment of grace. Autran sprang upon the man, delivering a sharp blow to the base of the skull, where the carotid bulged.

Two hundred euros!

No-one had seen a thing. Autran dragged the man between a car and a Volkswagen van, removed his jacket and the polo shirt with a Dodgers baseball logo on it, undid his shoes, stuffed them into his bag and fled in the direction of boulevard Richard-Lenoir.

Traffic was starting to build up on the arterial road, a tide of metal spreading slowly through the veins of the city. The first commuters were searching for a place to park, having come to Paris to while away their grey lives. Autran got changed on the central reservation. The brand new Nike trainers fitted perfectly. The polo shirt and jacket were a bit on the large side.

In the wallet he found two more twenty-euro notes, as well as some train tickets. He kept the money and tickets but chucked the wallet into a bush before disappearing into the nearest Metro station.

He was floored by a wave of pain. Everything felt rotten inside. His arm began to shake uncontrollably and his heart raced. Large drops of sweat trickled down his forehead. He bit his fist to muffle the horrific cry rising from his belly. He scanned his brain cells looking for some healthy synapses to try to re-establish the connections, but nothing worked. His fit went on and on, then like the Mistral withdrew, fleeing the coastal lands till it reached the sea and mysteriously disappeared.

He came out of the station. No visions, no voices. The contractions had stopped. The engine was still running smoothly. Passers-by with baleful eyes and sad expressions scurried past African shops. The air smelled of sugar cane, curry and salted fish. Groups of bearded men stood talking in front of Indian bazaars, while eyeing the traffic around them. Children zigzagged between the passers-by, satchels bobbing on their backs. Thomas assumed they were late for school. It reminded him of all the time he had spent in prison and asylums, removed from everyday life.

A gloomy melody swelled between the facades of boulevard de la Chapelle. The thunder of the overhead railway on its grey struts, the low throb of cars at a standstill, snatches of voices from bars, high-pitched horns, harsh barking, the wailing of sirens – it grew louder and louder, beating against Autran's temples, making him wince with pain. A pensioner waited for his poodle as it peed against the wheel of a delivery van. He stopped to ask the time.

"Eight-thirty, Monsieur."

He took a taxi to the Gare du Nord. The Chinese driver, a small anxious man, kept changing lanes, sucking air between his teeth. He exuded a smell of stale tobacco and wore the same cheap deodorant as the chief screw on B Block.

"Long night?" Autran asked.

"Oh, you last fare!" the taxi driver exclaimed, his smile like an old ivory keyboard. "Drive twelve hours . . . Too much!"

The taxi driver's bag lay in a compartment beside the meter. There should be a nice sum there.

"Can you stop just past the lights, I'll do the rest on foot."

The taxi parked outside the entrance to a textile wholesaler on boulevard Magenta. Autran handed the driver a ten-euro note.

"You no change?"

"No."

The driver picked up the bag. The blow landed that very same moment with flawless power and precision. Four hundred and ten euros! Enough to treat himself to a change of clothes, a sports bag, a new haircut and a good meal.

As he fled, First Man remembered the prints he must have left on the man in rue de la Folie-Méricourt. And on the seat of the taxi. Like a wolf, or fox, he knew how to throw hunters off their scent.

By that evening, if the dogs weren't too dumb, they would have all the clues they needed to trace him to boulevard Magenta. A beautiful dead end.

Then it would be the nutter's turn to deal.

# 20

A long stone wall with a watchtower rising at an acute angle. Opposite, a straggling village with an archway, two or three shops and a bar where local winos languished. Once in a while prisoners' families and friends would go there for a drink.

"It's on the left," de Palma muttered, flicking his indicator.

At the entrance two tricolour flags hung forlornly from their poles in the dressed stone walls, either side of the grey gate. Above, a recently renovated triangular pediment cut between the long brown-tiled roofs. Inscribed in the cold stone:

CLAIRVAUX PRISON

"I'll let you in."

The prison officer had done up every single button on his sky blue shirt. He blinked when he opened his mouth. A strand of blond, limp hair fell across his ruddy forehead.

"Are you armed?"

De Palma undid his holster and handed it to the officer.

A gently sloping yard ran down towards a formal classical building which contained the administration, as well as the Governor's office and his apartments. At the end there was a large windowless wall with a huge heavy gate. A watchtower. The closed world of notorious killers. The prison.

De Palma sneezed. The acrid air stung his eyes.

"We had a bit of trouble here last night," the officer explained. "We had to bring in the riot squad. They let off some tear gas in B Block."

De Palma felt his suit was too small for him. He couldn't help sneezing again. Two of his old 'clients' were festering here. He did some quick mental arithmetic: soon the older one would have been locked up for twenty years. He tried going over everything he had done in that period. It seemed like a lifetime. Marriage, divorce, the thousand and one little things that made him happy. The women in his life. And Eva. His was a whirlwind existence; the prisoners' lives at a standstill.

A man of about fifty appeared through a beige door, a welcoming smile on his face.

"Hello, Commandant. How are you?"

"I think I was better off outside, in spite of the cold."

"I see your point."

"May I introduce Captain Bessour?"

The Governor invited the two detectives into his austere office. There was a massive old oak desk. The only decoration was a portrait of a woman, presumably his wife, and a sign that read: Bernard Monteil, Governor. Clairvaux had been an abbey before it was transformed into a huge gaol, the most secure in France.

"We had a narrow escape with this Autran business," Monteil sighed. "A very narrow escape. We nearly lost control of the prison. The prisoners wanted to skin him alive."

He pressed a button on his telephone extension. "Can you get hold of Longnon for me?" he muttered to an invisible secretary.

Through the barred window frame, it was possible to see the woods overlooking the prison, rising stiffly in a mantle of mist. There was a knock at the door. Longnon appeared, holding his hands folded in front of him as men do at Mass.

"Good morning, sir."

Monteil did the introductions.

The officer looked flustered. Karim held out his hand to put him at ease.

"What exactly did he do before he went for Morales?" he said gently.

Longnon seemed surprised by the question. He turned to the governor.

"I remember quite clearly, he was reading *L'Histoire*."

"O.K. So was he reading any articles in particular?"

"It was a special issue on prehistory."

"Did he say anything?"

"Yes."

"Can you remember what?"

"He said: 'This is the sign . . .'."

"The sign?" de Palma looked surprised.

"Yes, that's right," Longnon said, nodding his head. "It's the sort of thing you don't forget."

De Palma ignored the officer's anxiety. "Can we have a look at his things?"

"Of course."

The Governor stood up and pointed to two cardboard boxes on the floor.

"It's all there. Clothes in the left-hand one. We'll get them sent on. In the right one there are some books and odds and ends. We've been through the clothes several times, but there's nothing at all."

"I'd like to have a look at the books."

Monteil put the box down on his desk, "That's fine, go ahead."

The first book was *Early Man* by Henri de Lumley, and the next a pocket edition of *The Shamans of Prehistory* by Jean Clottes. Autran hadn't made any notes. He had ordered the books a fortnight before the crime had been committed.

"He tore out this article," Longnon said. "He had it hidden on him. It's from *L'Histoire*."

De Palma opened the insert that Autran had folded carefully in eight and hidden behind a wooden shelf in his cell.

"Do you know it?" the Governor asked.

"It's a prehistoric cave near Marseille," de Palma replied. "From what we know he's obsessed by the place."

The Governor whistled. "The guy's really got a screw loose."

"He's looking for a different kind of world," de Palma went on. "A different sort of myth . . . a return to life as it was before the Neolithic revolution, when man didn't know about raising cattle or owning property, or that sort of thing. According to the psychiatric reports, he's a paranoid schizophrenic. So anything's possible. But would anyone make the same diagnosis now? When he was tearing those women to pieces, one shrink took the view he wanted to wipe out the image of his mother, and women represented being expelled from paradise, a bit like in the Bible, the fall. I don't really know if that's still the case today. After all those years in prison . . ."

"The mad people that come here," the Governor grumbled, ". . . and we get more and more of them − fact is, they leave their madness at home and only find it again when they come out. That's how it is. I've been fighting for years to get these problems addressed, but you can't rely on the authorities to do anything."

"They're clueless," Bessour chipped in.

"Tell me about it," the Governor replied, sounding disillusioned.

He got up and put his bony hand on the box. "Do you want these things seized?"

"Yes," Bessour said. "You never know. We want to build up a picture of his mental and intellectual state."

"If I may say so," Longnon put in, "he was always well behaved while he was here. A model prisoner he was, really. But I must admit he scared me sometimes. I was wary of him.

"With good reason," de Palma said. "Can we see his cell?"

"Of course. Longnon will drive you over there. There's still no-one in it. We don't have a problem here with overcrowding."

The prison gate opened onto a broad dirt track running between two perimeter walls; to the left and right were some glass screens perched on top of towers like the forecastles on a warship. From time to time armed officers looked down at the long dreary path enclosing the prison between two parallel ramparts.

A second grey gate, identical to the first. Then the huge courtyard and its modern white three-storey buildings with barred windows, standing to attention. A little to one side, the infirmary, where Buffet and Bontems had carried out their killings in 1972. On the right were the large abbey cloisters, containing the prison workshops, which had been awarded listed building status.

"Here we are," Longnon said, pointing at the white building.

A glass door opened, covered in bars and thick wire mesh. The prison had been freshly painted in cream and pale blue. It was spotlessly clean.

On the first floor was a square landing enclosed on three sides by grilles. The fourth opened on to the infirmary. To the right was a long corridor lined with cells, barred at intervals. The screw stared at his set of keys as he waited for each gate to open. The smell of tear gas was even stronger in this confined world.

Autran's cell was number seventeen, the last at the end of a row of doors. The room measured seven square metres, with a bed as you came in and a kitchen area beside the window. There was no radio or T.V. set.

Above the bed was a stencilled handprint with the thumb and index finger missing. De Palma took a photo using the small digital camera he had brought with him.

"Do you know what that means?" Longnon asked.

"It's his signature," de Palma replied, positioning himself by the window.

Beyond the perimeter walls the view stretched away to the forests overlooking Clairvaux. The cold had frozen the branches on the large oak trees. The sun was going down, spreading a bluish dawn light on the chalky ground. The prison was bathed in sadness.

"Anything else?" Karim asked the officer who was staring at him with pale eyes.

"No, only that drawing."

At the end of the day they left Clairvaux. De Palma was brooding. Eva hadn't called. He didn't dare phone her in front of Karim. She would curse him and be bound to ask what she was doing with a man who spent his time chasing lunatics. For more than a year she had taken up all the free space in his life. He didn't know if he really loved her, but at that moment he realised how much he missed her. Ever since she had found out about Anita's pregnancy, Eva seemed more distant, less available. Secretly the Baron was jealous. He often told himself that old people become self-centred. Old age is just a slow withdrawal into oneself. It must be fear of death, the fact of becoming gnarled like old wood. Does the heart dry up too?

Karim had booked them into a dreary hotel in the southern suburbs, on the other side of the ring road. The following day they had a meeting at Villejuif's secure unit. Karim was none too thrilled about it. Madness scared him. It was something irrational he could not explain.

As they passed Troyes a few snowflakes started to fall. De Palma reduced his speed. Karim twiddled the button on the car radio and found *France Musique*. It was a violin recital, the evening concert.

"I've heard you like . . ."

"Sibelius. Second movement of his Concerto in D minor. Must be Hilary Hahn. A great violinist. She's beautiful, too."

*

It was the first time Thomas had taken the tablets, as his mother said. He was eleven years old.

Initially, a small dose of Largactil. 25 mg white capsules, in an orange box.

"Are they sedatives?"

"Yes, of course. He'll feel better immediately."

Dr Caillol was wearing a white coat with a gold pen clipped to his breast pocket. His cropped hair and gold-rimmed glasses gave him a learned look. Unlike the other doctors, he didn't have a stethoscope dangling from his neck. His illnesses were his patients' bad dreams.

"If he has another attack, we'll need to increase the dosage. Or perhaps try Nozinan."

The door to Dr Caillol's ward was left open during appointments. Thomas had to wait in the lobby with Maman until the secretary showed them through to the waiting room. It took a few minutes, but it always seemed like an eternity. Maman was always impatient. She wore an austere suit, shiny stockings and plain court shoes.

The herringbone parquet floorboards still creaked the same as ever. The same Chippendale chair and leather armchair. A low table strewn with old newspapers. Each time they visited Maman immersed herself in *Jours de France* without so much as a look at him.

In his head Thomas asked, "Do you think I can get better, Papa?"

"Yes, son. With willpower you can overcome anything."

# 21

It was not a voice, but a tension that had to be alleviated otherwise your head would burst. A commanding force that made you think: Don't lose her!

"Why?"

"Remember. She's wearing a pencil skirt, high-heeled shoes and the finest stockings. But just like the others she's suffering. She needs to be freed."

The young woman crossed the boulevard and went down into the Metro.

The swift rhythmic clicking of her heels on the wet tarmac sounded like a monkey drum. Click, clack, click . . . Then the slamming of the gates, the stinking breath of the train, and the high-pitched sound announcing the closure of the doors.

The young woman sat down on a tip-up seat. Her skirt shot up her long legs. Her eyes were heavy, and so was her mouth. The train entered Richard-Lenoir station. She stood up and adjusted her coat.

"Follow her."

She lived on the ground floor of a block of flats in rue du Chemin-Vert. Opposite there was a shop that flogged incense and mystical books, crystal balls and Buddhist tat. Night fell gradually. The young woman switched on the light. The curtains at the windows were too thick to see through.

"Go on!"

A man entered the access code. He pushed open the large door and held it to let him through.

"Thanks."

No concierge or caretaker's flat. To the right, in the inner court-yard, a space for dustbins. It was the perfect place to wait, sitting behind the skips, his eyes fixed on the door and the little skylight that must look down into her flat. There was a sound of pots and pans, but no voices. She lived alone.

It seemed like an eternity, but then one by one the lights went out in all the windows.

"Don't wait!

The door did not present a problem. The young woman was watching a tedious television programme with the audience clap-ping when told to do so. She wore a Boubou African robe as a dressing gown. The sound was turned up loud. She didn't immedi-ately hear the strange prayer.

The slap took her by surprise. It seemed to pass right through her head. She stood up, her face stinging like the time she fell off her horse in a showjumping competition. She stared, she wanted to cry out, but a damp, sweaty hand gripped her by the throat. The scream stayed lodged deep in her belly.

The pain was nothing compared to the terrible feeling of being unable to make a sound. The T.V. audience was laughing at her.

A fresh blow split her lip. She swallowed some blood. A face passed in front of the television screen. A man with no hair was holding her. He smelled of old age and aftershave, reminding her of her grandfather languishing in the old people's home.

She knew the foul smell, the evil face. Expressions don't change, the only things that do are the layers of the past that cover them inexorably.

Long fine pointed fingers entered her. She felt a dull, warm pain.

124

Then the axe struck for the first time. Darkness and emptiness, falling endlessly towards the abyss. She saw herself again in that old café, the walls covered with cinema posters. The man with the shy smile who had looked at her. How many times had she told herself her life had come to a halt that day? That all the rest should never have existed? And before . . . she had no strength left for that.

She could no longer see out of her right eye. With the left one it was like looking through a dirty windowpane. There was no doubt it was him: the man who had smiled at her. In the end her suffering didn't mean a thing: her love had returned from nowhere, never to leave again. He would remain here forever, frozen like an image, in the place where she had wanted to end her life. The rest did not matter.

The axe struck for a second time.

## 22

Two banners were draped over the perimeter railings at Paul-Guiraud Hospital, Villejuif. Sprayed in red across a large white sheet:

### NURSES — NOT SCREWS!

Thomas Autran's escape had caused a storm within the prison administration. The National Governor laid into the Social Welfare Service, to which the secure unit at Villejuif was attached. Disciplinary action was taken against the nurse responsible for overseeing the common room, resulting in demotion and suspension from the service. Staff immediately went on strike, supported by trade unionists in other parts of the hospital. Autran's escape had highlighted serious shortcomings in the unit, particularly in relation to security issues that the understaffed personnel were unable to fulfil.

A nurse in a white coat with the words "on strike" written across it, and a C.G.T. union badge on the back handed out a flier to the two men from the Marseille serious crime squad.

"Thanks," Karim said.

"We need your support. It's really serious what's happening here."

Sympathetic as he was to such issues and inclined to protest, Karim was about to join in the discussion. De Palma cut him short.

"We're looking for the Henri-Colin building."

"The secure unit? You sure?"

"Yes."

The nurse looked defiant.

"You from the police?"

"You don't miss much," de Palma muttered. "You've obviously studied psychiatry."

She looked him up and down. "Five nurses have received warnings for doing nothing. They could lose three to four hundred euros a month. On the money we earn . . ."

"I see your point," Bessour said.

"It's the people who did the work on the building who are to blame for his escape, not nurses who are just doing their job. This isn't a prison."

"You're right there."

De Palma looked up at the sky. "We're here to get a killer back to the nuthouse, not discuss psychiatric problems."

"Alright, alright . . ." the nurse sighed. "It's at the back. You can't miss it. It's like a fortress! Last stop before the scrapyard, but you can't just go in, you know. Is someone expecting you?"

"Yes, Dr Kauffmann."

"Well in that case it's O.K."

The Henri-Colin building was at the back of the hospital. A formal courtyard as in a seminary; some deserted straight paths, lined with bare horse chestnut trees, alongside single-storey stone buildings. Passageways with corrugated iron roofs linked the different services.

Over the years most of the wards had been renovated, but the hospital retained an ascetic appearance characteristic of late nineteenth-century asylum architecture. The white limestone, reddish brown tiles and severe, high, rounded windows seemed to hold the secrets of the tragedies played out behind its walls – the dark side of the human spirit.

The weather was overcast. No rain, but a daubed sky reflected on the windows of the psychiatric services. An ambulance appeared at the end of a path and parked in front of the doors to a ward. A scruffy patient, wearing jeans and trainers, was escorted to the vehicle by two nurses.

"I hate this place," Bessour grumbled. "Madness scares me."

"In some cultures they believe mad people have special powers and can see things we can't."

"You really believe all that stuff?"

"Yes, but I'm not afraid of nutters."

At the end of a path was the Henri-Colin perimeter wall, a miniature prison with its stone palisade and grilles with thick bars. This was the end of the road in psychiatry, the final destination for those no-one wanted, not even the high-security prisons. These gates had closed behind the Japanese cannibal and former members of *Action Directe* driven crazy by lengthy sentences under Article 122 of the new Penal Code. *No criminal responsibility shall attach to any person who at the time of the events suffers from a psychological or neuropsychological condition, leading to the loss of their powers of discernment or control of their actions.*

An old entryphone and a reinforced door. Karim rang the bell.

"Commandant de Palma and Captain Bessour . . ."

There was a clicking of metal, and the door opened. Behind it stood an imposing prison officer.

"Good morning. May I see your I.D.?"

More palisades, more grilles. Patients locked up like shadows. Not one of them looked up at the policemen.

"This way. He's expecting you."

Martin Kauffmann, the doctor in charge, was a tall, skinny man with arms too long for his white coat. As he moved, he looked like a large spider with his shaved hair, friendly face, appeasing eyes and fleshy lips.

"You're the detectives from Marseille, I presume?"

"You presume right," de Palma said with a smile.

"Come on in."

The old buildings had been completely renovated. On the first floor was a gallery, secured by a tall gate. The interior looked more like a crèche than a unit for dangerous patients. Shades of pink and blue, green sections of wall and yellow edging strips. No straight corridors. The doors leading to the rooms and service areas all had observation windows; nothing could escape the nurses' view – at least in theory. All the rooms had glazed windows and the furniture was securely attached to the ground.

In cell number thirty-seven a man of about thirty was curled up in a ball asleep, his thumb in his mouth.

"Autran shouldn't have ended up here," the psychiatrist said. "Normally he'd have gone to Sarreguemines – it's closer to Clairvaux. But you know the problem we have with overcrowding."

"Afraid I do," Bessour said.

"And we're the ones who'll have to pay for all this."

They crossed the deserted common room. Most patients were either in the workshops or exercise yard, depending on their ward. De Palma noticed the blind spots that had been mentioned in the Versailles police report. There were observation windows in the walls.

"He was last seen here," Dr Kauffmann said, stopping a few feet from the table football. "He must have hidden in that corner, which is a blind spot, and then seized his chance to escape."

In the courtyard there were four horse chestnut trees planted at regular intervals. From the last tree on the right it was possible to reach the fence and cross the ditch.

"He climbed that tree and then jumped," the Baron said.

"Hang on, that's at least three metres!" the psychiatrist exclaimed.

"You obviously don't know him," de Palma shot back.

Kauffmann pulled a doubtful face and looked at Bessour, who also seemed sceptical about the Baron's statement.

"Can you tell us again what happened?" de Palma asked.

The psychiatrist looked irritated and nodded towards the room.

"There were five nurses on duty. Two of them were doing searches in the rooms, while another two were helping with the meals in the kitchen. The last nurse was escorting a patient to the lavatory. The ones in the kitchen could see the common room and the eight patients. The problem is that blind spot there. It took just two minutes and Autran was off."

Outside three nurses were playing footie with a patient undergoing "stabilisation". The man emitted little cries each time the ball bounced on his head, showing his teeth and looking up vacantly.

"Let's go and see his room," Kauffmann said. "There's something I want to show you."

A large corridor with green and white walls led to cell thirty-eight. Two nurses were trying to calm a hairy, naked patient who was bent double. Kauffmann stopped.

"This is what we have to deal with every day. Really difficult patients and a chronic shortage of staff. That patient refuses to have a shower. He's still very young."

"How old?" Karim asked.

"Nineteen."

Bessour peered through the observation window. The nurses had approached the patient, turning their palms to the ceiling in a peaceful gesture.

"You must know him. It's Jérémie Castel."

"Yes," de Palma said. "The guy who killed his mother and father . . . The Bordeaux case."

The fair-haired boy between the officers had been fourteen at the time.

"Come on," the psychiatrist said. "It's never a very good idea to watch."

Autran's room was the first on the right as you entered the ward. Kauffmann glanced at the nearby rooms and nurses' station. There was just one nurse for the whole of that part of the building. He pushed open the door. A fairly high metal bed with feet attached to the floor, no sharp angles, all rounded corners. The floor was covered in yellow and dark grey tiles.

Some books lay on a table attached to the wall. *La Provence Préhistorique* produced by a research group and some copies of *La Recherche*, devoted to the latest discoveries in the field of palaeontology.

The doctor picked up one of the magazines.

"Both times I saw him, we talked about prehistory. It seemed the only way of making contact and establishing a connection. When it came to science Thomas was a fount of knowledge. One of those exceptionally gifted people. During the two meetings he taught me a lot about the latest theories in anthropology and palaeontology. It was really impressive."

De Palma carefully inspected the walls in the hope of finding some marks or graffiti left by Autran. But there was nothing. The grey paint shone beneath the neon light in the ceiling.

"What was the last thing he read?" the Baron asked.

"I really don't know."

"The last book he talked to you about?"

"I'm not sure why, but he mentioned an old criminology book called *L'Homme assassin*. I had to do a search to find the author."

"Cesare Lombroso," de Palma cut in. "End of the nineteenth century."

"You know it?"

"Yes. But why did he talk about that?"

Kauffmann shook his head, "I've no idea. He just asked me if I'd read it and we left it at that. But there's something I wanted to show you. I forgot to mention it to the other detectives. Let's go to my office."

They went back past a series of doors with observation windows, encountering a single patient flanked by three nurses.

There were quite a few inmates in the workshop. Everyone who could make it was there. The idea was to re-socialise disturbed patients through simple tasks, the minimum for a care unit. It wasn't a prison, but the prisons treated it as something of a dumping ground, a way of getting rid of the really mad ones, the psychos. The dregs of society.

Kauffmann opened a door with a theatrical gesture, "This is my office. Have a seat."

On the left side of the table lay a medical dictionary as fat as a phone book, with some scattered sheets of paper and assorted felt-tips. On the walls were two posters of the Rocky Mountains and a painting with red and blue blotches that Bessour found rather beautiful and moving. A portrait stood out in the expanses of flat colour: two barely visible eyes, with daubed brushstrokes, stared out at the onlooker. The painting had been done by one of the patients.

Kauffmann slowly opened his desk drawer and took out a statuette. "Thomas was an artist. The first time I met him he asked for some sculpting materials. I gave him a ball of clay and some wooden tools. Things that weren't dangerous. And this is what he produced. Not bad, eh?"

De Palma flinched. The doctor had just put a man with an antler head on his desk. It must have been fifteen centimetres tall. The antlers were pretty successful. The eyes were not fully worked, just hinted at. This strengthened the overall effect.

"Why do you think he made this?" Bessour asked.

"That's really what I wanted to find out when he did a runner. Unfortunately I'm still waiting for his psychiatric files – they haven't yet reached me. I live in hope. It seems easier to escape from the unit than get hold of a file. Work that one out!"

The psychiatrist gathered his thoughts for a few seconds. A curved wrinkle had appeared on his forehead.

"Thomas knew he was ill. One day he told me straight out that he had been aware of it ever since they first put electrodes on that poor head of his. No-one ever thought to ask him if he could talk about the female voice that gave him orders. Nobody asked him. Yet that's probably where the secret lies."

*

Snow delayed the T.G.V. train bound for Marseille. On the station concourse at the Gare de Lyon, passengers thronged in front of the information boards. There would be a two-hour delay at best.

A handful of taxi drivers stamped their feet as they had a cigarette. A dry arctic wind sliced through the station esplanade. De Palma and Bessour strode off to the Brasserie des Deux Cadrans and sat down at a round table. The waiter, a chubby sort with jowly cheeks, immediately appeared. They ordered two coffees.

"Do you know what's in Le Guen's cave?" de Palma asked abruptly.

"Er . . . cave paintings," Bessour replied.

"There's a very rare drawing called 'the slain man.'"

"What's that exactly?"

"It's an image of a slain man . . . at least in a symbolic fashion. You could say it's the first depiction of murder in the history of humanity. You find it in other caves too, like the one at Chauvet."

"You seem to be an expert."

De Palma looked out at the street and smiled. "No, just someone trying to understand an extraordinary person: Thomas Autran. And his sister, Christine, of course. Our society always treats anything alien as savagery, whether it's distant in time or space. Autran is a man who lays claim to the distant past."

"He sees himself as a savage?"

"No. It's us who push him into that category."

Bessour stirred his coffee. "Who's this Lombroso then? I seem to remember hearing about him when I was at Police College."

"A great Italian criminologist who thought Criminal Man was a reincarnation of Cro-Magnon. A Palaeolithic castaway in our civilised genes."

"That's bullshit!"

"Maybe, but bullshit can be catching . . . It means we can fail to see the man behind the murderer.

"In the middle of the nineteenth century, Lombroso, an Italian doctor, worked on thousands of criminals' skulls, most of which had common features. The scientist worked out certain 'laws' from this, developing a criminal anthropology and linking criminality to heredity for more than a third of the offending population. Lombroso claimed they possessed distinct physical characteristics that could easily be identified. These all dated back to an earlier stage of humanity, to our ancestors, the apes. Some notorious murderers were even described as having abnormally long arms, which connects them to primates."

"Do people really still think that way?" Bessour asked.

"Of course," de Palma said. "These clichés never go away."

Lombroso used other anatomic criteria beside the skull. The most remarkable were probably imperfect teeth or having additional toes or fingers.

"For him," de Palma added, "there was general decadence – the whole of society was in decline. The unavoidable result was crime."

"So what's new?"

"The important thing is to realise that even today there are scientists who haven't abandoned these theories. You're about to meet one of them."

"Who's that then?"

"Dr Caillol, a psychiatrist who treated Autran."

The squad mobile rang. It was a brief conversation. The Baron nervously stuffed the phone into his pocket and asked for the bill.

"Sorry, son. We're going to miss our train to Marseille."

## 23

Three police cars blocked the road, forcing local residents to use a single lane. Men in white boiler suits were going in and out of a ground floor flat. They rummaged around in some large crates then went back inside carrying other tools. De Palma and Bessour made their way inside.

"Lucy Meunier," said Commissioner Reynaud from the Parisian serious crime squad. "I thought it might be the bloke you're looking for."

Bessour put his hand over his mouth. He had to swallow several times to stop himself vomiting.

"Shit," he blurted out. "I thought I'd seen quite a lot . . ."

"Well, you won't be able to say that any more," de Palma said.

Lucy Meunier's body rested on the television set: her arms either side of the screen, her chest ripped open. A morning shopping programme was touting a cut-price, high-pressure steam cleaner.

"The heart's gone," muttered a technician.

De Palma tried to absorb his first impressions of the crime scene. He was annoyed by the presence of his Paris colleagues, but it wasn't his territory, so he would have to put up with it.

He caught Lucy's dead eyes. One was half closed as a result of a haematoma, the other still wide open. He would have liked to go and hide, run away like a coward. He tried to write something on a pad, but his hands were trembling too much. He needed a whisky, or something strong that would burn his guts.

"You'll notice how he undressed her on the sofa," he said more loudly in an attempt to control his emotions, but Bessour had already gone out.

"You talking to me?" the technician said, raising his protective glasses.

"No, I wasn't," de Palma replied, trying not to dwell on Lucy's corpse. "Can I take a look at the other rooms?"

"Go ahead. We're done."

"Any prints?"

"Yes, two. A thumb and an index finger on some books. We've placed them under seal. It's number thirty, I think."

"Good. Can you pass them on to us as soon as you've lifted them? I want to be quite sure."

"No problem," Reynaud said.

There was just one room looking on to the street. Lucy Meunier had put some yellowed net curtains in the barred window along with some thicker material for privacy.

A few old books lay on a shelf. De Palma noticed *Shamanism and the Religion of Cro-Magnon* and *The Shamans of Prehistory* by Clottes and Lewis-Williams.

"That's the one we saw at Clairvaux," he said in a low voice.

"Look at the wall!" Bessour exclaimed.

A negative handprint.

De Palma searched among the photos he had taken in Autran's cell. "It's the same one."

Bessour leaned over his shoulder. "They're identical."

\*

You can never predict the lead story on the next news bulletin. De Palma would have put money on Lucy's killer not being mentioned in the press until the following day. But he was mistaken.

On the eight o'clock news everything he and Bessour had just experienced was recounted in grotesque detail. Who had leaked the story? Reynaud? The police press department, or just a simple beat cop?

On the radio they were in full flow: "serial killer", "animal", "monster" . . . no mention yet of cannibalism. That would probably come tomorrow, de Palma told himself. They had to make a saga out of it.

On the way back he avoided anything relating to the case. He'd had enough of police chiefs and magistrates leaking stories to the local press for a slice of the glory. Autran's face would soon be splashed all over the newspapers and T.V. screens. He would soon become everything de Palma hated: a name in big bold letters spread across the five columns of the front page.

*

Autran's file was in a box on top of an old mirrored wardrobe he had inherited from his parents. He took down the box, opened it, and spread the contents on the floor.

The statements recording the Autran twins' arrest had been drawn up by two police officers at the crime scene. De Palma moved on quickly, pausing at the list of objects seized. It was all diving equipment. Lieutenant Vidal had listed the following items:

Two well-worn diving suits. Black. Wet.
Two pairs of worn flippers.
Two diving masks.
Two compressed air cylinders, half full . . .

At the time of the twins' arrest it was possible to enter the cave through a shaft that emerged in the open air. A few years before, this entrance had been blocked by a rockslide. So there was no need to dive and no real reason for so much equipment. Quite an expedition! And yet the twins did not need to enter or leave the cave by sea.

De Palma rang Pauline Barton. "Did you search all the submerged parts of the cave?"

"Yes," Pauline replied. "All the tunnels leading from the flooded chamber. Nothing came of it. Why do you ask?"

"I don't really know. There are a few things I'm trying to understand."

Pauline wasn't alone. She asked him to wait for a few seconds, and then she returned.

"There's one part left to check," she said.

"What's that?"

"The lowest chamber."

"How do you mean?"

"The large shaft near the painted hands. No-one has ever dived down there."

## 24

The house was behind the rock that looked like a dog sitting up. Autran hadn't been there since the last holiday he'd spent with his sister. Some memories resurfaced, but he rationalised them away.

He looked at the sky. In a few minutes a lone cloud would pass across the moon. He put on his rucksack and walked as fast as he could over the pine roots on the stony ground.

The wind had got stronger; it whistled furiously in the hooked fingers of the oak trees. The embattled air smelled of resin, almond and carnation. Just before the moon disappeared behind the big cloud Thomas caught sight of the house and the white stone walls which reflected back a strangely dead light. The path wasn't long, but no-one had maintained it for years. He made his way through the bushes trying not to scratch himself. From time to time he paused to listen.

In his memory the key was always kept behind the small wash-house. He hoped the house hadn't been squatted or vandalised. There had never been anything there to steal. Just memories that no-one and nothing could ever take away. Even in the mad house the doctor hadn't succeeded in silencing his memory. Chemistry was powerless to do so.

An owl passed somewhere through the trees that had grown on the brow of the hill. The beating of heavy wings carried on the wind. Autran stopped and sniffed the air. No dogs, people or dangerous animals. Just an acid smell of thorns strewn across the ground.

He moved carefully, his senses on high alert. The curved roof tiles shone in the moonlight. The house had not changed. The shutter on the small garage had been forced and hung from the remaining screws in the rotten wood. No-one had been here for almost ten years. On the small terrace overgrown with brambles and ivy, there was a bench with twisted slats and a skeletal rattan chair. His father often sat there, watching his children play between the pines. Now there were thorny bushes everywhere.

The key was still behind the bowl, covered in a pile of leaves and needles left by the wind. Thomas grabbed it and stroked the metal with the tips of his fingers. In the forest some branches snapped. A wild boar grunted. He put the key in the lock and opened the door. Overwhelmed by a smell of old ash and rotten linen, he closed the door again and stood for a long while in the dark. The house creaked, buffeted by the wind. From time to time he seemed to hear his sister's voice still whispering unbelievable stories before they went to sleep. The sputtering of his father's meerschaum pipe; his slow breathing.

He opened his bag, took out the torch he had bought in Paris and switched it on.

It was all there. Wrapped in layers of time. The oak sitting room table, the chairs with straw seats on which he used to swing his legs as he waited for the inevitable pasta with tomato sauce at midday; and vegetable soup in the evening. His father was not much of a cook.

He decided to undress and steep himself in the cold. His body still hurt, but he wasn't shivering. He felt reassured by his toughness in those winter temperatures. He was still able to control his nerves and muscles. He wouldn't let himself go. His hands were probably stronger than on the day they had arrested him. All those hours of training in prison and in the secure unit had borne fruit.

On the bumpy saltpetre walls hung two prints of the *Passe Sainte-*

*Marie* in the era of the transatlantic liners. Setting sail for New York, or Rio, their giant frames shunted by tugs belching smoke.

In the fireplace a charred log looked like a lizard with charcoal scales. On the mantelpiece stood a vase of lavender and a modest painting by Christine of the fish market down by the old port.

Thomas took out a sandwich that he'd bought in Marseille, together with a litre bottle of water. He sat down and sank his teeth into the soft bread. He had two other sandwiches left in the bag and a second bottle.

The police didn't know this house existed. That meant he would be left alone and could, if necessary, hold out for weeks in these remote forests and hidden valleys. He knew how to survive. There was no shortage of game round here, and less than two hundred metres away, there was a spring in a rock crevice.

Once he had finished his sandwich he went into the first bedroom, the one his father had used. The bed had been overturned. Most likely the person who had broken into the garage had been looking for money under the mattress. He put everything back. The yellow sheets reminded him of the times he and his sister had spent listening to the old man's stories. The wallpaper with the small purple flowers was in shreds. A lump of plaster had come away from the ceiling and smashed on the bedside table.

Thomas retreated to the doorway and closed his eyes to banish the memories. He must not show weakness.

A small corridor led to the larger second bedroom, belonging to the children. Two beds, covered in blankets knitted from multi-coloured woollen squares, faced each other across the room. In the middle a faded rug was covered in dust and flakes of paint. Two books were lying in limbo on the bedside tables: Claude Lévi-Strauss' *A World on the Wane* for Christine; Peter Matthiessen's *Two Seasons in the Stone Age* for Thomas. The room was as spartan as a monk's cell. A small window looked out on the washhouse.

Autran felt under his bed and pulled out a rectangular wooden box that he placed in front of him and opened. An axe and a catapult made from reindeer antler were rolled up in a piece of chamois leather. The axe had a handle hewn from a slightly curved ash branch, about thirty centimetres long, and a large flint with two faces, as sharp as a metal blade, held together with gut. He checked the strength of the binding and swung the axe round several times in the ash-ridden air.

# 25

The Baron was searching for France Musique on his car radio. He had to turn the chrome button delicately since the little yellow arrow was temperamental. Ever since Eva had touched it, the radio stubbornly shied away from any public service frequencies. Though it should be said it had been stuck on the same waveband for decades.

De Palma was on the point of giving up, when he came across a tragic voice reading a news bulletin. French planes had attacked Libya. War and more war. The car radio spluttered with the President mid-speech. De Palma turned the knob so he could hear the rest and finally found France Musique. It was a concert series, with Stockhausen and Boulez on the menu. He turned up the volume and closed the windows on the convertible. Boulevard Michelet was not too congested and the random music gave a surrealist touch to Marseille's most chic district.

The Autran family had lived in rue des Bruyères, in the Mazargues neighbourhood. A private house set back from the traditional façades with their three windows; it had a garden and a few trees, a curved balcony, ochre walls and wide windows.

The Baron was not on duty, but he hated days off. He parked the Alfa Romeo Giulietta straddling the pavement.

Two old women were chatting, just metres away from the Autrans' house. He immediately recognised Lucienne Libri, with her dark eyes and bony chin. She had hardly changed since he'd interviewed her ten years earlier: she still had the same white hair done up in a bun, the same gnarled hands and stooping figure. Before she married, Lucienne had worked in the colonial hat factory; she then ran a stall at the market on place Castellane. Since her husband's death she wore black. The other woman could not have been much younger. De Palma greeted them both.

"Don't I know you?"

"You do indeed, Madame Libri. I'm the detective who came to ask you some questions ten years ago."

"That's it. I recognise your face. You must remember Germaine Alessandri too," Lucienne added, pointing to her companion.

"Of course I do."

"Any news?" Germaine asked. "They say he's on the run."

"Nothing much. I'm trying to piece things together from some old investigations so we can find him. I was wondering what happened to Thomas's parents."

"His parents?" Germaine exclaimed. "May God rest their souls! Fortunately they're not here any more. It's better they don't see all this."

"Holy Mary mother of God, much better," Lucienne went on. "The father was a good man, but as for her . . ."

She pulled a face.

"What do you mean?"

"A right bitch, she was! No other word for it. Treating the kids the way she did. They were bound to end up like that."

"Oh yes," Germaine added, nodding. "Poor boy. The sister wasn't so bad. But Thomas went off the rails when he lost his dad – and that woman, she was in ever such a hurry to have him put away."

As she spoke she nodded to emphasise each sentence. The twins' mother, Martine, was born in Cassis. Her maiden name was Combes. According to her former neighbours Martine was a real maneater. The local village bike: anyone could have a ride!

A scooter zigzagged between two delivery vans. As he came to the end of the street the driver revved the engine, drowning out Lucienne's voice for a moment.

Martine was devastated when she had the twins. She didn't feel up to having children and wept profusely. Motherhood can sometimes have dire effects. All the witnesses had testified to that effect ten years previously. Pierre Autran was a model father and the children were the apple of his eye. He was described as a responsible man who protected his children and took everything in his stride. De Palma didn't like these black-and-white descriptions of couples. Experience had taught him the reality was always different.

So he asked, "How did he react when he saw his wife treating the twins so harshly?"

"Oh, she didn't do anything in front of him," Lucienne said. "It all went on behind his back, if you get what I mean."

The Baron nodded several times.

Martine died driving a large green Mercedes. De Palma had always thought the children caused the accident; or at least had strongly desired it and gone as far as making a plan. Electra's words went through his mind:

*The dead are jealous: and for a fiancé*
*He sent me hate with hollow eyes.*

"The accident was on that winding road to Les Termes, near the village of Peypin," Lucienne said. "But I couldn't tell you where exactly."

The road goes up a hill that is familiar to Sunday morning cyclists – and Saturday ones as well – wanting to test themselves on the hairpin bends running through the scrubland. It leaves Marseille to the north, passes through the remote Logis Neuf suburbs and climbs the rocky hillside as far as the lonely pass above Peypin. In summer the heat is so oppressive, it's hell.

"Was the lad already having problems when his mother died?" the Baron asked.

"You could see it," Germaine said conspiratorially. "And he'd already been sectioned by then. I remember how he used to have terrible fits and then afterwards he wouldn't talk for days."

A tear appeared on Lucienne's cheek. She wiped it away with the back of her hand.

"How many times did he come to me so I could comfort him?" she said. "He was only seven or eight. His dad often used to take him to their house in the country – that did him good."

"A house in the country?" de Palma asked.

"Yes, I don't remember the place. Somewhere near Saint-Maximin, I think it was."

The Termes road certainly wasn't the most direct route from Mazargues to Saint-Maximin. It was much quicker to take the motorway to Aubagne and Aix-en-Provence. De Palma made a note of this. The neighbour at number thirty-two opened his window and watched inquisitively. The blurred sound of a T.V. game show came from his living room, then disappeared as he closed the shutters.

Lucienne's expression changed and she said in a strained voice, "Thomas was out of control with all these problems. There were a few times we had the police and emergency services here to cart him off to the asylum."

"Was he often with his sister?"

"They always hung out together. After his mum's death he was sectioned for a long time. I didn't understand it. But these mental illnesses are complicated."

She went on, "One day he came back from the hospital. You should have seen his face! He was white as a sheet. That's the drugs they give them. He wasn't a child any longer. I can still see him. He said to me, 'Those doctors, I'm going to kill them all.' He had an evil look about him. Holy Mary, that look, I'll never forget it. He wasn't the lad I'd known. That was all gone."

"Can you tell me about his friends?" de Palma said.

"He was friendly with my son until he was eleven," Germaine replied. "Then after that . . . Well, you know how it is, he wasn't here any more."

"Well, with my son," Lucienne said, "they did see each other again. They used to go diving together, with little Franck . . . Luccioni. Poor thing, they say it was Thomas who killed him. I was always surprised by that though – they were like brothers. You don't do things like that just because you're mad!"

Franck Luccioni's murder had been blamed on Autran a little too quickly, perhaps. The M.O. didn't seem right though: a murder disguised as a drowning just a short swim from Le Guen's cave. De Palma thought of Fortin and of Thierry Garcia. Imperceptibly, the wheels were turning.

"Tell me about the father. Do you remember him?"

"Of course I do. He was a nice man. But not like us. He was an engineer. Upper-crust people . . ."

"What were his hobbies?"

"He did a lot of diving. Seems he was good at it. He taught the kids. He used to go nearly every weekend."

"In the Calanques."

"Yes."

"Have you been to his house?"

"Oh yes, loads of times, I used to clean there for a while."

"Can you describe what it was like inside?"

Lucienne closed her eyes for a few seconds. "It was beautiful. Luxury armchairs and expensive furniture. They had money."

"Works of art?"

"It was full of the stuff. All over the place. But you weren't supposed to touch it."

"How do you mean?"

"They were prehistoric things," she said in a low voice, as though confiding a secret. "Well, he thought they were beautiful, but those things used to scare the living daylights out of me."

"Can you explain?"

"There was all this filthy junk, for God's sake. Little statues, knives and stones. What do I know? It looked like a museum to me. Especially in the corridor. But you weren't allowed to touch anything, or dust. Not one thing."

"And the children?"

"They weren't allowed either."

"You said there were statuettes. Do you remember what they looked like?"

Lucienne thought for a long while before continuing.

"I don't remember. But I know Monsieur Autran said they were very precious. Very unusual they were. Unique."

"Do you remember any of the objects? For example a statuette that looked like a man with antlers?"

Lucienne shook her head.

"No," she said. "No, it's all too long ago. And, you know, bad memories don't tend to stick in the mind like the good ones."

*

Back in his little office de Palma got down to some practical work. He had found a jar of natural pigments at the local hardware shop. He put two teaspoons of ochre powder and a little water into his mouth, laid his hand on a sheet of paper, and blew over it. The result wasn't great but it helped him to understand how Autran had gone about things.

He repeated the experiment on a section of wall. It was a total disaster. He had to give it several tries and finally produced a print that didn't dribble too much. At that moment Eva came in.

"Here we go. Who do you think you are? Cro-Magnon man?"

She gasped when she caught sight of the prints on the wall.

"Don't worry, I'll clear it all up."

"What's that music?"

"John Cage. *Roaratorio*."

"Ugh!"

She stared at him, uncertain whether to laugh or cry. The Baron's mouth was smeared with ochre, his white shirt spattered with the Palaeolithic mixture.

"I hope you're not thinking of carrying on with this experiment. Don't forget I'm called after the mother of all mankind. I'm not good to eat! It's taboo."

"I know that."

De Palma rushed to the sink to rinse out his mouth. For a moment he thought he was going to throw up. When he had recovered, he dialled Commissioner Reynaud's number.

"Have you got any D.N.A. from the print on the wall?"

"No," Reynaud replied. "Not a trace."

# 26

Dr Caillol saw his patients on Thursday afternoons, between two and six. The Édouard-Toulouse hospital was made up of two buildings set at right angles to each other, wedged between the large estates to the north of Marseille. De Palma presented himself at the Adult Psychiatry office. Everything was perfectly polished; soft colours gave the service a welcoming feel. A secretary with a thin smile greeted him. Her face was plastered in foundation and her specs perched on the end of her nose.

"Do you have an appointment?"

"No. Just say Commandant de Palma wants to speak with him."

"Are you from the Police?"

"No, the Navy."

Poker-faced, the secretary tapped away at her switchboard.

"Dr Caillol will see you in a few minutes. If you'd like to go to the waiting room at the end of the corridor ... "

It was a long room lit by wall lights. Pictures of green countryside hung next to some A.I.D.S. awareness posters. On the table was a pile of mindless magazines, just like in any doctor's waiting room. The patients were evidently captivated by the glossy photos, depicting the lives of powerful people and their hangers-on.

A young woman with a waxen face and tearful expression was flicking through a tabloid magazine. As she turned the pages she moved her chewing gum from one cheek to the other and looked up vacantly at de Palma. Tattooed in blue ink on her hands was the name of her boyfriend, Marc, a heart and the outline of a flower. The scars of prison.

In a few minutes the doctor appeared. The same smouldering expression as ten years before; the same rectangular steel-framed glasses; a stern, broad forehead and feverish temples stretched tight like a kettledrum. His face was more wrinkled than when de Palma had last seen him. It seemed an age ago.

"Hello, Monsieur de Palma. I have to say I never expected to see you again."

His voice was worn, the handshake stiff. The surgery was decorated with a collection of drawings and aboriginal paintings.

"These are wonderful," said de Palma in an attempt to ease the atmosphere.

Caillol shot him a courteous smile, which failed to mask his impatience.

"Dream time," he said. "The essence of Australian Aboriginal culture. Most of my patients find these things moving, it seems they understand the meaning of these works better than anyone."

The artist's brushstrokes formed complex curved patterns in yellow, red and white. In the centre was a human figure, with a semi-circular headpiece. Next to it smaller figures. A dreamtime mother and some star people.

Caillol sat down and picked up a pen lying on a blank sheet of paper. He looked anxiously at de Palma.

"The last time we met was at the court in Aix."

"At the Bouches-du-Rhône criminal court," de Palma said. "Not a nice memory. For either of us."

"Thomas has escaped. So you could say we're back to square one . . ."

"Unfortunately, yes. That's why I'm trying to find out what I missed years ago. He needs to be foun, and quickly."

The secretary came in and put down on the table a thick

cardboard file, tied in grey ribbon. Autran's name was written in large letters in green marker pen.

"This is his medical file," Caillol said. "In theory it's confidential, but should you need any of the documents . . ."

"I'd like to get a sense of Autran's past. Understand what sort of man he is exactly," de Palma said.

"He's an extremely intelligent boy, someone who thinks faster than you or me. Even as we speak he probably knows you're here, and we're looking at his file to try to catch him."

Caillol went on, "In psychiatric terms Autran is a particular type of schizophrenic. The medical records show a loss of contact with reality. There are times when he becomes totally detached from the external world. He has auditory hallucinations when he believes his thoughts are imposed on him. Violent episodes you rarely see in other patients. His schizophrenia was diagnosed very early, before he reached adolescence. Usually it arrests normal development. By rights Autran should be an idiot. But that's not the case at all, quite the contrary. His intelligence resists the illness."

"Is that the reason you're so interested in him?"

"Yes."

"How do you see his current mental state?"

Caillol let his gaze wander over the file, "It's impossible to say. They must have stuffed him full of drugs. Provided they're administered correctly those medications can be quite effective. But I don't need to tell you that when you stop taking anti-psychotics, you relapse and become completely unpredictable. It's a bit like driving a racing car without any controls. You're heading for a collision. There's a high risk of carnage."

Caillol took off his specs and rubbed his eyes. Fatigue, no doubt. Saddled with the psychoses of an entire service, he must be exhausted. He didn't look the same without his glasses. He seemed much less severe, and had an air of naivety due to a slight squint.

De Palma asked about Autran's time in prison. But he didn't find out much that he didn't already know.

Thomas had been imprisoned in Marseille while still very young and then spent time at Ville Évrard, a huge asylum in Neuilly-sur-Marne on the outskirts of Paris. When Thomas was there it was one of the best equipped institutions. The young patient received initial treatment, some of it very aggressive. In psychiatric terms this meant electroconvulsive therapy, which the general public know as E.C.T. It is used for delusional psychoses that can't be treated with drugs. He underwent eighteen sessions at the age of fourteen: six weeks of treatment, three times a week. Each time the doctor would trigger an epileptic fit lasting for about thirty seconds.

"Did you care for Thomas at Ville-Évrard?" de Palma asked.

"No," Caillol replied, putting on his glasses and looking stern once more. I referred him to another service run by my colleague Dubreuil, if that's any help."

Thomas then returned to his parents' house in Marseille which was considered to be an open environment. A new approach to psychiatry was emerging. They were shutting down hospitals with a vengeance. Thomas was just as alienated from society as he had been behind the asylum gates. He swallowed pills, cowered and withered. His sister erected invisible barriers around him.

De Palma abruptly shut his notebook. He decided he would lead Caillol on to different territory.

"Tell me about the man with the antler head."

"I beg your pardon!" Caillol protested, clearly shaken. "I have nothing to say."

"Not the right answer, Doctor. About ten days ago you went to Porquerolles to visit Rémy Fortin's boat. I want to know why."

"Have you any evidence for what you're suggesting?"

"Of course. I wouldn't be here otherwise."

"Well, I'm sorry to tell you I couldn't have been at Porquerolles.

I was in the States. I left three weeks ago and came back the day before yesterday."

"In that case why did you leave your phone number with the harbour master? Well?"

Furious, Caillol stood up. There was something terrifying in this sudden anger that he had such difficulty controlling. His expression had gone cold, devoid of all humanity. He took a moment to calm down. De Palma returned to the offensive.

"I'm waiting for an explanation."

"I've already told you. In your language: I've got an alibi."

"For someone who considers himself to be so intellectually superior, I find you very lacking in common sense. I'm not going to take you to court, which I could do, legally. But you should be aware, sir, that I believe you're one of the people who pushed Thomas Autran to the brink. Out of scientific interest – and perversion, I should add."

"Our conversation is over. I'm calling my lawyer."

"You can call the Human Rights League, if you like. From a legal point of view your prospects don't look too good to me. And there's more."

De Palma pointed a finger at the psychiatrist. "Thomas Autran isn't far away. I know that, I can sense it. I'd advise you to be careful. He's going to come here. I'm just an old policeman, not a prophet or a magician, still less a shaman, but I can tell you you're going to receive a visit. It's only fair after all!"

\*

Eva was on her way back from a long walk along the Mont Puget footpath and the crests that towered over the sea. She had gone off on her own early in the afternoon, as she often did. In the Chèvre pass she had savoured the east wind rising up the small rocky valleys.

De Palma had come to appreciate her passion for long walks. Each time she returned from a hike, he loved to see her glowing face tanned by the sun, and smell the lentisc in her hair.

"You're back early, gorgeous," Eva said. "Though I don't much like that expression on your face."

De Palma gave a faint smile.

"On the lookout for evil ideas?"

"No, Eva. I'm trying to understand one man's madness."

"The one who escaped from the mental hospital?"

"Yes."

She put her hands on his shoulders. "I think you need to move on. Thirty years with the police should be enough. Why do you need to understand?"

"Because I can't live with myself if I think my work is just about putting killers in the nick. It's unbearable if you don't try to find the reason for all the blood and deaths. And you need to deal with your anger. To begin with, I was happy just to receive orders, and then one day I asked myself that simple question. After all, Autran could be my son or my brother! I've read loads of books about it."

Eva turned pointedly to the bookshelf and his proud criminology collection. "So what's the answer?"

"They've all got one thing in common: immense suffering in childhood. Sometimes you can't see it. Sometimes you don't find it. But it's there and it's done the damage. We get the murderers we deserve. There are many cultures where killers like Autran are unknown because they look at them differently before it's too late. There are cultures where mad people live within society. But we haven't learned a thing."

"He nearly killed you ten years ago."

"From man to true man, the path goes through the madman."

"Nice one."

"It's Michel Foucault."

She stepped away from him. "That madman of yours nearly killed you . . ."

"I know that and it's no excuse. It wasn't me he wanted, but what I represented. You can't change what's happened. The play's over, the

155

curtain's come down. We're going to kill Autran, or lock him up forever. It comes to the same thing. That's all we can do."

Eva sat on the sofa. Her hands were scratched from the thorn bushes on the hill.

"I read in one of your books that we can understand and treat madness through poetry," she said. "I think that's interesting."

"Me too," de Palma replied, looking for an L.P. on the shelves. He picked out "Electra" and put it on the turntable.

*Now comes the hour,*
*The hour when they cut your throat,*
*Your wife and the man who shares*
*Your royal bed with her.*

Eva stood up. "I'm going to have a shower, and then let's go out," she said. "The walk's made me hungry and I don't want to play the housewife listening to music from my great-grandfather's time."

"It's so beautiful though."

"No-one said it wasn't."

*They murdered you in your bath,*
*The blood ran over your eyes,*
*And the bath steamed with your blood.*

De Palma watched her disappear down the corridor, with her lithe walk and the slight swaying of the hips she had never lost. He felt he was living in a parallel world to the people he was close to. And there weren't many of them.

The previous few days seemed to have lasted forever. He was finding it difficult piecing together the different clues he had found on Autran's trail.

*Father! Agamemnon! Your day will come!*
*Just as time always flows from the stars*
*So will the blood of a hundred throats pour on your grave.*

Christine and Thomas's mother had died on the Termes road, by the junction known locally as "Regage", not far from Peypin. De Palma dialled the number of the *Gendarmerie* in Gréasque. A young voice answered.

"De Palma, C.I.D. Marseille."

"How can I help you?"

"I'm looking for some information. When you have an R.T.A. on the Termes stretch who's responsible for clearing the vehicles from the highway?"

"Please hold the line a moment, I'll just find out."

De Palma waited. The switchboard played "A Little Night Music", announcing every ten seconds, "You are connected to the *Gendarmerie* Nationale, please hold the line . . ." The voice was smooth, erotic even.

"Yes, I'm sorry about the delay. The Gilbert garage in Peypin takes care of that. He's accredited by the *Gendarmerie.*

*The dead are jealous: and for a fiancé*
*He sent me hate with hollow eyes.*

## 27

Past the smart estates of Plan-de-Cuques to the north-east of Marseille, the D908 crosses the main street in Logis Neuf. The last houses in the village cling to the white hillside, their gardens laid out in the scant earth.

De Palma didn't dare have a go at the car radio – tuning it was always a perilous exercise. So he had brought along his MP3 player and was listening to Zemlinsky's "Lieder" sung by Ann Sophie von Otter. It was a recent recording which he didn't think was too bad. *The Song of the Virgin* was his favourite.

*To each soul that weeps, to each sin that comes to pass,*
*I raise to the stars my hands full of grace.*

The road followed capricious hairpin bends, climbing through the harsh foothills of the Étoile and Garlaban mountain range. Steep sides with pine trees and loose stones towered overhead, until he came to a pass. The fires had left blackened tree trunks in the middle of a forest of creeping broom.

*No sin lives when love has spoken*
*No soul dies when love has wept . . .*

High up on the plateau, in the bright light, the view extended as far as Sainte Baume hill to the east, Grande Étoile, to the north, caught in the fires of the setting sun, and the huge Auriol valley scarred by the Aubagne-Aix motorway.

*And if love should wend its way below,*
*Its tears will find me and will stay . . .*

As he passed the sign for Peypin, the Baron ruefully turned off the music. Gilbert Car Repairs was near the village entrance: a blue sign bleached by the sun and two enormous plane trees with knotty fingers. A breakdown truck with chrome fittings was parked in front of the workshop. A mechanic wearing a crumpled expression appeared from behind a clapped-out B.M.W.

"What do you want?"

"I need some information," de Palma said. "I'd like to know the location of an accident that took place in 1982."

The mechanic, who couldn't have been over twenty-five, stared, his eyes nearly popping out of their sockets. "I'll have to get my dad; he's in the office."

He disappeared behind a glass partition covered in stickers. A large notice spattered in grease set out the minimum charges and hourly labour rates. The father appeared.

"Hello. Are you in charge here?"

"That's right, Gilbert Monteil. Which accident do you mean?"

"It was in 1982. On the Termes road. A woman called Martine Autran. Seems she was killed instantly."

Monteil looked him up and down.

"You from the police?"

"You don't miss much."

Monteil rubbed his chin and went to the front of the workshop. A Renault Scenic had just pulled in to fill up.

"I only know of one and that was at the Regage junction. On your way back to Marseille, a bit higher up after Termes, there's a track that goes off down to the left."

He pointed the way.

"Just after the turning there's a track that comes off the hill. From l'Étoile, as it were. Well, it's just opposite that. The car ended up in the ravine. It had rolled twice."

Monteil turned and called to his son to come and cash the notes the driver had handed him.

"You've got a good memory, I see."

"You're telling me. It's like it was yesterday. Such a beautiful woman. Killed instantly. You think I can forget that?"

He put his hand on the wing of a Peugeot that had recently been filled in.

"Were there any tyre marks? Anything that struck you as unusual?"

"No, nothing. I remember the Gendarmes couldn't understand how it had happened. The car had rolled bonnet first."

He mimed the accident with his hand. The front of the Mercedes was damaged. The sides were almost intact, the steering jammed.

"Could the impact cause that to happen?" de Palma asked.

"No, it wasn't that."

Gilbert looked down and picked up a bolt lying by his feet. "I remember it was a Mercedes 300. It had power-assisted steering. They were quite rare at the time."

He stopped. "I had a colleague with the same car, but without the power-assisted steering. So I said to him, 'I've got one at the garage, Jacques. If you want I can change the steering for you.' He bit my hand off. Those things cost a fortune."

Monteil took a cigarette from a greasy packet and wedged it between his lips without lighting it. "So I start to dismantle the steering column and then I realise there isn't a drop of fluid in the cylinder. No steering oil! It was bone dry. I thought to myself: Shit! You don't get that on a new Mercedes!"

"So how do you think it happened then?"

"No idea . . . could be a leak or a join perhaps . . . a hose . . . who knows? I didn't look any further. I told my mate the steering had gone and there was no point. And that was it."

Monteil was lying. It was obvious from the way he rolled his eyes. The real version was undoubtedly different: the owner of the garage simply didn't want any hassle. De Palma thanked him and got back into his Alfa Giulietta Sprint Veloce, styled by Bertone. Monteil hadn't seen a coupé like that in thirty years.

*

The Regage track was barely two kilometres away. The Baron parked on the verge and walked back up towards the accident site.

The road was quiet. In the evening the ridges of the Étoile glowed pale pink, emphasising the deep shadows cast by the cliffs. The accident had happened on a straight stretch of the track. The car had gone head first into the ravine and rolled, hitting the bonnet and radiator grille.

De Palma was baffled. He had gradually developed a theory that now seemed to be confirmed: the steering oil had been syphoned off, somehow. Either by cutting a hose, or draining it with a syringe. The steering wouldn't have seized up immediately – that would take several hours' driving. It meant the saboteur knew Martine Autran would be driving along this winding stretch of road.

A light wind started to blow, bringing a thousand scents from the scrubland. A car went slowly by. The driver shot de Palma a ferocious look.

The accident had taken place at almost exactly that time. Virtually no traffic. On a difficult road.

What on earth was Martine doing in a place like that?

De Palma went a few metres back up along the track and looked at the accident site from a higher vantage point. The car had toppled head first into a deep ravine – that was impossible from the road. It seemed clear Martine had been coming from the track where he was standing. There was no other possibility.

Only one theory held water: Martine was returning from a drive; she had stopped before taking the side road; the steering wheel jammed as she accelerated and that led to the accident.

But who had called the emergency services? The Gendarmes and the fire brigade had arrived in less than thirty minutes. The car couldn't be seen from the road. It definitely wasn't a passer-by.

Three hundred metres away a small house was tucked away in a hollow that funnelled towards an oak and pine wood. It was a pleasant spot for a drive, but a long way from the Mazargues district where the Autran family lived. It was close to the Calanques and Mont Puget. The scenery was much nicer over there.

The Baron returned to his Giulietta, his mind in disarray like the Grande Armée at Waterloo. He found "The Song of the Virgin" on his MP3 player, put in his earphones and turned up the volume, to drown out the surrounding noise.

*And if love should wend its way below,*
*Its tears will find me and will stay . . .*

# 28

Before the Alcazar became a state-of-the-art library it was one of the most taxing theatres in France. Music hall stars and novices alike were met either with thunderous applause or with an unbelievable din of boos, catcalls and rotten vegetables.

Maistre and de Palma had agreed to meet in the reading room. There was nothing to remind one of Réda Caire, Andrex, or that maestro of operetta, Serge Bessière. This put a dampener on de Palma's pathological nostalgia. He didn't like all the glass cases filled with books, C.D.s and films.

"I feel like I've just gone back to Uni," Maistre joked, pointing to the pile of books in front of him. "Not bad for an O.A.P. I've found quite a lot of stuff."

After five minutes de Palma felt suffocated. The bank of computers opposite was not inspiring. He looked around for a good old manual filing system, where he could have flicked through dogeared records while daydreaming about the titles. But there was nothing. The poetry of the card index was gone forever.

Most of the tables were empty. There were not many young people, mainly women in their sixties. Is that what I'm like? de Palma thought. Not yet, a voice inside replied, but it won't be long. He watched Maistre for a few seconds, with his greying temples and glasses sitting on the end of his nose. Maistre liked progress as much as he himself detested it. He fitted in rather well in this setting.

No-one would have guessed he had been in the police force for over thirty years and was still capable of abseiling down the Calanques in the middle of the night!

"I've found four books that are relevant, and there are some academic publications as well," Maistre said.

Christine Autran's *Religion of the Caves* was intended for an informed readership. She had written the book in the mid-nineties. Three hundred and forty-seven pages of erudite references and footnotes: far too numerous for de Palma to focus on anything in particular.

A lengthy introduction of more than fifty pages was devoted to the methodology of scientific study. Christine Autran described two journeys. The first visit, to the last remaining San communities in South Africa and Botswana, took place in the winter of 1992. She had brought back a set of notes on cave painting in that part of the world. The other journey during the spring and early summer of 1993 had lasted for more than three months. Christine described encounters with Evenki and Even shamans in the Altai mountains of Siberia.

The first chapter was an overview of earlier works on symbolism in cave painting. Most of the writers cited were unknown to him. The names Leroi-Gourhan and Abbé Breuil cropped up frequently.

Two subsequent chapters gave examples of the depiction of human figures in prehistoric caves: 'slain men', to use the specialist terminology.

On page 134 there was a description of a birdman. Christine Autran assigned him the role of prehistoric shaman. She claimed that similar symbolism was found among the San in southern Africa.

Towards the end of the book, Maistre had inserted a bookmark. For several pages Christine dwelt on a drawing in the Trois-Frères cave: a strange being, half-man, half-stag, drawn three and a half metres above the ground. According to her sources this creature was referred to as the Sorcerer or Horned God. De Palma thought of what the Autrans' neighbour had told him about statuettes in the house. Was one of them the man with the antler head?

Christine Autran devoted a long passage to a drawing from 1705, depicting a man with a stag's antlers on his head, playing a drum A Tungus shaman. Had she encountered one during her visit to Siberia? Did her brother accompany her? Shamans predicted the future, cured the sick, and brought rain or sunshine. They could talk with human and animal spirits. Shamans were not murderers. In ancient times priests believed they were under the influence of the Devil, who appeared in the form of a crow or similar bird or, more rarely, as a ghost.

Christine later wrote:

*"This is the 'slain man' found in Le Guen's cave. The question is often asked, what exactly does he represent? Is it the depiction of a real murder, a symbolic one or simply a hunting accident? It should be noted that as far as paintings or drawings are concerned the portrayal of humans is extremely rare. They are more often found in the form of statuettes and in almost every case they are half-men, half-beasts. Which is odd. Prehistoric man is hardly represented, if at all. It's as though he ceded his place to the animals. As though he was ashamed of his face and was at the same time compelled to assume the mask of another being, for example a face with a bird beak. That's a fairly common feature. The body by contrast is very crudely drawn and often takes the form of a large potato! Only the head is stylised . . ."*

De Palma returned to the "slain man":

*". . . lines that visibly pierce our man. It is for this reason he is thought to have been killed, but such an interpretation could not be more risky. For my own part I prefer to see magical allusions.*

*Like many of my colleagues I believe in a magic of represen-*
*tations. Of course we don't yet know how to decipher this.*

*"The 'slain man' is arresting for several reasons, but the first*
*is these lines. Were they done at the same time as the rest of the*
*drawing, or are they a later addition? It would not be the first*
*time in the history of cave painting that additional elements*
*have been introduced in this way. In this case it would be like a*
*desire to strike out, to deny the individual that is drawn in*
*outline in the rock. We find mysterious lines of this type in a*
*number of caves, including Chauvet, Trois Frères and Le Guen's*
*cave."*

Christine went on to describe a host of mysterious symbols and
drawings drawn on top of one another, interwoven to the point of
almost making the original material disappear. Then she mentioned
one of the most enigmatic paintings, the famous horned god:

*"It is of course an imaginary being. It has the head of a snowy*
*owl. The expression is truly penetrating. Once again, this crea-*
*ture is endowed with several animal characteristics. It has, for*
*example, reindeer antlers on its head. Man and beast are linked.*
*The sizable phallus takes us back to our age-old fantasies. As*
*though a kind of unconscious has endured . . . a merging of Man*
*and beast. Sexuality is there. The paths of the psychoanalyst and*
*pre-historian cross."*

De Palma closed the book. He looked tense. In the other world
voices whispered something incomprehensible to him, snatches of
incoherent sentences emerging from a mirror.

"We need to make sense of all this," Maistre whispered, glancing
towards a group of women reading.

"I know, Jean-Louis. But Fortin wasn't killed by Tungus shamans,
diving at Sugiton at night."

166

"Do you think that man came to look for the statuette?"

"We can assume so. But it's only an assumption. The cave still has a secret," de Palma said. "And it's one we're no closer to finding. Unless we go back and take another look."

"How do you mean? Surely Pauline Barton did a proper job."

"She's a pre-historian, not a policeman. It's not her role."

"And you think our methods are any better?"

"They're not the same, that's all. We've got to search that cave, no two ways about it. Fortin must have secretly gone there and seen something. And unless you believe in spirits, that something was very real. It's up to us to find out what!"

Maistre put his notes back in a folder and placed his glasses on top.

"And Thomas Autran's role in all this?"

"Same story. Just the same. Autran escapes from prison because we're about to uncover the cave's last secret."

"You sure?"

"Of course not. But at least it's a theory that makes sense. He left some clues. There's the reading material in prison and the statuette he made when he was at the secure unit in Villejuif. It all points in the same direction."

"Unless it's a false trail. His sister is due out soon. Who's to say that wasn't the reason he escaped? He wanted to find his twin sister and do a runner with her."

It was a strong motive. But communication in prison between the twins amounted to nothing. There were no letters or phone calls. Their lawyers hadn't seen them since they first went inside and did not particularly want to receive any news either.

# 29

Caillol rose stiffly behind his desk. "I don't want to see you, Monsieur de Palma."

"I'm not Monsieur de Palma, I'm the police. Would you rather I issued a summons?"

Caillol caved in. He sat down and took off his glasses with an exasperated gesture.

"Tell me about this rather unusual therapy you used to treat Autran."

Caillol looked embarrassed. "I think I told you everything there is to say on the subject nine years ago. There's not much to add."

"My memory's playing up. I forget things."

Caillol cleared his throat. "Autran was fascinated by prehistory. Well, I am too. I knew his sister well. She was one of a long line of remarkable scientists who saw a link between Palaeolithic cave painting and magical practices, things connected with shamanism . . . to tell the truth that was really Autran's delirium."

The doctor collected his thoughts, his eyes fixed on the files. "During Thomas' therapy his sister became an ally. Together we developed some sessions that were appropriate for him."

"You were copying the Magdalenian shamans!"

Caillol looked self-important. "Well, in a way, yes. I wanted to use magic to reproduce the effect of the electroshocks on Thomas's brain. It isn't easy to explain to the layman."

"You need to try, doctor. Get off your high horse."

De Palma had raised his voice just enough to intimidate Caillol, then fell silent. During a face-to-face meeting, such pauses could seem like eternity. It was an old technique he had picked up at the police station. He flicked through his notebook, turning the pages at random, then stared at the psychiatrist. "You asked Thomas to go into a trance and then you observed his reactions, is that right?"

"I start from the principle that it is not psychology that explains madness, but the other way round. Truth lies in madness. So we tried to control the fits, not by using electricity but by triggering them in other ways. We then channelled them into harmless areas. The madman became a doctor, someone capable of entering into contact with the spirit world, interceding with the elders to resolve problems that were quite real."

"And that worked?"

Caillol looked sombre. "Yes, it did, I have to say. I know I've been criticised for that, but I insist. The epileptic fits triggered by these shamanic sessions helped Thomas."

"What I mean is, was he able to communicate with spirits and treat the living like shamans do?"

"Is there any point in my agreeing? You won't believe me."

"You're wrong there. I genuinely think Autran has these powers. I also know he's a killer and can see you were using a very dangerous man as your guinea pig. But let's carry on. And believe me, I won't doubt what you say."

Caillol stared at his fingertips. He couldn't stop them shaking very slightly. "Thomas once told me what he felt during one of these sessions. He was in a huge area of long grass. The spirits had taken possession of him and decapitated him before leading him to a cave. The cave was painted with magical symbols, including handprints. There the spirits made him whole again by placing crystals in his body and other substances that had special powers. When he came round he was in a state of temporary insanity.

But then it disappeared, because the madness could be tamed.

"Do you understand, Monsieur de Palma? He had given me a description of a shamanic rite practised by the Arundas in the Australian outback. At his age, and at the time he told me all this, he didn't know the Arundas existed, let alone anything about these practices. Not a thing. How do you explain that?"

"Are you telling me shamanism and madness are connected?"

"I'm telling you what I believe to be true, Monsieur de Palma. It seems to me that's why you're here."

The Baron nodded. Caillol continued in the same vein. "Thomas' sister, Christine, thought that artistic drive and the shaman's mental disorder were connected. In fact it's not a new theory. It was put forward by Andreas Lommel in the sixties and served as a prelude, if I may say so, to the hippy era and the New Age movement, a time when shamans were held up as the sanest people of all. You remember psychedelic drugs and that sort of thing?"

De Palma got up and stood in front of one of the two windows. He could see the tower blocks and lowrise flats on the estates to the north of Marseille.

"In such cases you reach the deepest, most unpredictable part of the human psyche," Caillol added. "Shamanism is still practised in many cultures across the world. It's probably what man has preserved from the earliest stages of humanity and what he has retained best. From the Tibetan plateaux to Siberia, through Australia and North America, these practices exist and are respected. I think Christine was right to believe those handprints you see in the caves are shamanic symbols."

"The problem is, doctor, in societies where shamans live they aren't different in the way we imagine. They are quite ordinary people, insignificant even. If you'll forgive me, they know how to be mad at the right time, while Thomas Autran is a pervert who uses these symbols as a signature for his crimes. For him shamanism is just an excuse. A delusion."

"Yes, I agree," Caillol said.

A silence ensued. Shadows from the past rose up around the old policeman and psychiatrist.

"Autran hatched something in prison," de Palma said. "Detention forced him to become introspective, and that's never very good for that sort of patient. Monastic living and schizophrenia don't go together. You know that, doctor. The dark prison with voices that stalk the mind."

Caillol turned, so his face was hidden, "His father died young, after returning from a dig. In an accident."

"An archaeological dig?"

"He was working with Professor Palestro, whom you'll have heard about. One of those volunteers lucky enough to work on a dig with real scientists."

"What do you know about his death?"

"I've been told it was a stupid accident. He fell off a stool and banged his head. A sad story."

Caillol kept his back turned.

"You seem to know a lot about the Autran family."

"I treated Thomas."

The doctor swung round.

"It's pretty basic for any practitioner worth his salt to know about his patients' lives. This is psychiatry, you know."

"Tell me about his mother."

Caillol looked flustered.

"A beautiful woman. She also died – twelve years after her husband."

"Of natural causes?"

"No, in a car accident."

Caillol grabbed a pen from his desk and twirled it in his fingers. It was the first time de Palma had noticed this tic.

"And where were the children at this point?"

Caillol struggled for words. The pen twirled faster and faster.

"Thomas was sectioned," he said finally. "At Ville-Évrard."

"Why not in your department? Why so far away?"

"They were more advanced than us in terms of care. Psychiatry had changed. At Ville-Évrard they were doing things that were more appropriate for Thomas."

De Palma saw a key part of his theory collapse like a pack of cards. Martine's children had not killed her. Perhaps that was an end to Electra's song. But he was still convinced the twins' mother had been murdered.

Caillol kept hold of his pen. He looked drawn. De Palma noticed his fingers were long and thin, feminine almost.

"So, what was Thomas's reaction when he learned of his mother's death?"

Caillol's hands started to shake. He gripped the pen tightly. Then he answered in a strangled voice, "There was no reaction. No sadness or joy. It was terrifying."

# 30

"This way."

The prison officer was rather short and masculine looking. She shuffled over the glazed tiles in her soft-soled shoes. "Autran's one of our best inmates. She's no problem at all. Spends all her time with her nose in her books or else in the gym. She's in great shape."

It was de Palma's first time in a women's prison. He knew all the rumours that circulated about them: the harshness and the inhumanity. The officers could be tougher than their male counterparts. At Rennes, there were no Christmas decorations; no reminder at all that this was the festive season.

The buzz preceded the Baron and followed in his wake. He felt ill at ease in the gaol, ugly even, in his black cotton trousers and sweater. Everywhere the sound of whispering and raised voices from the cells. A high-security prison is one long hum that never ceases, day or night.

"The problem with Autran is she hardly ever speaks. Just a few words when she needs to ask you something."

Twenty metres or so further on, the woman stopped by a double door. Another officer with a bun on her head looked up from the screens and nodded.

"I'll open up."

She released the first lock and then closed it after the detective and prison officer had gone through. A second bolt squeaked in its guides.

"I'll leave you here. My colleague will take you to Autran. I don't know if anyone's told you, but she hasn't had a single visit in the nine years she's been here. I don't think she'll tell you much."

"We can always try," de Palma said, darting a smile.

"You never know, she's not a bad girl."

The visiting room was square, with white walls and green edging. There was a table fixed to the ground and two metal chairs. De Palma threw his briefcase on to the table and put his jacket over the back of a chair. Without really knowing why, he dreaded meeting Christine Autran's eyes, seeing the face that had left such a strong impression at their only meeting at the criminal court in Aix-en-Provence.

"I'll fetch her. I'll only be a couple of minutes."

The officer had an agreeable face, with alert blue eyes and brown hair tied at the back with a black silk scrunchie – her sole concession to prettiness in that drab world.

De Palma tidied his hair and put a pen and piece of paper in front of him. The seconds slowly ticked away as he waited. A loudspeaker in the yard announced exercise time for B block. Immediately doors started to bang one after the other. The buzz swelled. A ray of sunlight came in through the window. Sea birds could be heard seeking their fortune in the prison rubbish skips.

"There you go," the prison officer said.

De Palma stood up, looking solemn. Christine Autran stared coldly, letting him know she already understood why he had come to interview her.

"Good morning," de Palma said. "Have a seat."

Christine wore a synthetic sky blue tracksuit that showed off her figure. A firm bust jutted out from her white T-shirt. Prison hadn't broken her physically. She retained the haughty look of a woman who had never let herself go. There was something stunning and scary about her face. Her short hair, cut back from the ears, emphasised the thinness of her cheeks and heightened the ascetic look. She

174

sat down, crossing her long, delicate hands in front of her. Her deep-set grey eyes shone, filled with profound pain.

"I'm Commandant de Palma. The man your brother nearly killed."

The Baron's words seemed to bounce back off an invisible wall.

"Your brother has escaped from the secure unit at Villejuif. We're looking for him."

There was no response, no physical reaction. Just a very slight flicker in the eyes.

"Listen, Christine, I know you don't want to talk to the police or lawyers because we put you in here. But you're the only person who can help. The man is sick. I've come to appeal to you as a woman, who wants to put an end to his atrocities."

Autran turned to the window and took a deep breath. A cloud passed in front of the sun, nibbling away at the light.

"Are you listening, Christine?"

She looked back at de Palma.

"I've come to ask for your help, Christine. The smallest clue could be important."

De Palma cursed the fact that he was just a policeman, coming to beg for information from someone far brighter than himself. A soul battered by her time in prison. He had planned to speak to her about Lucy Meunier's death, but something told him not to mention it.

"If you agreed to cooperate I could ask the sentencing judge to allow you some privileges. Do you understand?"

Christine crossed her hands and stared at him coldly. Eventually he looked down.

"You've only got a few years left. I think you could expect a pretty substantial period of remission."

The officer standing behind the door jangled the keys in her hand.

"Do you think the days are long in this prison?" Christine said in a whisper.

"I imagine so."

"They are the eternity within life, constantly renewed. For most of the hysterical women here this dense layer of time soon becomes unbearable. But for me it's the other way round. I thrive on time at a standstill. I am steeped in eternity."

A faint light stirred in her eyes. She leaned against the back of her chair and gazed at the drab walls.

"Are you still working on prehistory, Christine?"

Her fingers clenched, "Yes," she said in a silvery voice. "Why would I stop?"

"Still the same subject? Shamanism and prehistory?"

She nodded. De Palma wondered whether to continue. Each word counted and the woman before him had a head start. Prison had certainly sharpened her capacity to concentrate on the essential.

"Lots of specialists find your theories pretty far-fetched," de Palma went on. "To explain cave painting in terms of shamanism is just an easy shortcut."

Autran stared at her fingers. "They don't have my experience. And I don't think you do either!"

"Siberia, Africa . . . I've read all about it."

"The stuff you've read is dated. There are new things I've discovered."

"Such as?"

Autran had turned to the window. Her profile was very sharp, as though sculpted in white marble.

"Tell me about the man with the antler head."

"Antler head?"

"Yes."

Her lips hardly moved, but it was enough. De Palma knew his words had hit home.

"I've read what you've written about the Horned God," de Palma continued. "Do you think the same about the man with the antler head?"

176

"Yes."

"Can you elaborate?"

"What do you want to know?"

De Palma hesitated. He didn't know how to pursue his line of questioning. He wasn't sure about anything. He was steering between different assumptions that might make him look credible.

He decided to try his luck. "I think that statuette belonged to your father and someone stole it from you. Is that the case?"

Christine looked up at de Palma and scanned his face. "Where's the little god?"

"Only you can tell me that."

"I don't know."

De Palma put his hand on the folder opposite him. Christine watched. The hand settled on the elastic binding. He had slipped several photos of the statuette inside. A sudden flash of intuition told him not to show them. He withdrew his hand. Christine hadn't missed a thing. She slowly raised her eyes again towards de Palma's face, lingering on his mouth for a second or two.

"Do you know someone called Rémy Fortin?" de Palma asked.

"I know he's dead."

"So you read the same papers as your brother?"

"I think so."

"You haven't answered my question."

"Did you come here to talk about Rémy Fortin, or about my brother?"

"Both. I think your brother's escape is connected to the opening up of the cave, the recent finds and the man with the antler head. Am I wrong about that?"

"I don't know."

"You haven't answered my questions."

Christine looked straight into his eyes, boring right through him.

"You know the answer to the first question. The man with the antler head is one of two statuettes that belonged to my father."

"Where did he find it?"

"It's a long story and it's not important. But it did belong to him."

"It is important and I want to hear about it from you."

She stared at him for a long time. De Palma didn't take his eyes off her, in spite of the unease this woman's intense expression stirred in him.

"My father was only ever dishonest once in his life," she said. "Just once. He was working on a dig with Palestro. One evening after the site closed, he went back and took that statuette."

"Why?"

"He thought the man with the antler head could cure my brother."

"And that wasn't the case."

Calmly she laid her hands flat on the table. "How can you say that?"

"It's just an assumption," de Palma replied.

"As long as my brother had the man with the antler head, as long as he could touch it, pray to it, talk to it, nothing happened. It was only when it was stolen that all these terrible things started to happen."

"Who stole it?"

"How do you expect me to know?"

For all his experience, de Palma had come up against a brick wall.

"I'll repeat my question. Who stole it from you? I'm convinced you know."

She was cut off from him, hidden behind an invisible barrier.

"Was it Dr Caillol?"

The question produced no response. Christine was lost in some inaccessible place. She seemed to be looking straight through him.

"The great hunter has returned," Christine said in a sombre voice.

"Who are you talking about?"

"The sacrifice requires a forked larch tree on a small hill. A stick symbolising an arrow is placed in the fork of the tree. The direction of the arrow shows which spirit the sacrifice is intended for . . ."

De Palma leaned over and put his hand on hers. It was cold. Christine left her hand there, as though she felt nothing.

"Tell me where your brother is. It's your last chance to save him from certain death. I beg you."

"If the stick points south and upwards, the sacrifice is intended for an *Abaahy* from the upper world. If it points north with the tip down it's for an *Abaahy* from the underworld."

"What is an *Abaahy*?"

"A spirit," replied Christine, looking up as though she was emerging from a subterranean universe.

De Palma summoned the prison officer with a nod of his head.

"I'm going to leave you to have a think about things. I'll be in touch in a few days' time. I hope by then you'll have something to tell me."

The door opened. Christine stood up mechanically and left the room. "Goodbye."

Thomas' sister went down the corridor, her arms by her side. She stopped at the first grille.

"Try to find out who Rémy Fortin really was," she said.

De Palma followed her. "How do you mean?"

Christine stared at him with a sardonic smile, "Try to find out who Rémy Fortin really was . . ."

She passed through the grilles and disappeared into a forest of barred gates and the sound of locks turning. The door to the visitors' room closed again.

"When is she due to be released?"

"Very soon," the officer replied. "Probably by the spring."

# 31

De Palma hated work meetings, especially when they took place early in the morning. He had woken late and hadn't had time to enjoy his usual coffee with Eva. It was a habit he'd developed since they'd been living together.

Bessour sat opposite, looking shattered. He must have spent a good part of the night turning things over in his head. Legendre chaired the meeting in his usual style, anxious despite his good-natured façade.

"Karim's taken care of border control, the railway stations and the airports. He's done a good job, but nothing's come up so far. Either Autran has already left France or he's outwitted us. Which is not impossible. Michel?"

"I'm caught between getting nowhere and going backwards. There's a lot of stuff, but nothing concrete. Nothing at all. It feels like we're swimming in porridge. Right now, Autran's got the lead. What's more, I'm sure there's someone either following in his footsteps or out there ahead of him. I think it's the diver who killed Fortin and nearly sent Thierry Garcia to an early grave. And, I should say, very possibly killed Lucy Meunier."

Legendre and Bessour looked at each other, bewildered and confused.

"I know Autran. I've agonised about it. Lucy Meunier isn't his style."

"So who do you think is killing all these single women?" Legendre asked.

"I'm torn between Dr Caillol and the diver. Unless of course they're one and the same."

"Interesting," Legendre said, stroking his cheek. The skin was still red from razor burn.

"The hand on the wall, that isn't Autran. The person who tried to imitate him got two things wrong."

De Palma liked to make his audience wait, like in Verdi's operas where the expected note comes only after a lively cavatina. He stood up and went over to the wall.

"The technique isn't the same. Autran drew on sheets of paper. He mixed some water and pigments in his mouth and then blew, like this. Just like prehistoric men. You still find that today among the Aborigines and in other societies, such as indigenous people in Borneo or the Kanaks."

De Palma pressed his hand against the wall, as the ice age painters did.

"Autran left his D.N.A. behind. But there was none on the trace found at Lucy's house. The outline of the hand shows it was drawn with the help of a blower or spray gun. The outline is too sharp. So, that's it."

They both nodded: Bessour to acknowledge he'd been given a lesson by the maestro, Legendre because, once again, he'd been out smarted by his subordinate.

"Nice demonstration," Legendre said. "But there's still the question of the motive. Why butcher that poor Lucy woman?"

De Palma hesitated. He had nothing left to impress his audience. "We'll soon find out."

"And Christine Autran?" Legendre asked.

"She remained completely impassive. I think I tried everything, but nothing worked. As I left she told me a sort of riddle. I've made a note of it and I'm trying to work it out. But I must admit none of it makes any sense to me."

"How do you mean?"

"She talked of a sacrificial, spiritual place and about the religion of Siberian peoples. I've a feeling she was giving me a coded message."

"You don't think she was a bit shaken? She was kooky enough already; prison can't have sorted her out."

"There's some truth in what you say, boss. But I think her brother is going to kill someone and she wanted to warn me. A very perverse way of thinking. And of course it's all going to happen right here under our noses, or just about."

Legendre smoothed down his tie, as he always did when anxiety set in. "Karim's done a lot of work on the case. He's got a few things to tell us. Karim?"

Bessour bent down and picked up a bulky file lying at his feet. He had trawled through the interviews from the time of the twins' arrest a decade earlier. "At no point . . ." he said. "At no point . . . did Christine or Thomas ever make any admissions. We don't have any genuine confessions. There's almost no proof of their guilt."

"What are you trying to say?" de Palma thundered. "That they're innocent?"

Karim dodged the question. "I don't mean that at all."

"Then why are you poking your nose round in this shit? Of course they're guilty. The court had no doubt."

Legendre smacked the table with his hand. "Calm down, Michel. This could be interesting."

The Baron clenched his teeth.

It had not been possible to follow up every lead at the time the first Autran case was closed. Whole aspects of the case had remained obscure and these were now coming to light. Bessour had looked into Autran's family and tried to find out if he had a bolthole with some relation. An old cousin from Avignon turned up out of nowhere. Grudgingly the cousin finally admitted he had spent holidays with the family in a house in the country, which did not appear in any statement or other document. The Autrans had a house in the country and no-one had noticed.

"Do you have any idea where it is?" de Palma asked.

"Afraid not. The cousin's getting on and this all took place about forty years ago. He said it was somewhere near Marseille. I need to get stuck into the archives and that could take time."

De Palma immediately saw a link with the location of Martine Autran's accident. On the Termes road, by the Regage turning. But he kept his thoughts to himself. The Commissaire brought the meeting to a close. Bessour immediately disappeared with the file under his arm. De Palma rang Maistre and gave him directions to the Regage track.

"I'll be there in half an hour," Maistre said. "But why don't you go there with Legendre and the rest of the gang?"

"Because they're the gang, that's why."

*

The autumn rain had washed away the track in several places. De Palma stopped by a rocky outcrop and gave his exact location to Maistre, who was still on his way.

Two hundred metres away a small house stood out in the scrubland. The path leading to it was overgrown with bushes. It was the only nice spot in the Étoile foothills; the rest of the track was torrid and bare in summer.

The Baron went down to the fork with the small path. He was about a hundred metres from the house. To his left a large rock protruded like an ogre's head from the dwarf vegetation; all around were charred stumps, rusted stone and dense thorn bushes.

Further to the right some pine trees had escaped a fire. The house was just a stone's throw away. The thick vegetation forced de Palma to wind his way through, taking huge strides.

After a few minutes he was sweating. He stopped to take off his jacket and tie it round his waist. He could feel his heartbeat pounding in his temples. He was about to go back and wait for Maistre when he heard the sharp, snapping sound of wood breaking. Then there was silence. Only nature, the incessant buzzing of flies and the distant throb of a lorry struggling up the side road.

He decided to continue. He nearly stumbled on the root of a holm oak tree. He became angry, wondering if he wasn't wasting his time. Then he spotted a figure passing between the main house and a little hut that must be used for storage purposes.

"Hey!" the Baron shouted. "Who's there?"

The figure appeared for a second time. De Palma froze. A face he could not forget. Thomas Autran was standing there in front of him. Then, in a second, was gone.

The Baron drew his Bodyguard and went into the undergrowth. The dense thorns scratched him. His heart was thumping. If he arced round he would have the front door in his line of fire. Nothing moved.

"Police! Come on out, Autran. You've no chance."

A closed window, a door ajar, no other exit at the back. He raised his weapon to eye level.

There might be a second opening at the side, hidden to view. He continued to skirt round, never taking his eyes off the house. To the left of the building was a small structure that looked like a washhouse. A sheet of corrugated iron fixed to a small shed banged against the wall in the wind.

Suddenly something shot out between the washhouse and an old dry-stone wall. Instinctively de Palma stepped aside. The assegai caught him in the shoulder, making him cry out.

Taking advantage of the unexpected hit, Autran leapt from behind the washhouse and ran towards the pine trees. He was wearing jeans, a leather jacket and a rucksack. De Palma fired. The bullet went wide of the mark and shattered the trunk of a young pine. Aiming as best he could, he fired for a second time. Autran wasn't running; he was springing up and down, zigzagging towards him. He stopped. A louder shot rang out behind the Baron. The bullet hit a rock, throwing up a cloud of dust. Autran turned and fled towards the wood. A second shot. De Palma looked round. Maistre was standing behind him, a semi-automatic hunting rifle on his shoulder. He fired twice more. But Autran was now out of range.

De Palma was bleeding. The spear had gashed his forearm, but it was nothing serious.

By now Autran was well away and no-one knew where to find him. There was no chance of catching him. Lady Luck is miserly: she doesn't allow a second bite at the cherry.

De Palma felt deeply humiliated. All alone, holding a gun he imagined he would never use again. He was in pain but refused to show it, burying the shame away deep inside. Maistre was just a few metres away. He came over.

"I – I don't know what to say," the Baron stammered.

"Don't say anything then," Maistre replied, looking at the assegai.

They were the words his father had used when he did something stupid as a little boy. "Don't say anything then" – that simple little sentence stung him. He was worthy of contempt and he couldn't even find the words to apologise.

It was Maistre who spoke. "I'd've done the same in your position."

"Is that right?"

"Yes, if it's any comfort."

Maistre put down the assegai and glanced around.

"I can't get his face out of my head," de Palma said. "Can you understand that?" He had raised his voice.

Maistre turned and looked at him. "You're starting to scare me. Are you serious?"

The Baron took off his jacket and examined the wound. The tip of the assegai had torn the fabric, causing a gash in the skin three centimetres long. Correct procedure was to use his mobile and call in the choppers and the squaddies with their sniffer dogs. He hesitated.

"Let's go," said Maistre.

"Where to?"

"Take a guess," Maistre replied, pointing at the house.

"Give me some cover, Jean-Louis."

Maistre picked up the spent cartridges and slipped three new ones into the magazine. He looked momentarily over towards the little wood where Autran had vanished. Further away, some tender green, ancient meadows extended across a narrow valley.

"There's no risk," he said. "He'll never try and take on two armed cops. Go inside. I'll stay in front of the house."

De Palma slipped four new bullets into his revolver and put the empty cartridges in his jacket pocket. "Right, I'm off."

There was a concrete terrace cluttered with old wicker chairs and a table warped by the sun. Two narrow windows in the bare stone façade. Some dense brambles had thrived in the shade, wrapping their clawed hooks around the rusty hinges of a shutter.

Inside a smell of old clothes, ash and stale sweat permeated the air. There was very little light. The first room was quite large. In the middle stood four chairs with straw seats gnawed away by rats, two pairs facing each other. Marks in the dust showed that one of the chairs, opposite the small fireplace, had been moved recently. Thomas' place, the Baron decided. He used to sit opposite his father, perhaps, with his mother on his left and sister on the right. The Baron imagined the twins teasing one another while their mother bustled about cooking. The thought embarrassed him. How could he imagine the childhood of a man who, only a few minutes earlier, had tried to kill him? He went through into the bedroom. Autran had been disturbed as he prepared to leave.

A flint lay on the ground, a biface shaped like a willow leaf, about twenty centimetres long.

"He didn't kill you," Maistre said behind him, keeping an eye on the outside.

"I don't know what you mean, Jean-Louis."

"I hope you realise he spared your life. He had you at his mercy. All he needed to do was wait for you to come into the house and then kill you."

*

"I don't think Maman loves us!"

Pierre Autran looked down. When Thomas talked about his mother, he looked like thunder.

"Maman loves us all in her own way."

"You're lying, Papa! One day she's going to kill us all. She doesn't want us."

Pierre Autran covered the tears on his face. He had married Martine because she was so beautiful. She had always cheated on him and had made no secret of the fact. He didn't really know why he was so crazy about her, but that's how it was. All he had was her intoxicating body, the slightly full mouth that made him go weak at the knees. Encounters were few and far between but he would give everything he had – and more – just for a moment with her. He couldn't stop thinking about it. It was an obsession that sometimes scared him, which he kept to himself.

She had become pregnant before their marriage. She had tried to have an abortion, but he managed to stop her. She had taken her revenge ever since. He wanted her to go away, to die. He wanted to kill her. But he didn't have the guts.

*

Today Thomas was at the doctor's.

"Come here, Thomas."

The boy went into the surgery. His mother looked away.

"How do you feel?"

He didn't reply. He knew what the doctor meant when he said that. Hospital!

"We need to do some more tests, Thomas. You're going to Ville-Évrard – it's a large clinic near Paris. Is that alright?"

Thomas did not reply. The doctor had the same smile as the car dealer – the one who had tried to persuade Papa to choose a Renault 16, with gears on the steering wheel. Papa had sent him packing.

"Do you agree with my decision, Thomas?"

"My decision" meant the electrodes and strange fluid that went inside his brain and made the visions go away. But he liked the visions of the ancient world. They gave him the strength to live.

# 32

On Thursdays Dr Caillol offered private appointments until eight in the evening, for the benefit of patients willing to pay a fortune to jump the queue.

The Édouard-Toulouse hospital held no secrets for Thomas. He had learned the ropes there as a disturbed and dangerous patient. He went round by the maintenance department. Two African men were emptying the bins. He gave them a friendly nod.

The laundry was on the right. The smell of washing and disinfectant turned his stomach. It reminded him of the sour stench of prison. Those places always smelled the same.

But Thomas knew that was all in the past. Once you've killed someone there's no going back. It's like a leap into the void. He had been evil incarnate. One journalist had even called him a monster. He knew he had done things you shouldn't do, but he hadn't been able to stop himself.

He opened the door to the laundry. A warm blast hit him in the face. He walked fast. There was no time to lose.

In his memory, the door to the consulting room was at the far end of the corridor. He needed to avoid it, keeping close to the wall so the secretary wouldn't see him. Even if it had all been refurbished that sort of thing couldn't have changed much.

He had to wait in the lobby with his mother until the doctor's secretary showed them to the waiting room. It took minutes, but it seemed to last for hours. Invariably his mother was impatient, dressed in her suit, shiny stockings, and plain court shoes.

Thomas crept along the corridor. Everything was quiet. A couple of nutters were talking to the secretary. With a bit of experience you could spot them at once. The unfocused eyes, faces shiny from the sedatives, features that always looked different. Little things set them apart.

The two patients were complaining about the ban on smoking in bedrooms. Nutters always smoke a lot. Thomas' friend, Bernard, was a chain smoker.

Dr Caillol was in his consulting room. He had raised his voice and Thomas was able to catch a few words. He was talking in English, using medical terminology. He had a thick accent, lisping as he pronounced the words: "zis" and "zat". Thomas tiptoed quickly forward.

The door was ajar. The psychiatrist had his back turned, one buttock resting against the edge of his desk. His words were clear now. He was preparing for a psychiatric congress on early dementia due to take place at the faculty of medicine in Marseille.

Thomas slipped inside like a shadow, waited for him to hang up, then moved closer, brandishing the axe.

Caillol turned. Unable to utter a word. Autran's eyes moved from the doctor's trembling hands to his face contorted by fear.

Caillol stammered, "I . . . You know . . . Good to see you."

His voice was hoarse. Fear oozed from his body: a fetid smell that Thomas hated more than anything. Dr Caillol, the man in the white coat who leaned over him after each electric shock session, with that same benevolent smile. The psychiatrist, who had sought to uncover the secret of schizophrenia by dabbling with shamans, now stank of sweat and urine.

"You've come back to see me? Oh Thomas, I'm so pleased."

Autran remained impassive, his arms by his sides. No longer could he be seduced or charmed by the doctor. In a world where everything had become blurred since his father's death, this man had been his sole male reference point.

In the past the doctor had known how to calm him. Talking to nutters is an art. You have to be tough and gentle, not rush things. But that was all over. Today he no longer listened. He was impervious to that smile.

Caillol's little eyes darted round his office. There was a press cutting about Lucy Meunier's murder. He pushed it under his in tray. It was a clumsy gesture. He was losing control. He seemed to have gone into a trance: his face quivered from the corner of his lips to his chin.

"I've come to sever my links with you," Autran snarled. His eyes had settled strangely on the picture on the wall, it was as though he could read between the brushstrokes.

"Dream time," Caillol said, to gain some space. "Do you remember, you understood better than anybody what that picture meant?"

Autran's eyes moved from the canvas to the doctor's forehead.

"How are you feeling?" Caillol mumbled.

The doctor received a sideways glance by way of response. The sort that wild animals give when they know they can toy with their prey.

"I'm going to tell you our secret, Thomas . . . we do have a secret. I've only spoken to your sister about it up till now. But of course you need to know too. You're ill, but that doesn't mean you can't know everything. I want to talk to you about your father. Would you like to talk about that?"

Thomas feigned indifference. He gave another sideways glance.

"Your father was never a friend. He was a man of rare intelligence. He used to say he loved you more than anything in the world. That's what he said. You were his only son. I have to say he did prefer you slightly to your sister and she was jealous of that. But, well, those are childhood matters . . . Isn't that so?"

Caillol's voice brightened. "Your father never came to your appointments. It was always your mother who brought you. She wore herself out looking after you. Oh yes. You always thought your father was better than your mother, but you were wrong."

Caillol started to shout, "You were wrong, Thomas! You've built your whole life on that error. Deep down inside you there is that lie. Your mother loved you more than anything in the world. But for your dad you were just a sick child he was too proud to accept. A child who had to be treated, because it was important to keep up appearances. The Autrans were a well-known family. To have a son who was mad . . . it was unbearable. In his eyes, your mother was the one who introduced the mad genes into the family. It was all her fault. Do you want me to tell you the secret?"

Caillol was losing control. He was bawling, "Do you want me to tell you?"

Thomas gave a piercing cry and raised his hand, "This is the sign. This is First Man."

The blow floored the doctor. He saw the face leaning over him. He felt a warm breath that made him blink.

"The voices must go."

It was all he heard. Just that one sentence, somewhere in the distance. He lost consciousness as he felt himself lifted from the ground like a sack of potatoes. A human parcel that weighed so little in those powerful arms.

*

When Caillol awoke the cold gripped him in its iron jaws. He was tied to a tree, naked, the bark digging into his back.

Thomas watched, emitting strange clucking noises. Two long streaks of blood were smeared across his chest. It was snowing heavily, and the dead claws of the trees were fringed with white. A crow cawed, muffled in the snow.

Caillol screamed but no sound emerged. An evil spirit had cut off the sound of life. He looked up at the heavens and saw the great arrow. He cried again. No sound.

"The voice must be silent," Autran muttered, his eyes rolling upwards. "The voice must not speak."

Caillol was gripped by a demented laugh that he could do nothing to contain: a laugh that overwhelms those about to die. An irrational impulse when faced with the loss of all coherence. Life was draining away with each contraction of his stomach, every beat of his heart.

He sensed Thomas was watching his mouth and straining to listen. The coarse sound of laughter did not reach him. He was trying to make out a last message, but as he hovered on the brink Caillol was unable to say a word.

"The voices are going away," Autran growled, "going back into the dark."

He picked up the stone axe and struck it into the middle of the doctor's chest. Caillol didn't feel as much pain as he had expected. He looked down and saw the blood spurting and trickling down to his feet. A whirlwind of images exploded in his head. Women's faces, all with the same hairstyle and a slight eye defect. Eyes that had seduced him.

"The heartbeat is stopping," Autran said. "The spirit must depart."

Caillol saw only glowing eyes piercing through him. The axe rose high in the pale sky.

# PART THREE

# THE MAD HOUSE

Mounting evidence demonstrates that before the Neolithic shift from a foraging or hunter-gatherer mode of existence to an agricultural lifeway, most people had ample free time, considerable gender autonomy, or equality, an ethos of egalitarianism and sharing, and no organized violence.

John Zerzan – *Why Primitivism?*

# 33

De Palma showed his police I.D. card as he went through the security tape. A chubby brigadier from the northern unit greeted him with a serious face. Outside Dr Caillol's consulting room, Bessour and Legendre were studying an object being shown to them by a forensic technician. Cameras flashed.

"Hello, Michel," Legendre said. "We decided to wait for you."

"What about Autran?"

"No idea," Bessour replied.

The psychiatrist had disappeared. His secretary hadn't seen him leave at the usual time. Worried, she had knocked on the door several times and had finally gone in. Caillol was not there. She waited for some time, but he hadn't returned. His briefcase lay on the floor by his desk and his coat hung from a stand, with his mobile inside. The log of incoming and outgoing calls did not reveal much: just numbers that featured in the doctor's phone book.

Autran's signature was missing. There were no negative handprints.

"I think he wants to show us something, or lead us somewhere," Bessour said.

"Wise words," de Palma said wryly. "I'd say he wants to lead us to Caillol's corpse."

Bessour couldn't help smiling. His eyes fixed on one object after another. Suddenly he stared. On the desk was a scrumpled ball of newspaper.

He prodded it open with the tip of his pen. "It's a finger! A human finger!"

He looked at his own hand then back at the finger. "A right index perhaps."

On the scrumpled paper, spattered with blood, only the headline was legible, in big bold letters:

LUCY'S ORDEAL

The automated fingerprint database came up with Thomas Autran's name and a note to say he was in prison. The file was out of date.

De Palma stared for a long time at the fingerprint on his computer screen with its large dark lines, long intricate curves, line breaks, enclosures and bifurcations. This print was telling him something, but in a language he didn't yet understand. He hadn't ever come across self-mutilation by murderers before. The thought alarmed him. He told himself that contrary to received opinion Thomas Autran's insanity had evolved after nine years in prison.

Why a finger? And why in a newspaper article about Lucy Meunier's death?

A search of Dr Caillol's house seemed in order. At first Legendre refused to allow it. The psychiatrist was not officially dead; the police couldn't just go into his house without a valid reason. But the situation was urgent. No-one could stand by and do nothing. Legendre relented. When Bessour and the Baron arrived at Caillol's town house the front door had been smashed in. There was an overturned chair in the hall.

They did a rapid tour of the first floor: a large sitting room, study and two rooms that couldn't have been used for years. A huge kitchen and dining room overlooked a small neglected garden. In the study the shelves were stuffed with scientific publications. The door leading to the basement was open. A spiral staircase went down to a part of the cellar that was hewn into the rock. At the bottom of the steps a lobby led to the boiler and a disused laundry. The floor had not been swept for a long time.

Bessour spotted fresh traces of bare feet. "He's been here."

"You can take a cast later," de Palma said.

Two prints stopped by a cupboard. De Palma opened it, taking care not to disturb anything. Inside were some old white hospital bed sheets and towels of the same colour, carefully folded in four. The linen smelt mouldy and had started to yellow.

"What was your idea in coming here?" de Palma muttered.

At the other end of the lobby was a room that must have been a children's games room. An old rocking horse stood covered in dust. An array of tins and cardboard boxes lay by the wall.

"Put the lights out, Karim! And give me your torch."

The beam swept the ground. There was no sign of any footprints. Bessour switched on the light again.

"If he doesn't come here but goes into the laundry, that suggests he knows the place . . ."

"Or he's looking for something in particular," de Palma cut in.

"Cloths or towels. It seems like he wants to wipe something clean."

A long corridor led to the other rooms in the cellar. The floor was covered in red hexagonal tiles, the walls painted white. Two shelves, on either side, contained stacks of *American Research*, crinkled by the damp. There were no prints visible to the naked eye.

Bessour stopped in front of a heavy door, the only one in the cellar that was closed. He took a handkerchief from his pocket and turned the handle. A long, tapered room had been converted into a clinic. In the middle was a bed fitted with leather straps.

"What's this?"

"It's Dr Caillol's little lab," de Palma exclaimed.

At the head of the bed, a box with some electric wires rested on a stainless steel trolley, itself connected via several cables to an oscilloscope and a tracer.

"Looks like an E.E.G. machine," Bessour said.

"Unless it's E.C.T.," de Palma corrected him.

"You think?"

De Palma passed his hand over the edge of the bed. Some multi-coloured wires had been thrown on the pillow.

"This is where Caillol must have brought his patients to trigger seizures. Normally that's done under anaesthetic. The current is very weak, less than five seconds."

The Baron turned a Bakelite handle on top of the box. The joule ratings were inscribed in silver figures on a semi-circular scale: 20, 30, 40, 50 . . .

"It's normally forty joules."

"You seem to know all about it, Michel."

The Baron picked up the electrodes. "I've read quite a lot. Psychiatry is fascinating but repulsive."

The tone of his voice was cold. His eyes saw only the instruments in front of him. "Succinylcholine is used for general anaesthetics," he said. "Two to four seconds, 70 hertz, between 50 and 70 joules. Manual ventilation of the patient. You come out of it in a state of severe confusion, with varying degrees of memory loss . . ."

"What a nightmare that thing is!" Bessour said.

A thick layer of dust covered the equipment. Several fresh fingerprints were visible.

"He's been here," de Palma grumbled. "I'm sure those are his."

Under the fine tracer needles, there was an encephalogram on a yellowing sheet of graph paper. The waves were regular. In red pen the name: Bernard Monin.

"We need to find that bloke. Quickly."

At the back of the room a grey steel cupboard had been left open. On the top shelf some phials and boxes of drugs with bleached labels. Chloral hydrate solution, Largactil, Haloperidol, Leponex . . . A musty, chemical smell wafted out. On the lower shelf, other electrical apparatus was stored. A mass of wires ended in bunches of rubber and silicon suction pads that time had turned into dirty flower petals.

"Wow, they're ancient," Bessour exclaimed. "Just like the old radio sets in the fifties."

"It must be a while since he stopped playing the sorcerer's apprentice," de Palma muttered. "But he'd have had to use old equipment in any case. Those things cost a fortune."

On the middle shelf there was a row of white porcelain pots, each bearing names written on strips of sticking plaster: Ayahuasca, Iboga, Peyotl, Cannabis, Psilocybe Semilanceata, Psilocybe Cubensis.

Bessour lifted the lids. "Leaves and dried mushrooms," he said in a disappointed tone.

"Hallucinogenics," de Palma observed. "Some are well known, others less so. The oldest and most natural ones that exist."

"So you think the doctor was getting stoned between the E.C.T. sessions?" Bessour quipped. The joke bombed.

"He must have given them to the patients before or afterwards," de Palma said. "Maybe both."

"That's outrageous!"

"It was a time when psychiatrists were exploring new avenues. We're talking about the seventies, the era of L.S.D. and other drugs. Caillol was a man of his time. He experimented and took things to their logical conclusion. He probably thought it was best for his patients."

Bessour looked up. In the bland neon light his face betrayed his anxiety. He was venturing into unknown territory.

"There are some boxes missing on the bottom shelf!" he said suddenly.

On the left-hand wall was a locked wooden cupboard. He tugged sharply at the handle, but the door didn't budge.

"So what do we do, Baron?"

"We open it."

De Palma inserted the blade of his penknife into the gap and forced the lock. Some folders were lined up in alphabetical order. Three of them caught his eye, on the top at the left. De Palma took down the first one and flicked through it. "It's one of Autran's medical files, probably the most complete record since the beginning of his treatment . . . Caillol has even made a note of the first doses of Largactil."

He thumbed through the paperwork and stopped at a section relating to a spell in the hospital at Ville-Évrard. Several psychiatric reports were filed in a transparent folder.

Bessour picked up the third folder and put it on a table not far from the bed.

"There are photos!" Bessour looked closely at the first one, then pushed it away, "Those things freak me out."

It was a black and white photo, taken in the lab. Autran lay on the bed, electrodes attached to his shaven skull.

*

Caillol's files recorded Thomas Autran's early psychiatric history from the age of eleven to twenty-one. It was a dark chronicle of madness. He had been sectioned after a violent punch-up at the local school in Mazargues, and placed in the care of Dr Caillol. He had been massively sedated and restrained for a whole night.

"What does restraint mean?" Bessour asked.

"A straitjacket, or straps that tie you to the bed."

Bessour looked disgusted.

"He was dangerous, Karim. Extremely dangerous. To himself and to others."

"Yes, but he was only eleven, just a child!"

"We're talking about the sixties. In those days, psychiatry was a bit like prison. If you didn't toe the line they used force."

"And that's all changed?"

"In psychiatry yes, but not in gaol."

Bessour placed the second folder on the table.

Autran was sectioned after the death of his father. He was released in 1972, apparently cured. Dr Caillol had diagnosed childhood schizophrenia. This was the period when everything was broken up and the asylums closed. Anti-psychiatry was all the rage. Treatment switched from institutions to care in the community, giving patients the dignity they deserved. But society wasn't up to it. People said murderers had been put back on the streets. Patients like Autran are extremely rare. You get one in a decade. Not more. A single case in the Baron's entire career . . .

Bessour watched de Palma lost in his reading. He had known him for some years but had never seen him this way before.

"Can I ask you something?"

"Fire away, son."

"How come you know so much about psychiatry?"

"I've had dealings with it at several points in my life. It's something you don't forget."

"Do you mean professionally or personally?"

"Both."

Bessour immediately regretted his questions. They put the Baron in a strange mood: his face was as grave an undertaker's.

Just then Legendre came in looking anxious, as he had done all day. Caillol's abduction had started to cause a stir. Journalists kept telephoning one after the other. They had not yet made a connection with Autran's escape, but it was only a matter of hours. For the moment there was no speculation about Lucy's murder.

The Baron took a large photo from the pile of paper he had left on Bessour's desk: a shot of the handprint Autran had left on the ceiling in his cell.

"Who's going to be next? A man? A woman?"

"I don't get you."

"There are three fingers missing on this hand. The thumb, index and little finger. Well, he's already cut off his index finger."

Legendre went pale. "Shit, Michel. You think . . ."

"I don't think, I just observe. If he's sending us a sign, maybe that's it. He's going to kill three times. Three people who have close connections to him or to his illness. It's up to us to guess who. We're going to need a lot of courage."

Legendre sat down, legs apart, an elbow resting on the corner of the desk. The Baron put away the photo.

"So how's he going to kill them?" the Commissaire asked.

"It's not the how, but the why that bothers me," de Palma replied. "Why Lucy Meunier? Why leave the finger in a press cutting about her murder?"

At that moment the prosecutor's office called. A hiker had discovered Caillol's body in the Saint-Pons forest, about twenty kilometres from Marseille. The *Gendarmerie* had dealt with the initial investigations at the crime scene. The psychiatrist was already in a freezer drawer at the medico-legal institute. Taking his secrets with him.

# 34

The car radio finally gave up the ghost as he sat in a traffic jam near La Joliette. He had been listening to Dutilleux's "Mystère de l'instant" recorded at the Salle Pleyel.

De Palma hated driving without music. In that situation he usually started to talk to himself, rambling on about anything under the sun. That morning he tried to tie up several chapters of the Autran case. He had a little dialogue about Lucy's murder, which was raising lot of questions.

Time passed quite quickly. Beyond Gémenos the road had been gritted after the recent snow. Two cars had already ended up in the ditch.

The Saint-Pons forest had turned white overnight. De Palma parked by a woodpile and thought for a while. Caillol's body had been discovered at the end of an icy track, about a hundred metres from the winding road that rose towards Sainte-Baume. The Gendarmes had done the reports and collected the forensic data. A book of photos provided a meticulous picture of the crime scene.

Bare branches sagged under the hoar frost. Everything was still and magical, like in scenes from Christmas stories. The Baron rubbed his hands to warm them and opened his notebook. He was taken aback by the cold. Snow had fallen along the coast the day before and the hills looked like the North Pole.

He wrote the word 'car' in large letters at the top of the page. It was the only way Caillol and Autran could have come here.

The diagram produced by the crime scene technicians was very precise. Legendre could say what he liked, but their peaked-capped rivals had done a good job. They mentioned some woodland, a forest path and a large, lone conifer, set amid oaks and beech trees. A little further off there was a waterfall, a large meadow, and at the end of this unusual green space a Cistercian abbey that had been used as a convent in the Middle Ages. In the summer concerts drew crowds of hikers, but in winter the place was gloomy, or romantic, according to your taste.

De Palma inspected the ground first. There were no tracks. The cold had left a layer of crystals that scrunched underfoot. As he brushed the crust away, he recognised the Gendarmes' vehicle tracks as well as some earlier horses' hoof prints.

A car went past on the side road. Some branches snapped nearby. De Palma was surprised to hear a sort of echoing through the trees. The noise came closer. He tensed and strained his eyes. Something was moving about forty metres away. He turned towards the sound of the steps and placed his hand on the butt of his Bodyguard. Everything was silent. He undid the safety strap on the holster and walked on.

After twenty paces, he took a photo of the scene. From where he stood, the conifer mentioned by the Gendarmes was clearly visible. He had been through enough files to know that most policemen missed things on the ground. "Keep going back to the crime scene" an old cop at the quai d'Orfèvres had taught him. "As often as you think it's useful. They always overlook something."

The first rays of sunlight came through the tall treetops. The frozen path, hard as an anvil, became a blinding mirror. De Palma felt in his anorak pockets for his sunglasses, then cursed as he realised he had left them in the car, twenty minutes away on foot.

According to the technicians' drawing, some size forty-five footprints had been found just metres away from the corpse. The report stated that they were produced by Vibram soles: a very common brand for walking shoes.

"So he probably planned to come here. That's his size."

The trunk of the tall tree must have been over a metre in diameter. It rose straight up before splitting into two like a huge fork prodding the sky. This conifer was a larch. De Palma suddenly remembered Christine Autran's premonition in the visiting room at Rennes prison.

He hadn't written it all down, but he could remember her final words, "The sacrifice requires a forked larch standing on a hill."

He looked up at the tree. The first branches had been cut to head height by the foresters. The frost hadn't covered the carpet of needles lying at the foot of the conifer. Caillol's bloodstains were still clearly visible. De Palma had to walk ten steps back to take a shot of the larch. Underneath the fine ice, like glazed paper, he spotted one of the footprints seen by the technicians. It led straight to the trunk of the tall conifer.

One thing was clear. Autran had wanted the body to be discovered. Up till that point, he had followed his usual practice. He had left prints in the mud ruts. He had laid the body as an offering, on the large, knotty roots protruding from the dark earth.

"It's some kind of signature!"

De Palma recalled the crime scene photos the Gendarmes had sent him. Caillol's face was turned to the east, his arms extended in a cross.

The Baron stepped back under the larch. The carpet of needles had been disturbed. According to the report there were visible signs of a struggle.

"It's a Friday evening. He comes here by car. He parks close to this bit of the woods. Caillol is still alive. Then he kills him."

Once again some branches snapped. Then came a heavy, irregular treading sound, brushing through the bracken. De Palma strained to listen. The footsteps receded. The place must be full of large animals, he thought.

There were some notches in the bark of the larch tree. The technicians had said these were probably caused by a knife. A branch had been broken off at the end. De Palma searched around the trunk for the missing bit, but without success. He opened his notebook and took down a few details. The rest of the crime scene told him nothing new.

"At least you've got an idea."

He looked up at the fork in the tree. A long pole of dead wood was caught in the place where the trunk split; the tip formed a large arrow pointing east. The branch could not have fallen from higher up, as all the other branches above were smaller.

"Someone has gone and put that piece of wood up there," de Palma thought to himself as he took another photo.

Once again he recalled Christine's words, "If the stick points south and upwards, the sacrifice is intended for an *Abaahy* from the upper world. If it points north, with the tip down it's for an *Abaahy* from the underworld."

"An *Abaahy*," de Palma repeated aloud. "A word that comes from the far reaches of Siberia and a ritual that has nothing to do with our culture. No connection with Cro-Magnon either, unless it's one of Christine Autran's more outlandish theories."

The silence was broken by a whistling sound not far from the path. A dark shape passed between the trunks of the oak trees. De Palma stood rooted to the spot, incapable of reaching for his weapon.

There was a powerful breathing sound: some kind of animal stood behind him. He turned sharply, his whole body shaking. Less than two metres away a large stag was watching him, its eyes black, a foreleg raised. Its antlers seemed huge. With each slow, deep breath, a thick plume rose from its muzzle.

"You scared me," de Palma shouted to release the tension in his stomach.

The stag gave a deep cough and lowered its neck as though about to charge.

"Easy," de Palma whispered, "I won't do you any harm. Easy now."

He put his hand on the butt and slowly drew his weapon. The stag raised its head as it pawed the ground. There was something almost human about its expression.

"No, no . . . I don't mean you any harm. Easy."

The stag grunted and took a step forward. The Baron backed away without taking his eyes off the animal, until he came to the edge of the road. Several times he nearly slipped and lost his balance on the icy patches still untouched by the sunlight. The animal watched as he beat a retreat, then turned and disappeared into the forest.

## 35

Christine Autran's flat was on boulevard Chave. It still belonged to her, but had remained unoccupied since the time of her arrest. Requesting a search warrant would take hours, days even, and might not be granted. De Palma told Legendre he was going there and would try to gain entry. Legendre grumbled, but finally agreed, while refusing to cover for him if things went wrong. He could be courageous, but not on Christmas Eve.

Christine had lived in an opulent-looking building dating from the end of the nineteenth century. There was no concierge. De Palma rang the bells for all the floors. The heavy door finally opened. On the first floor he recognised the face leaning over the banister: Yvonne Barbier. She was probably over ninety years old. He had thought she had died a long time ago.

"Do you remember me?" de Palma asked with a smile as broad as he could manage.

"No." Yvonne Barbier frowned.

"I'm the detective who did the Christine Autran investigation. I came to see you a few times. Don't you remember?"

"Holy Mary, of course I do! Come on in . . ."

Nothing had changed since his last visit – there was still the same smell of frangipane and ilang-ilang, mingled with vegetable soup. Yvonne was dolled up in black silk and make-up to go to a party. She was wearing a long dress, had painted nails and honey-blonde hair.

She led the Baron into the living room and invited him to sit on the pink velvet sofa.

"Would you like a coffee, or something else?"

"No thanks. I don't want to disturb you."

Yvonne sat down opposite and watched him for a few seconds. Her eyes were not as as blue as a decade before, but they had kept their sparkle.

"You see, I'm on an assignment," de Palma said, looking serious. "I need to check something in Christine Autran's flat. Do you still have the keys?"

"Of course I do. It's been a bit of a nuisance, but I've still got them. I'll go and fetch them for you, then you can have them."

She got up and disappeared into a far corner of her huge flat, leaving the Baron on his own, surrounded by bunches of silk flowers, paintings by minor masters and baroque ornaments.

"There you go," she said. "I've forgotten which is the key for the top bolt, but the big one's for the middle lock."

"Thanks."

"Why do you need to see her flat? Has she been up to no good again?"

"No. She's still in prison, but we've been asked to do a further investigation."

"Oh, I see."

De Palma thanked her and went up to Christine Autran's flat on the next floor. He closed the door behind him. Dust tickled his nostrils. Long shafts of daylight filtered through the shutters, leaving the corners of the rooms cluttered with furniture in the shade.

The Baron switched on his Maglite torch. He looked down at the floor, covered in grime. No-one had been there for a long time, probably not since Christine's arrest. Most of the drawers had been left open by his colleagues, when they carried out the search.

"Neither Palestro nor Caillol have been here."

De Palma was looking for just one thing. He wanted to see if there was any sign of the man with the antler head. The twins' father, Pierre Autran, had statuettes in the Mazargues house. De Palma had developed a theory that the man with the antler head was one of them. What had happened to the others?

De Palma didn't know where to look. He spent a long time in the little room by the kitchen. Christine had put all her publications, course materials and lecture notes on a shelf to the right. On the wall opposite there were some books on prehistory, carefully arranged by author and in alphabetical order. He didn't have time to look through all the publications, let alone the books. He turned to the piles, lifting them up one after the other. No feasible hiding place. He went through into Christine's bedroom.

The bed was unmade. Ten years earlier the police must have searched under the mattress and in every nook and cranny. He went to the fireplace and opened it. It was a classic hiding place, but then Christine didn't specialise in handling stolen goods.

He found nothing in the bedroom, so he returned to the living room. A marble fireplace occupied the back wall. He opened it and put his head inside, an even more classic hiding place. There was nothing but soot, which spattered his face.

He started to think he was on the wrong track. His intuition was playing tricks on him. He removed the panel on the bath and searched around the pipes and U-bend, but there was no sign of the statuette. He went into the dining room and rummaged through the drawers.

"If you had something that valuable, where would you put it?"

He sat down to think. Christine's flat wouldn't tell him anything. This had been a waste of time. Thomas hadn't been here and certainly wouldn't be coming back.

"If he hasn't returned, it's because there's nothing here to take. I should have thought of that before."

A bronze medal on a shelf caught his eye. It was heavy and measured about five centimetres across. The face was edged in red, white and blue. In the centre was a diver. On the reverse side an inscription was engraved:

CHALLENGE DES CALANQUES
CHRISTINE AUTRAN
CLUB LA GRANDE BLEUE
MARSEILLE

De Palma recalled Christine's remark, "Try to find out who Rémy Fortin really was." He contacted Bessour, who told him straight away that Fortin had been a diving instructor at La Grande Bleue. He then rang Pauline Barton. She was staying down near Toulouse for Christmas. He asked if she was aware Fortin and Christine knew each other. The question drew a long silence, then Pauline eventually said that her old assistant had never mentioned any connection. Pauline had only met the diver a couple of years previously, while preparing for the excavation at Le Guen's cave.

"Did he dive in the cave without you?" the Baron asked.

"Of course. Just like I dived without him. You can't expose yourself to those pressure changes every day. It's too dangerous."

There was something about Fortin's accident that jarred. The diver had only been under water for about ten minutes. De Palma called the pathologist who had carried out the autopsy. He replied that decompression problems only happened if the diver remained under water for more than thirty minutes. As a general rule that sort of thing happened to people who had done a lot of diving and hadn't taken their rest days. In which case the smallest thing could have dire consequences.

The Baron was puzzled. He dialled Pauline Barton's number once again. The accident had taken place on a Monday. There had been no dig over the weekend. In theory access to the cave was closed and Fortin had been resting.

"Did he have keys to the gate?"

"Of course he did," Pauline replied.

*

The Baron locked up Christine Autran's flat and went down to say goodbye to Yvonne Barbier.

"I've kept her mail too. Do you want to see it?"

"I'll take a look."

Yvonne put a cardboard box full of letters on the kitchen table: it was mostly administrative stuff and letters from Christine's bank, the Crédit Lyonnais. De Palma quickly checked the postmarks. The majority were at least eight years old. He found follow-up letters, reminders from the inland revenue, and then he came across some more recent mail. A letter from Crédit Lyonnais dated June 2007. The head of the business branch had written to Christine to say that without a response on her part he would be obliged to initiate a search procedure. She had some money in a savings account, as well as a safe deposit box.

"Thanks, Yvonne, you're a darling!" the Baron exclaimed.

The old lady looked puzzled.

"I'll keep this letter," the Baron said. "It could be useful."

He accepted her cup of coffee, lingered for ten minutes or so and then said goodbye. "Happy Christmas!"

"I'm off to my daughter's," replied the old lady with a wink. "We're having a knees-up."

De Palma left his business card and asked to be kept informed if anyone came to see her about Christine, or if she heard any suspicious noises from upstairs.

*

The Crédit Lyonnais on boulevard Chave was about a hundred metres back up towards place Jean-Jaurès. De Palma brandished his I.D. card and asked to speak to the manager. He was seen immediately in an office behind the tills.

"How can I help?" the banker asked, with an expression as welcoming as an overdrawn bank statement.

"Someone we're actively looking for is the brother of one of your account holders, who has a deposit box at this bank. I'd like to know if you've noticed any recent activity."

The manager pulled a face indicating he hadn't fully understood. De Palma waved the letter that had been sent to Christine Autran in 2007.

"She's in prison at the moment," the detective explained, "but her brother's on the run. He's killed one man already. It's urgent."

"I completely understand, sir, but this is confidential information. We can't just pass it on to you like that."

"Obstructing a police officer in the execution of his duty. Do you know how much that could cost you?"

The banker mulled over the problem in his head.

"There have been some receipts and withdrawals. That's all I can say. Otherwise, you'll have to clear things with my superiors."

"That's all I'm asking."

The banker turned to his screen and entered a series of codes before obtaining access to the information he was seeking. "Someone has a power of attorney on this account."

"I need his name."

"It's a bit sensitive."

"I'm asking for his name, not his account number. If you won't give it to me I'll have to call in the heavies and I promise you there'll be a right stink, Christmas or not."

"Alright, alright, it's a Monsieur Pierre Palestro."

"Has he taken anything out?"

"No. In fact the box is empty."

"Since when?"

"Oh, a long time ago."

The banker moved his mouse around. "1999, on 23 December."

"Who asked for the box to be opened?"

"Christine Autran herself."

"Can you tell me what was in it?"

"No, there was no declaration of content value."

"Is that normal?"

The banker looked sheepish.

"I think so," he said, adjusting his jacket collar.

Once again de Palma was up against a brick wall. He called Palestro, but only got the answering machine. It would soon be evening. He had just enough time to return home, fetch Eva and put on his Christmas best.

\*

Maistre had laid on a big spread. *Foie gras*, lobster tails and caviar canapés. De Palma and Eva brought the champagne and wine.

"I've spared you the venison stew," Maistre quipped.

De Palma pretended not to hear, as he eyed up the tins of caviar.

"For Christ's sake, Jean-Louis, I've never had caviar before!"

"Me neither," Maistre replied. "I've dreamed of trying it for years. Since my wife left, I've indulged in the worst depravities."

Eva burst out laughing. She had put on a black dress and was wearing her mother's jewellery – a touch on the heavy side, as favoured by elderly Italian ladies. De Palma felt as if the veil of time had lifted. Here was the young girl he had known decades before. Her radiant diva's face reminded him of his mother and the women who had come from Genoa, the gulf of Naples, or the mountains of Sicily. The women of his childhood, always in widow's weeds, who wore a lace veil over their faces for Mass on Sunday and muttered endless prayers in the sonorous tongues of Italy.

"The little ones are only coming in the morning," Maistre said.

Eva watched him rushing around, trying to make sure everything was perfect. He had refused to let either of them help.

"Did you remember the thirteen desserts, Jean-Louis?" the Baron asked.

"I went to get the *Navette* biscuits from the Saint-Victor bakery and the nougat from Allauch."

"What about the *Pompes*?"

"The *patissier* in L'Estaque does the best ones I know. Any other questions?"

"Over and out," de Palma said, winking at Eva.

He went outside for a smoke in the garden. The view extended across the entire bay of Marseille, from the deserted docks and shady inner harbour to Cap Croisette. Eva joined him and put her arms round his waist.

"What are you thinking about?"

"For the first time in a long time, not very much."

"It's beautiful," she said.

"Yes. It's one of the most beautiful views I know. Maistre really is lucky to live here."

# 36

Ever since he left the car rental agency, de Palma had been fiddling with the car radio. But the only stations he could find were ones churning out electronic music with a heavy beat. After a while he realised he stood no chance with the pre-programmed stations. Things went from bad to worse. When he pressed button six, it was that old crooner and cops' favourite, Michel Sardou. Admitting defeat he turned off the radio and concentrated on the traffic instead.

The N34 passed through a suburb that wavered between town and countryside. Endless green railings revealing glimpses of burrstone and red brick detached houses with deserted lawns.

The entrance to the Ville-Évrard psychiatric hospital was welcoming. There were no security guards or fence and no-one to ask you the reason for your visit. A broad path ran down to the woods and canals, not far from the muddy river Marne and heavy barges laden with goods. The exterior was neat and tidy, like a barracks, with well kept lawns and flowerbeds. Nothing to indicate that this was one of the oldest and largest asylums in France. No reminder of the hundreds of patients who had once inhabited the huge hospital. Camille Claudel and Antonin Artaud had dragged their tormented souls through the massive wards, where the demented scratched their pain on the walls.

"Dr Dubreuil is in Orion ward, Blue Sector," the young receptionist told him from behind her thick glass screen. "He's expecting you. You can go on foot, but it's not that close. If you're in the car drive to the end of the big avenue and it's on your right."

De Palma found a space for his little hire car directly beneath a huge window. The panes were decorated with Father Christmases and fake snow stars. Two tall cedar trees towered above the old building which looked more like a provincial *lycée* than a hospital for the mentally ill.

"Hello, Monsieur de Palma," Dubreuil said, appearing on the doorstep. "I've found those things you're interested in."

Dubreuil was an affable sort. Impressive, broad shoulders, chunky hands and a face that exuded *joie-de-vivre*.

"I've worked here for over forty years. Things have changed a bit, I can tell you."

"Are you retired then?"

"Not yet, but it's well overdue."

They walked down a long corridor on the left side of the building. It was painted sky blue and flooded with light, even on a dull day. Dr Dubreuil's office was huge. In the middle in pride of place was a desk as old as the hospital itself: at least a hundred years old.

Autran had stayed at Ville-Évrard on three occasions. The first time, in the spring of 1967, he had been in the children's ward. His second spell, in autumn 1970, was when his father had just died. He had been through some extremely hard times and on several occasions was placed in a special cell under heavy medication. The final episode, in the winter of 1973, had been just as serious. But by then 'sectorisation' was underway – the asylums were being closed down. For someone to be sectioned there had to be a real crisis or security risk. Autran's file described him as "posing a danger to himself". He had narrowly failed a suicide attempt on 27 January, 1973.

"Why did he come here?" de Palma asked.

The doctor rummaged through the papers spread out in front of him, "Because he was living in Paris then, with his mother."

"Do you have an address?"

"31 rue de la Chine. It's in the twientieth arrondissement."

De Palma made a quick note. "Did he have any friends? I mean patients like himself, whom he got on with?"

"Indeed," the psychiatrist replied, suddenly raising his voice. "People imagine that patients like Autran don't talk to anyone and only express themselves through violence. Well, it's not like that. Outside periods of crisis he was a perfectly sociable young man. Pleasant even, if I'm to believe what the nurses say."

"You talked about friends."

"That's right, I think you're in luck there. We've got Bernard Monin here, a friend of Autran's. He's an old hand, if I can put it like that. Been a patient of mine for many years."

"Do you think I could speak to him?"

"Of course." Dubreuil winked. "He can't wait to see us. He'll have nearly finished his packet of cigarettes by now! Come on."

They went through the hospital to the Alizé ward. It was identical to the one they had just left. Dubreuil walked slowly.

"Does Bernard know what Thomas did?" de Palma asked.

"Hard to say. Perhaps he found out and suppressed it. When he was younger Bernard was no angel himself."

"Tell me about him."

"There are things I can't say. But you should know he's been inside since he was eighteen and he's spent ten years in secure units."

"How old is he now?"

"Sixty-five."

Dubreuil climbed the steps two at a time. He gripped the handle of a large glass door and paused before opening it. "One thing: don't push him or ask too many direct questions. Keep calm and give him space."

"I'll do my best," de Palma replied.

Bernard was sitting by a window smoking a cigarette. The index and middle finger on his left hand were stained with nicotine, the nails brown from the smoke. He had a neatly trimmed moustache, yellow from the tobacco. His hair was swept back and he wore an elegant beige jacket and dark trousers.

"Hello, Bernard," Dubreil said. "This is Monsieur de Palma, he's come from Marseille to find out a bit about Thomas Autran."

Bernard sat up straight and then stood up. He was quite tall, heavily built and paunchy.

"Hello, sir," he boomed. "I was waiting for you both."

"Bernard is a famous poet," the doctor said to de Palma. "Have you written anything recently?"

"Yes, sir."

De Palma noted how he said this in a whisper, deliberately avoiding any mention of the word 'doctor'. Bernard stepped aside and turned his face to the pale pink wall. Then in a nasal voice he recited his poem:

*I have turned cold, it wearies me*
*This roof it weighs so heavily.*
*The tormented sky weeps over the praying woman.*
*Does she know how I was smitten*
*With her black hair across my face*
*Dancing like an ancient shaman . . .*

"It's wonderful," Dubreuil said, "Beautiful. But isn't that an old poem? I think I've read it before . . ."

"Stop!" Bernard shouted in a high-pitched voice. "I haven't finished yet."

He closed his eyes and waited for them to be silent.

*Along that path to the hereafter*
*Here and there grow drops of rain;*
*They wipe away that gentle face.*
*Will my heart know some relief?*
*No. I'm just dead and frozen flesh.*

*A clover draws life from my frozen nostrils,*
*My eyes see nothing but my eyelids;*
*If only I knew at least one prayer!*

Bernard turned to his two visitors, his face radiant. "Thirty years ago I wrote that. Thomas was by my side. I remember it just like yesterday."

"When was that?" Dubreuil asked.

Bernard pulled a funny face that made his moustache bristle.

"When I was just a load of horseshit. It was in the seventies. During the winter. Unless it was summer. When you're on medication you forget the colour of the seasons."

He tapped his temple with the palm of his hand, "Here. This is where the madness lies, sir."

He started to recite again:

*Tireless as an insect I will build the universe*
*That you destroyed with your iron words.*
*I will give you more than my feathers and my bloodied mind*
*More than my weary eyes, more than this slimy world.*
*I will show you the beauty you cannot see.*
*I will show you the warmth of love in the evening.*

Bernard went back to his seat like a schoolboy who has just acquitted himself well. Dr Dubreil had moved away and was leaning on the little table that served as his desk.

"Which was Thomas's favourite poem?" he asked.

Bernard did not reply. He took a cigarette from a half-empty packet, "I haven't got a light," he said after feeling in his pockets.

De Palma handed him his lighter. Bernard snatched it as though it would be taken away from him before he had a chance to use it.

"Thank you very much, sir."

He took a long drag, drawing in his thin cheeks and blowing out the smoke through his nostrils.

"Thomas's favourite poem – I'm not going to tell you that. It's a secret between him and me. He asked me not to tell anyone. I never break my word."

Bernard stared straight ahead. Every now and then he winked at de Palma.

"When did you last see him?" Dubreuil asked.

"Oh, not so long ago."

De Palma was on the point of saying something, but the doctor stopped him with a gesture of his hand.

"I think I passed him walking round Ville-Évrard," said the doctor in a monotone. "Am I wrong about that?"

"No," Bernard exclaimed. "He came here and told me it was the last time he'd see me. I cried and then he comforted me."

"What did he say to you?"

"He told me he was going to be a free man and he'd be waiting for me in the nutters' paradise."

There was a long silence. Somewhere in the grounds a man was screaming. De Palma suddenly pictured himself after his brother's death when he had seen a psychiatrist at Conception Hospital in Marseille.

"I don't recall which day it was when Thomas came," the doctor said.

"It was last Wednesday."

De Palma and Dubreuil looked at each other, astounded.

"He arrived at two o'clock on the number 113 bus. He came straight to my room. He left at four. On the dot."

"Do you know where he's living now?" de Palma asked.

"I don't know. He didn't tell me. He's not stupid."

"Why do you say that?"

"Because you're a detective and he must have done something wrong."

De Palma beat a retreat. Dubreuil had probably described him as one of Autran's close friends. But Bernard had seen right through it. He started to sway backwards and forwards, faster and faster.

"We'll leave you now," Dr Dubreuil said, signalling to de Palma to leave. "You go and have a rest. Thank you for your help."

Bernard went on swaying and staring into space. Each time he moved he gave a little moan and sniffed. Then suddenly he stopped and took a cigarette from a packet on the window ledge. He had a lighter in the right-hand pocket of his trousers.

It had started to rain. De Palma and Dubreuil walked beneath the covered passage towards the central path. They passed a nurse escorting a young girl with a vacant expression, her pyjama bottoms trailing along the ground.

"Do you believe in this visit then?" the Baron asked.

"There's no reason not to believe Bernard. I must admit I was gobsmacked. Autran coming here!"

"And no-one realised."

"Of course they didn't. It's an open hospital. No-one apart from me would recognise him and I wasn't here last Wednesday."

"In any case, you showed a hell of a lot of intuition getting Bernard to talk like that."

"Sometimes it works. You've seen for yourself, Bernard is no fool. He's very sensitive, very intelligent. He told us what he knew. It's possible he cooperated because he knows what Thomas is capable of."

Bernard suddenly appeared at the corner of the Orion building. He must have gone round another way. He was holding something in his hand.

"Leave this one to me," the psychiatrist said.

He slowly approached the patient without taking his eyes off him. De Palma followed a couple of metres behind.

"Something wrong, Bernard?" Dubreuil asked in a tone that was suddenly commanding.

Bernard shifted uncomfortably from one foot to the other.

"I didn't say goodbye to the gentleman like I should have."

He gripped the Baron's hand firmly. His eyes were red.

"Your car is over there," he said with a sob. "I'm waiting for you to go."

De Palma went back to his Clio and set off at once. Thomas Autran's fellow patient watched him leave. On the passenger seat there was a package with Autran's name written in large fluid letters.

As he headed towards Paris, Ville-Évrard now far behind, de Palma drew into a supermarket car park. He carefully removed the Sellotape from the package. Inside were a cassette and an old copy of Lombroso's *Criminal Man*.

## 37

Number 30 rue de la Chine was on the side of the road running from avenue Gambetta towards the rue des Prairies. On the corner was a bar. At that time of day there were few cars or pedestrians. Whenever a brighter spell drove away the rain, the sun beamed down on the limestone buildings.

De Palma had to tap in a code to enter the building. He looked at the keypad. It was a device that reflected a society closeted away in its anxiety. He waited for a few minutes, but no-one came in or out of the door. He decided to ask at the local shops, starting with a bakery that seemed to have been there for ever. The large woman behind the till assured him she had been working there for over forty years and had never heard talk of a mother and her son. The Baron thanked her and headed for the nearest bar.

"A woman and her son? At number thirty?"

The landlord was a local boy. He must have done time before he flourished as a barkeeper. "Doesn't mean anything to me. Is it important?"

"Yes, it is quite," said de Palma, realising the other man had sussed his profession.

"Something serious?"

"Yes. The lad I'm after is about fifty now. He's a killer on the run."

After a few observations on lax prisons, the dangers of madness and the death penalty as a panacea, the landlord poured out a half to a stooping pensioner.

He looked pensive, his forehead lined with three ugly wrinkles, "Are you from Marseille?"

"Can't hide anything from you," de Palma said.

"Funny thing is," the barkeeper said, "I don't remember the woman or the young man you're talking about, but I do remember a bloke living at number 30 who often went to Marseille."

"Do you know his name?"

"Oh, that's going back a long way, but I remember he used to come and have his coffee in the morning and we'd talk about the footie. He was a bit of an O.M. supporter, so the customers used to take the piss. Just a bit of banter."

"Was he from Marseille? I mean, did he have an accent like mine?"

"Not really. Well, come to think of it, yes, he did have a bit of one though not like yours."

"Do you know what he was doing in Paris?"

"Yes I do, because he once treated my daughter. He was a doctor."

"A G.P.?"

"No, a consultant. Psychiatrist, or something like that. Though he dealt with other illnesses too. My daughter kept on vomiting. Our family doctor wasn't around, so he gave us a prescription."

"Did he live on his own?"

"No, I've got a feeling he was married, with a son."

\*

Eva had gone out. De Palma put down his case as he came into the flat and rushed off to have a shower. He took his time, hoping the water would revive him. Towards midday Eva returned with a baguette under her arm.

"How's the weary traveller then?"

He gave her a kiss. "Like someone who's just been to a mental hospital. Head full of questions and with a heavy heart."

"Better than when you left, I hope."

"No, just the opposite. It's like I'm on a ghost train and I don't know what's waiting for me round the next bend."

He put on some jeans and a clean shirt, gave his boots a quick polish and went out on the balcony for his first Gitane of the day. He realised he had been smoking less and less, though he wasn't really sure why.

"We need to find something for you to do when you retire," Eva said.

"I was thinking of buying a boat, but I never got my sailing licence."

"You can always take it again."

"Not so easy. I'm getting old and I don't want to go back to school."

"How about a cottage in the country then?" she said, closing the refrigerator door.

"Why not? I don't know where though, but we can think about it. Find a place to do up."

The conversation shifted to Eva's daughter, but he had too much on his mind to listen. She noticed and lost her temper. He apologised and fled to the little room that he used as an office.

*Criminal Man* was in his suitcase. He had taken the precaution of wrapping the book in a plastic bag. He wondered if he should drop it off at the police laboratory. Forensic examinations could take days yet reveal nothing. He took out the old book and lifted the cover with the tip of his paper knife. There were no markings or dedication. It was a 1902 edition, probably the first translation into French. De Palma had read the book some years earlier, out of curiosity.

Lombroso belonged to another century. At the time they talked of 'criminal anthropology', following on from Darwin's ideas. A Frenchman, Bénédict Morel, had just written his *Traité des dégénérescences humaines*. There was much discussion about atavism and phrenology. The Italian doctor had set out to examine 5,907 living offenders and 383 skulls belonging to criminals. On some of the murderers' skulls he had discovered a pronounced occipital dimple. He went on to suggest five criminal types: the born criminal, the insane, the impulsive, the occasional and the habitual. He accepted that social factors played a role in the last three categories, but in the first two cases – by far the most dangerous – he stuck to his guns: atavism was present.

De Palma turned the pages one after the other, taking care not to leave any marks on the paper. The book taught him nothing new about Autran. There were no paragraphs underlined and no book-marks to indicate passages to be read, but he felt there was some kind of link. He opened the old wardrobe where he stored all the note-books he had kept throughout his career. He had little difficulty finding the one where he had made some notes the first time he read *Criminal Man*. There were very few of his own thoughts, just some words in red: "Importance of social context. See Lacassagne, and Durkheim's *Suicide* (1897)".

The two authors' views were at the other end of the spectrum to Lombroso, suggesting that social factors were determinative in the study of crime. The Baron had made a note about some pretty far-fetched theories, but others were genuinely scientific.

More recently, during the sixties, researchers sought to establish that, given what they termed a favourable biological terrain, a karyotypic anomaly comes into play. In the twenty-three pairs of chromosomes in a cell there could be disorders of the same type that trigger Down's Syndrome. Other British, American and French biologists worked in secure units at psychiatric hospitals. They spotted the particular frequency of this abnormal karyotype among notorious criminals. It applied to one to two per cent of the crim-inal population, as against one to two in a thousand for the rest of society.

The only man de Palma knew in Autran's circle who might be interested in such studies was Dr Caillol.

"I have to go out this afternoon," de Palma said.

"Where?"

"To the Édouard-Toulouse hospital."

"Off to find another ghost?"

"Got it in one."

# 38

"I want to see everything he left here."

De Palma flashed his magic red, white and blue I.D. card. Dr Caillol's secretary sighed. She got up from her swivel chair and fetched the keys from the board.

"There's not much there," she warned, her heels clicking on the white tiled floor. "Just patients' files, that's all."

"We're following up any lead we can," de Palma explained. "It's a difficult investigation."

The secretary flung open the door to the consulting room. She stopped in the doorway, suddenly overwhelmed.

"I'll let you look," she said, turning away. "I can't leave my desk for long."

De Palma opened the desk drawers one after the other. He found a stethoscope, a box of surgical gloves and some medical bits and pieces, jumbled up with pens and packets of post-its.

"Not very tidy, Doc!"

The inside of the cupboard proved to be more interesting. De Palma had to ask the secretary for the keys. No-one had touched the contents, not even Autran. At the bottom medical books were piled on top of one other. On the top two shelves there were articles – some typed – on exorcism, shamanism and magnetism. The names of several precursors of psychiatry, such as Mesmer, featured. Caillol had sketched an outline for a thesis on a couple of pages, with the title: *Early Man, the Murderer: An Alternative Approach to Clinical Psychiatry.*

"So he was planning to publish something," de Palma said aloud.

The writing was in Caillol's hand and looked like a first draft. There was an exercise book of photos: some showed ritual objects from primitive cultures; others featured a group of five people, one of whom was a woman. Caillol had written below: magnetism session. Next came a series of shots taken inside a cave. The faces were unrecognisable but the clothing looked the same as in the previous prints.

De Palma searched further in the piles of papers. He didn't have time to read everything; he was looking for just one thing, but Thomas Autran's name appeared nowhere.

"Has anyone been in here since Dr Caillol disappeared?" he asked the secretary, putting his head round the door.

"Well, it's possible. I'm not here all the time."

His colleagues hadn't sealed the entrance to the consulting room: at the outset the case had been treated simply as a disappearance. Anyone could have gone through Caillol's papers.

In parts of the text a page or two were missing. Sometimes more.

"That's not like Autran," the Baron thought, "He may be insane, but he's no fool. He knows us well enough to understand we'd expect him to come here."

The image of the diver who had tried to enter Le Guen's cave suddenly came to mind. Rémy Fortin, Pauline Barton's assistant, had paid with his life for his encounter with a diver thirty-eight metres down.

Was someone following in Thomas Autran's shadow? Or were they even out there ahead of him?

The text of the manuscript began with a fairly short introduction summarising the classical definitions of the unconscious and locating the murderer within the typology of schizophrenics.

The first chapter was called: *Voices that Kill*. The psychiatrist made some general observations about the criminal instinct and the build-up to the deed. Examples of notorious murderers were then cited.

A second general chapter dealt with the evolution of criminology. Caillol devoted a long passage to Lombroso's theories, drawing mainly on *Criminal Man*. The genetic legacy of prehistoric man.

Caillol went further than Lombroso. If the Italian criminologist's theory no longer held good, his thinking still had an impact on the way murderers were depicted. The psychiatrist concluded the second part of his study with the following words:

"*Western society has always equated the remote with barbarism, whether it be remoteness in space or time. In the same way that we have long depicted early peoples as savages close to a state of bestiality, we have always described prehistoric man as a dim-witted brute capable of killing without any qualms. Both of these assertions are false, but very strong cultural assumptions remain, as can be seen from the following case study.*"

The next chapter was headed: *The Case of Le Guen's Cave: Cro-Magnon Among the Killers.*

The doctor was on the brink of producing his greatest work: retracing step by step the original discovery of the unconscious. Through the centuries scholars had shown that human beings weren't really masters of their minds; well before Freud, the founder of modern psychoanalysis. It was similar to the way in which Galileo established that because the earth goes round the sun and not vice versa, it isn't therefore at the centre of the universe.

Caillol belonged to a generation which believed in the virtues of primitive life. The world was seen as a jumble of illusions and pretences; a place that had regressed in comparison to a life closer to our origins.

De Palma turned the pages of the manuscript, stopping at a photo from the Criminal Records Office that Caillol had pinned inside. It showed a man of about forty, with a beard and a tormented expression, wearing a red shirt. Theodore Kaszynski, alias the Unabomber, American mathematician and terrorist. The man who had fought against the demon of technological progress. The F.B.I.'s longest manhunt. For almost twenty years the Unabomber had sent parcel bombs to his targets, who were mainly people he considered responsible for the decadence in our society: I.T. specialists, airline bosses, scientists . . .

The Unabomber was an anarchist who believed in anarcho-primitivism. He believed that man is alienated by technology and needs to be rid of it, and advocated a return to life as it existed before the Neolithic revolution – an era when men didn't know about raising animals or private property. There was also a Green anarchy movement, which followed the theories of another American, John Zerzan, who dreamed of returning to the dawn of humanity.

Zerzan claimed that before the Neolithic revolution, man had been happy and unconstrained by authority. He was not a property owner, had no possessions and moved from one hunting ground to another, his sole preoccupation being his own happiness.

De Palma had suspected for some time that Caillol was a supporter of anarcho-primitivist theories and had taken his experiments as far as he possibly could. He had pushed back the limits of what at the outset was mere speculation, believing that to find the real human being – laid bare as it were – you first had to pass through a stage of insanity.

The Baron thought through the logic of what he had learned in the last few days. Caillol was a man who had suffered from psychosis while still very young. He had been sectioned but had extricated himself in the most beautiful way imaginable: by becoming a consultant in a psychiatric hospital. He had gone on to treat patients, having been one himself.

"He's found a path," the Baron whispered, "a path that links us to our most distant ancestors."

# 39

The *Archéonaute* caught a big wave as it passed Ile Maïre. The wind traced long white flurries at the whim of the swell. Pauline Barton smiled at de Palma as he watched the waves breaking on the starboard side. The boat was rolling heavily and taking on water.

"Fucking wind," the helmsman shouted from the bridge. "It'll be more sheltered when we reach Cap Morgiou."

"It's the return journey that's the problem," Pauline said. "We don't want it to get any worse."

"No, it's alright, the forecast says there won't be a change before the end of the afternoon. That's when the wind's going to pick up. So we'll collect the carbon samples and come straight back. There's no way we can anchor in this weather."

Gusts of damp air whipped across the bridge. Pauline and de Palma went down to the cabin. She had laid out a dozen plastic boxes on the central table.

"We'll put the carbon samples we took yesterday into these boxes, then close up the place."

"Today?"

"Either today or Monday. Maybe we'll wait for the wind to die down a bit."

Spray crashed against the cabin porthole. De Palma watched the grey and white sea. He loved stormy weather, the smell of salt in the whirling air – it was nature at its wildest.

"Thank you for letting me come on this little journey," he said to Pauline.

"I hope you like it."

"That's not really why I came."

De Palma spread the photos out on the cabin table. "Can you spot anything?"

Pauline bent over the photo that de Palma showed her. "That's the silhouette I talked to you about. You see, there's a human figure."

"Did it come from the cave?"

"It certainly did. Those were the last pictures we found on Rémy Fortin's camera."

"I know that, I meant which part of the cave?"

"Let me think. Is it important?"

"Extremely important."

She remembered Palestro's suggestion that the photos hadn't come from Le Guen's cave. She opened a drawer, took out a magnifying glass and examined the photo more closely. "I don't really see what you want me to find out," she said.

De Palma handed her some other shots of the cave. All were general views. "How do they compare?"

He left Pauline to concentrate on the photos and went out for some fresh air. He was starting to feel seasick. Cap Morgiou loomed through the fine spray in bright sunshine. The *Archéonaute* changed course, catching a wave as it sank into a hollow.

"I think I've worked it out," Pauline shouted from the cabin.

De Palma went back inside.

"That photo is a set-up. It wasn't taken inside the cave. The stalagmites and concretions are not the same. We should see negative handprints. I'm sure of it."

"Do you mean not Le Guen's cave, or not the same chamber?"

Pauline looked at the Baron in surprise. "I don't understand."

"The photo was taken as part of a sequence. The pictures next to it on the memory card are from Le Guen's cave. We're sure about that, but not the ones with the silhouette and the statuette of the man with the antler head."

Pauline shook her head. "I don't see what you mean."

"We need to go to the bottom of that cave," de Palma said. "Much of what we're looking for is there."

She didn't reply and put the magnifying glass away in the drawer.

"Fortin went diving in the cave the weekend before he died," de Palma said.

"How do you know?"

"The only explanation for the decompression sickness is that he'd been diving too much. When he left you on the Friday before the accident he already had some lethal gas bubbles in his body. The bubbles were in his blood because he'd been diving all weekend at the bottom of the cave and perhaps didn't make his decompression stops. Even if he did, his body couldn't cope."

De Palma concentrated before continuing. He was in the cabin. The windscreen wipers squeaked as they moved across the portholes.

"He went diving on the Saturday. He must have taken a first look at the cave. Maybe he spent the night in the first chamber. And then he went back down the shaft and carried on. I'm willing to bet he found a second chamber."

Pauline was staring into space. "You're probably right," she whispered. "It scares me."

"I can see why. That photo is from the second chamber. He only had time to take one shot. He caught sight of something in the flashlight: a hideous shape. Then he realised he was in danger."

"And the man with the antler head?"

De Palma took a deep breath. "He'd probably just discovered it when he was disturbed. He decided to flee and took the same route back."

De Palma put his index finger on a photo of the statuette.

"We'll never know the truth, but I can't think of any other explanation."

Pauline Barton was amazed. She had always trusted Fortin implicitly. With hindsight she could see some of the things he had done weren't entirely normal. He had insisted on guarding the entrance to the cave at weekends and arriving there first. He had often lingered behind.

Sugiton appeared on the starboard side, with its large jagged cliffs over a hundred metres high. In the middle of the little bay the waves worried away at the torpedo boat, hurling torrents of white water. Some technicians were dismantling the red tent that had housed the expedition headquarters. The canvas flapped, buffeted by the wind.

"I'm going to go behind the torpedo," the helmsman shouted, on the starboard side as always. "We'll be sheltered, but there are shallows. We can't afford to hang around."

"Do you want me to make a call on the radio?" Pauline asked, looking up at the gangway.

"Done that. Your carbon samples are out of the cave. Manu and Claude are going to join us in a Zodiac."

As he saw the *Archéonaute* heading for the entrance to the creek, Claude, a research engineer, raised his arms in greeting. Pauline replied with a wave.

"Alright?"

The helmsman cut the engine and let the boat drift in the waves towards the front of the torpedo. Then he corrected his course and put the motor into reverse to slow down. Pauline looked around sadly at the white stony landscape, as though the Baron had stolen away her last remaining dreams.

The Zodiac came alongside the hull of the *Archéonaute*. Claude handed a sealed box to Pauline, who clutched it to her stomach and took it straight to the cabin. The last carbon samples from Le Guen's cave had left a world of total silence. Seeing them in their cotton swaddling Pauline felt tearful. Everything was spoiled. Fortin had used her. The dig hadn't given her what she had wanted so badly.

"Will you seal up the entrance this afternoon?" de Palma asked.

"No," she said.

"So on Monday we can go down to the bottom."

"Who? You and me?"

"No, I'm going to ask a couple of the police divers to go with you."

"I'm scared all of a sudden."

"You've got nothing to fear. The men I'm sending aren't novices."

De Palma asked them to let him disembark. The *Archéonaute* went out to sea again, disappearing in the spray and the squalls. The Col de Sugiton wasn't far by the footpath. De Palma rang Eva to ask her to pick him up at Luminy, on the outskirts of the city. That evening they would go to the cinema and treat themselves to a meal at a restaurant in town.

Before leaving Sugiton, de Palma turned one last time towards the Calanques and the islands of Riou and Les Impériaux. The sea was covered in creased brown silk. Saint-Exupéry's plane had plunged into these waters, not far from the ancient Greek Massaliot triremes, German fighter planes, old roll-on roll-off ferries and those huge frescoes slumbering in the silence of the caves. The sea never returns the secrets it has swallowed.

*

When they played together, Christine was always the leader. She decided which games they would play. Especially since her small breasts had swelled like beautiful apples.

There were a thousand places to play along the path coming from the road. When Maman was there, the children weren't allowed to go beyond the small embankments that bordered the furrowed earth track, but the children didn't care.

Thomas preferred the rock that looked like a sitting dog. He felt comfortable in the cool shade of the stone. It was his second home.

The last time he had been there, he had spotted a yellow and grey toad by a bush. Christine had wanted to catch it and show it to Papa, but Thomas didn't agree. They had an argument, a big one that made Thomas have a fit. He was sure she had done it on purpose, to make him do what she wanted. He thought his sister was a bit of a monster. Especially since her body had changed. It had happened just like that. His own body was not the same either. A strange force now inhabited him. It came from his belly and sometimes spread to his legs and chest. Then he felt himself getting hard, so hard it almost hurt.

Christine had shown him what happened to girls: the blood of life running down between their legs. It disgusted him and he felt nauseous. He had gone to hide under the rock. Nobody knew that was where he had hidden the man with the antler head, behind a large piece of limestone. No-one knew. Not even Christine.

August, 1961. He was still little at the time. That morning Papa told Maman she had bad genes; that there were mad people in every generation. She was a beautiful woman, still very young, with hair as soft as honey. He liked to smell her sweet perfume like the scent of acacias in bloom. Whenever he could, he brushed against her. Sometimes he even dared to touch her, his finger stroking the nylon pleat in her skirt or the woollen hem of the jumper she often wore in winter.

But Maman was wary of him and his strangely frozen expression; the way he had of looking beneath reality, showing the whites of his eyes. When he started to shake – arms rounded, body rigid – she panicked. It was as though an electric current passed through him, from head to toe. He watched her run away, with her long face and eyes the colour of mustard.

Every time Maman complained about his fits, the doctor locked him in the room with the 'no entry' sign.

Then came the anti-psychotics, the hypnotics, the anxiolytics and the tranquillisers: drugs which put the beast to sleep and lightened his mood. It was a long list, but he knew the names off by heart. All those chemical formulas and mysterious molecules. He had pinched a formulary from the hospital and often read it in the secrecy of his room.

# 40

Near Saint-Eustache church, in the heart of Paris, an evangelist in a tie was handing out 'Good News' cards. Three Japanese tourists went up the gleaming stone steps, turning to pose for a photo in front of the heavy wooden doors; grinning meekly at the camera for the umpteenth time.

Thomas watched for a while: it seemed such a simple, happy life. A smell of sugar candy and bird droppings lingered in the cold air. The insistent music of a merry-go-round hung over the rectangular lawns of the Parc des Halles. Sounds from his distant childhood.

In front of the church some pigeons had crowded round a crust of bread like a bunch of bold marauders. The ceaseless flow of passers-by emerging from the gloomy shade of the old buildings on rue Montorgueil was immediately swallowed up by the mouth of Les Halles Metro station. Autran followed the weaving throng. The patch of blue sky shrank as the escalator took him down into the bowels of the capital. His eyes were red; the eyelids seemed to droop towards his mouth. His face was flushed and he sniffed repeatedly.

Thomas felt suffocated by it all: the escalators throwing up streams of bored travellers, bland lighting, endless passages oozing out big city pus. He walked along, fists clenched in his pockets, gazing at the shoes in front of him. He went through the barriers and looked up to check which way to go for Saint-Germain-en-Laye. It was off to the left, following the small rectangular signs on the ceiling. He had to go deeper into the belly of the earth, caught up in the slowly moving crowd which he did not like at all.

The train arrived, its steel nose shunting the fetid air laden with grit and ozone. Without thinking Thomas got in and sat down on the first available seat. A large woman stared at him for a few seconds before returning to her glossy magazine. As the train left Paris he fell asleep. He didn't wake until they reached Saint-Germain-en-Laye. It was only as he came out on to the esplanade opposite the Château that he noticed the weather. Big raindrops fell from a grey sky, raising dust from the ground. Since he had left the knacker's yard for psychos, it hadn't occurred to him to look up at the sky. He missed the sun.

The Museum of National Antiquities occupied one wing of the Château François 1er, just by the station. It was a huge stone building with a severe facade, adorned with mullioned windows and diamond-shaped panes.

Thomas bought a ticket from a bored official and followed the arrows indicating the way for visitors. As he walked past the museum shop he caught sight of the young woman working there. He stared at her fleetingly and she smiled back.

It was his second visit. The first time was long ago with his father, shortly before he died. His sister Christine had been there, as she always was. They had looked at the collection of bi-faces; the harpoons; the lance throwers, needles and scrapers. It was here that the twins' passion for prehistory was born.

The museum had been modernised. It was better organised. He had to go through the Celtic antiquities room, with its bronze weapons and gold torques; then past the Neolithic revolution and the Menhir statues, before reaching the cradle of humanity. That ancient era, the age of free men.

It was a Wednesday. A group of children burst onto the scene, crowding beneath the huge antlers of the Megaceros skull on the wall. The guide – a small blonde woman with a sharp expression –

pointed at a grinning Cro-Magnon skull in an attempt to subdue them. She needn't have bothered.

Thomas paused to let the din subside. In the semi-darkness, inside illuminated cabinets, the great hunters' weapons were displayed in all their rough nobility. He lingered without daring to go near. Two visitors moved in front of him, making inane comments about the collection. A snivelling child tugged at his father's coat, but First Man no longer heard anything. Slowly, he approached the main display cabinet.

There she was: tiny and supreme. He had waited so long to see her.

For ten years, in his mind, he had caressed tenderly that finely chiselled little face: oval shaped with full cheeks and braided hair falling down on her shoulders. He knew her every little secret. She had the face of a young virgin, with huge eyes – just a hint of the pupils – and a straight nose. The label read:

THE LADY WITH THE HOOD,
OR, THE LADY OF BRASSEMPOUY

It was twenty-three thousand years old: the oldest depiction of humankind. Divine purity sculpted on to the tip of a mammoth's tusk. Then he caught sight of the words beneath it, "Copy of the original".

He felt a great emptiness. He was looking at a fake. A perfect copy perhaps, but it had not been sculpted by the hand of First Woman. The museum was like a prison: the best of humanity was locked up there in dark chests, hidden away from view.

Everything started to spin. He sat down on one of the wooden benches opposite the display cabinet. Beads of cold sweat appeared on his brow. He began to feel spasms in his calves, then his arms. The brown museum walls blended into each other, spreading in large pools across the floor. Somewhere a T.V. set was showing a programme about the sizes of flints. He looked up and saw a screen to his left. Then everything went blurry.

After a long while the attack passed. He stood up, walked through the Neolithic, Iron and Bronze Age rooms to the museum bookshop. The young sales assistant greeted him shyly. She was wearing a straight skirt with thick black tights, a coarse woollen jumper and a necklace with some large silver balls. She had a discreet parting in her hair. It fell down in amber curls over her slender shoulders, framing a long elegant face with sparkling hazel eyes.

Immediately, he found her attractive. "I'm looking for *Les Réligions de la préhistoire* by Leroi-Gourhan."

The well-known title was the first thing that came into his head.

"I'm sorry, but we're out of it."

He looked surprised. "It's a good book."

"Yes, but it's out of print."

"That's a shame. It was really useful."

He understood from her expression that she was still a student, but already quite an expert. It was clear too from her slightly awkward manner and the way she looked at the books. He wasn't wrong. Scholars cherish books.

"Have you got anything on Le Guen's cave?"

"No, I'm sorry, we haven't, but there's a book due out in a year's time. It's an account of the last two digs there."

Her name was Delphine. There was a curious liveliness about her body. It gave off vibrations that Thomas experienced as a slight tingling at the base of his neck. He was shrouded in a strange veil.

They spoke for a long time about the cave. He explained in remarkable detail about the Magdalenian hunters' drawings on the limestone cliff faces.

"In my opinion the 'slain man' is probably the most important. He's about twenty-eight centimetres long, with his arms raised. A jet spear strikes him in the back and pierces him through."

"I've heard about it, but why are you so interested in him? It's not that beautiful. I prefer the small horses or the bison shown in three-quarter view – they're wonderful!"

"Why the 'slain man'? I find it very moving. It's a simplified portrayal of a man slain by an assegai and is probably the oldest portrayal of a murder in the history of humanity!"

"A murder?"

"Yes, he's struck in the back by the assegai."

She was impressed by the depth of his knowledge. Few passing customers knew about these drawings, which were sometimes mere scratches in the fragile rock. Most people only remembered the paintings. Thomas explained that he had done his thesis on cave painting and been lucky enough to visit the cave, in the Calanques near Marseille.

"Must be amazing to find those paintings," she said.

"Yes, it's more than that. It's like going back into your mother's womb."

His words left her pensive. The museum was about to close. Thomas suggested they have a drink in the bar opposite the Château. Delphine agreed. He could see traces of the gauche adolescent in her expression and gestures. In spite of the self-assurance, there was a great loneliness about her.

*

It was night-time and raining hard now. They ran across the square and took refuge in the bar. It was packed with business school students. They were greeted by a deafening noise of clinking glasses, high-pitched laughter and coarse remarks.

Delphine tried to make herself heard. "Come on, let's go and have a drink in my flat. It's nothing special, but I can show you my dissertation. It's only a draft, I haven't got very far yet."

They took the first turning left, then walked down a narrower, gloomy street running through the historic centre of the city. Driven on by the wind, curtains of rain lashed the facades with their closed shutters. The lights in the shop windows were reflected in the rain-splattered paving stones. After two hundred metres, Delphine stopped outside a detached house and took a bunch of keys from her pocket. The roof was covered in small rusty-looking tiles. Outside was a little garden with a larger plot at the back that merged into the semi-darkness.

"This is where I live. It's on the ground floor."

"Nice place."

The shutters on the first floor were closed.

"The owners aren't here at the moment. They're due back next week."

She opened the door and turned on the light. The flat smelled of incense and stale tobacco. A bunch of fading flowers sat proudly on a wrought iron pedestal table, straight out of IKEA. The kitchen area was separated from the main room by a thick wooden counter. A collection of little pots of jam was arranged along the edge.

She had covered the tiled floor with a cheap Persian carpet that clashed with the pale walls. A flowery quilted bed stood against the right hand wall; the desk opposite was strewn with paperwork. A dictaphone lay on a copy of de Lumley's *L'Homme premier*. Dissertations, books and magazines were piled on the floor.

"Your hair's all wet," Delphine exclaimed. "I'll get you a towel, the bathroom's in there."

"You go first, you must be freezing."

She refused, but he insisted.

A small clock on Delphine's desk chimed seven-thirty.

"I'm looking at how man was depicted in the Palaeolithic era," she said, returning from the bathroom with a towel. She handed it to Thomas. "I'm interested in children's skeletons. We're recon-structing them in 3D, using a virtual system."

"I've heard about that, but I thought it was a Swiss lab that did it."

"That's right, but I'm only looking at Neanderthal art. I'm trying to understand how we portray that today. It's important. Have a look."

She clicked on the mouse and refreshed the screen. A series of skulls appeared. The parts recreated by the software were coloured in.

"Here's the result. It's impressive, don't you think?"

"Fantastic! I imagine you've got some skeletons too?"

"Certainly have."

With two clicks she brought up another page. "This one is almost complete. It's of a child . . ."

"Why a child?"

"I'm trying to collate the data I get from the lab. I interpret it and try to compare it with previous studies that have been published."

She shot him a tender look. It was difficult to assess how old he was. He could have been her father, but she didn't mind the age difference. She found him attractive.

"Perhaps we could address each other as 'Tu'?" she said hesitantly.

He gave her a knowing smile.

She carried on with her demonstration. "We're almost certain Neanderthal children developed faster than the Homo Sapiens ones did. The teeth and the main parts of the skeleton seem to be more mature than in a Homo Sapiens child of the same age."

She displayed several other skeletons, "You see, there's no chin, like we have. They're stocky. In the other pictures of the adult specimens, you can see their pelvis is longer than ours, the hands are broad and powerful, the skull is quite a bit bulkier and the trunk wider. In short, real Neanderthals."

She moved away from the computer screen. "The most important thing is when you decide to put a face, skin and flesh on these skeletons. That's when you leave science behind and enter the realm of fantasy."

"How do you mean?" Thomas asked.

"We still think of Neanderthal man as a mindless brute, so we give him hair everywhere, a bony face . . . a killer's face. And we do the same with Cro-Magnon man."

"A killer's face?"

Delphine moved the mouse again. Two pictures of Cro-Magnons appeared, dating from the middle of the nineteenth century. There was a strong similarity with great apes. In other pictures from the beginning of the twentieth century the facial features became finer and closer to contemporary human beings.

"Between these two portrayals science has moved on," Delphine said. "We no longer view primitive people that way. Nowadays we go for images that make Palaeolithic man seem more like us. I want to show that we add what we like to the skeletons. You can turn Cro-Magnon into a sensitive, civilised being or a rude barbarian. It all depends how you see our heritage. Have you heard of Lombroso and his theories?"

"Yes."

"I've read *Criminal Man* and all the other stuff that's been written on atavism. I think it's a good illustration of this. I'm going to do a chapter about it in my thesis. What do you think?"

Thomas' face clouded over and went cold. He closed his eyes and tried to summon the strength to dispel the turmoil he felt.

"I've got to go," he said suddenly.

Her jaw dropped. "Are you sure? You don't want to . . ."

He put his hand on her shoulder. "No, I must go. I'll drop round soon, when I've got time."

She wanted to stop him, but his powerful silhouette had already disappeared through the doorway. He turned and looked at her for a moment and there were tears in his eyes.

# 41

The cassette which Bernard Monin had left on de Palma's car seat at Ville-Évrard had been returned by the laboratory. As with *Criminal Man*, there were no fingerprints on it. There was nothing for the experts to go on.

Bessour opened up the large exercise book that was lying in front of him along with a pencil and brand new rubber. "Shall we make a start then, Baron?"

"Right you are."

De Palma put the cassette into the dictaphone and pressed the play button.

Street noise. The sound of a door being closed.
*"Are you ready, Thomas?"*
*"Yes, I'm ready. Are you recording?"*
*"Of course. Is that O.K.?"*
*"Yes."*
A series of rustling sounds and then some tapping on the table.

De Palma had immediately recognised Caillol's calm, rather dull voice. "It's unusual for a patient to be on such friendly terms with his doctor," he said, pressing the pause button and then releasing it. Bessour frowned, straining to listen.

"*Thomas, do you want to talk about the voice that sometimes speaks to you?*"

"*It's hard.*"

After a long silence.

"*Why is it hard?*"

"*Because of that thing.*"

"*What thing?*"

After another long silence, "*When I see a woman, I always start thinking of Maman and . . .*"

"*And what?*"

"*There are pictures with blood. Like there's blood everywhere.*"

"*You mean you see blood?*"

"*Yes.*"

Autran was close to the dictaphone. His slow, deep breathing was clearly audible.

"*There's blood and then the voice . . .*"

"*Tell me about the voice. Whose voice is it? Is it someone you know?*"

"*Yes.*"

"*You've heard it before?*"

Autran's breathing quickened.

"*It's Christine's . . .*"

"*And what does the voice tell you?*"

"*It talks to me.*"

Caillol coughed.

"*It talks to you?*"

"*Yes. It's all muddled in my head.*"

"*But you should try to answer.*"

"*No, not now.*"

The conversation stopped. A period of calm followed with no voices. Then there was a metallic tapping sound.

"*Why have you tied me up?*"

"*Because I need to do some tests and you might get a bit restless.*"

*"I don't want to be tied up."*

*"It has to be done."*

Once again a metallic tapping sound.

De Palma stopped the tape recorder.

"He must be lying on a hospital bed," Bessour said.

De Palma nodded.

"It could be the one we saw in the basement at Caillol's house."

"You're probably right," de Palma replied, pressing the button. "Let's see what happens next."

Clicking sounds. Grunting. Thomas was probably writhing beneath the restraints.

*"Calm down, otherwise I'll have to tighten the straps. Is that what you want?"*

*"No!"*

Autran was panting. Caillol had stood up. The sound of his footsteps was unmistakable.

*"Right. Just relax and you won't feel a thing. We're going to try a little experiment. Have you heard of Amanita Muscaria?"*

*"Yes, it's a kind of mushroom."*

*"Some people say it's dangerous, but we're only going to use it in a small dose, like the shamans of old. You'll be able to travel in time and leave your body. It'll help you to get better."*

*"I don't want to!"*

*"Do you want us to stop that voice?"*

*"Yes."*

*"Would you rather be a medicine man, or a stupid nutter who gets locked up in a ward for disturbed patients?"*

*"I want to get out of here."*

*"That mushroom contains a substance that's good for you. I've tried it myself. Look at me. I was a patient once, now I'm a doctor. Worth trying, isn't it?"*

*"Alright."*

*"Right, I'm going to attach the electrodes in the usual way."*

De Palma stopped the tape and turned to Bessour, "Do you have any idea what *Amanita Muscaria* is?"

Bessour typed the name into the search engine.

"Fly agaric. It's a common type of mushroom. Very toxic. It can put flies to sleep without killing them. I assume it's a hallucinogenic if given in the right dose."

"Christine Autran wrote something about that. A short piece on how nature provided for Palaeolithic men. She talks about mushrooms. We need to look into it."

De Palma pressed the play button on the recorder.

*"Swallow it. It won't harm you."*

A long silence. The only audible sound was the humming of the loudspeaker.

*"There. You'll soon start to feel the effects."*

Autran was becoming increasingly restless. His arms and wrists tugged at the restraints. The bed squeaked on its legs.

*"You're going down a long tunnel,"* Caillol said. *"Soon you'll see the light."*

A strange rattling sound came from Autran's chest. Caillol was moving around some glass objects.

*"Can you see her now?"*

*"Yes."*

*"What's she called?"*

*"It's Hélène Weill. She often comes to the surgery."*

*"Tell me what you feel when you see her."*

*"She's suffering a lot. The chains holding her are strong."*

*"So she must be freed?"*

*"Yes, she's suffering too much."*

*"I'm going to bring her here. Release her. You'll be able to watch her."*

He walked away from the microphone until his footsteps were barely audible. A door opened. He said something impossible to hear, then more footsteps.

"There are two of them," de Palma exclaimed.

At this point the recording stopped.

"I'm not going to sleep tonight," Bessour muttered. "What a nightmare!"

"It's terrifying. Hélène Weill was his first victim."

"I know. We'll send it off to the lab. We might find out what he said when the door opened."

*

The sound lab was situated at the end of the corridor in Forensic Medicine, past two neon-lit rooms used for taking D.N.A. and seal samples. There were some bloodstained clothes on coat hangers, a balaclava recovered from the scene of an armed robbery and a torn silk nightdress.

"I don't like it here," Bessour grumbled.

"Me neither," de Palma said. "I'll be glad to see the back of it."

He opened the door to the Audio section and was a little surprised to find a new colleague there, bent over her oscilloscope.

"I'm Sabrina," the young woman said, holding out a hand. "How can I help?"

"We need to identify some words on a tape."

"Let's have a look."

A tall brunette with dark eyes, Sabrina couldn't have been much over thirty. Bessour went weak at the knees. De Palma hung back.

"Have you marked the clip?" Sabrina asked in a reedy voice.

"Er, yes. It's just after the sound of the footsteps."

Sabrina isolated the clip and digitised it. "It's very faint, but we should be able to sort it."

She brought up a graph of the voice onscreen. The different sounds appeared in blue and red, depending on their intensity. Caillol's voice was in green.

"There we go," Sabrina said, "that's the frequency you're interested in."

She put on some headphones and fiddled with a series of equalisation buttons. "I'm having difficulties with the end of a word."

"Which one?" de Palma asked.

Sabrina took off her headphones. "He says: 'Come in, Hél . . .' or something. It's really garbled."

"Hélène Weill!" de Palma said.

Bessour searched through his notebook. He stopped at a date where he had made a note at the foot of a page. "Two days later she was dead."

# 42

Christine Autran followed the Baron's every move with her cold eyes. She was wearing a very old-fashioned flowery blouse. Her hair had grown a little since his last visit, forming two ringlets on her gaunt cheeks. She stared at the notebook he had just put down front of him. The page was blank. The Baron clicked his pen and placed it on top.

"Dr Caillol is dead," he said in a muted voice. "I don't think you'll be surprised to hear that."

Christine's hooded eyes stared at the Baron's face. "And what did you find?"

"A tall, forked larch tree. An arrow pointing east and God knows what else! But there's worse to come. Do you know what?"

"I'm not in the police."

"I know that, Mademoiselle Autran. We found one of your brother's fingers on Caillol's desk. One finger. One death. My question is a simple one: who's going to be next? A man? A woman?"

Christine turned towards the window. Her hands hadn't moved on the table. They were like wax.

"One thing surprises me . . ." de Palma said, his voice trailing away.

"What's that?"

"Why did you tell me about the tall larch tree?"

"You should know that by now."

257

"I know lots of things, but why give me that lead?"

She gazed sternly at her hands, "To show you up for what you are, Commandant. A big know-all who hasn't been able to predict a thing."

"It's not just that."

She looked up. For the first time de Palma could see a vestige of humanity behind the hard expression.

"So what else is it?" she asked.

De Palma had spent a good part of the night working out how much to say. Thinking what his old mentor from the quai d'Orfèvres would have done in his place, he would have been bold, he told himself. But he wouldn't have tried to trap her or be clever. He would have struck when Christine least expected it.

"I think you've had enough," de Palma said calmly. "Deep down you only want one thing and that's for your brother to be arrested."

The silence that followed told the Baron he had possibly hit the mark.

"That's outrageous!" Christine exploded.

"In that case why give me the lead on Caillol's murder? Well? Are you trying to get one over on me? No, I think you're too intelligent. You just want to be able to live without your brother."

Her manner became frosty and haughty again, as at the beginning of the interview, but her fists were clenched.

"There's you thinking that soon you'll be out, but your brother might show up. That'd be pretty tragic! You and him, face to face. After nine years apart."

She stayed silent. De Palma felt he had hit the bull's eye.

He decided to press home his advantage. "I think it's time you helped us."

Christine sniggered and shrugged her shoulders, but there was something about her contemptuous manner that jarred. "Help the police!"

De Palma got up and stood by the window, hands on hips.

"You see, Christine, we can never know what's going on inside the head of a lunatic like your brother. In the past you could manipulate him, but now?"

He pointed at her. "Now he might well turn on you. Have you thought of that? You yourself could be the second or third finger."

She clenched her fists more tightly. The bones jutted beneath the delicate skin.

"Well, have you?" de Palma pressed her.

"My brother, harm me? If you only knew how gentle he is."

De Palma walked towards Christine and stood behind her.

"I'm not an archaeologist, I'm a policeman. Crime is my line of business. And believe me I know quite a bit about it."

He moved his face closer to hers. "Thomas is a sociopath. The only person he loves is himself and he kills for pleasure. He has no taboos. He wouldn't find it difficult to kill you. He thinks of you as his property. He treats everyone as an object. Something he can chuck away when he no longer needs it. It only takes the voices to ask him to do these things."

De Palma went over to his chair and put his fists on the table. "Now for some good news. The Judge has contacted us about your release. He asked what we thought and I think we'll give him a favourable response. Very favourable, even."

Christine fixed her eyes on the drab wall opposite. Once again she was in control of her emotions. De Palma allowed a few minutes of silence to pass by. Time enough to create a different atmosphere. The sounds of the prison could be heard through the visiting room windows.

"Tell me about the second chamber at Le Guen's cave."

It was an unexpected question.

"I don't know what you mean."

"Stop messing around. A man you know went there. Rémy Fortin. And paid for it with his life."

"Too many sanctuaries have been desecrated."

"Do you know what he saw in the second chamber?"

She bowed her head and whispered, "The man with the antler head."

Her hands were in the same position. Lifeless.

"Tell me about Caillol," de Palma said. "Why kill him?"

"My brother must have blamed him for all the tragedies we've suffered."

"Your mother was his mistress?"

"Yes. Long before my father died. Did you know he was seriously ill?"

"No, I didn't."

"He suffered from a brain tumour for many years. Why do you think he took up shamanism? He was using my brother as a healer. Thomas has rare powers. He was a lot more effective than scalpels or chemotherapy. The tumour should have killed him a long time ago, but he fought it."

"Did you know your mother and Caillol were both sectioned at the same time?"

A tear trickled down Christine's thin cheek. She made no attempt to wipe it away. De Palma was moved. There was a long pause, then he resumed his questioning.

"Did Caillol know of the existence of that statuette?"

"Of course."

"Did he know about the second chamber?"

"You seem to have got the picture."

There's just one problem, de Palma thought. The doctor doesn't match the description of the diver given by the man at Scubapro.

"Was Caillol the only one who knew about this statue?"

"I don't know," she said.

He stood up and took from his briefcase the two photos that Bessour had found in Caillol's cupboard.

"These photos make no sense to us. Do you recognise the people?"

She didn't look at them. "How do you expect me to recognise anyone when their faces are cut off?"

"Have a try."

A long silence. Then she added, without even glancing at the photo, "I'm the third from left. Lucy's the fifth one."

# 43

Against all expectations the surveillance system set up by the police had finally produced results. The hotelier had got in touch. Autran was staying in a no-frills Hotel Formule 1, on an industrial estate in Versailles. He had left his room that morning but was due to return the following night. Legendre was very edgy.

"Are you sure about what you're saying?" he asked Bessour.

"Positive. Our colleagues in the city have had a look at the hotel register. He checked in under his own name."

"It could be his namesake!"

Bessour stiffened, his pride hurt. "I rang the owner. He's very well informed. He was dead certain about Autran because of an article in *Le Parisien*. He called the police right away."

"You see what prison does to people's minds," Legendre said. "You've got to be pretty careless to use your own name to check in, but it's not the first time I've noticed that with blokes on the run. They lose all touch with reality."

"Especially when your name is Autran."

"In any case, nice work. Congratulations!"

Legendre contacted his counterparts in Versailles and they put the Special Intervention Units on a war footing.

"We move in tomorrow morning at 6.00 a.m. You can come to Versailles with me."

"And de Palma?"

"He's in Rennes, but I'd prefer it if he stayed away. There's no knowing what he might do. In any case, he should be on the train by now and we need to catch the first plane. I'll leave a message for him."

*

The hotel was at the far end of a retail park. Warehouses stood between rows of wire fencing and tarmac alleys where articulated lorries languished. It was freezing as the night drew to a close. The cold air cast halos of light round the lamp posts. An unmarked van had been parked there since the day before, just a few metres from the entrance to the hotel. There were four men inside, all tooled up for war.

"His car hasn't moved since yesterday."

"Is that the 307 there?"

"937, X-ray, Papa 13 . . . yes, it's definitely the one."

Legendre glanced at his watch. "Only five minutes to go."

Two unmarked cars moved down the alley. Karim recognised a huge man from the Special Intervention Unit: he had met him at a New Year's Eve function organised by the head of the force. As he passed, the big guy pulled his balaclava down over his face.

The two cars parked at an angle.

"Shit, those people always impress me," Legendre said. "Just like clockwork."

He racked his Sig-Sauer and stared at Bessour for a few seconds. "You O.K.?"

"Yes," Bessour replied, trying to sound assured. "It's not the first time I've nicked someone."

"Exciting, eh?"

"Er, yes."

Karim was scared. He had butterflies in his stomach and a taste of bile in his mouth. That morning nothing had gone down, not even the dishwater which passed for coffee that Legendre had brought along.

The hotel reception suddenly lit up, throwing a yellowish light over the asphalt surface of the car park. Eight men jumped out of their vehicles and strode towards the glazed entrance.

"Our turn now," Legendre said, putting on his police armband.

They got out of the car and ran to the hotel. The manager looked grim. He smiled broadly at the man from police headquarters: his big day had come. Bessour found the décor terrifyingly mundane. The yellow walls, the machines selling drinks, toothbrushes and condoms, it all seemed horrendous.

The anti-terrorist ninjas had taken up position by the door of the room where Autran was sleeping. The group commander appeared in reception. Two grenades dangled from his navy blue bulletproof vest.

"Are we good to go?" he said through his balaclava.

Legendre looked at his watch one last time, in what he hoped was a solemn gesture. "Go!"

He nodded at his female assistant and clumsily drew his weapon.

"Get back," the commander ordered, holding out a black-gloved hand.

In front of the hotel two snipers were posted on the lawn, their dark silhouettes barely visible as they crouched on the ground. They slid a round into the chamber of their rifles and aimed the infrared sights at the bedroom window.

By the time Legendre hurtled down the second floor corridor two men had grabbed a shiny metal battering ram and were drawing it back. A dull sound shook the hotel. The door to room number thirty-eight exploded in pieces.

Two men rushed into the room armed with submachine guns. "Police! Don't move!"

The commander sprinted inside, holding his Manurhin revolver at eye level.

"Where's the fucker gone?"

Legendre heard the muffled sound of doors opening and shutting. Then the rattle of rifles being unloaded. It was over.

"For fuck's sake! We've been had."

"We fell for it," Legendre muttered.

For a few seconds he looked uncertain.

"Here!" the commander exclaimed.

A finger lay on the pillow.

# 44

"Why have you brought me here?"

The D16 to Milly-la-Forêt passed through some sparse woodland. Delphine was driving fast.

"I have to go down south," Thomas said. "I wanted to give you a present and I felt I could only do that in the right place."

She looked at his bandaged hand. "Doesn't it hurt a lot?"

"I'm getting used to it. That's twice in a fortnight."

On the left was a clearing, with a wooden sign that said 'Mandatory Parking'.

"It needed to be somewhere heavy with meaning, a bit magical."

"Not so common round Paris."

"No. Let's park here. Then we have to walk for a bit. You don't mind, do you?"

A path wove between some sandstone mounds jutting out from the ground. To the right a winding trail led to a copse of pines and dwarf chestnuts.

"It's that way, if I remember right."

All around the scent of dead leaves and heather still wet from the morning downpour.

They walked for some two hundred metres before they came to a huge clearing. Some climbers had laid a mattress on the ground and were testing themselves on the Bilboquet overhang: an enormous rock in the middle of a sandy heath that looked a bit like a sphinx.

Thomas suddenly turned left through a clump of waist-high bracken. Between the straight pines a mass of round boulders suddenly appeared, like a gigantic elephant towering over the slope they were about to climb. "Almost there," he said, turning round. "That's it up there."

She paused to get her breath back as she watched him move away. With every step a strange force seemed to drive him on. She had difficulty taking in the fact that more than twenty years separated them. He was handsome and the sight of this man with the powerful shoulders filled her with pleasure.

She looked up at the sky. The sun shone through the thorn bushes and spread slanting rays of pale gold over the rusty bracken. A breath of wind carried laughter from children who were trying out some easy rocks. When she looked down now, Thomas was just a dot in the gap between two crags. Then he disappeared altogether.

She followed, lengthening her stride. As she climbed, the rock in the shape of an elephant's back turned into a man with a beret on his head. Another seemed to point up at the sky like an angry finger. She knew the origins of these geological oddities. In the Oligocene era, thirty million years earlier, the Parisian basin was covered by sea, with sand on the bottom. Once the water disappeared patches of sandstone formed, some harder than others. Erosion had got to work and the boulders had toppled over. Others had rolled down the slopes to form this maze of gigantic rocks and fabulous cathedrals.

When Delphine reached the summit she called out, but there was no reply. She scanned the heap of rocks. Nothing. She went round the stones, stepping over the gaps in between. Thomas had disappeared. She sat down and smiled at the childish game he was playing. Suddenly she heard a voice from the other side of a level piece of ground. She moved forward without saying anything, taking care not to tread on any dead wood, hoping to surprise him. She passed

267

under a sandstone canopy and caught sight of some holly that screened the entrance to a small cavity.

"Delphine!" The voice, distant and muffled, came from the bowels of the earth.

"Delphine!"

She walked towards the semi-circle of rock. Thomas had hidden behind some holly. She parted the branches carefully to avoid getting scratched. A dark, damp hole gaped in front of her.

"Thomas!"

He did not reply, but he wasn't far away. The heavy smell of his body worn out by all the exertion rose towards her. The hole went a long way down and ended in a cave, barely visible in the darkness. She moved forward a few metres. The smell of moss and wet sand was becoming stronger. She had to duck to enter the cave. A second chamber appeared; it was pitch black. She held out her arms and turned round. She was lost.

"Thomas! Thomas!"

She could hear his breathing, echoing softly on the sandstone roof.

"Thomas, it's not funny."

At the far end of the chamber a yellow light appeared: a second tunnel. She walked towards the luminous rock shelf framing a third chamber, bigger than the others. Thomas was standing in the middle with one hand behind his back. There was a torch by his feet, the kind that campers use. He stared intently at her.

"You scared me. What do you think you're doing, bringing me here?"

A strange light reflected in his china-blue eyes. "Don't you like it?"

She shook her hair. "Yes, I do, it's great. And it's certainly a surprise!"

"I discovered this place with my sister when she was at the Sorbonne. We used to come to Fontainebleau quite a lot, and especially here to Trois-Pignons."

"It's a magical place. You'd think you were back in the time of the skeletons I'm studying."

"You don't know how right you are."

He brought out his hand from behind his back. An enormous flint gleamed in his fist: a biface, worthy of any collection.

"I wanted to give you this."

She went towards him and gently picked up the stone blade.

"It's magnificent," she said crouching down so she could study the weapon by the light of the torch, "But it's a . . ."

"It's authentic, Delphine. Take good care of it; it belonged to First Man. He'd be angry if you didn't."

She stood up. She was almost within touching distance. He remained impassive. She took his hand and drew it to her. The tension in his body made her shiver. He raised the torch above his head and disappeared into the darkness.

"Look," he said in a whisper.

A multitude of geometrical drawings appeared on the ceiling. A small horse, on a flat surface.

"It's beautiful!"

"Put your hand on the rock and you'll feel the power of the spirits . . . all the mystery of cave painting."

He took her hand and pressed it gently against the rock. "Just breathe and let the fluid rise inside you."

A long silence ensued.

"Can you feel the spirits hiding behind the invisible wall?"

A strange sensation came over her. It was as if a very weak electric current was spreading from her fingers throughout her body. After a moment that seemed like an age everything started to spin. The cave and their shadows entwined.

# 45

Professor Palestro was dozing outside his front door, some high-powered binoculars resting on his expansive stomach.

"Hello?"

Palestro sat up with a jolt and stared. "Who are you?"

"Commandant de Palma, Serious Crime Squad."

The pre-historian looked astounded. He had difficulty recognising the policeman who had questioned him, at times aggressively, a decade or so earlier. In fact he had never expected to see the man who had arrested Christine ever again.

"Been doing some bird watching?" de Palma asked in an attempt to ease the atmosphere.

"There's a couple of eagles nesting over in those cliffs."

Palestro pointed to the two grey crags obstructing the horizon. Black veins ran through them from top to bottom.

"I must have been asleep for an hour," he grumbled, looking at his watch. "Sleeping is such a waste of time. Early man had little space for it. Life was dangerous."

His voice was thick, his speech slurred. He must have been drinking.

"What do you want from me?"

"Just a few questions," de Palma said with a smile.

"Questions? Last time I saw you, I nearly ended up in gaol."

Palestro put on some worn slippers that were lying by his chair.

Around the corner, barely hidden behind a pile of firewood, the barrel of a shotgun peeped out.

"Tell me about Pierre Autran," de Palma said. He had no intention of going easy on the prehistorian.

"He was a friend. A guy I liked a lot. He was passionate about prehistory. A great expert."

"And one who stole the man with the antler head from you?"

"Who said that?"

"A little bird told me."

Palestro sneered, his yellow teeth showing. His condescending expression seemed out of keeping with his character. "Your little bird is an informer, but you have no proof."

"Alright, tell me about the man with the antler head then."

"We found it in a Gravettian stratum not very far from here. I didn't even have time to write it up or take a photo. It was stolen the minute we discovered it."

"How many people knew about it?"

"Two apart from me. Pierre Autran and a student called Jérémie Payet."

"What happened to the student?"

"How should I know? He didn't pursue prehistory as a career. I don't know anything about him. I assume he's teaching history somewhere out in the sticks to kids who couldn't give a damn."

"How far had he got with his studies?"

"He'd started his Ph.D. I know he sat the teaching diploma and passed that. He must have tried the top teaching qualification too."

Palestro didn't dare look the Baron in the eye.

"Did you see Payet again after the dig?"

"To tell the truth, no."

"Did you suspect him of stealing it from you?"

"Yes, but nothing came of that lead – to use your jargon."

De Palma's glance quickly shifted from the binoculars to the shotgun. "You seem a little on edge, Monsieur Palestro."

"Why do you say that?"

"I seem to remember eagles don't nest close to villages, let alone in cliffs like that."

"So you know about eagles then?"

"I love them. I've got a real thing about our feathered friends."

Palestro shrugged. The Baron went over to the gun. It was a 16-bore, loaded with two buckshot cartridges.

"You must be after prehistoric bison with a gun like this!"

"I'm afraid."

"Of what?"

"Thomas Autran. He's on the run, as you know."

Palestro looked at his weapon with a tinge of regret.

"Are you going to confiscate it?"

"I've no reason to. It's legal to possess one and you're in your own home."

De Palma closed the gun and put it back. Palestro feared a visit from Thomas Autran because he had been his sister's lover. De Palma couldn't help him there. Palestro might end up like Caillol. He lived all alone in this wilderness of lavender fields and thick scrubland.

"Why would Autran have it in for you?"

"He's jealous. Whenever Christine and I saw each other, we had to meet in secret. It made life very difficult."

"Was his sister scared of him?"

"Yes. She would have liked to lead a more independent life, but it was virtually impossible. He was too possessive."

"You need to understand . . . all his life he knew only two things: hospitals and his sister – the only family he had. She was his last link to normal life."

Palestro put his binocular strap around his neck and sat down. Clouds had gathered over the foothills of the Alps. Snow was on its way.

"Let's go back to the man with the antler head," de Palma said,

"Was Pierre Autran ever investigated by the police? It was some theft!"

"He didn't have time."

"What do you mean?"

"A few months later he died. When he left the site, I didn't know it would be the last time I'd see him."

"How did he die?"

"I was told he had a stupid accident. He was changing a light bulb. Apparently he got a shock and had a bad fall. I was amazed."

"Why?"

"Have you ever heard of an engineer of his calibre putting his fingers in a socket?"

"Why not?"

"Pierre was careful and meticulous. Obsessive even. Everything was just so at his house."

"Are you trying to tell me he was murdered?"

"That's what I think."

"Can you explain?"

"It's just a theory."

De Palma took out a packet of cigarettes and offered one to the old professor, who accepted.

"You must have good reasons for thinking that. Did Christine say something?"

"She told me her mother despised her father so much she constantly wanted to humiliate him. She was afraid of her mother and often told me she was dangerous. It was the fact that Pierre Autran left the site that made me think about it. With the benefit of hindsight."

"How do you mean?"

"We had just found the man with the antler head when a car turned up. It was his car, with his wife in it. She didn't get out, or even turn off the engine. She was wearing a large pair of sunglasses. He went over to talk to her, then he came back to say goodbye and rushed off."

"Why did that shock you?"

"I don't know. I got the feeling he was saying goodbye for the last time. He had tears in his eyes."

Several days before Pierre Autran left the site his son had been sectioned. This was confirmed by his medical file: two forms, one from the department and one from the psychiatric hospital, explaining that Thomas had nearly killed one of his girlfriends.

The bells from the Quinson church struck five o'clock.

"Did you try to get the man with the antler head back?" de Palma asked.

"No."

"What did Christine say?"

"She thought that was why her father died."

"So you know for sure that Pierre Autran had it?"

"Yes, I found out long after he died."

"Who told you?"

"Christine did."

"Did the statuette disappear when he died?"

"No, I think Thomas hid it."

"Did his sister tell you where?"

"No, that's all I know."

De Palma concentrated for a few seconds. A solitary crow settled in the field between the dense rows of lavender.

"So Pierre Autran came back to steal it from you?"

"I can't answer that," Palestro replied.

A second croaking bird landed not far from the first. They must have been fighting over some carrion.

"What exactly does the man with the antler head represent?"

"It's hard to say."

"Please try."

Palestro took his hands out of his pockets and rubbed them hard. "Have you ever thought that prehistoric man might come to our aid if only we could listen to him?"

"I've never thought anything of the sort."

"Man has always been an artist, Monsieur de Palma. The man with the antler head was certainly conceived about thirty thousand years ago. If you're looking at the history of human evolution that's almost like the present day. That half-man half-beast is a prehistoric artist's representation of the unconscious. There's a link between him and us, and it's never been broken. Do you understand me?"

"I'd like to believe what you say!"

"You should. If we compare what we call *Homo Habilis* – man the maker – who produced tools, with Homo Sapiens, the Cro-Magnon creator of the paintings at Le Guen's cave, Chauvet and Lascaux, the only difference is the size of the skull. The brain of the man who made that statuette is infinitely more productive than that of his predecessors."

Palestro had rediscovered his academic eloquence. He seemed to be addressing a lecture theatre.

"At a symbolic level, that sculpture is very powerful. It forms part of the individual's day-to-day imaginary world. It is truly modern. Unsurpassed even by the surrealists . . ."

He went on, "In the Trois-Frères cave at Ariège in the Pyrenees, a few hundred metres from the entrance, there is a hidden chamber called the Sanctuary, and another one known as the Chapel of the Lioness. These two chambers contain hundreds of fine wall paintings thirteen or fourteen thousand years old.

"A wild cat stares out at you: an incredibly rare painting. It is covered in symbols and abstract geometrical shapes. It's a male; the phallus is clearly visible. It also possesses what seems to be a human upper limb. The hand is clawed like a wild cat's. A fantastic image: half-man half-beast. There are other examples: a bison with its head turned and human lower limbs, or a rhinoceros whose hind leg obscures a very small owl. Another painting is a mask combining human and animal features.

"The bison-man looks to his left at a bison head on the body of a reindeer. A reindeer with a bison's head! In front of it on the same wall is a stag, with forelegs that resemble human limbs. Both drawings have strong sexual themes . . . Do you know about the Horned God that Abbé Breuil described in 1952?"

"Yes," replied de Palma, who had come across this very sexualised "God" in one of Christine Autran's articles. The drawing combined sexuality with animality.

"In the end," Palestro said, "psychoanalysts, psychiatrists and prehistorians occupy the same territory. All are confronted by the unconscious that Freud talked about, and faced with what makes us authentic human beings. It's frightening and fascinating."

# 46

The prison administration invariably notified people at the last minute. It was a habit for which there was no real explanation. Prisoners were moved, transferred or released with the minimum of publicity.

Christine was due to be released the following morning. The news caused quite a stir in the Marseille serious crime squad. And as news, good or bad, is invariably followed by more news, the police learned that the person standing bail for Christine was none other than Professor Palestro. De Palma wasn't too surprised. Communications between the police and the judiciary had been garbled for years.

Legendre put some special measures in place. Half the squad would keep tabs on Christine Autran and Palestro, never letting them out of their sight. The powers that be at the C.I.D. thought a trap was a brilliant idea, though it was hardly new. Neither de Palma nor Bessour thought it would work. How could Autran be that stupid? Never underestimate the enemy; you end up making mistakes.

De Palma and Bessour would take care of the tail from Rennes prison to Quinson, the next destination of prisoner number 91890. It wasn't Legendre's finest idea: the two detectives were known to the people they were following. But it was a good way of removing de Palma from wherever Thomas Autran might be. And in the meantime he could get in a hard day's work.

In the morning Bessour found the documents relating to Pierre Autran's death. He had fractured his spine and was killed instantaneously. According to his wife's testimony, he had wanted to change a light bulb without turning off the electricity. A mundane story. Bessour didn't believe it. To break the third vertebra, a strong blow to the nape of the neck was required. That would mean him falling against the edge of a table or piece of furniture.

"I think Palestro's right," de Palma said. "He did receive a blow to the back of the head."

"From someone bloody strong. You need brute force to fracture a vertebra, which rules out his wife . . ."

Bessour had ordered a vegetarian pizza and a Seven Up. He wolfed down a slice and offered one to de Palma, but Eva had prepared something more civilised. Watching Bessour, de Palma saw himself a few years earlier when his relationship was on the rocks and he couldn't tear himself away from an investigation.

"Why don't you go home, son? Pierre Autran died over thirty years ago. It can wait."

"There's no-one there," replied Karim, his mouth full. "Anyway, I prefer the company of dead men to the telly."

"Slippery slope!"

Karim opened his notebook and turned a few pages.

"According to the death certificate, Autran died at seven in the evening, but there's a problem."

"What's that?"

"Well, we're talking about a Tuesday and the dead man would have been working at the time the doctor certified his death."

"Meaning?"

"Autran was a civil engineer working for the Highways Agency. On 17 September 1970 at six in the evening he was attending the official opening of the final stretch of motorway between Marseille and Aix."

De Palma whistled in admiration. "How did you find that out?

Did you pray to the wizards of prehistory?"

"No, just the great spirit of Google. We knew the older Autran had done stuff in civil engineering. All we needed to do was consult the online archives."

"So to sum up, he couldn't have been on the motorway and at home at the same time. Unless he was into quantum physics."

"Don't go there. Let's just say it was Dr Caillol who certified the moment of death."

*

From time to time the gates of Rennes prison would open to admit a visitor. Bessour was able to guess without too much difficulty which ones were the lawyers, psychologists or magistrates.

"If someone had told me I'd be doing a stakeout here this close to retirement," de Palma grumbled, "I'd never have believed them."

"Me neither, I must admit," Bessour said.

"Yes, but you're not retired."

"I'd love a coffee."

De Palma was wearing shades, old jeans and trainers. He had slipped a cap into his jacket pocket in case they had to do the job on foot. Bessour had brought along two outfits.

Christine Autran's release was scheduled for ten o'clock in the morning. According to the sentencing judge, Pierre Palestro was due to come and fetch her by car. The professor was standing bail and acting as her moral guarantor. He had suggested taking his protégée directly down to Quinson. Christine had to pay her first visit to the *Gendarmerie* the following day as part of her bail conditions.

De Palma looked at the clock on the dashboard: it was five past ten.

"Do you have any idea where the good professor might be?"

"No, Michel. I've been searching high and low, but nothing doing. I reckon he's going to drop from the sky."

Suddenly, the prison door opened. Bessour trained his binoculars on the doorway where Christine appeared. She waved, presumably to someone behind her, and came outside. The door immediately closed behind her. She put down a small suitcase at her feet and waited for a few moments, arms hanging stiffly by her sides. An old Mercedes drew up with its headlights on. A man of about seventy got out, his shoulders hunched against the rain. He embraced Christine and put her luggage in the boot.

De Palma set off and drove to the end of the car park. Neither Christine nor Palestro had noticed the unmarked Vectra. They passed him and moved into the fast lane outside the prison. The policemen followed about two hundred metres behind until they reached the main road. Then they left a bigger gap between the cars, only catching them up every fifteen minutes or so.

Bessour rang Legendre and gave him a quick update. For the moment there was nothing very exciting to report. Palestro and Autran were heading for Paris.

At Quinson a rather more substantial operation had been organised. Two lieutenants from the squad would take it in turns to keep a round-the-clock watch on the comings and goings around *Empreintes* publishers. The company's phone lines had been tapped, as had Palestro's mobile. Legendre preferred to keep the plan secret to avoid a leak to the press about Christine Autran's release. He wanted to seal his success, ensuring promotion to the position of Controller General, with his own unit to manage.

De Palma switched on the radio and tried to find some music, but there were just rappers ranting about the filth and the toffs.

"People hate you when you're a cop," Bessour said. "Too often for my liking."

"Nothing new about that," de Palma replied, switching off the radio.

The rain was pouring down now. The Brittany countryside looked like England: chequered with bald hedges and drowning in grey. From time to time church towers rose up from dark, unmoving villages. Cattle stared, waiting for the rain to stop.

"Aren't you sleepy?" Bessour asked.

"Let's just say I'm used to it."

About thirty kilometres from Le Mans, Palestro and Autran stopped at a service station. De Palma took the opportunity to fill up with petrol and buy a sandwich. As he came out of the minimarket, Bessour caught sight of Christine standing in the rain in the picnic area, facing the woods that bordered the motorway.

"It's nine years since she's seen any trees," de Palma muttered. "She must find it strange."

He was moved by the thought. Palestro appeared with an umbrella and ushered her towards the restaurant. Bessour flung himself into the back of the Vectra and took a sandwich from a bag lying on the seat.

There was water everywhere. The wind had started to blow, forcing the rain on to the tarpaulins of the parked lorries.

"Let's turn on the radio," Bessour said. "I want to hear the forecast."

The forecast was incontrovertible: rain across the northern half of France, cloud everywhere else, with patches of sunshine on the south coast.

"This is really getting me down, Michel. Change the station."

He found a performance of Mahler's Fifth played by the Berlin Philharmonic. The sombre tones went well with the muddy light outside, he thought. Large electric eyes peered through sheets of rain and lorries raced along the motorway raising plumes of water.

"Alright let's have some classical then," Bessour said between mouthfuls. "Just so long as it's not opera!"

In less than twenty minutes Palestro and Christine Autran came out of the restaurant and headed swiftly for their car. De Palma took a bite from his second sandwich as he turned the key in the ignition. He went up the slip road in front of the Mercedes and tucked himself into the right-hand lane doing ninety. Palestro soon overtook him, driving much faster than before the service station. Something had happened. Their meal had been cut short for some reason. De Palma accelerated until he was just fifty metres behind them. A hundred and seventy, according to the speedometer.

"Do you reckon this professor fella has taken some lessons from our hoodie friends?" Bessour asked.

"I don't know, but it's a trick they use when they want to see if they're being followed. It's the sort of thing Christine would have picked up in the nick. What she doesn't know is I've been at this game for the last thirty years."

Suddenly the Mercedes slowed and moved into the right-hand lane, doing a hundred and ten. De Palma overtook one lorry, then another. He reduced speed. They had passed Le Mans. There was a sign for Chartres.

"They want to see if they're being followed," Bessour said. "That's clear enough."

"But why? In theory they've done nothing wrong."

"Porridge paranoia! She's spent ten years being spied on while she was inside. Those warders are like Dobermans."

"She can't believe she's free. She thinks someone must be watching her."

"Well, she's got a point, but it's not just that."

"Are you thinking about the brother?"

"Yes."

"Is she scared of him?"

"Of course she is."

Two hours passed. As they drove across the vast Beauce plains, the road became monotonous, the sleepy fields merging with the sky. From time to time a solitary tree threw its bare silhouette against the flat horizon. At nightfall they went through Gap, gateway to Haute Provence. Patches of dirty snow covered the pavements which were strewn with hailstones. Higher in the starry sky the ridges of Champsaur sparkled in the white moonlight.

They continued for another hour before they reached Quinson. Christine was going to live on an estate by the Marseille road. The surveillance team had moved into an empty flat on the other side. Lieutenants Martino and Fernandez were already in place.

"The Mercedes has just turned up," Martino said on his walkie-talkie.

"Roger," Bessour replied. "We'll go the back way and meet you."

The stakeout smelled of mould and cigarettes. Fernandez and Martino had chucked their sleeping bags over some airbeds. In the kitchen a plank resting on two trestles served as a table. An electric cafetière stood on top.

"I hope we're not going to be hanging round here for too long," Bessour moaned as he opened the door.

"I was never in favour of this," de Palma replied. "We've just gone all the way across France for nothing. Autran isn't stupid; he won't come here."

"What a pain in the arse!" Bessour said, pouring out two cups of coffee.

Martino was at the window, hiding behind a thick lace curtain. Some binoculars were lying on the sill.

"They've just closed the shutters."

"Fascinating!" de Palma said, shaking his hand.

"I reckon he's already taking her in every position and here's us lot playing gooseberry."

Bessour joined them.

"You think he's giving his nuts a bit of an airing?" Martino said, grabbing hold of the binoculars.

"After nine years in the nick that'll be something!" Bessour exclaimed, not wanting to be outdone.

The shutters suddenly opened. Palestro came out on to the little balcony and looked down the street for some time.

"They're not having a shag," Bessour said, "and they're keeping a lookout. They must be worried."

"Yeah, I think the professor's overdoing it a bit," Martino said. "Is he afraid of the police or what?"

"He's really afraid of Christine's brother," de Palma said. "He's the real danger."

"You think?"

"I'm almost sure. He'll take his time, but he's going to strike."

Bessour pulled a face and threw his coffee down the sink. "How can you say that?"

"In nine years Christine only wrote to her brother three times. It seems to me that speaks for itself. She wants to start a new life. She's still young and Palestro's loaded."

Martino looked anxious all of a sudden.

"A car's just stopped in front of the building. Looks like a blue Peugeot 307."

He lifted a corner of the curtain. "What the fuck is that bloke in the car up to?"

"Do you want me to go take a look?" Bessour said. "I can always play the passer-by."

"Do you want them to spot us?" Martino asked.

"An Arab in the dark? No-one'll guess I'm a cop."

"Alright then, off you go."

Bessour put on his jacket and went out. As he passed the building where Christine lived, the car moved away, disappearing along the road towards Marseille.

"That's weird," de Palma said. "Is there an entrance at the back?"

"No," Martino said.

"Any windows?"

"The lowest ones are over two metres high. It'd be difficult to get in that way. Also Autran's flat doesn't look out on the back."

The Baron glanced at his watch. "It's eleven o'clock. We're going to have to shift it. It's two hours back to Marseille."

Martino put down the binoculars and rubbed his eyes.

"How much longer are we going to be in this shithole?"

"I don't know," de Palma said. "The boss seems to think it's a good idea. We just have to go along with it. Two colleagues are coming to relieve you late tomorrow afternoon."

"I shouldn't have told Legendre that Autran might come and see his sister," de Palma went on. "Ever since, he's been obsessed with setting a trap for him."

Bessour came back, his face red from the cold. "I think the bloke in the car spotted me."

"Did you see his face?" Martino asked.

"Hard to say. Fortyish, maybe? He had a woolly hat pulled down over his ears."

"Did you get the number plate?"

"937, X-ray, Papa, 13."

Martino called a colleague from the northern unit. The answer came back in less than five minutes

"The vehicle was stolen last month."

# 47

Delphine was in tears. The day before, she had rung the central police station in Saint-Germain-en-Laye. The pictures of Thomas Autran in the press and on T.V. had done the trick.

De Palma went to see her immediately. "Thomas is a very dangerous man," he said, taking her hand. "Trust me."

"I find it hard to believe. He's so sweet and considerate. At the same time I have to face facts. What you say is probably true. He could be weird sometimes. I should have been more careful. Though it's hard to accept he's a bad person."

"Bad isn't the right word for it. It doesn't mean anything when you're at the stage he's at. He's seriously ill."

De Palma looked through the window. Out in the Jardin des Plantes, men were jogging in the cold. He made a mental note of all the faces he could see, then turned back to Delphine.

"We're going to think things through," he said. "Let's go over each of your conversations with him, starting with the most recent. When did you last see him?"

"Three days ago, before I went to the museum. He spent the night here."

"What did he say?"

"Not much. It's hard to remember. We talked about this and that and then I told him about my Ph.D. He gave me some tips on Neanderthal art."

"Neanderthal art?"

"Yes, he thinks those hominids weren't as primitive as people believe and says their art was quite sophisticated. He believes some of the pieces attributed to Homo Sapiens could in fact be Neanderthal."

De Palma thought for a few seconds. He had never read anything about Neanderthal art in Christine Autran's work, or that of her colleagues. No connection with Le Guen's cave, he decided. He shelved the idea for the time being.

"How long has he been coming here?"

"I never know when he's going to turn up. He hardly ever goes out. He's really helped me with my Ph.D. That's why I find it difficult to understand . . ."

"Tell me how you met."

She took a deep breath. "He dropped in at the bookshop and we had a chat."

"What about?"

"Mainly about pre-history. And Neanderthal man."

"Anything else?"

Delphine shook her head.

"And that first evening?"

"He came here because it was raining like today and the bar was crowded. We talked and then all of a sudden he felt faint. His mood changed and he left."

"Do you know why?"

"No, not really."

"What were you talking about at that point?"

"The same stuff. I told him Neanderthal man was a bit like Homo Sapiens' twin brother. I remember he repeated that phrase several times."

De Palma nodded, but couldn't see any connection.

"What day did he come back?"

"Hang on a minute," she said, standing up. "I've got a note of that as I'd asked for the day off."

She flicked feverishly through her diary, her long slender fingers moving from page to page.

"That's right. It was the 21st, Saturday. He arrived on the midday train. I went to collect him from the station and we went to the forest at Fontainebleau."

"Fontainebleau?"

She blushed and looked away.

"So what did you talk about that day?"

"We took shelter. There were some sculptures in the rock and . . ."

"What did he say to you?"

"I . . . it's difficult."

"I understand."

"We . . . we made love."

"And then?"

"Nothing special, we just came home. He gave me this flint. It's a Neanderthal one. Very rare. I was really touched."

De Palma raised the curtain and gazed out of the window for a long time. The street was veiled in sheets of rain, driven by the wind against the neat facades.

"He told me about a cave he knew in Provence," Delphine said suddenly.

"Did he give you the name?"

"No," she said. "He just promised he'd take me to see it."

"You must try. Did he describe a place by the sea, or near a mountain?"

"No, not by the sea. More inland."

"Which mountain?"

"He told me it looked like a large beak and the view from the summit spread right across the ancient world."

The mountain overlooking Quinson, with its overhanging spur, had the rough shape of an eagle's beak.

"Did he tell you anything else?"

"No."

She dried her blotchy red eyes.

"What are we going to do now?" Delphine asked.

De Palma was taking away the man she loved, but at the same time opening her eyes to the enormity of what might have happened.

"To tell the truth, I don't know," the Baron replied.

"That's terrible!"

"I know, but that's how it is. Do you have anywhere safe where you can hide? I mean somewhere he doesn't know about.

She thought for a while. "Only my mother's place."

"Is it far from here?"

"No, it's on the other side of Paris, in the eastern suburbs. Nogent-sur-Marne. There's a direct train from here."

"O.K., get your things we're leaving."

"But what if he comes here?"

"He won't, Delphine."

"How can you be so sure?"

"Let's just say I've finally realised he has a sixth sense about danger."

Delphine stuffed some of her belongings into a holdall. The journey to Nogent-sur-Marne only took an hour. De Palma informed Legendre, who rushed two men over to keep watch on her parents' house.

Then he took the evening train back to Marseille.

*

The next morning a phone call from Martino left the Baron with little chance to linger. There was just time to give Eva a kiss and have a shower before he went off to Quinson with Bessour.

"Palestro left the flat early yesterday afternoon," Martino said. "He got into his Mercedes and drove off towards the centre of this fucking village. Then he went home."

"Is that why you brought us here?"

"No. Christine didn't show up yesterday."

"Now that's something!" Bessour said, closing the door to the flat.

Inside the stakeout Martino had closed the living room shutters and stationed himself by the kitchen window.

"I'm starving," he said.

"To tell the truth so am I."

"There's a pizza place down the road, shall I go out and get us something?"

De Palma eyeballed Martino. "I reckon you look even more like a cop than me. Karim can go."

"Facial discrimination, bruv, facial discrimination," Bessour quipped.

"Get on with it," de Palma said. "And fetch us three bottles of wine. I think we're going to need them."

He joined Martino at the window. A delivery lorry had parked in front of the building. In the right-hand lane a long queue of cars had formed, the roofs loaded with skis.

"Some people have all the luck," Martino muttered.

"I hate skiing," de Palma said.

Martino offered the Baron a cigarette. He had rolled up his shirt-sleeves to reveal a crude tattoo, showing the insignia of the 2nd parachute regiment.

"How long were you in the Paras for?"

"Six years."

"Do you miss it?"

"No way. I left after Africa. Couldn't stand it any more."

A sad expression came over the policeman's face. He screwed up his eyes and drew on his cigarette.

"The lorry's off," he grumbled. "That's exciting."

Bessour came back with an armful of pizza boxes. "King size deluxe all round."

He put his haul on the table and produced three bottles of Bordeaux. De Palma took out his Swiss army knife and opened the first one.

"I'll have a coke," Bessour said, refusing the glass that Martino handed him.

"Is that your religion?"

"No. Just want to stay sober."

De Palma had already downed a glass of wine and taken a bite of pizza. The alcohol made him shiver. He noticed a child's drawing on the living room wallpaper. A police car, with a blue bonnet, white doors and a large light on the roof. He was touched by the naïve depiction.

Bessour filled the Baron's glass.

"Thanks, son." He looked at his watch, "One o'clock! This is starting to drag."

The Baron had finished his meal and threw the remains into a rubbish bag. "I'll call Palestro. He must be at his place now."

The phone rang about twelve times before Palestro finally picked up.

"I saw Christine yesterday morning. She had to go and report to the *Gendarmerie*."

"Any news since?"

"No. She should call me. I'm seeing her tonight."

The Baron had a sinking feeling. He hung up. "Let's go."

"You might fuck everything up," Martino said.

"I don't give a shit. Something's wrong. I can feel it in my bones. Karim, you come with me. Martino, you keep watch. Got it?"

"Loud and clear."

De Palma and Bessour raced across the road. The door to the building was shut. There was no concierge.

"Shit," the Baron said. "Stand back.

He gave a kick just below the lock. The door flew open.

They went up to Christine's flat.

De Palma tried the handle. The door gave way. Bessour drew his gun. Ahead of them was a corridor. To the right was the kitchen. A bottle of orange juice stood on the table.

De Palma opened the door on the left. "This is the bedroom."

The bed was unmade, with no sheets. The flat smelled damp. Shafts of sunlight filtered through the metal shutters.

De Palma switched on the light and went through to what must have been the living room. The door was closed.

"Careful," Bessour said. "I've got a bad feeling."

"Why?"

"You don't shut the living room door before going out shopping."

The Baron took out his Bodyguard and cocked the weapon. Bessour looked panic-stricken.

"What the . . . ?"

"Not now. Just give me cover."

The Baron took up a position by the wall and slowly turned the handle. The door squeaked. Bessour took aim through the doorway. His face fell.

"Shit, Michel."

He took three steps backward and put his hand over his mouth to stop himself from vomiting.

For a few seconds de Palma turned his face away from the nightmarish scene in front of him.

Christine Autran was lying on the bed, her throat slit.

De Palma suppressed his disgust and slowly went up to her. The acrid smell of haemoglobin had spread through the room. The walls were streaked with blood that had coagulated but not yet turned black. Death must have occurred several hours earlier at the most. Martino hadn't seen anything coming and he was one of the force's best detectives.

The Baron leaned over Christine's body. "Will you ever let me know your secret?"

He would have liked to close her eyes and cover her gaping throat. No longer hear that voiceless cry from within his gut. Just one thing was missing from the barbaric scene. One little detail: Thomas Autran's signature.

*

The autopsy provided no further information. Nothing at all to give the forensics experts a lead.

"He's changed his M.O.," Legendre said. "That's all."

"It's not the how, it's the why that bothers me."

"Why?" the murder squad boss grumbled. "Because he's nuts."

"There's always a logic to the way nutters act. He's just killed his sister, his own twin sister. You could say he's killed a part of himself. I don't get any of it, I must admit."

"Maybe he wants to destroy himself," Bessour countered. "He's taking any remaining attachments with him to the grave. He wants to put an end to his life as it no longer has any meaning."

"Well said," de Palma concluded. "There's only one place his life can end and that's at Le Guen's cave."

*

"Tell me a story!"

"Which one do you want?"

"The one about the sacred cave."

"Not again! You always ask for that."

"That's because I had a dream last night."

"You dreamed about the cave?"

"Yes, and I was really scared."

"Why?"

"There was loads of water. It was all flooded. The big paintings and the hands all disappeared."

Papa suddenly looked sad. "What you dreamed really happened."

"Tell me."

"More than ten thousand years ago the ice covering the earth melted. The sea kept rising and rising. It rose so much it flooded the plains near the coast, swallowing up the caves and the great hunters' shelters."

"It all disappeared?"

"No, not everything. I know a cave where everything stayed just the same."

"You've got to take me."

"When you're bigger. It's very dangerous. Now go to sleep."

But during the night the water kept on rising and rising. It was so high he thought he was going to drown. He thrashed about. Water everywhere. No-one could stop it. Not even Papa.

The policeman held the photocopied form ordered by the Judge: a certificate sectioning him on the grounds of imminent danger. It was very unusual for a child. Dr Caillol had noted down the psychotic episodes and drawn up the certificate.

*This patient requires care as a result of a mental disorder endangering the safety of persons and/or posing a serious threat to public order.*

The second document was signed by the local mayor. Maman had secured this one.

*Thomas Autran is afflicted by an illness rendering him a danger to himself and to others . . . His condition requires immediate hospitalisation . . .*

The doctor at the hospital had said, "We're going to try some E.C.T. It will do him good." Though he himself knew the current travels through the head down other wires, showing the world in its most sordid light. You're nothing but an alimentary canal. Food and shit.

He searched for Papa in the fog. Everything was hazy. He could see the grey faces of the nurses and hear Caillol's voice.

The man with the antler head had told him that Papa had gone to join the world of the spirits. The current in his head stopped him from seeing the invisible. It silenced the voices. Without Papa's voice, life was meaningless.

# 48

The first vision hit him. A flash of lightning, followed by silence. Strange geometric shapes. Long broken lines and spirals. A man covered in scratches. Then shadows once again and the total darkness of the sanctuary.

Thomas hadn't eaten for more than ten days. His strength was gone. The cold, damp air slithered over his skin without penetrating it. Nothing could get inside him any more. The visions only came after much suffering.

He could see the kitchen in the rue de Bruyères. The bulb on the ceiling had gone. His father was standing on a stool and Christine was in the dining room. They had a guest that night. Maman was sitting next to Dr Caillol.

The stool wasn't high enough. Papa stood up on the table, his legs shaking while he tried to balance, as if he was drunk.

The doctor must have told one of those jokes he was so fond of. Maman burst out laughing. There was a clinking of glasses and a tinkling of knives and forks. Thomas didn't like the sound. It reminded him of hospital instruments.

Papa gave a small cry. He must have received an electric shock. His legs wobbled. His arms beat the air, but it was no use.

Thomas shouted. A moan, that tore through the silence and bounced off the walls of the vast cave. He opened his eyes. There was nothing but the dark. A darkness so deep it was known to no-one. The visions wouldn't come, only memories.

Christine was in a corner of the kitchen. Biting her hand because she was so scared. Dr Caillol was bending over Papa, Maman looking over his shoulder. The doctor made some strange movements; Papa's head went back and forth between his large hands like a balloon. The vertebrae cracked.

Caillol turned and said, "That's it."

Maman didn't cry. She bent down too and put her hand on the doctor's shoulder. They looked at one another. Caillol spoke in a whisper, but Thomas could hear.

"It's what you wanted."

Christine cried. She always understood things more quickly than Thomas. Her face slowly contorted with pain. Maman made a phone call. She said there had been an accident. They must come quickly. Her husband was lying on the floor.

A few minutes later a blue light turned into the street. It was the light he had seen at the hospital. Thomas had to get away. He went down to the bottom of the garden to hide. As he walked along the corridor he took the man with the antler head from its nice display case.

He clutched it close to him and said, "Papa, do you think I'll get better?"

"Yes, son, with willpower you can overcome anything."

"Except death!" Thomas shouted.

Dr Caillol was in the garden. He went straight to Thomas's hiding place.

"There's no need to hide. You're a big boy now."

Thomas hid the man with the antler head under some dead leaves, where no-one would find it.

"Come on, you're a big boy now."

He was, but childhood never goes away. Dr Caillol didn't know that.

The blue light in the street had gone. There was only darkness.

\*

Thomas searched in his head for a vision. Everything was muddled. The man with the antler head should have been there. Christine and he had put it in the sanctuary before they were arrested and sent to prison. Behind the big stalagmite. But he couldn't find it. Someone had taken it.

Would Christine come?

An image appeared. A face he knew: Hélène Weill, Dr Caillol's patient. She wore that smile that sad people have. She suffered from depression. She must be freed, the doctor had said.

It was night. The stone axe struck several times. Hélène had no time to cry out.

A second image: Julia Chevallier. She was also very depressed. She no longer saw Caillol, but went to her local priest instead. First Man struck her down in her sleep. She had no time to cry out either.

Thomas needed some light. The diving torch was in the other chamber. He couldn't find it in the dark. It was impossible.

*"With willpower you can overcome anything."*

He crawled in one direction and banged against the rock face. He wanted to stand but his legs could no longer support him. The stone was cold and clammy. His feet slipped. He lay down, defeated.

A third image: Lucy walking, with her vacant eyes wide open. Wearing an ugly sky-blue dressing gown and padded mule slippers. No longer a woman, but a robot fed by chemicals that polluted every cell in her body. The machine had to be broken to free the soul within. Dismantled to the core, taking the vital organs apart piece by piece. For the spirit never dies.

"I've liberated them all. Every one of them."

# 49

"Once you're inside, let yourself go, O.K.?"

De Palma nodded. His wetsuit hood squashed his cheeks. He was in a hurry to be in the water. Captain Franchi of the police diving section was a big burly man who inspired confidence.

"You've got one bloke in front of you," Franchi said, "and another behind. There's no risk. None at all. Sure you're O.K.?"

"Yep," the Baron replied in a small voice.

Franchi toppled into the water first. In less than five minutes the three divers were dark silhouettes against the wall, with its covering of soft corals, sponges and sea anemones. At regular intervals de Palma released long streams of oxygen bubbles, which raced up towards the silvery surface.

Thirty-eight metres down the seabed was covered in sediment. The drop-off came to a sudden halt, slicing through a heap of fallen stones and recently dislodged concrete blocks.

Captain Franchi undid the padlock, pulled back the gate to the cave and left it open. His movements were slow, punctuated every five seconds by the breathing from his regulator.

The entrance was barely a metre wide. It was like a menacing hollow eye, peering through the murky water. Charles Le Guen, the diver who discovered the cave, had described it as a noxious hole; there was little doubt about that.

De Palma paused for a few seconds. A shiver ran down his spine.

The primal fear of a man who knows he is at the mercy of his surroundings.

Franchi went first, de Palma following two metres behind. Twice, his cylinders scraped against the rock. With each breath the sharp sound of the regulator hurt his eardrums. The divers made a first decompression stop before they reached a bottleneck. De Palma closed his eyes and clenched his fists. The passage narrowed into a bend barely wider than his shoulders and then suddenly rose back up again. He had to twist his body to remove the cylinders and place them in front of him, while keeping the regulator firmly between his frozen lips and his teeth clenched over the nozzle.

Franchi had passed the obstruction and was now out of sight. De Palma could feel the breath of the sea coming through the cavities in the rock. He moved forward using his elbows until he found himself virtually upright in the sump. He was hindered by his flippers, his belly brushed against the pebbles, and his lead belt caught on some snags. He had to retreat a few centimetres and try again. Behind him the other police diver was watching his every movement.

A little further on there was a huge cave that was completely flooded. Some stalagmites had been stranded by the returning sea. At the back the black hole led directly into another chamber, in the open air. The Baron used his fins to save breath. Soon he would be out of this tunnel. The second passage was a narrower, shorter one. After a few minutes a mirror appeared on the surface, which rippled each time a drop of water fell from an invisible roof.

Franchi was already at the surface. De Palma emerged beside him, and took off his mask and his regulator. The air was saturated with cold and damp. It had a bitter taste of camomile. He breathed deeply, happy to find himself in the open air once more. The captain put his waterproof container on the small stone slab, then hoisted himself up on the ledge and sat down. De Palma joined him there. They took off their flippers and removed the heavy cylinders, their legs still painful from all the crawling through the passage.

On the left, a maze of wet rocks sank away deep into the darkness. De Palma shone his torch to the right and ran it slowly over the tapering concretions. As the light swept back and forth, a scene of webbed rock unfurled before him to disappear immediately again into the shadows. He knew it all. A few metres away there was a handprint, symbolic of time immemorial. Then another hand and another, all stencilled on the stone lacework. Some had fingers missing; other smaller ones were barely visible.

Captain Franchi looked at his watch. Time was precious. He asked his colleagues on the surface to illuminate the cave.

"The others shouldn't be long now," he said.

"They're in the flooded chamber," the second diver said, pointing at two white beams that had just appeared in the dark water. "I can see Madame Barton and her assistant."

Had there not been a break in the slope, only about thirty metres would separate them from the open air. But that was in an ideal world: the sort of assumptions made by scientists and policemen; the stuff of fantasy. The channel might equally well plunge down into the depths again.

"Can we go?" de Palma asked.

"Soon," Franchi replied. "We'll send two scouts ahead first."

The police divers checked their weapons and went down into the dark water of the chasm. During the first expedition Pauline Barton's assistant had swum back up to ten metres below the surface. He hadn't gone any further and had left a guideline. The divers followed this and paused where the line stopped. It was time to make a radio call. The voice only reached the surface with difficulty, a robotic tone interrupted by static and the whistling of the regulator.

"Receiving you, that's three out of five now. Over."

"We're at the end of the line. It's getting narrower."

"Alright, carry on," Franchi said. I'll send two men as backup. Over."

"O.K. I'm entering the last stretch of the tunnel. If all goes well I should be out in less than ten minutes. Over and out."

As they stared at the radio, the anxiety on their faces was palpable. De Palma was dying for a cigarette. Pauline bit her nails, looking tense. Two divers jumped in the water and joined their colleagues in less than ten minutes.

"All fine," the radio sputtered. "We're going up."

Pauline needed some space. She stood up and took a walk round the cave. De Palma went over to her.

"Don't worry, it'll be alright."

Her nerves were shot. She was about to say something when once again the radio broke the silence.

"The team leader's reached the surface. Over."

"Franchi here. Is the air O.K.?"

"Yes, we're in a large chamber. Bigger than the one where you are."

"Alright, stick together and don't budge. I'll send a third group along with de Palma."

The Baron got ready and followed the two divers into the water. The fear that had overcome him in the first passage had now almost vanished. He felt relaxed. On his way down he caught sight of the drawings Pauline Barton had spoken about. At the bottom of the cave he filled his lungs with oxygen and slowly moved towards the mouth of the passage, his weapon case in his outstretched arms. If everything went to plan he wouldn't need a decompression stop; there had been too little time under water. He moved faster. The passage started to narrow. Twice he banged his head against the roof. Beyond the sump the rock sloped upwards. Rays of light reflected on a grey surface. Fresh air!

"This way, Michel."

He landed on a flat surface. The police divers surrounded him.

"Did you hear anything?"

"No, nothing."

The Baron removed the heavy diving gear and took out his weapon from its waterproof container.

"A killer could have come this way before us," he said. "It's possible he's out there, somewhere in the cave. He could be watching us at this very moment. It's true he's dangerous, but we need to take him alive."

"O.K., boss."

De Palma switched on his torch and shone it inside the chamber. It was much higher and wider than the one he had come from. To the left of some concretions a passage receded into the darkness. Water oozed from a large cleft in the roof.

"I'll go first," the Baron said. "Let's try to make as little noise as possible. I'll go about ten metres ahead and then you can join me. When I switch off my torch, you do the same. Got it?"

"O.K., understood."

Just past an indentation in the rock there was a fairly large second chamber. De Palma took some time to adjust to the dark and overcome his first pangs of anxiety. A large limestone slab sloped away towards the passage. Patches of red earth had accumulated in the uneven rock.

Bent double beneath a slanting roof, de Palma advanced step by step. After about thirty metres a huge pool of water on the right reflected in the torchlight. The ground was stony; there was no visible trace of footsteps. An icy draught hit the Baron as he reached the end of the passage.

He sat down in the dark and switched off his torch. The lights from the divers who had remained behind in the first chamber still cast a white glow over the cave walls. He listened for a long time to the sounds from the sinkhole until each of them became perfectly clear. Then he switched on his torch and ran it over the rusty rock faces. The shadows seemed to flee before the beam, coming to life in the dark then appearing again in some unexpected corner.

He saw the first sign on a bump formed by the concretions: two black diagonal lines. Further along, on the wall itself, there was a second drawing depicting what some pre-historians have described as female sexual symbols. Outlines of fingers covered another wall. The charcoal lines and scratches were covered in concretions, a sign of their authenticity.

The Baron shone his torch towards a well. There were some recent footmarks on the muddy ground. He went closer, taking care not to tread on them. The air smelled of wet rock and saltpetre. The well must have been little over two metres deep. On the ground were some clearer footprints.

He made a call on the radio and waited for the police divers.

"He jumped here."

"Are you thinking of going down?"

"Yes. Keep three metres behind."

He went to the bottom and stopped for a moment. Two narrower passages led off in different directions. He inspected the ground and the rock faces carefully. Inside the right-hand passage fine scratches were just visible. He went in. It was pitch dark. The only sound was the heavy drops falling from the roof of the large chamber.

De Palma stopped several times. He felt short of air. There was a bitter taste in his mouth. Had the temperature risen or was it simply anxiety? He was sweating profusely. After about thirty metres the passage veered off to the right. The sound of the drops ceased. There was total silence. De Palma's breathing filled the space. He held his breath and strained to listen. The silence was so complete he felt quite dizzy. He stayed still to give himself time to adjust.

Two divers arrived, covered in mud and making a lot of noise. De Palma decided not to wait.

The passage went down steeply. The slabs were slippery. Once again he heard the slow rhythm of drops of water falling on the ground.

At the end of the passage another huge chamber opened up like a predator's mouth. In the beam of the torchlight, he saw a stencilled hand drawn on a pure white stalagmite. It was a right hand, with the tip of the thumb and middle finger missing. Two other hands, fully formed, had been drawn on a flat piece of the wall, each covered in a thin, transparent layer of concretions.

There was an outline of a bison with the head in three-quarter profile; the rest of the body unfinished. Further on a lion, with several lines through its body.

Suddenly there was a strange, low sound, apparently coming from beneath the ground. The Baron switched off his torch and listened. A distant hissing; a wail. He froze. Someone was moaning: the sound rising, then falling, in waves.

It took him a while to locate the source of the sound: a narrow opening in the rock face that ended in a tight gully. The only way was to drag himself forward flat on his stomach. Using his elbows de Palma crawled to within a metre of the end of the passage. The moaning hadn't stopped. He cocked his revolver, switched off his headlamp and hurtled into the chamber.

A man with dishevelled hair was sitting leaning back against a rock. He was naked from the waist up, his chin down, his eyes dead. There were white stripes across his chest. A pendant like a shell hung from his neck. He was holding something in his right hand. The left one was hidden behind his back.

"Autran?"

The only reply was a low groan. De Palma didn't dare approach the figure. He kept his weapon trained on him.

"Who are you?"

The man struggled to raise his head. His eyes glared in the white light of the Baron's torch.

"Thomas Autran!"

De Palma recoiled. Autran's cheeks were mere hollows; his eyes shone brightly, deep in their sockets. A trickle of saliva foamed at the corner of his lips.

"So we've come full circle, Monsieur de Palma." Autran's voice was barely audible.

The Baron shuddered. His stomach tightened.

"We're going to get you out of here."

Another long moan.

"No," Autran said at last. "This is the end. Time no longer creeps along the rocks. I'm on the threshold of a new life."

"Did you find the man with the antler head?" the Baron asked.

Autran shook his head slowly, as though every movement required more energy than he could summon.

"He's the one who knows the world behind these rocks. Who can see what is invisible. "

De Palma took time to find his words.

"Thomas, who stole the man with the antler head from you?"

Autran's head dropped again. His tousled hair formed pointed horns on his skull.

"I'd hidden it here, but someone came. It doesn't matter any more."

There was a faint movement at the other end of the passage, then a soft sound of breathing. The police divers had just entered the chamber.

"What do you mean 'someone'?"

"It doesn't matter. It's too late."

Autran's chest rose. His breathing quickened then became constricted.

"The first time they hosed me down with water. That's how they wash them, the patients. They wore aprons and white boots like in abattoirs."

Autran tried to catch his breath. "I've been through dark lands. I . . ."

His mouth was horribly contorted and muscles bulged beneath his skin. Slowly he brought his hand out from behind his back.

"This is the sign."

His breathing was becoming more and more laboured.

"This is the sign."

Then a long silence. De Palma waited. Autran must have taken poison. There was nothing he could do to save him.

"Death is like a Mercedes," he whispered. "A big car going back up the lane. Maman's at the wheel. She's left me to my fate. In the nut house."

Autran sat up straight, his eyes already rolling up. "And then she went for Papa, bringing death in her wake. It's been a long journey."

Thomas stared at his mutilated hand. There were only two fingers left.

"Christine will come," he said. "It's our last meeting. She'll come and then we'll go for a long walk. She's wearing Papa's hat that's too big for her. She's put on her trousers and her boots and we'll walk. Nothing can stop us. Evil's behind us, we're walking towards the light."

Autran coughed. A trickle of blood ran from his nose.

"There's a large stag over by the rock that looks like a wolf's head. I've never seen such large antlers. The stag is a god. It's full of strength and grace. It's waiting for us. Christine must come."

He dropped his arm. His hand was lifeless.

"Christine isn't coming," de Palma whispered, "You know that."

Autran seized the Baron's arm and gripped it with all his might. "What are you saying?"

"Christine's dead, Thomas. Remember?"

Autran started to shake, "Christine . . . Where is she?"

"She's dead. DEAD."

Autran put his hand to his stomach, then he fell on his side, spitting out blood.

"Help!" de Palma shouted.

Three men appeared.

"No!" Autran shouted. "No!"

He struggled for breath. "For nine years I've waited to see my sister. Nine years behind bars, staring at the gloom. Nine years with that scream inside that tears you apart morning, noon and night, and only stops when you go to sleep. Could you live without your other half? Tell me that. Could you breathe normally in a prison where every creak, every squeak, every cry, vanishes into thin air? Could you bear all the emptiness without the woman who means more than anything to you?

Autran's fingers scrabbled in the mud. "All the time you think of her eyes, her smile, her drawling voice. Her little hands that can do anything. She was the one who used to tie my shoelaces. I could never do that myself. Christine taught me everything I know. You don't learn anything in those mental hospitals. There's just a void like prison. It's where they dump you to keep you apart from the rest of society. If you're mad they take away everything that makes you what you are. They siphon it off through drugs or solitary. I remember Caillol's pills and electrodes. I'd never have been evil without them. I'd never have been the angel of death, but I was on the edge, my head was spinning. I killed so I'd stop hearing the doctor's voices."

Autran was racked by increasingly violent convulsions. His legs beat against the rock.

"Why did you kill your sister? Tell me."

De Palma leaned over the face with its rolled-up eyes. Autran's lips were moving. His voice was just a breath now.

"What myth do you live by?"

"I don't know," de Palma replied. "I don't know any longer."

Autran's head slumped.

"Out of the way, Commandant," Franchi ordered.

De Palma stepped back.

"His heart's about to go."

For three minutes the policemen took turns trying to bring him back to life – this man who was death personified. Cardiac massage achieved nothing. Autran had taken a very toxic poison. At 5.43 p.m. his heart stopped.

"We did everything we could, Michel."

"I know."

De Palma crouched beside the body. The eyes were still clear, staring up at the dark ceiling. Autran's head was thrown back, his features frozen in intense pain.

"You nearly killed me," de Palma whispered. "A long time ago. I thought about it for weeks. I thought I could kill you and if I didn't, then one of the other men here would. Your death would be just a small chapter in the long fight against notorious killers, if it hadn't happened at the end of this long journey. Are you going to tell me your last secret? Come on, tell me."

Autran's muscles relaxed. His face softened and his mouth stopped trying to cry out. His hands turned, as though begging for mercy. Dark blood ran from his mouth, as though draining an excess of life. Autran's torso bore some old scars, stripes that had cut into his skin.

"Listen," one of the divers whispered.

A strange dirge rose, a wild litany of blurred vowels. The voice of the angel of the Apocalypse.

"Look!"

A huge shadow danced in the topaz light. As it moved it stretched out the large deformed body over the concretions and sent it lurching across the rusty walls. One by one the harsh syllables of the incantation bounced off the fragments of rock, making the prehistoric sanctuary judder.

"It's just a hallucination," de Palma shouted. "That's all it is."

The shape vanished. Everything was calm once more. Autran's hand opened. Inside was a finger: the ring finger.

"The third one was him."

Over the corpse was a drawing of a strange creature: half-man, half-beast. A Horned Sorcerer. A long charcoal line pierced him through.

Dr Dubreuil was in the library at Ville-Évrard psychiatric hospital.

## 50

Dr Dubreuil was in the library at Ville-Évrard psychiatric hospital. His stubby fingers flicked through the yellowed forms in one of the large filing cabinet drawers.

"Bernard had a terrible fit after you left," he said without looking at de Palma. "He smashed everything up. We had to sedate him."

"Do you know what caused it?"

"I think it had something to do with your visit, and Autran's. But there was another reason too."

"What was that?"

"I can't tell you, unfortunately."

He pushed shut the drawer and went over to the bookshelves where psychiatric classics slumbered alongside lesser tomes.

"I want to show you a couple of things, Monsieur de Palma, so you'll understand better."

He took some old books from the top shelf. "These are two of Dr Caillol's lectures which we found amongst the rest of the stuff. He spent hours on them."

Dubreuil put the books on a table and offered de Palma a chair.

"And this is Kerner's *Magikon*," he said, slamming down his hand on the leather cover. "Here are some collected articles on Gassner, the exorcist who achieved great therapeutic success in his time. And here is one by Mesmer, whose discoveries have been compared to those of Christopher Colombus. We're talking about the eighteenth century. I'm showing you works by some of the founding fathers of dynamic psychiatry. Gassner and Mesmer did a lot of experiments in their time. They were seen as great therapists and people came from all over Europe to be treated by them. I'm giving you their names to show that Caillol broke completely with the psychiatric mainstream. By returning to the past, and the earliest forms of treatment, he was looking for something else. He was trying to grasp why magnetism and shamanism had been effective in their time. Caillol was very well read, but he was mad: as mad as the patients he treated."

"What do you mean?"

"Just that he himself was a patient at Ville-Évrard."

"How did you find that out? Did he tell you?"

"No, not at all. One day when he was here we had a conversation and then he went off to the lavatory leaving one of those bloody patients' forms on the table. Curiosity got the better of me and I had a look. Imagine my surprise when I found out it was his!"

"Can I see it?"

"I'm afraid not. It's disappeared."

"I must admit, I'm a bit lost."

"I can see why."

Dubreuil stared at de Palma, just as he no doubt did with those strange patients of his.

"You should know that Caillol treated himself. He was a schizophrenic, but quite aware of his condition. He was in B Block on several occasions."

"B Block?"

"Yes, that was the place where, in Caillol's time – I'm talking of the fifties now – they locked you up for ever. It was the ward for acute patients. The playwright Antonin Artaud also had several spells there."

"Is it possible he recovered?"

"Oh yes, I think he feigned madness to be as close to her as possible."

"How do you mean?"

"This is where Caillol's reading comes in. What witchcraft did he practise? I can't answer that. But one day he said to me: 'I think I've found a way of doing without anti-psychotics.' When you know the side effects of those drugs, you can't help being interested in Caillol's findings."

"Did he share his secrets with you?"

Dubreuil looked downcast. "No, of course not."

A man of about forty entered the room. He had greasy, unkempt hair and a beard. He wore rubber boots and a camera was slung across his body.

"Have you come to do your research?" Dubreuil asked.

"Yes, the Science Research Council rang me again this morning."

"But the library's about to close. Could you come back tomorrow?"

"Of course. I don't live far away."

The man turned and disappeared.

"He's been with us for three months now. His family had him admitted. He's a danger to himself and to others."

De Palma shivered. This was a part of human nature he had always refused to confront.

"Was Caillol like that?"

"I don't really know if he was dangerous. I do know he managed to pursue his studies to the highest level. So his mental state didn't disrupt his life that much. But he was sectioned here."

"Do you remember the dates?"

"No, I'm sorry. It was some time in the fifties. He was quite young and still a student at the time. It should all be in the police archives."

"When did you meet Dr Caillol?"

"It was here. Probably the eighties."

"What was he doing?"

"He didn't have any patients apart from Thomas Autran, though he didn't come here because of him. He was looking through our archives. We've got thousands of files on all the patients who have passed through here. Some of them are quite famous. Caillol claimed he was planning to make a systematic study that linked epidemiology and history. Looking at pathologies to see how they had developed according to the treatments used in this hospital at different periods. I have to say it wasn't such a bad idea. Understanding how the treatment of mental illness has evolved is something that hasn't ever really been done."

"But what exactly was he looking for?"

"He did tell me once. He wanted to write a revisionist history of the discovery of the unconscious – from the earliest times up to the present day. You can imagine what that involves."

"What did he mean by the earliest times?"

"He was thinking about prehistory, of course. For him, cave painting represented one of the first attempts to depict mental images. An illustration of what was going on in early man's unconscious."

"Was he the only person to study that?"

"I don't know. I assume so, but I can't be sure. I've always thought Thomas was helping him, but I can't be certain about that either."

De Palma thought of the diver who had got away. He believed he was close to Caillol, but did not really know why. Or could it be a rival? An idea came to him.

"Could I take a look at those files myself?"

Dubreuil suddenly turned serious, his expression becoming hostile.

"No. They're strictly confidential – doctors only. Medical confidentiality, as I'm sure you know . . ."

De Palma decided to work around the problem. "I just want to know if any of Caillol's friends or family was an inpatient here. If I give you the person's name, would you be able to confirm or deny it?"

Dubreuil relented. "I'd be happy to do that for you. What's the name?"

"Combes. Martine Combes. She was born in Marseille in 1938."

The Baron realised that he was venturing onto unknown territory, but he had to break the impasse in the investigation.

"Hold on. I'll let you know in a few minutes."

Dubreuil disappeared behind a door with a sign that read: "Medical Staff Only". The researcher in rubber boots reappeared, looking lost. De Palma avoided his eyes.

"Is the library open now?" the man asked.

"No, no. We're just closing. Dr Dubreuil won't be long."

"I need some batteries for my camera. Have you got any?"

"Er, no," de Palma replied. "What type do you need?"

"Triple As."

The man spun round. The soles of his boots squeaked on the lino. "A-A-A. It's a secret code."

De Palma felt at a loss. He wondered how the situation would develop in Dubreuil's absence.

"I'm going to take your photo," the man said. "The Science Research Council wants me to be thorough. Everyone has to be done. I've already delivered three million or so photos. The whole population of Paris has to be done and the suburbs too."

"That's an interesting study," de Palma said.

"It's never been done before."

"What's the focus of the research?"

"Madness: people in the capital are mad. You can see it in their eyes. It's all in the eyes. Especially madness. We analyse the expressions of nutters and divide them up into numbered categories. After that it's not up to me. Paris and the suburbs are like a big research lab. There's no need for test tubes; all you need is a camera."

Dubreuil opened the door and slammed it behind him.

"So has our friend from the Science Research Council come back?"

"Yes, doctor. We were talking to this nice gentleman about our experiments."

"I see," Dubreuil said, "But we're about to close."

The man in the rubber boots took his leave, sniggering.

"Come along," Dubreuil said, switching off the library light. "I have to lock up otherwise our friend will come back and tell you all about his latest findings. He can talk the hind leg off a donkey. Eventually he collapses and we have to bring him round."

De Palma followed the doctor. The corridor leading to the small museum and reading room was decorated with photos from the First World War. It was a collection that had come from an army psychiatrist.

"In the Great War Ville-Évrard was used as a barracks," Dubreuil explained, stopping by a picture. Some soldiers with bland smiles posed in front of the buildings. "During those years the patients were transferred and other people stayed here. Everyone was starving and many people died. Did you know Camille Claudel died of hunger and ill-treatment, Monsieur de Palma?"

"No, I didn't," the Baron replied, unable to take his eyes off the photos.

"I've got the information you need," Dubreuil mumbled as he opened a wire mesh gate. "Now let's get out of here."

Night had fallen. A patient in pyjamas and a woollen dressing gown was out watching the stars and smoking a cigarette. In the distance, shouting could be heard permeating the walls of one of the wards.

"Martine Combes *was* here, between 1952 and 1958. I can't tell you any more than that."

"You can," de Palma said. "She's dead now."

"Schizophrenia. She was sectioned, treated, and then went back home to the Marseille region. She returned a few times, but nothing too serious. It's not the fifties now."

"Was she violent?"

"She must have been for them to section her. Her illness probably evolved. We'd need to find the file. I can look for it, if you like."

"Yes, we've got time. I need to pull together everything I've just learned. So she was here at the same time as Caillol? There's a pattern emerging, I need to see things more clearly."

"So who was Martine Combes?"

"Thomas Autran's mother. Combes was her maiden name."

## 51

Two days later a package arrived from Ville-Évrard.

"It's from Dr Dubreuil!" de Palma exclaimed, tearing open the envelope. "It's Martine Autran's file."

On a separate sheet of paper Dubreuil had written, 'Madness is difficult to understand, I hope this will help. Keep to yourself.'

He had photocopied about a hundred pages. Some of the original documents were handwritten; others were typed.

Martine Autran had been admitted to Ville-Évrard at an early age. She was just fourteen when she was first sectioned. 'Alcoholic father and clinically depressed mother', the consultant in charge of the juvenile ward had written. She was fairly subdued initially, but then an exceptionally violent attack had brought her to the acute ward. On two occasions she had been isolated and placed under restraint.

"Fortunately they've changed their methods since then," de Palma said, handing Bessour the first two sheets of paper.

On the third page the consultant psychiatrist in charge of the women's section disclosed that Martine had become pregnant at sixteen, probably as a result of rape. In her third month of pregnancy she suffered a miscarriage. The associated trauma led to a second spell in the acute ward. And while she was there a homicide attempt followed, against one of the male nurses. She could no longer bear the hospital. No-one came to visit her there.

Shortly after her miscarriage Martine attempted suicide, taking an overdose of sedatives she had stolen from the hospital dispensary. She spent two nights strapped to a bed with a tube in her stomach, and was then sent back to the women's section.

Three months later, her doctor noted a marked improvement. Martine was reading again and taking part in the study groups. She worked every other morning in her ward laundry. According to her notes, from the age of fourteen to eighteen she never once left the hospital: it was the only place she knew.

"A bit like spending four years in gaol," Bessour said.

"Well, not exactly."

On 22 May, 1957, there was an entry by a nurse named Robert Vandel. Martine had formed a relationship with a patient in the men's ward. Another patient had informed on her, probably a woman who was jealous. In his entry for 23 May, the nurse wrote that there must be holes in the fence separating the women's sector from the men's. Martine had no further spells in the acute ward after that date. The nurse made it clear the relationship had 'settled' her.

On 17 June she received a brief letter, signed by Caillol himself.

"Ever since I've been released, I can't stop thinking of you and those intense times we had together. Tell me that you love me – again and again."

"How touching," Bessour said. "In those days shrinks used to open the patients' mail and add it to their files. Charming. Just like they do in gaol."

"Don't get so worked up, son. There must be a reason."

De Palma turned the page. "And here it is . . . On 24 July Martine escaped. So the people you accuse of inhumanity were just keeping her stuff in case . . ."

Bessour frowned. "Did you say 24 July?"

"Yes."

"Doesn't anything strike you as odd?"

De Palma struck the notebook with the palm of his hand.

"The twins were born at the beginning of January! Nine months earlier she's getting sweet nothings from Caillol."

"Yes," Bessour said. "Something's not right."

"There's nothing in the correspondence about Pierre Autran."

De Palma searched through the Ville-Évrard file, but at no point did Pierre Autran's name appear.

"It looks like we're going to do some forensics this afternoon."

\*

Caillol's D.N.A. profile arrived early that evening; later than anticipated. The analysis was carried out at the national database, where Thomas's profile was also stored. The psychiatrist was indeed Thomas and Christine's father.

"Well, I've come across some pretty sordid stuff in my life," Bessour said, "But this really is the pits. Any worse and you'd be roasting in hell."

"I don't know if madness is hereditary," de Palma whispered, "but this is a textbook case. Poor boy."

"You're not going to start feeling sorry for him?" Legendre exclaimed.

"I think I am. Like it or not."

Legendre changed the subject. "We're all tired. Let's take the evening off and get a good night's rest. We'll see things more clearly in the morning."

\*

"Do you think he knew Dr Caillol was his father?" Eva asked.

"Thomas came to kill Caillol because he knew that: D.N.A. doesn't lie."

"How can anyone kill their own father?"

"How can any father do so much damage to his own child?"

"What about his mother?"

319

"From what I know that's even more sordid. She thought the children were chained to her, and the chains had to be broken."

"These stories of yours send shivers down my spine."

"That's my life though."

"Don't bring it home then. Out there society's breaking down and here we are living in a relatively normal world. You need to keep the two separate."

"I'm sorry."

De Palma recalled the ancient tragedy of Electra and her brother Orestes, and the horrors experienced by their family, the Atrids. Society hasn't really changed, he said to himself. Not a very original thought when it came down to it.

Eva was deep in her book again – Albert Camus' *The Outsider*. From time to time her face betrayed her feelings.

"How's your daughter?" de Palma asked.

"Better," she said. "I saw her while you were out chasing monsters. She's got bigger."

Anita was four months pregnant. She wasn't sure if it would be a boy or a girl and didn't want to know either.

Eva returned to her novel.

He sat down at the other end of the sofa. "I'm late because we've just been sent Martine Autran's psychiatric file. It's pretty hard to take. I wanted you to know."

She pushed back her glasses and stared at him. "I know why it's getting you down, Michel. I remember when your brother died. You were angry at the whole world. You fought with everyone."

He bowed his head.

"That's over, Michel. I know your mother sent you to see some shrinks. But there wasn't a single one of them who thought you were mad."

She put her hand on his shoulder. "You get trapped – you need to free yourself and let go. Stop getting so involved in this case."

"I've often had to use my gun," he whispered. "Far too often."

"Stop talking rubbish."

"I've never talked to anyone about this. Even Maistre. It's that urge, you know. I didn't think when I fired. That urge, it haunts you and you dread it more than anything."

"You've shot people?"

He stood up and went over to his record collection.

"Do you want to go out tonight?" he asked without turning round.

"I don't think so."

"Well, in that case I'll put on some opera."

He chose Handel's "Caesar". For some time he had found that Baroque music stirred up emotions he hadn't felt in a long while.

# 52

The last person connected to the man with the antler head was Jérémie Payet, the student who had discovered it at Quinson in 1970. According to the records at the University of Provence, Payet was living in Saint-Henri when he joined its department of prehistory. Having checked this out, the Baron discovered that Payet's elderly mother still lived in the same place and he often used to visit her. De Palma had no difficulty in finding the address: a boat in the port of Les Goudes. Payet was indulging his passion for scuba diving. He had even opened a club with the evocative name: *La Grande Bleue*.

The little port of Les Goudes is like a horseshoe, enclosed by a sea wall made of large stones and a concrete wharf. In the centre is a crane corroded by the sea, a few speedboats and other small craft. Old rigging moulders away; the decks are all white from the insatiable spray.

De Palma approached a man of about sixty who was lugging the aluminium cheek plate of a pulley for hauling nets.

"Payet? He's over there on his boat. If you can't find him, he'll be at Chez Georges. It's a bar that does food."

The man sized up de Palma. "What exactly do you want from him?"

"I want to join the diving club."

The man nodded.

He went through the gate that controlled access to the wharf and walked towards the boat belonging to the diving club. "Hey, Jérémie, are you there?"

Payet stuck his head out of the cabin. His eyes immediately settled on de Palma.

"I think the police want a word."

The other man went on his way with an easy rolling of the shoulders. Payet jumped onto the wharf and wiped his hands with a rag cut from an old polo shirt. De Palma showed him his I.D. Payet showed no surprise.

"I've come to excavate some old memories," the Baron said, "The man with the antler head . . . Have you got a couple of minutes?"

Payet glanced around at the houses overlooking the harbour, as though to reassure himself no-one was watching. In this little village that had harboured a fair few smugglers and other shady characters, talking to the pigs didn't go down too well.

"The man with the antler head . . ." Payet began. "I was the one who found it at Quinson, in a stratum from the Gravettian period."

"What happened that day?"

Payet thought for a while. "Palestro and Autran were there. Nobody else. I had a feeling I might come across something in the place where I was digging. For days I'd been finding arrowheads and that sort of thing."

"And then you discovered the man with the antler head?"

"The Horned Sorcerer, yes."

De Palma was surprised. He took out his notebook.

"Who stole it?"

Payet baulked at this.

"It's alright, you can tell me. Nothing will happen. You won't be taken to court."

Payet relaxed.

"It was me, I must admit," he replied, looking down. "I stole it a few days after I'd found it."

"Why?"

"Palestro was a right bastard. He sidelined me and claimed the find as his. It wasn't him who dug up the statuette."

Payet blinked nervously. "So I took it from the safe."

"And what did you do with it?"

"Listen, at the time . . . how can I put it? At the time I'd received a phone call from Pierre Autran. He knew about the theft. He knew it was me. He offered me a shedload of money."

"How much?"

"Enough to buy the boat we're standing on."

De Palma cast an eye over the deckhouse and the fittings for the diving school. "Did you know Pierre Autran?"

Payet had straightened up, he looked uneasy. "Not really . . . we met on the dig. We often used to chat together."

"What did you talk about?"

"He knew I was a good diver and I'd found some cut flints thirty metres down, near the Calanque de la Triperie."

De Palma suddenly realised that Payet was the director of the diving school where Fortin and Christine Autran had met. The wheel had come full circle.

"Is this the only diving school in Les Goudes?"

"Yes, always has been."

"Are you the director?"

"I certainly am."

"Do you know anything about what happened in Le Guen's cave, before Christmas?"

"Only vaguely. A man had an accident, is that right?"

"Spot on."

De Palma paused to give Payet time to think. All of a sudden the light changed. The sun had tipped beyond the seawall rocks, casting its last rays over the picture windows of the restaurants.

"It was an accident," the Baron went on. "A stupid decompression accident."

Payet's little eyes shone. He had large hands, like tennis rackets. "That's awful," he said.

De Palma leaned over the boat rail and let his gaze drift across the oily waters of the harbour.

"You don't know what happened to the man with the antler head?" he said, standing up again.

"No. The Autran family must still have it."

"Of course, of course," de Palma said.

Payet grabbed hold of a frayed nylon rope on top of the engine bonnet and twisted it between his hairy fingers.

"That's all I know."

De Palma handed him his card. "Sorry to bother you, Monsieur Payet, but if you remember anything else give me a call."

De Palma walked back to the car. A bluish shadow spread over the small road leading to the Passage de la Croisette and the Île Maïre.

Coming into Pointe-Rouge a traffic jam had formed in front of the little marina. De Palma grabbed his mobile.

"Hi Karim. Do me a favour, will you?"

"Go on."

"Autran's first victim was called Weill, but I've got a feeling that wasn't her maiden name. Can you find it out for me? She was killed eleven years ago. The first name on the list. The other two were spinsters, I'm sure of that."

"I'll ring you back in five minutes."

On Friday evenings, the town is buzzing, from its choked centre to the outlying districts, which form constellations of electric stars at the foot of the dark hills.

After five minutes the phone rang.

"Any news?" de Palma asked.

"Yes," Bessour replied. "Hélène Weill's maiden name was Payet."

# 53

Hélène's mother clasped her crumpled handkerchief. She had a small face with pale, delicate skin, grey hair tied back and eyes red with grief.

"Men are animals. There's no other word for them."

Claire Payet looked up and stared at the Baron coldly.

"Even her father," she said, pointing at a photo of a young man in uniform, on the marble top of an Empire-style dresser. "He sometimes hit me. Hélène never knew that, but that's how it was. We stayed together for her sake and for her brother, Jérémie. I never knew if she'd noticed anything . . ."

The house was obsessively clean: the herringbone parquet floor gleamed, each ornament was just so, and a pot of freshly cut flowers sat beside a corduroy armchair.

"Why wouldn't they let me see her body?" Hélène's mother said sourly.

"You need to remember your daughter as she was when she was alive," de Palma said softly. "That's the important thing."

Claire Payet sighed and sat down by the dining room table, her hands clenched between her knees. "I suppose you saw her?"

Her voice was reproachful and tinged with sadness. De Palma didn't reply, feeling any words he might use would be wrong.

The old woman looked at him grimly. "Those things can't be very nice to look at," she added in a whisper.

Her shoulders slumped. She lived alone in a small detached house in the impoverished Saint-Henri district, at the end of a street that climbed towards the hills. There was a garden with two clumps of bamboo and an ancient, slowly rotting swing. De Palma imagined Hélène begging her brother to push her higher and higher, up into the immense sky. Her mother seemed to guess what he was thinking. She went over to the window.

"I haven't touched a thing," she said. "Her brother doesn't want that. It's what she wanted too – no changes. Since their father died her brother has tried to hold on to his childhood memories. Sometimes I find him sitting on the swing, dreaming of I don't know what . . ."

Hélène was married for some years, then divorced. She taught history to 17 and 18-year-olds at the Institut Saint-François, a private school in Aubagne.

"Did she have any friends? I mean, did she know any . . ."

"Men," Madame Payet cut in with a bitter smile. "No, not many. She worshipped her father, but no boy ever really found favour. None of them were half the man her father was. Her marriage was a disaster."

All daughters worship their fathers, de Palma thought to himself. His eyes settled on the bare stems of some rose bushes in the garden.

"What did your husband do?"

"He was an archaeologist," Claire Payet replied, rolling her eyes. "Imagine that! An archaeologist!"

"It's a fine profession."

"You think so? It wasn't his profession, it was his passion."

"What else did he do?"

"He was a doctor. Dr Payet was the best G.P. in Saint-Henri, or so they said."

Hélène's mother was mocking, her face a tragicomic mask. De Palma wondered if she was on tranquillisers. The type of pill where going cold turkey can bring out the best as well as the worst.

"Did she go out much?" the Baron asked.

"Sometimes. She'd go to the cinema or with her friend, Florence. Our neighbour."

Claire Payet looked away. She was shaking.

"Can I see her room?" de Palma asked, glancing at his watch. He reckoned Jérémie Payet wouldn't be long. Bessour should have been there by now.

"It's on the first floor. I can't bear to come with you. It's the door at the end of the corridor."

The oak staircase was glazed. De Palma went slowly up the stairs, feeling as though a spirit was leading the way. On the landing, a couple of bronze dancers stood out on a small table in the feeble light. Mauve and white striped wallpaper covered the walls. A red and gold oriental rug adorned the wooden floorboards. A couple of portraits, probably ancestral, gazed down with pinched smiles on the comings and goings in the corridor. At the end there was a closed door. De Palma had a feeling the spirit was telling him to stop, as though a sacred relic was waiting on the other side. He inhaled deeply before turning the handle.

The room was large and light. A Henri II double bed was covered in a pale pink eiderdown embroidered with flowery patterns. The white cotton curtains on the windows overlooked weeping willows which sadly brushed against the slow waters of the Marne.

A chest of drawers stood against the left-hand wall. A doll with half-closed blue eyes and immaculately combed hair sat on the polished wood. Its clothes harked back to the seventies: a kilt and a dark green, rollneck sweater. De Palma found a collection of out-moded lingerie in the top drawer. There were socks and tights in the others. As he rummaged through the silky fabrics the detective experienced a strange sensation. It was as though the woman who had worn all this finery, and whose secrets he was uncovering, was watching him, outraged.

He closed the drawers and moved over to the wardrobe.

Everything was perfectly arranged and ironed. The suits and skirts were in a variety of materials, all in either green or dark purple. There was a smell of mothballs. He closed the wardrobe doors and looked around the room. Opposite the bed, Hélène Weill's desk was still meticulously tidy: pens on the right, a stapler on the left and to the side a pile of photocopies, probably documents for the classes she taught. A photograph that must have dated from the time of her death hung up above: Hélène was arm in arm with a young man of a similar age.

De Palma leaned over to look at the print; its colours had faded. He shuddered: the man beside Hélène was Thomas Autran. An inscription was etched on a wall in the background of the grainy, slightly blurred photo. The letters above her head weren't visible, but the rest made him think the word was 'university'. Then came a capital 'P' followed by an illegible lower case letter. De Palma held the print up to the window and took a photo using the camera on his mobile. The result was not very satisfactory, but it would do as a visual aid. He put the photo back in its place, feeling a bit sheepish about having disturbed this well-ordered room.

A clinking sound came from the ground floor. Claire Payet must be busy in the kitchen. De Palma went downstairs and paused for a moment in the living room. A bookshelf filled with biographies and history books covered a whole wall. Some women's magazines lay on a coffee table. Hélène's mother appeared.

"Which university did your daughter go to?"

"Aix-en-Provence. She was very bright."

De Palma asked about the photo on the desk.

"Who's the young man with her?"

Claire Payet blinked nervously.

"I've never really known."

"How do you mean 'really'?"

"I think he was her boyfriend at the time. It's not for lack of asking . . . She just wouldn't tell me."

She looked up at the stairs and the dark rectangle opening onto the floors above, as though trying to recover some lost memories.

"I think she was in love with him, but I don't even know his name. To be honest I didn't know a thing about her love life."

She pushed back a lock of grey hair that had come away from her bun with a trembling hand.

"I didn't teach her about loving men, you see. Just the opposite, in fact. I always told her to be careful of anyone who got too close. She was beautiful, you know."

"Do you know why the relationship ended?"

"It seems the man was deranged. That's all I know. My son knew him a bit, he could tell you more."

De Palma stared at the windows. Would Jérémie Payet turn up as he anticipated?

"You told me your husband was interested in archaeology. Which period?"

"Prehistory, or prehistoric art. He used to go off on digs – I don't remember where. It seems there are quite a few sites in Provence.

"Did your daughter go with him?"

"Whenever she could. She always went with her brother. He studied prehistory."

"And what about you?"

"No, when he was with his children I didn't count. Anyway for me all those old stones . . ."

"Did you ever hear him talking about statuettes?"

She shook her head and threw up her hands, exclaiming, "Certainly not! And even if my husband had talked about them, I wouldn't remember."

"Would your son, perhaps?"

"No."

A door slammed at the end of the garden.

"Oh, there he is – that's my son back."

The Baron drew his revolver without Claire Payet noticing. He positioned himself in the doorway and stared at the only exit to the garden. Jérémie Payet came through the kitchen and finally appeared, concealing something behind his back.

"I knew you'd come here," he yelled at the Baron. "I knew it. Come on, let's get it over with."

At that moment Bessour rang the bell. De Palma opened the door.

"You're under arrest for the murder of Christine Autran," de Palma said quietly.

Payet dropped the speargun that he'd been hiding.

"It's six thirty-four," Bessour added. "We're arresting you under a Rogatory Commission issued by Judge Landi."

Bessour put on the handcuffs and made the man sit down. When she realised her son was now a prisoner, Claire Payet cried out in terror.

"Oh my God, what have you done?"

Payet lowered his head. "I miss Hélène so much."

"I know you do. So do I . . ." his mother said.

"I saw Hélène. I saw her. Someone had done terrible things to her. And that person, I knew him. Often I couldn't sleep because of that. Everything in my head was upside down. I remember her laughing. I remember her smelling of those strawberry bonbons you wouldn't let us eat."

Claire Payet had turned towards the wall. Her lips quivered, the words wouldn't come.

"She smelled of sweets . . . when I saw her on the stretcher in the morgue. I thought of the times we used to play in the garden together. I thought of that when I saw the stitches the doctors had put in to patch her up. I saw the little girl I'd known cut into tiny pieces."

Payet raised his head; face crumpled; lips twisted. "I suppose that when you see things like that there's nothing you can do to blank them out. No clean slate. The memories stay deep inside you until the day you die. Is that right?"

"Yes," de Palma replied. "You don't forget. The best you can hope for is to tame them."

Payet clenched his fists. He wanted to cry, but no tears came. "I've tried to live my life as best I can, I've tried to do something good, find comfort in love, but nothing came of it. I chose the sea instead. That belly of water; that great belly. It was only in the water that I stopped seeing my sister all stitched up. I forgot about her delicate fingers scrabbling at the earth to escape that monster, her feet beating on the ground, but then when I came to the surface, it all came back. Every little detail. Even how she smelled when I saw her."

Payet turned to his mother as she got up.

"Do you want to know what she smelled of on the stretcher? Tripe. She stank like a fetid marsh."

Claire Payet left the room.

"And then we opened up the cave. At least that's what he thought. I knew Thomas Autran had hidden the man with the antler head there. That was all I wanted. Without that statuette, nothing would have happened to my sister."

"How do you mean?" de Palma asked.

"My father wouldn't have known Pierre Autran. It was only because of that . . . his monster of a son got to know my sister. Pierre Autran was a charming little man. A weak person who allowed his children to do anything, and wealthy just like my father. They knew each other well. I knew Autran and his sister well too."

"And you got your revenge. You killed Christine, but you missed her brother."

"Missed her brother?"

"He's dead," de Palma said. "It's all over."

Bessour put a hand on Payet's shoulder. "Where's the man with the antler head?"

"It's on my boat. You'll find it in a parcel tied under the chart table. I want people to know I was the one who found it, not that shit Palestro."

"I'll have a word with Pauline Barton."

Two patrol vans stopped in front of the house. They took away Jérémie Payet. His mother stood frozen in front of the swing in the garden where her children had had so much fun. Neither Bessour nor de Palma dared go near.

The moon rose early. Tiny, frail clouds raced across a sky that was hard as stone. The Mistral was blowing, carrying away the dry scents of winter.

# EPILOGUE

The Baron was going through his record collection looking for something that would sound "young". But he had little success.

"Opera's not bad as background music, is it?" he said tentatively.

"I don't think so!" Eva shouted from the kitchen.

"Alright then, how about some Baroque?"

"Not that either!"

De Palma tidied away the records. "Well, I'm not going to put on the Clash," he muttered, "Too precious. They're vinyl."

He had bought the complete set in London during the eighties. Maistre, who saw Joe Strummer as the last of the prophets, called it the end of El Dorado.

"I've got time to buy something. Any ideas?"

Eva appeared in the doorway to the living room.

"No, don't go. Anita'll be here any minute."

"I need to get changed."

She eyed him, amused, "No, it's O.K. You look quite smart like that. Apart from the slippers."

She was wearing a purple silk dress that would have driven a Franciscan wild, and some gold jewellery that was a teeny bit flash. She had inherited them from her grandmother, a reminder of her Sicilian roots. De Palma liked the honeyed glint on her olive skin. He remembered the old women – Corsican, Sicilian and Neapolitan – who went down to Saint-Jean church on Sunday mornings in their black dresses and absurdly shiny shoes. The only concession to luxury: jewellery as heavy as their endless mourning.

"We're off to Rome soon," de Palma said, holding Eva close.

"Our first trip together."

"Yes."

She planted a kiss on his lips.

"Will you try to be a little romantic?"

"I'll sing you Tosca in front of the Castel Sant'Angelo. *Recondita armonia, di belezze diverse . . .*"

"How about you put on that aria?"

He hurried over to the C.D. player with a name in mind: Mario del Monaco, a recording from the sixties, with Renata Tebaldi in the title role.

"I've invited Maistre to join us for dessert!" he said, putting the C.D. in the machine.

Eva looked up at the sky. "Are you scared of meeting my daughter on your own?"

"Don't be daft!"

"She's been talking about you for months."

"Exactly, that's what's worrying me. Maistre knows about this kind of thing. His two boys have brought round their girlfriends."

"I hope you're not going to treat us to any of your police stories."

"No, I promise. I'll talk about opera instead. Women like it when you talk about music."

She nibbled his ear. "Maistre doesn't need to stay late . . ."

"Er, no. Just give the order and we'll wind things up."

"Perfect. I'm going back to the kitchen then."

De Palma went over to his bookcase. *Criminal Man* was lined up alongside *Crime: Its Causes and Remedies*. A thousand pages in all. The first book dated from an era when they tried to explain man in terms of nature; the second from a time when they said that people are not born criminals, but become so as a result of tragedies and breakdowns in relationships. Listening to the radio that morning

335

de Palma had heard on the news that they now claimed to be able to spot children at risk from early childhood. It was the fantasy of a minister, who knew nothing about killers or children. He flicked though *Criminal Man* and sniffed the paper and old ink. All that knowledge was no longer of any use to him.

In three days' time he would hand in his gun and his I.D. card just like in the old detective stories. He was neither happy nor sad about it. There would be no more corpses stretched out in front of Dr Mattei, no more shaking in his shoes at the time of an arrest. He had gone through hundreds of them and remembered nearly every one. They were always fractured moments; lives shattered by the letter of the law.

Bessour had taken over and was winding up the Autran case. He had interviewed Payet in police custody and brought him before the examining magistrate, who solemnly informed the killer of his indictment for murder. The Criminal Court and life imprisonment lay before him. De Palma swore that if he was called to give evidence, he would try to persuade the jury to spare Payet a life sentence with no remission.

Bessour no longer had anything to learn from the man who the entire squad had nicknamed the Baron. Legendre had entrusted him with a team that he led with finesse – something de Palma had never known how to do. Karim was already working on another case. A settling of scores between drug dealers on the Busserine estate in the north of the city. A kid of fifteen had been gunned down in a hail of Kalashnikov bullets. He endured three hours of death throes before he died.

De Palma would have liked to help Bessour, but he knew nothing about the estates on the outskirts of Marseille. Even the old French Connection chemists no longer understood what was going on, but for Karim this war held no secrets. He knew its roots, the terrain and the forces on the ground. He was expecting at least a dozen adolescent corpses, kitted out like their sporting heroes: *Made in the USA.*

Their designer tracksuits would be shot through with an 11.43 – the older generation's gun of choice. The conflict between generations focused on knowhow.

De Palma closed the book. The doorbell rang.

"You going to answer?"

"No, you go!"

"I've got my hands in the puff pastry!"

De Palma looked at himself in the hall mirror for a few seconds, pulled up his shirt collar and adopted a serious expression as he opened the door. Anita held out a fine, bony hand. The Baron's heart missed a beat; she was the spitting image of her mother at the time when he only had eyes for her.

"I guess you must be Michel?"

"Er, yes."

Her belly was already round and was covered with a large scented scarf.

"Please come in."

De Palma hoped for some help from Eva, but she didn't appear. Anita was holding a bunch of blue lilies.

"It's funny," she said in a faltering voice, looking down at the Baron's slippers. "I'd imagined you differently."

De Palma stopped himself from replying. He took the bunch of flowers and carried them through to Eva.

"Look what your daughter's brought you."

"They're not for Maman, they're for you. She told me you love opera and I'm sure you like flowers."

He was speechless, but then rallied again.

"That's the first time anyone's given me flowers. They're beautiful. I'll put them in a vase."

He turned away to hide the tears he struggled to hold back.

A little later that evening Maistre rang to say he would not be coming. The man who was never ill now used a sudden fever as his pretext. De Palma suspected Eva had put him up to it.

"It's a boy," Anita said, as de Palma popped the champagne cork.

"How long have you known?" Eva asked.

"For a month now, but I wanted the three of us to be here when I broke the news."

"A boy," the Baron whispered, "A boy . . . What myth will you live by?"

# ACKNOWLEDGEMENTS

This book owes much to the celebrated diver Henri Cosquer who discovered a prehistoric cave in the Calanques near Marseille, which today bears his name. Henri had the courage and audacity to venture down into the abyss in search of First Man's footprints.

My thanks also go to Laure and Pierre, for their unfailing support over many years; Eliane, my indefatigable, caring and indispensable reader; and Christopher and Koukla, my British publishers who believed in this book long before it was completed.

Thank you to all those who have helped me: especially to Maurice who knows the beginnings of this journey, and to Ursula for her friendship and precious advice.

X.-M. BONNOT

XAVIER-MARIE BONNOT has a Ph.D. in History and Sociology, and two Masters degrees in History and French literature. He is the author of *The First Fingerprint*, *The Beast of the Camargue* and *The Voice of the Spirits* (winner of the 2011 Crystal Feather award for crime writing), all featuring Commandant Michel de Palma.

JUSTIN PHIPPS is a translator from French and Russian, most recently of Barbara Constantine's *And Then Came Paulette*. After studying modern languages and social anthropology, he has worked in overseas development and as a solicitor specialising in employment law.